AGAINST THE ODDS

AGAINST THE ODDS

Ben Igwe

AFRICAN HERITAGE PRESS
NEW YORK LAGOS LONDON
2009

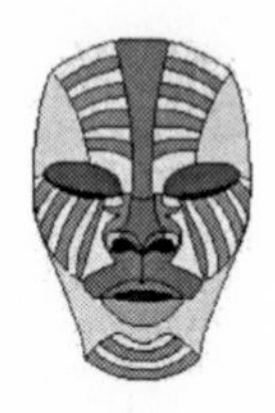

AFRICAN HERITAGE PRESS

NEW YORK	LAGOS
PO BOX 1433	PO BOX 14452
NEW ROCHELLE,	IKEJA, LAGOS
NY 10802, USA	NIGERIA

TEL: 718-862-3262
FAX: 718-862-1440
Email: afroheritage9760@aol.com
www.africanheritagepress.com

First Edition, African Heritage Press, 2009

Library of Congress catalog number: 2006937598

Igwe, Ben

Cover Design: Dapo Ojoade

Distributors: African Books Collective,
www.africanbookscollective.com

ISBN: 978-0-9790858-3-3
ISBN: 0-9790858-3-7

ACKNOWLEDGMENTS

I owe a debt of gratitude to many who in various ways contributed to the development of this novel; the late Mazi Okechukwu Iheukwumere, Gerald Washington, Ms. Joan Adetayo and Diane Moore at the Martin Luther King, Jr. Memorial Library in Washington, D.C. for their suggestions. To Sekum Boni-Awotwi and Basil Maduka both of Howard University Health Sciences Library in Washington, D.C. for their kindness. Ms. Patricia Elam and Obi Iwuanyanwu gave me thoughtful ideas and Kalu Ogbaa provided much needed encouragement.

DEDICATION

To my parents,
Nze Titus Ukawunne and Elizabeth Ada Opara-chukwu Igwe.

To live in the hearts of those who love you is not to die.

I have a past, my past is my life
the mother of my future.
Like every other journey to the peak
I am ready to take care of the
ups and downs,
To be loved and cherished in the crown of my heritage
I have a past.

Chidi A. Okoye

One

The mist that settled overnight on the village in dry season cleared quickly in the morning. A big bowl of sun appearing on the horizon could be sighted through tree branches and drooping palm fronds. Some villagers had emerged from their compounds to start the day. Women with long baskets on their heads were on the way to farms to dump trash or start work, while others returning from the stream balanced clay pots of spring water on their heads. Men who had gone into the bushes earlier on were returning with fodder for goats, machetes in hand, before setting out for other daily activities. A wine tapper with a ladder and oblong safety harness slung across his shoulder was on his way to tap palm for morning wine. Fowls that sauntered across the road into neighborhood farms had begun scratching through debris and soil for food. Occasionally a rooster stretched its neck, head, and combs high to crow, embracing a new day.

Uridiya walked briskly along the dirt road in the direction of the half-walled village hall with its roof of rusty corrugated iron sheets. She looked pitiful in the black mourning outfit that consisted of a loose blouse, a single wraparound loincloth, and a head-cloth of the same fabric knotted loosely at the back of her neck. Her temper was short. Quite easily she would call out all the evil spirits of the land if provoked, especially by relatives of her deceased husband who took advantage of her. She would put a curse on everyone who abused her or planned to do so:
"*Chi-ne-eke*, any man or woman who does not wish a

widow well, or who wants to see her head buried in the ground will not meet good fortune. Anyone who wants to stress me to death from talking will follow Nnorom to the land of the dead. May all the dead of this village and the great Imo River take them? The evil spirits will not allow anyone to rest who has sworn that Uridiya will have no rest. May all the evil things you wish for me follow you, your children, and your children's children, both born and unborn. May evil visit you—reincarnation after reincarnation. May you be cursed, not me. You say I am a lunatic, wait till you see what a lunatic can do."

Uridiya would conclude by saying that she was certain that those who maltreated her would never leave her alone. She likened herself to the chick picked up and lodged irretrievably in the sharp talons of a fleeing hawk, shrieking hard not because the predator would let go. Alas, no, she is crying out so the world would hear her voice.

Village youngsters and siblings who gathered in cool sandy shade looked forward to hearing Uridiya at some point during the day because they expected someone to upset her. Her curses had almost turned into a song and ritual for them. If children saw her standing with two hands clasped across her head staring intently into space, they knew she was about to invoke evil spirits on persons who might have wronged her. They would giggle and provoke her by throwing out some words so she would say something funny for their amusement. One very windy afternoon, after she was done cursing and breathing heavily, a townsman, Nzeadi, coming down the narrow road on a bicycle, greeted her as he approached.

"Uridiya, I greet you. How are you doing?"

"Are you asking how Uridiya is doing? Can't you see how I am doing?" She spread both hands and projected her chest. The cyclist stopped. Still on his bicycle with the right foot on the pedal and the left foot on the ground, he looked at her.

"To tell the truth, you look well."

Uridiya laughed mischievously.

"Do you say I look well the way I am or are you mocking me?"

"How can I mock you, Uridiya? To mock you is to mock myself. Your late husband and I were age-mates and friends too."

"Is that true? I did not know that." Uridiya's voice rose. "Then you are in the group of those who want me dead. They are the people who call themselves Nnorom's friends and relatives."

"What would they do with your corpse, Uridiya? They can't eat it." The cyclist dismounted and with his right foot pressed down the bicycle stand and turned fully to Uridiya.

"The meat from Uridiya's body will be tasteful. You didn't know that?" she said.

"I did not know anybody who wants you dead. Please don't count me in that group. I am hearing it for the first time from your mouth." The man held on to his hat and beat back the wind that attempted to take it off his head.

"If you have not heard it, then you do not live in this village. You must be a visitor. What town are you from?"

"Uridiya, please don't worry about it. I did not say anything bad. All I said is that you look well." A woman who turned to look at them after she passed almost walked off the road. The cyclist let go of his hat, having pressed it firmly down on his gray-haired head.

"Come on, man, you said it again. Are you looking at Uridiya, or are you looking at someone else?" She pointed at herself.

"I am looking at you, and I see you do not look sick." Nzeadi moved closer.

"Oh, is that true? It is only when I look sick that you will know that my death is near?"

"At least everyone will know that Uridiya has been sick."

"So, you have not seen anyone who died without being sick?"

"Uridiya, please don't die. To whom will you leave this one child of yours? Stay alive and raise your child. Nobody takes care of a child like a mother does."

"Did you say that? Did you say that?" The cyclist struck

a cord in Uridiya, who wheeled herself around and even came closer to him. "Did that come out of your mouth? I hope all the creatures of God and man heard you. May you live long, you who have seen the truth and voiced it! Nobody raises another person's child. All those who plan my death should hear you. Your statement is that of a prophet. Anyone that it pleased God to give a child should stay alive to see the child become somebody, be the child male or female. God made it so."

"Uridiya, I must continue on my journey now. May life be good to you."

"Go well, may you be blessed." The cyclist, still talking to her, pushed his bicycle for a while, then mounted and rode away.

Villagers who took advantage of Uridiya would attempt to rob her of farmlands as well as the fruit trees that sustained her. They harvested her oil bean tree in the early hours of the morning before she woke up, carried away her breadfruits when they fell and no one was watching. They would not leave a widow alone to have breathing space until she started to behave like a lunatic with a sharp abusive tongue, spitting out curses on them and their children.

The black two-piece mourning outfit with matching head-cloth was Uridiya's attire for one year during the period tradition required that she mourn her husband. A merciless haircut compounded her miserable condition. Her head was shaved to the bare shining skull. This duty was dexterously performed by widows from the kindred who themselves had been through the same rite. They shaved off her hair with a piece of broken bottle or sometimes with a locally made razor. It was done to perfection and, her head polished with palm kernel oil, shone reflectively.

Uridiya Nnorom, a widow in the village of Aludo in Igboland in Eastern Nigeria, suffered the fate of a widow. The condition of the widow in the village in the 1950s evoked sympathy and pity. Her life was a struggle. Suffering was her lot and endurance her virtue. Because most people did not care about her, she went about her harsh living saying as little as possible. Widowhood leaves little for words. Resignation to the will of the gods and protection by the spirits of her ancestors bespoke her condition. Widows in the village most often were helpless. This is the reason malevolent persons would pounce on a widow's farmlands, fruit trees, or domestic animals such as dogs, goats, sheep or her fowls, attempting to dispossess her. Ironically, it was the close relatives of the widow's deceased husband who were the first to try to disinherit her, especially if her children were minors.

Uridiya was forty-five years old, tall and brown skinned. She looked far older than her age due to hardship. Her cheekbones, set on a slightly square face, highlighted the wrinkle on either side of her drawn cheeks. Before her mourning outfit became regular wear, she used to sometimes walk around bare-bodied to the waist, her flat breasts pendulous and her one-piece loincloth knotted firmly with a cloth string around her waist. Above the cloth and below an exposed navel were many rope-like rings of red and black beads that adorned her hips and swung with the undulating movement of her buttocks when she walked.

Everyone in the village knew Uridiya well. Wherever she appeared, persons around would be aware of her presence because she would be complaining beyond conversational tone about what someone had done to her. Sometimes she walked briskly barefooted along the village dirt road wringing her hands at man's inhumanity, cursing, and invoking the god of thunder and other evil spirits to visit quickly and snatch away all those oppressing her. When rain threatened, thunder roared, and lightning flashed in the sky, Uridiya would raise her hands to the sky and entreat,

"The strong one! No living person doubts your work. Anyone who crosses your path does not stand again. Whoever doubts you does so to his or her peril. You know those who are after Uridiya, I don't know them." She takes a pause and then continues. "What am I saying? I know some of them. I beg that you come down and do your work on them. Strike them so all will see and know that you do not want mistreatment of anyone. We know that nothing will happen to anyone who does nothing wrong. Follow the evil ones; follow them even if they run into a rat hole. They are the reason why the world is not good."

Jamike was Uridiya's only child, born to her late in life. She became pregnant just as her husband, Nnorom, was seriously thinking about taking another wife, after years of barrenness and the concern and pressure of his relatives to take another wife. In their imprecise counting, the villagers said that it was nearly two decades after her marriage that Uridiya gave birth to the boy, Jamike. Fate, however, was cruel to Uridiya and the baby, for her husband, Nnorom, died just two years after her son was born. He fell to his death off a palm tree. Villagers considered this an abominable way to die. Such deaths were believed to be the handiwork of Amadioha, the god of thunder, showing his wrath over an offense against the god.

When Jamike was young, Uridiya always carried him on her back with such a narrow piece of cloth one would think the boy could fall off, but he clung hard on her shoulders. When he was older and able to walk, she would hold him by the hand along the uneven road, she walking briskly, he holding, crying and running to keep up and sometimes stumbling. Uridiya cursed along the village road whenever she was aggravated. Because of that, the villagers said she was on the verge of becoming a lunatic.

"No," she would protest, "I am not a lunatic. I am never one to talk too much. You turned me talkative after my husband died." Then she thought for a moment, "No, after you killed him."

After Nnorom died, villagers did not believe Uridiya would survive his death. Her grief could not be controlled. Passers-by would look at her and shake their heads in pity as she flung a sick and tired child, Jamike, on her shoulder from one native doctor to another. If she tied him to her back, the boy's neck and head would feebly tilt to one side or another. People close by would ask Uridiya to situate the child right before he would break his neck. She carried eggs, lizards, white-feathered fowls, and tortoises to divining priests for ritual offerings to propitiate Jamike's chi so he might live.

Uridiya and Jamike eked out a harsh existence. Living for them was based on small quantities of farm products. Cassava, cocoyam, and green plantain were staples. Uridiya sold some of these, including pepper, small quantities of palm oil and palm kernel, vegetables, and ripe banana, to buy other things like crayfish, kerosene, onions, matches for the hurricane lamp, salt, soap, and other commodities. Whatever she could not afford they did without.

When Jamike started elementary school, he would come back from school and there would be no real food available. Dropping his raffia school bag, Jamike would look into every pot in Uridiya's dingy kitchen in search of food.

"Is there nothing to eat in this house today?" Uridiya would keep silent. She heard him.

"Mama, I am asking you."

"Jamike, find something to eat and leave me alone to think about my life and my world. Crack some nuts. Palm kernel is food. It is not always that one has to have a full stomach."

Jamike would gather and crack palm nuts for kernels to chew. If there were dried slices of cassava, he would either eat them so or soak them in water to soften before he ate them. During harvest time Uridiya would bring out cocoyam for him to eat before she would leave for the market. Without taking off his school uniform Jamike would put the cocoyam in the fire to roast. Once it was ready he dipped it in peppered palm oil and ate zestfully. Soon a bulge would appear on either side of his stomach like a well-fed lizard. Jamike was full and ready to do his errand. Uridiya would always attach a chore to after-school meals. She educated Jamike on her philosophical belief that wherever there is something to eat, there is also something to do. Jamike would speed off to get palm fronds and twigs for their two goats or go to the stream to fetch water. He could do his little homework or prepare materials for his school handiwork for the next day. Sometimes he went into the forest to cut sticks for building or mending school fences.

Despite their condition of poverty, Uridiya had a strong faith in her god and an indomitable will to survive with the only seed, as she called Jamike, which God gave to her. She believed the god of Nnorom would not allow this one seed of his to be taken away. Nnorom, she said, never harmed anybody while he lived, nor did he commit an abomination or anything forbidden by custom or tradition. She could not understand why the god of thunder chose to take him. The divination priest told those who went to the oracle to seek the reason for his death that it was on account of some oath he took but did not fulfill in his previous life before he reincarnated. The Priest said Nnorom would have reincarnated as a stump of a tree but for the intervention of benign fate. If his parents had appeased the god when he was born he would still be living.

To make sure that Jamike would not suffer the same fate as his father, Uridiya sold off many of their farmlands to appease Amadioha. The chief priests of the god carted away most of Nnorom's property, as is the custom when the god of thunder is responsible for someone's death.

Most mornings when Uridiya visited her farms there was an unwelcome activity in one or two of them. It might be that a villager who farmed the portion of land adjoining hers had encroached beyond the boundary with one or two tongues of hoe strikes. It might well be unintentional or even intentional just to see if they could get away with a little piece of her farmland. Sometimes youngsters in search of firewood had removed dried palm fronds that covered germinating seeds. If she found out, then it was time to call up the neighborhood to witness the hatred visited on her. Villagers farming in the vicinity would stop work for a moment to listen to what problem the widow had to warrant her yelling. They knew immediately that someone had wronged her.

In the evening when she returned from the farm, there was always something that would cause her voice to be heard beyond the rampart that surrounded their family compound. It could be that someone had made use of a little bit of her meager pile of firewood or taken water from her clay storage pot, or that someone had left the barn open for goats to eat her little quantity of cocoyam. Each day, at some point, she would scream and curse the machinations of evil people against her. Some days, though, Uridiya would walk along the road silently, saying nothing to people she passed on the way. If Uridiya were greeted while in this mood, she would mutter a response to herself, saying, "How can you greet me when you too are in the plan to have me dead?" She was suspicious of everyone. When she walked along the village dirt road in silence, Uridiya was in her own world.

"What am I going to do so people will leave me alone?" she would reflect. "In fact, if they ever cause my death, they would be the worse for it because I will promptly return as a witch and snatch away all who destroyed me. They cannot run me to death and stay alive here. They must join me in the land of the spirits. But what I cannot do now is to take my own life. If I do, what will I tell this seed that the gods gave to me? Those who caused my death would make sure he died too so they could take over Nnorom's household."

Two

Jamike and his mother lived off the products from their farms. Cassava, cocoyam, green bananas, yams, and plantain were their main foods. In a bad harvest, things were difficult for them. Uridiya would sell pepper, vegetables, and a small bowl of palm oil to buy a handful of crushed crayfish to give taste to their soup. Meat in their food was a rarity. If they wanted beef broth to season their soup, Jamike would take a pot of water or a bundle of firewood to the village butcher so he would give him some broth in exchange after he cooked meat for sale. But as a village boy, Jamike would go into the bush some nights with a palm oil lamp or a lit bundle of sticks tied together to pick snails following a heavy rain, or he would pick mushrooms the morning after. On Saturdays during the planting season he accompanied Uridiya to the farm and helped to make mounds for cassava or cocoyam planting.

Other times he would go on insect-hunting excursions in the farms and low bushes in the village. Early in the morning sometimes, when dew had dulled and weakened the insects, Jamike would go into nearby bushes to catch edible insects like grasshoppers, praying mantises, crickets, and beetles for food. After Jamike removed their wings, Uridiya would fry the insects and put them in their soup.

During the season for edible caterpillars, when greenish voracious caterpillars, like locusts, descended on trees and shrubs, a season that came around at long intervals,

Jamike would climb trees to shake caterpillars off branches and leaves so that persons on the ground under the trees would pick them. Once he was on the tree, he would climb from branch to branch, shaking some branches with his hand and thumping his foot on others while he held strongly to another branch. When he came down, he would collect a handful of these wormlike caterpillars from each person.

Sometimes a stingy villager would not contribute enough caterpillars to Jamike. Jamike would be upset and would show it. An old woman was once tightfisted with Jamike.

"What is this you are giving me? I would rather not take any caterpillars from you than for you not to give me enough." He attempted to walk away, refusing the handful the woman offered.

"Go ahead, young man, and collect from others. By the time everybody gives you their share you will have more than enough."

"Mama, just give me a fair share from what you have. Don't worry about what other people may give me."

"Are you ever satisfied, you little boy? Did you do any other thing except to climb a tree? You are not God that put caterpillars on the tree." People standing around laughed as they watched the old lady and the young boy exchange words.

"I am not God, but I am the one that climbed the tree. If climbing the tree is nothing why didn't you climb it yourself?" Jamike was firm.

"If I were a man I would climb it."

"Now you know you are a woman, please give me the caterpillars."

Another villager in the group who got tired of waiting for Jamike while he argued was getting ready to leave her share for Jamike at the foot of the tree.

"Please don't do that. The caterpillars will crawl away." His simmering anger rose to a boil.

"Please give me the caterpillars. If these other people leave without giving me anything I will seize this big bowl that you have," Jamike warned.

"I did not get all these caterpillars from here. I have been out all morning." She gave him a little more.

By early afternoon, before the sun got too hot, Jamike would have climbed over ten trees, and his sizeable calabash bowl would be filled with a big mound of caterpillars crawling in a slimy mass over one another, raising and shaking their tiny heads. When cooked and dried in the sun or fried they became delicacies for different types of soup. Sometimes Jamike and his mother would have more than they required, in which case Uridiya would sell some.

During the rainy season, Jamike and the other boys went to the community pond at midnight to catch frogs. They carried lanterns or brightly lit bundles of dried thin sticks that showed the water of the pond under illumination. They would then surround the pond at different points. On noticing the light the frogs would attempt to jump into nearby bushes. As they tried to jump out, they would be apprehended. Each frog caught had its long legs broken so it wouldn't jump out of the bag.

As he grew older, Jamike began to hunt rabbits and squirrels with other young men in the village. Sometimes he followed older men on their hunt, carrying their hunting bag like an apprentice. After they slaughtered their catch for the day, he would go home with a leg, thigh, or even the head of a small animal. On these occasions, Uridiya would welcome and embrace her young son with a broad smile and shower praises and sweet names on him for bringing home meat for their soup. She would call him *Nwachinemere*, one who God takes care of, and *Nwadede*, my beloved. Jamike was proud to hear his mother call him those names of endearment.

By the time he was ten, Jamike had appropriated one of Uridiya's old machetes. He went to a relative who was a blacksmith and had the handle changed by the blacksmith's son. He was proud of his machete. Early on Saturday mornings Jamike would spend a long time sharpening the machete at the grindstone. He used it to cut firewood in the bush and to cut palm leaves and twigs for their goats. Ownership of a machete was a mark of incipient manhood for a young boy in the village. As a weapon, he could use it to defend himself and his family, and he used it as a tool to work on the farms or at home. Every village boy was eager to own a machete, usually one that his father was not using anymore. He sometimes played with it and learned about its many uses from parents and relatives. Jamike had to learn fast. Having lost his father very early in life, he had to come to manhood faster than his age-mates if he and his mother were to survive in a widow's harsh environment.

Jamike started elementary school at about the age of twelve. It had not been but a few years ago that he wore his first pair of shorts. He was seven or eight and liked shorts that had belt loops. Before that age, he was naked in the village like every other boy or girl. Skinny Jamike wore his long oversized belt so tight in those days that it almost went twice around his waist. His mother always feared the boy would crush his intestines with the belt he drew too tight around his stomach.

School was for anyone who could afford it. Most children of Jamike's age in the village were apprenticed to learn a trade. Blacksmithing, bicycle repairing, and carpentry were popular choices. With meager capital received from the selling of farmland or cash crops, some youngsters engaged in petty trading. School meant fees, uniforms, levies, and numerous other requests by teachers. But Uridiya, a woman of determination, had sworn that Jamike would attend school whenever she could afford to put him there. She always said that since she did not know her ABCs, her only child must go to school to learn them. Through him, therefore, she would be enlightened.

Harvest was bountiful the year Jamike started school. Uridiya sold vegetables, palm oil, palm nuts, kernels, and other crops to pay his first fees. Jamike even helped out. He gave his mother the little cash he earned from the baskets he wove and the crude kitchen knives he learned to make at the local blacksmith's workshop. These he constructed with the help of the blacksmith's son who was his age-mate and who was learning his father's trade. It was generally the custom in the village for first sons to learn the trade of their fathers. Because Jamike occasionally visited the blacksmith to help fire the furnace for him, he was allowed to tinker with bits and pieces of iron and scrap metal. He learned to make crude kitchen knives and simple types of cutlasses for grass cutting. It became known in the village that he was talented in things technical.

At school Jamike showed a remarkable brilliance that villagers did not expect from the son of a widow. At the end of every term, results of examinations were called and report cards given out to pupils in the assembly hall with parents in attendance. Parents who could afford school fees but whose children did not do well in schoolwork were quick to point to Jamike as a kid whose widowed mother could ill afford his fees, but who came first in class most of the time. He missed classes only when he was sent home for not paying his fees. Uridiya knew well that once in a while she would not be able to afford the fees, but this did not deter her from putting her son in school. She believed that somehow her god who had provided for them through all these years would not abandon her.

Each time Jamike returned to school after staying away for a couple of days for not paying his fees, he was quick to catch up and would still be among the top students, scoring the highest marks in class tests and examinations. Being sent home from school was what Jamike expected whenever he did not have his fees. Even with this knowledge the boy still went to school when fees were due, hoping he would be lucky not to be sent home.

What happened to Jamike one Monday morning was a situation he had been through often for not paying his fees. To make the matter worse, he was late to school too. It was a cloudy and chilly morning in January during the dry harmattan season. There was dryness everywhere as trees reeled in the wind that sent leaves and debris spiraling high into the sky. Smoke and sparks rose from many compounds where fires were made in the open air and children surrounded them to warm their ashy bodies.

Uridiya got up early to gather palm nuts to cook. They needed palm oil for use and for sale toward his fees. She noticed that she did not have enough water and wanted Jamike to run to the stream three miles away to fetch water before going to school.

Jamike came out from the room where he slept on a mat on a ribbed bamboo bed. Stretching himself and rubbing his eyes he approached the fire for warmth, extending his open palms toward the rising flames. He was the first child by the fire. Shortly after, other children in the compound crouched around stretching their hands toward the flame like Jamike. At this time of the year it was a ritual to warm up before getting ready for school.

"Jamike, I noticed I will need more water to cook these palm nuts," Uridiya said to her son who just got out of bed.

"How did you plan to cook palm nuts when you didn't have enough water? Were you going to borrow water?"

"No matter what else I may borrow, son, I will not borrow God-made water. I will not cook with empty hands, anyway."

"That's what I wonder about."

"Please, son, can you run to fetch me a pot of water before you go to school?"

"Mama, I will be late for school. Each time I go late, I get flogged. I am not going to the stream this morning." He stood and staggered away from Uridiya, upset and shaking his head.

"If you go right away you will not be late."

"I am not going." He leaned angrily on a mud wall and wiped tears with the back of his palm.

"Jamike, please go fetch your mother some water. I am not going to drink the oil I am making. This is the palm oil I will sell to get money for the fees your teachers never tire of asking you to bring."

"I know, Mama. I will be late to school and I will be flogged." Jamike began to look for a bucket so he could take his bath.

"Jamike, please, my son. Please, my husband. Just one pot of water will do. You will not go a second time." Uridiya called him such an endearing name like "my husband" whenever Jamike did something special or she wanted to cajole him to run an errand she suspected he would resist. Jamike put down the bucket he wanted to use for bathing and picked up a clay pot. He held it by the neck.

"Jamike, do not hold that pot by its neck. It is clay and not iron and will easily break. Before you know it you will be holding the neck while the pot is in pieces on the ground." Jamike placed the pot on his head and moved toward the wooden gate of the compound.

"I will fetch a pot of water and only one pot. I will not go two times to the stream this morning. I don't want to be late to school. The teacher told us we would learn new arithmetic today."

"No, darling, one pot is all I need. Take quick steps. Let me see you back right now." While he was gone Uridiya set the big earthen pot on a roaring fire with the water available. It was for the second or maybe the third round of cooking that she would need more water.

Jamike was late to school as he worried he would be. There was already a line of latecomers kneeling outside the school gate. The assistant headmaster, Mr. Ndu, was standing with a bundle of canes to administer strokes on each student's buttocks. The headmaster, Mr. Ahamba, a disciplinarian, stressed punctuality to school, but it was his assistant who enforced it through corporal punishment. The assistant headmaster was notorious for flogging. Students nicknamed him "Eze Nkita," dogtooth, because students said his teeth were set like a dog's and he showed no mercy when flogging as a dog would show none when biting.

A woman who once brought her son to Mr. Ndu, against the youngster's wish, to protest the severity of the strokes that gave her child a bruise on the head had to leave his office in haste because Mr. Ndu threatened to flog her too. Until the student in question passed out from that elementary school he was made fun of by his classmates because of the speed with which his mother hurried out of Mr. Ndu's office to avoid being flogged too. When the story reached the village those who heard it thought the woman showed no common sense by protesting to a teacher who disciplined her child. She should rather be thankful to the teacher.

On every school day, once morning assembly was in progress, Mr. Ndu would close the school's big gate, and every latecomer would kneel outside the gate waiting for no less than six strong strokes of his cane on the buttocks. If the pupil did not scream loud enough because of the pain inflicted, he would be called back for two additional strokes, sometimes on the pupil's back, head, calf, or anywhere else Mr. Ndu determined the pain would be more severely felt.

But students soon devised ways to cope with the harsh strokes of Mr. Ndu's canes. Some students who knew they would be late for school or who committed an infraction would take time to pad their buttocks with layers of dried banana leaves or rags in readiness for him; others wore two or more khaki shorts. The young boys looked odd with raised buttocks, obviously disproportionate to their small bodies. It seemed, though, that Mr. Ndu knew their trick, because suddenly he began to raise his hand higher in the air, and the strokes came down harder on their backsides. Each latecomer would step up to him and receive his strokes. Brave students would step forward faster, while the chicken-hearted would move behind others as if to shield themselves until the inevitable encounter with Mr. Ndu's cane. Jamike stepped up this morning and the sound on his stuffed buttocks went "tu-wai, tu-wai," six times. He ran in with the expected scream to fool Mr. Ndu, grabbing his raffia school bag on the run, with laughter in his heart.

Jamike was not in class for more than ten minutes this particular morning when his teacher, Mr. Ekweariri, sent him away for not having his school levy. He went outside and stood by the window trying to peep at the blackboard where the teacher had set the new arithmetic for the day. What pained the boy most were not the strokes he received for lateness to school. It was the new arithmetic that students would learn that day. Jamike wished he could stay but he would go home to help his mother prepare palm oil.

On a day like this Monday morning when he was sent home, as soon as Jamike stepped into the compound, his raffia bag slung across his left shoulder, Uridiya would move up to him and ask,

"My child, what did they say you did today? You may have to leave this schooling alone." She knew the only reason for which her son could be sent home from school.

"They said I did not bring the money I told you about when you came back from the market the other day."

Uridiya sighed and continued to stir the pot full of palm nuts cooking in the open on a dry season day. A goat came close to her feet to eat peelings of the cocoyam she would cook with the nuts. Uridiya hit the goat on the waist with a clenched fist. She examined her fingers and cursed the goat for making her hurt her knuckles. Jamike wondered why his mother would worry about a goat trying to eat cocoyam peelings that would be trashed later.

"The cocoyam peelings will become manure for crop when they are spread on the farm. Why should the goat be allowed to eat them?" Uridiya chastised the goat and responded as if she'd read her son's mind.

Uridiya walked away from the hearth, cleaning her sweaty forehead with the back of her palm. She asked Jamike to add firewood to the decreasing flame burning outside the periphery of the big pot. Jamike added firewood and pushed back wood burning away from the pot. He went down on his knees and lowered his head toward the smoldering firewood to blow air into the fire. After drawing in air and blowing rhythmically for some seconds, the dry firewood logs ignited and flames rushed from under the pot, causing Jamike to move his face away quickly and rose. A woman whom Uridiya asked for help arrived late because her child was still breast-feeding. She apologized. On seeing Jamike she asked why he was not in school.

"I was sent back." She inquired no further.

After a short while, Uridiya behaved as if she was just

hearing what Jamike said for the first time.

"Jamike, what is the reason you said they sent you away from school today?"

"It is because of the money."

"Which money is it, now? Did you say you told Uridiya about it?"

"If you bring an oath I will swear I told you. Maybe you forgot."

"You will swear no oath, my son," the visitor chimed in.

"This time, Jamike, you are going to swear that oath for me, because you always claim to tell me these things." Uridiya did not mean it.

"Bring the oath. I will swear it."

"You see, this is the reason why people do not go to this thing you call school." She stirred the pot filled with palm nuts while standing, with steam enveloping her. She pulled her face, sneezed, and continued, "Everyday there is one kind of money or the other to pay. Do these teachers ever spend the money given to them before they ask for more?"

"Mama, you talk as if I am the only student asked to bring money." Jamike was irritated.

"No, my son, you are not the only one. That is the way those teachers are," Uridiya's helper added.

"Well, I cannot get money by magic or through the movement of my bowel. The palm oil I am making is for sale."

"I am still waiting for the oath."

"You are not swearing any oath for Uridiya."

"Jamike, find something to do. Two of us can handle the palm nuts; do not stay idle. No living person stays idle. See if the goat has something to eat. Do we have drinking water in that pot? Do we have enough firewood? You can visit the farm near the market square and see what mischief has been done to the yam stems. Jamike, I tell you this all the time, and I will not tire of saying it. You are the husband I have today. You are not a child anymore. Remember what the elders say, that no matter how young a male child is when his father dies, he starts from that point to stay awake at night. It is a true statement, and I hope you understand it."

"So when others are asleep I would be awake. What would I be doing?"

"When the time comes, son, you will understand the meaning of what I am saying. I will not be the one to remind you to stay awake at night while children whose fathers are living would be sleeping. An orphan learns these facts fast. You are an orphan on your father's side. Do not forget it. That's what I am talking about."

Some days, like Saturdays or during the holidays when Jamike was not at school, he would busy himself constructing mousetraps for sale. He hunted lizards, rabbits, or squirrels with some of the adults in the kindred. He usually held their hunting bag for them. At the end of the day, they gave him a share of their kill. On one occasion when he hunted by himself, Jamike gave a squirrel a long chase, the animal dribbling him around. He tripped twice before the animal hopped onto the nearest tree and sat on a very high branch. From there, the squirrel viewed Jamike with disdain. Anger and desperation filled Jamike as he stood arms akimbo, looking at the prey that got away. Said he,

"Since you are a runner, why did you not continue with me on the ground? If you are not a coward, why do you sit where I cannot reach you?" Jamike shook his fist at the animal.

He broke a cassava stem, held it at one end, and with all his might threw it at the squirrel. The stick went in a different direction from where the animal was comfortably perching, twitching its whiskers. By the time he broke another cassava stem and readied to hurl it, the squirrel saw Jamike's movement and was nowhere to be found.

"Thank your god, you escaped today," he said. "Your luck cannot continue forever. Try coming my way tomorrow and find out if your head will not cook in a pot. Idiot!"

Jamike moved deliberately in the bush in search of a quarry, attentive to every noise or movement on the ground or on the trees. He used his machete to cut impediments on his path. Suddenly he stopped. His foot stepped on a hard object. He cleared the ground with the tip of his machete. It was a big snail and would make good meat.

Three

Years of widowhood and harsh living took their toll on Uridiya's body. The furrowed forehead, the gray hair, and slightly drawn cheeks bespoke this as she continued to survive the machinations of relatives who constantly wronged her when Jamike was growing up. Jamike proved brilliant in primary school. Many times he would come home and inform his mother he came first in class at the end of the school term. If Uridiya asked for the "piece of paper" the teacher gave him to prove what he told her, Jamike would explain that his report card was withheld because of fees he did not pay. Each time this was the case, Uridiya would curse the death that took Nnorom away, depriving him of the joy of seeing his only child grow up and excel in school.

"They can hold your report card for as long as they want. If they want, they can chew and swallow it too. But one day it will be given to you. Anyone who seizes a child's possession and holds it high beyond the child's reach will bring the item down when his or her hand starts hurting. Uridiya didn't say this, it is a proverb I heard from the elders."

On occasions when Jamike announced that he passed his examinations, Uridiya would come out in the middle of the compound to rejoice, calling her ancestors to join her. She would bend low at her waist and take successive dance steps in different directions and at the end of each routine, raise her leg and slap her loincloth. Then she would raise both open hands toward the sky, with or without Jamike's report card, saying:

"If only Nnorom were alive this day! Alive to see his little seed of yesterday make him happy! Death, did you do this to me?" Uridiya would slap her open palm on her chest. "Did you say that a man who suffered would not see the fruit of his labor? No, death, do not rejoice, you are not victorious. I say you have not won. For as long as Jamike is alive, Nnorom is alive. Shame on you and the devil."

Other women in the compound hearing her loud voice would come out to rejoice with her. Some would give her high five. Uridiya did not think they were all happy for her, but she couldn't care less.

"My God, if Nnorom lived, maybe I would have given him another child," she continued; "It is not a law that he would have only one child because he was an only child himself. But I swore I would not bring forth a child with another man. Shame to all those who promised heaven and earth to give Uridiya another child." The women laughed and thought the menopausal Uridiya should be thankful to God for the miracle of Jamike rather than talk nonsense.

"*Chineke*, what did I do to deserve this? But I know it will be all right, that you will wipe my tears away through the son you have placed in my hands to look after. He does not belong to me. He is yours. I am only a caretaker. My Lord, the power is in your hands, not in mine."

Jamike could not have finished primary school were it not for the village headmaster, Mr. Ahamba, who took over the payment of his fees. The headmaster was a middle-aged man from the distant town of Emekukwu where the missionaries first settled in that part of Eastern Nigeria. He was portly, and his head was beginning to bald. His people had been long in contact with the missionaries, and he was one of those to receive education early in the nineteen forties.

Though Jamike's examination report cards were often

withheld, Uridiya managed to pay the fees in the end. It happened that for two consecutive terms, the same bright pupil that came first in Primary Standard Three examinations had his results withheld for not completing his fees. The headmaster was aware of this but did not know who the pupil was. When Jamike's result was again withheld at the end of his first term in Primary Standard Four, the headmaster asked to see the pupil. Jamike was petrified when Ekweariri, his teacher, took him to see the headmaster, Mr. Ahamba, at the beginning of the second term.

The headmaster's office was in fading blue color. Roof rafters and crossbeams were visible in the room with no ceiling. Jamike and his teacher stood a good distance from the headmaster's wooden table with a green blotter that covered half the tabletop. There were class registers on one side of the table and teachers' notes of lessons on another side. Three bottles of black, blue, and red ink, pencils and fountain pens were obvious.

"Good afternoon, sir. This is the pupil, sir."

"What is your name, young man?" Ahamba asked the boy who stood at frozen attention.

"Jamike," he replied, shaking in his knees.

"Who pays your school fees?" he asked in a deep voice, as he looked at him straight in his face. Jamike dropped his head.

"My mother."

"Why does your father leave your mother to pay your fees?"

"My father is not alive," Jamike stated.

"How long ago did he die?"

"Sir, I don't know. My mother said I was a little boy then," he answered.

"What type of work does your mother do to get money for your fees?"

"Sir, she sells whatever she gets from the farm." Jamike began to sweat.

"Things like what?"

Jamike told the headmaster that his mother sold vegetables, cocoyam, pepper, palm oil, and palm kernel.

"Does your mother not have some other person in the family who can help her pay your fees?" The boy regained his confidence.

"Sir, it is my father's brother but he is not on good terms with my mother. They quarrel all the time. He did not want me to attend school."

"What did he want you to do?"

"Sir, he wanted me to learn how to repair bicycles."

"You know your last term's result was withheld because you did not complete your fees?"

"Sir, I know." Mr. Ahamba looked at the teacher and shook his bald head.

"What a waste of talent if this boy does not finish schooling."

"There are many like him, sir, but this boy is different because he is always first in class examinations." Jamike did not fully understand what the headmaster said about talent.

Jamike's teacher noted that very soon students would be sent home for non-payment of the present term's fees, and Jamike would be among them. At this point the headmaster told Mr. Ekweariri, and Jamike thought he heard him well, not to send the student away for lack of school fees until both of them discussed it. He asked Jamike to return to his classroom while his teacher stayed back. As he left the headmaster's office, Jamike tried to think about why the headmaster would ask his teacher not to send him away if he did not pay his fees. Did he mean Jamike would not pay school fees anymore, or is it that the headmaster would now pay for him? He did not understand it. The teacher came closer to the headmaster's table.

"Who will take care of his fees, sir? You know it would be unfair to send other students home without Jamike being sent home too."

"I will take over the payment from now on. A bright young man like this should be assisted, or he would leave school and begin to waste his life in the village and never realize his potential."

"Do you mean this, sir?"

"I would not say so if I did not mean it."

"What you have said is true, sir, about children not being able to realize their potential because of lack of money," the teacher said. "What you have done, sir, has no comparison. It is wonderful, sir. You know, sir, that you need to arrange to see his mother so she won't have to worry herself to death about this term's fees. Parents lose sleep and pine away when it is time for school fees and money is not available."

"I plan to do so. I will, however, need someone to direct me to his home." The headmaster thought for a few seconds. "No, I think the best thing to do will be to follow Jamike home after school next Friday. That's what I am going to do."

"That would be the best way to go about it. Thank you, sir." Teacher Ekweariri left the office thinking how lucky Jamike was among other students. "Well, he is intelligent," he muttered.

That night the headmaster and his wife, Asamuka, discussed his intention. She said it was worthwhile and gave her support. That was not the first time the headmaster and his wife had helped an indigent student, but for Jamike they planned to be responsible for his fees until he completed elementary school in Primary Standard Six, three years away.

It was a little after two o'clock in the afternoon on a Friday. The sun was still hot. Hawks flew high and drifted in clear skies. Dry oil-bean pods exploded on trees from the sun's heat, and children ran with speed into bushes in different directions, not minding thorns, shrubs, and other impediments to pick oil-bean seeds. Though the market was settling to its usual noisy business at this time, some men could be seen strolling leisurely and chatting on their way while women with baskets of goods to sell walked at a more than normal pace.

Most villagers had gone to the market, and the village was generally quiet. School children who played ball along the road were still heading home. Uridiya, usually prompt for the market, was still in her backyard arranging and tying her basket. Akudike, her late husband's brother, tired from the day's farm work sent his grandson to the market for tobacco and palm wine while he swept out the goat shed and organized his veranda.

The headmaster dismounted his white Raleigh bicycle at the gate of the compound and stood it to the left of Akudike's out house. School children who saw him on his way down the dirt road were surprised but excited that he was in their neighborhood. Some ran off to tell their parents that their headmaster had gone into Jamike's compound with him, but they were doubted. Others stood and stared, wondering what might have happened. They thought the boy must have committed a serious offense at school for the headmaster to bring him home. Uridiya answered her son from her backyard. Jamike hurried back there and in a moment was out with his mother.

Uridiya was gripped with apprehension when Jamike introduced the headmaster. She greeted him but did not know what to make of this unusual visit.

"Headmaster, what brought you to our compound this day? Whatever it is, it must be your spirit that has been delaying me. I would have long been in the market by now. I hope it is nothing bad. Children are very rascally these days."

"Your son brought me, but it is for a good reason. I like to visit in the village from time to time, but I just haven't made it to this area before now."

"God bless you that you remember us. May it be good to you." Akudike raised his head and kept an ear in the direction of the conversation.

Uridiya called on Akudike to come out to see who had come to visit them. He chided her for keeping the headmaster standing while she talked to him.

"Find the headmaster a seat," he scolded Uridiya. He shook the headmaster's hand and motioned him to his veranda. Once they sat down, he offered kola nut and alligator pepper, which he fished out of his bag, and apologized for not having any palm wine.

"Please pardon our inadequacy."

"You have offered kola nut to welcome me and that is enough in our tradition. After all, I did not inform you I was coming to visit."

Jamike was standing and holding on to the wood column that supported Akudike's veranda, his feet crossed as if he was about to swing around the wood.

"I thank you for the kola nut. Let me not hold you from leaving for the market. It is past time. Uridiya, is this your son?" He looked at Uridiya and pointed at Jamike.

"He is the only child God gave to me and his father."

"He did not ask you for a story, Uridiya, storyteller. If you begin your story I will leave you to continue. He asked you a simple question. He hasn't told you why he is here," Akudike cautioned.

"Oh, I will shut up. When he asks me the next question, you tell me what to answer. Pardon me, headmaster. This is the way they shut me up in this compound. I have no say, not even to tell you that Jamike is my child without a rebuke from those who own me." The headmaster was amused. He understood family squabbles.

"The reason I came here is to talk about your son, Jamike. He is an intelligent student and does well in class, coming first in examinations most of the time. I found out from his teacher that his end of school term result is always withheld, either because he has not completed his fees for the term or he failed to pay anything at all..." Uridiya cut in.

"Your observation is right. I pay, as I am able, when I can. Things are hard for the two of us. But I have sworn to my god that he will go to school. Let God do his wish on him."

Jamike listened to every word that came out of the headmaster's mouth and watched as well the look of consternation on his mother's face. Jamike had told his mother about the meeting with the headmaster and his teacher early in the week but Uridiya did not think much about it. She thought the boy did not understand what he was talking about.

"Hold on, Uridiya." Akudike interjected. "Headmaster,

though she took the word from your mouth, what she said is true. Since the boy's father, my brother, died, the woman you are looking at here has suffered in raising this boy. Whether they see what to eat or not they carry on. It is from what she scratches out of the farm that she uses for both of them. These days the farm does not yield much. However, God has blessed her with a good boy. Of all the children in the kindred, this child is number one in character. Just mention the errand and he is on his way. If you give him a message for someone he does not forget it while playing, like other children do these days. He is a good boy. Please, continue your statement," Akudike said.

"Woman, you have tried very much. I praise you for your determination that your boy will be educated."
Uridiya adjusted herself on the bamboo bench in Akudike's cool veranda. On hot days this bench serves as a bed for the old man.

"Since I did not go to school, let him go there and read the books for himself and for me," she cut in again. Akudike was irritated.

"Headmaster, do you see that? This is what I am talking about. Uridiya, please allow the man to talk. You have started the behavior that brings you in conflict and gets you in trouble with the village people. Keep your mouth shut."

"I have kept it shut. God gave me a mouth to talk with, but all of you in our kindred say Uridiya will not talk. I agree. Jamike, do you see what I tell you all the time? Thank God these things keep happening before you."

A kinsman came into the compound to see Akudike but he was asked to wait outside for him. This man heard that the headmaster was in the compound and had come to verify. He asked to tell Akudike he would return, but did not.

"I don't have a long statement to make. I come to talk about Jamike, your son. He is a bright young man who does outstandingly well in schoolwork. I found out that he has continuous difficulty in paying fees or school levies. He informed me that his father died when he was a child, leaving his mother the burden of raising him and now struggling with his school needs. I fully understand his plight. My own father died when I was a schoolboy, but my situation was different. Not many children attended school in those days, so the Catholic mission helped to support me. I am here to tell you that starting from this term I will take over the payment of your son's fees until he finishes Primary Standard Six in three years. I will give him what is called scholarship. It is from me and not from the mission or the government."

"What did he say he is giving Jamike?" Uridiya asked Akudike.

"It is scholarship. It simply means I will pay his fees and buy his books while he attends school. So, let's leave it at that so you can go on to the market. I need to leave too to take care of school matters." He did not say that, Uridiya thought. She moved closer to Akudike and held his lap. Her body shivered.

"Akudike, what did he say? I doubt if I heard him right. Please tell me what he said, so I won't misunderstand him." Akudike could not believe what he heard, either.

"I am not deaf yet, but hold on while I ask the headmaster to repeat what he said so it would not be that we did not hear him properly.

"Headmaster, what did you say? Please say it again so we may hear it well."

Jamike himself thought he heard the headmaster very well. He was now thinking about the flogging and being sent away for school fees. These would be no more, and he would not have to cry on his way to school because Uridiya did not have the fees to give him. His school report card would not be withheld anymore, and he could now jubilate like other students when school results were announced at the end of the school term instead of leaving the assembly hall downcast. He believed he heard the headmaster clearly. The headmaster answered Akudike and repeated what he just said.

"I said I will take over the payment of Jamike's fees from now on. This means from his present class, Primary

Standard Four, up to Standard Six. I will be his father in this respect. You only have to provide him food, clothing, and other things a boy needs. Do not worry about his school fees and books." Uridiya fell to the ground on her knees. Her hands up and palms open, she said:

"Headmaster, I thank you. Who said that man is not God to man? Yes, man is the God we see everyday. He works His miracles like this one through man. Headmaster, you are God this day for my child and me. Nnorom, are you seeing the good that is coming into your household? Death be shamed! Akudike, can you see? You said I should shut my mouth. This time I don't have the mouth to talk. You can do all the talking now. How do we thank him? How will I be able to thank this savior? I leave that in your hands." She moved closer to the headmaster and held his knees, tears welling in her eyes. Imagine not paying school fees any more!

An arrow of envy shot through Akudike because Uridiya's hardship was about to lessen. He had mocked that Uridiya had a grand plan to educate her son when she had no means to do so and failed to heed his advice that the boy should learn bicycle repairing or blacksmithing, for which he seemed gifted. He used to comment that Uridiya thought education would be cheap or something one could obtain by hoping and praying God to provide. The boy, Jamike, he told people, would have been a blacksmith by now instead of all these years he was wasting in school he would never complete.

"Headmaster, I thank you," Akudike said. "Our Lord bless you. You saw a widow's son, and you want to do the work of a father for him. May God reward you and bless your family. I am speechless. I will pass on this good news to our people. They will be overjoyed. It has been a long time this woman has been suffering. She tries to borrow money from here and there but villagers have their own problems. How can you give to someone when you have none to eat?" He turned to Jamike.

"Jamike, you have heard it. Your headmaster said you would complete your schooling. You have nothing else to worry about but only to read your books. The heavy load has been taken off your mother. So wherever the book goes you follow it. The headmaster has said you have brains. I am not surprised. I, myself, have known you have brains since you were born."

Jamike, still standing, his eyes roving over everything on Akudike's veranda, nodded his head. A goat suddenly jumped out from the goat shed and made toward the gate to enter a neighbor's farm. The woman who owned the farm had complained that Akudike's goats are never reined in but instead left to eat her vegetables.

"Jamike, go after that foolish goat and chase him right back." Jamike grabbed a long stick and went in pursuit as he always did. The gate was closed. The goat gave him a couple of run-arounds, racing and galloping all over the compound and kicking down a clay pot of water in his path before jumping back into the shed with speed. There was water everywhere. Jamike followed the errant goat into the shed and gave a good hit of his stick.

As the headmaster got up to leave, he said to Jamike,

"I will talk with your teacher on Monday. I will introduce you to my family. Obi is in the same class with you, though you are much older."

"Sir, I know him. Is there nobody who doesn't know the headmaster's son?" Jamike said.

"Yes, everyone ought to know the son of the headmaster. If the headmaster's son is not known, whose son will be known?" Uridiya joined.

"Come to me if you have any problem in school. I don't expect any but do not be afraid to come to my office or my home. I will introduce you to my family."

"Jamike, did you hear him? Everything is now in your hands. The headmaster said you are now his son and a member of his family." Uridiya was pleased.

They all saw the headmaster off to the road. He mounted his white bicycle and they kept looking at him until he rode out of their sight. Akudike asked Uridiya if the headmaster said that the fees should be repaid. He wished that would be the case.

"I watched his mouth to see if he would say so, but I did not hear him say that."

"It must be free then. This is your own gift from God for the year. My son, Jamike, rejoice because your brain gave this to you."

Uridiya left late for the market, remarking that what God had given her through the headmaster she could not get on her own even if she sold herself a hundred times over. She asked Jamike to eat the leftover plantain porridge they had the previous night and to be sure to fetch some firewood.

After his meal, Jamike went out to play soccer with his age-mates along the dirt road. They were envious of him because the headmaster came to their house. They did not believe him when he told them what the headmaster said. Later he went into a nearby bush and quickly got some firewood. Uridiya had warned Jamike about that particular bush, because the owner swore to put some evil charm in it against intruders searching for firewood. Jamike did not worry about that, because he had seen the farm owner's children enter the same bush too to pick firewood.

Another person who played a role in Jamike's education was Reverend Father Thomas Murrow, Aludo's parish priest. He was a tall and thin Irishman who walked with a slight stoop. Villagers liked him because he was very kind to them. But they wondered why he remained thin if he ate all those large quantities of eggs, fowls and other food items that female parishioners donated every week. The Catholic mission gave Jamike the scholarship that enabled him to attend Teachers' College for four years after primary school and later employed him as a pupil-teacher in the parish. It was Bishop Kelly's policy to send the top three students of the graduating class in each elementary school in the diocese to Teacher Training College. It was his way of preparing future teachers for the Catholic mission.

Jamike was already eighteen years of age when he arrived at Bishop Shannahan Teachers' College to begin his four-year teacher's training. On the successful completion of this course, he would become a trained teacher. It was the first time he would leave home for another town.

Life began to change for Uridiya and her son during Jamike's first year at the teachers' college. The little stipend he received from the parish priest enabled him to help his mother with food money. At first Uridiya refused the offer, because she did not think Jamike had enough for himself. But Jamike insisted. For Easter he bought her some cheap new clothes. Uridiya thanked her son and commented that she could not remember the last time she wore new clothes. Villagers could see a gradual difference in Uridiya's clothes and behavior while her son was a student.

Jamike completed the four-year teacher-training course successfully, scoring merit and distinction in many subjects. As was the practice, after teacher training, newly graduated teachers were employed in their respective parishes as trained-teachers in the primary schools. Father Thomas Murrow employed Jamike as an elementary school teacher at a new school in the village. He taught Primary Standard Four and soon became popular as Games Master. Life for him and his mother would never be the same again.

The headmaster continued his mentoring. At his urging, the first project Jamike embarked upon was to add a two-room house next to Uridiya's. It took less than two weeks for the mud walls to reach roof level. Jamike's class pupils fetched water needed for mixing the mud. His age-mates spent a Saturday helping him to put the bamboo roof and thatch. Attached to the sidewall of his mother's house, Jamike's house was higher than other houses that dotted the compound in a semi-circular form.

In three months, Teacher Jamike was settled in a two-room mud house. The frontal side of the outside walls was plastered with a thin layer of cement, an achievement for that time. Headmaster Ahamba gave Jamike the whitewash that was painted on the cemented surface. Uncle Akudike marveled at the sudden turn of fortune for Uridiya and her son. Some people in the village felt proud of the young man, others were envious.

While Jamike was having his two-room addition built, he also turned his attention to other matters he had vowed to address as soon as he began to earn money. He wanted to get back a couple of the farmlands and fruit trees that his mother pawned to put him in primary school. Surprisingly, Jamike did not have any problem in regaining the three pieces of land involved. One particular person who it was feared would not return the land Uridiya pledged to him was Mr. Ngere, a petty businessman in the village. He had money by village standards and was known to put difficulties in the way of debtors who wished to recover any property pawned to him.

Despite his meanness, however, he was the last resort, the lesser of two evils, for villagers in dire need of money. Mr. Ngere sometimes took them to court or threatened to do so if they did not pay his exorbitant interest when it came time to recover their property. Because these debtors could not afford court costs, some abandoned their property or farmland to him. Mr. Ngere accepted back the money Uridiya borrowed from him and returned their farmland to Jamike without difficulty. Some villagers believed the reason he quickly gave back the land was because his son had been a pupil in Jamike's class or because he feared he might be challenged if he contemplated appropriating Uridiya's land.

Four

It was during his second year of teaching that Jamike met Paul Laski when he went to play tennis on the secondary school lawn. Laski was a member of the American Peace Corps who was posted to Aludo's new Saint Silas Secondary School where the town's parish priest, Reverend Father Thomas Murrow, was also the principal. Father Murrow had almost given up on his request for a science teacher when the Ministry of Education sent Laski, a man in his late thirties. Laski had a Bachelor of Science degree in chemistry from the University of California at Los Angeles and was teaching in a high school in Richmond, Virginia, when he joined the Peace Corps. Africa fascinated him, and while at the university he decided to join the Peace Corps upon graduation. On his application form he indicated he would like to be sent to any English-speaking country in Sub-Sahara Africa, and he was glad to be sent to Nigeria.

Laski was a fitness addict who enjoyed lawn tennis. Jamike learned to play tennis at the Teacher's College where he was engaged in various sports. Saint Silas Secondary School was not far from Jamike's home, and he always went there to play tennis, often playing with novices he taught the game. After watching some tennis games one evening Laski identified Jamike as a good player and invited him to a game. They enjoyed playing each other, as both were good at it though Laski had more experience.

Jamike became Laski's tennis partner and they played on weekends and some evenings. Jamike's tennis partnership with the American grew into friendship. Most evenings, after a game, Jamike would go to Laski's house located in the secondary school compound to refresh and talk. He asked many questions about America, some of which Laski found funny or even silly. Jamike wanted to know many things about America because of the fantastic stories about the country. Each person in the village who heard something about America had always added one or two more fantasies. In addition to questions about the land and people, Jamike also wanted to know if everyone in America was a millionaire and if there were cowboys on the streets shooting people.

Jamike was also curious to know if many Americans engaged in magic. He told Laski that when he was a boy, itinerant magicians went from one primary school to another performing amazing conjuring and disappearing acts. Before the magician began his act, he would work the crowd up into frenzy, exhorting them to chant:

Come and see America wonder
Come and see America wonder
Come and see America wonder
Come and see America wonder

As the crowd sang and clapped their hands, the magician would exhort them to sing even louder and faster, while shouting "Abracadabra, abracadabra." Then he would open his mouth so they could confirm it was empty. After much dancing and joining in the singing, he would start pulling out handkerchiefs tied end-to-end from his mouth. He would further amaze the crowd of school children by igniting a blaze on a rod and shoving it deep into his mouth and down his throat to extinguish the flame. Many children closed or turned away their eyes because they thought the magician would choke.

One Sunday evening when Laski invited Jamike for dinner, they talked about education in America, among other topics. Jamike was fascinated by the differences between education in America and in Nigeria. He was surprised to learn that what was called college in Nigeria was high school in America, and what was called college in America was called university in Nigeria. Jamike showed so much interest in American education that Laski thought it might be good for his tennis partner to be exposed to it. He put a question to him.

"Have you considered studying in the United States?"

"Well, I believe to consider that would amount to dreaming. I cannot even begin to entertain such a dream. I think people usually stretch their hands as far as they can reach."

"Not exactly, at times people stretch their hands beyond their reach and hope to attain their goal. They may not always succeed, but they wouldn't succeed unless they tried."

"You may be right, but I don't have any basis for hoping to go to America to study. As the saying goes around here, who would give a toad a gift of a coat?"

"That's funny. You are not a toad, what are you talking about?" Jamike laughed.

"That would be an impossible dream. It was almost impossible for me to finish primary school had it not been for the school headmaster, Mr. Ahamba."

"How then did you go to get a teaching diploma?"

Jamike always felt emotional when he had to recollect aspects of his growing up. They reminded him of the hardship he and his mother went through, and especially of relatives who were unkind to them. It was a past he would rather put behind him.

"It was the Catholic mission that gave me the scholarship to go to Teacher Training College,"

"How did that come about?"

"After completing primary school, I wanted to go to the city to look for a clerical job. My mother said she would commit suicide if I left her for the city, because she was informed that people who live there easily forget home and parents for a life of enjoyment and rascality. She did not want her only child so exposed. She wanted me to stay in the village and engage in some petty trading or learn some handiwork."

"What did you intend to be?"

"I wanted to be a clerk. I admired the clerks who were sent by the bishop to invigilate primary school final examinations."

"Being a clerk is not a bad ambition."

"It was while my mother and the headmaster considered what I would do after primary school that the parish priest sent for me."

"Was that Father Murrow?"

"Yes. He informed me that I was one of few students in the diocese selected by the bishop to attend Teacher Training College."

"Was there any basis for this?"

"It was at the time the diocese needed teachers for local primary schools. The bishop decided to select and train as teachers the top three students in the First School Leaving Certificate Examinations, the final examinations in primary school. In addition to this there was also the diocesan examination set by the Catholic mission. Father Murrow told me I had one of the best results in both examinations. The bishop gave all three of us scholarships."

"How long did this training last?"

"It was a four-year teacher training course. Each student was bonded to teach for two years in one of the primary schools in the diocese after completion of the course. When Father Murrow invited me to his house and mentioned the possibility of furthering my education, I told him my mother could not afford any more schooling for me. Then he asked if I would further my education if someone else paid my fees."

"I would," Laski interjected.

"That was exactly what I told Father Murrow. He then informed me I had the Bishop's Scholarship to attend

Teacher Training College. I could not believe it. He brought out the college prospectus and went through the requirements with me. After that, he gave it to me, blessed me, and wished me well. When I informed my mother of it, she doubted me. Her response was, "I will believe it the day I see you bring out your portmanteau and tell me you are on your way to whatever place you call it." The following Sunday, during church service, Father Murrow announced my name as one of the students who received the Bishop's Scholarship for Teacher Training College. It was then my mother believed it." Jamike noticed that Laski showed keen interest in his story, because he smiled and nodded approvingly many times.

"Your mother is an interesting woman."

"She did not want to hear anything about more education. She believed I had enough, and she had no illusions about how expensive education was."

"I would say you have been lucky. It is an amazing story."

"That is my story, and I thank God." Jamike asked for a drink of water.

"I believe I told you in one of our conversations that I will be returning to the United States at the end of this year when my tour of duty ends. I intend to obtain an advanced degree and later look for a teaching job in a college in a rural part of the country. If I do I might be able to help you come to the United States to continue your studies. I am not making any promises, but I will try. I think you will benefit from an American education." Jamike was baffled.

"Are you serious? Even if in the end it is not possible, the thought alone is sufficient. But I tell you, that will be in my wildest dream. As they say, seeing is believing."

"No, just think positive about it. It is when you believe strongly in a thing or want it badly that it actually comes to pass. It is a fact that is not easily appreciated."

"You are right. The Igbo people have a saying similar to what you just said. They say that whatever one affirms, his chi or god will also affirm it. Now, I am going to believe it will happen. I will be in America! Alleluia!" Jamike hit both hands on the table; they laughed and shook hands. For the rest of that evening before he went home with a flashlight, they played a card game.

Paul Laski left for the United States in December of that year and within six months after his departure a civil war broke out in Nigeria. The Eastern part of the country seceded and declared itself the Independent Republic of Biafra. The war lasted thirty months, and during that time young men were conscripted into the armed forces. First, Jamike worked in civil defense and later for CARITAS, the Catholic relief organization. He assisted Father Murrow in overseeing the distribution of scarce food items like salt, stockfish, corned beef, corn meal, milk, baby food, and other essential commodities needed for life's sustenance. Uridiya's friends enjoyed her generosity during the war.

The ravages of war did not get to Aludo, located in the heartland, and villagers believed that had to do with their ancestral name, Aludo, which meant land of peace. Villagers could hear the sounds of heavy military artillery like mortar shells from the faraway city of Umuahia. One time a fighter jet plane flew over Father Murrow's house but dropped no bomb. The two-storied building had a huge Red Cross sign painted on the zinc roof. Apart from one letter Jamike received from Laski before the war broke out, the two friends lost touch for the duration of the war. In the meantime, Laski had gone on to the Pennsylvania State University to get a doctorate degree in science education and began teaching at Regius State College in rural western Pennsylvania.

When the civil war ended, Jamike received Laski's letter inquiring whether he made it through the war. He was worried about his friend because of horrible pictures of the war on television and news stories from Voice of America. These and the images that appeared in magazines and newspapers, gave Laski concern for his friend. Soon correspondence was re-established between them. Shortly after their renewed contact, Laski informed Jamike that he was leaving for a two-year teaching contract in Okinawa, Japan. For about six months, Jamike did not hear from Laski. Once he settled in his new teaching position, Laski wrote Jamike, and their correspondence continued until Laski returned to the United States.

Not long after Jamike began teaching, Mr. Ahamba suggested that he inquire from older and more experienced teachers in the school about the correspondence courses some of them were taking from Woolsey Hall and Rapid Results College in London, England. These courses prepared one who did not attend or finish high school to sit for the Ordinary Level of the General Certificate of Education examinations as an external candidate. He urged Jamike to start such a course so that after he passed the necessary examinations, he could move up to become what was called a pivotal teacher with a high school equivalent and a teacher's training certificate. It would enhance his status and prestige. Two years later, Jamike obtained the General Certificate of Education in four subjects: Economics, British Constitution, English History, and Government.

Laski returned to Regius two years later. Not quite three months after he was back in Regius, Jamike received an application package that included forms for tuition remission for Regius State College.

Fate was about to smile again on both Uridiya and her son in a way that would marvel the village. No one believed that the little boy who walked about naked in the village, hunted rodents, chased rabbits and squirrels wherever he sighted them, and who many didn't think would survive ill health as a child, would one day become a teacher. And little did they think that Jamike would be the one to make the village proud, for he would now travel to America to further his education. He would be the first in his village to set out on an educational mission to a land that the most imaginative villagers could only dream about —a land they had only heard by name, a fairyland, America.

Five

A week after Jamike studied the various documents in the application package, he made his first trip to a major city. A bicyclist took him to Umuahia Township from where he joined a lorry to make the three-hour journey to Enugu, the capital of Eastern Nigeria, the location of the United States Information Services (USIS). The three hours that the trip took did not seem long for Jamike, because he was able to see other towns and villages as well as changing vegetation as they rode through. The villages along the road were bustling with activities. At each stop, hawkers pestered motorists and passengers alike with all kinds of edibles in baskets and enamel trays carried on their heads. Enugu was bewildering to Jamike. The many people on the streets, the roads, electric poles, big and tall buildings, and the hustle and bustle mesmerized him.

The motor park where he was stopped seemed in a state of confusion with too many people moving in all directions; traders had their wares displayed up to the roadway, taxi drivers hustled passengers and everyone seemed to be pushing and shoving their way through. When Jamike finally made his way out of the motor park, he took a taxi to the United States Information Service. The Information Officer whom Jamike met readily made handbooks, brochures, and other materials for foreign students going to the United States for studies available to him. He learned about the necessary steps and requirements for obtaining a student visa and where the United States Embassy was located in Lagos. Jamike went through different college catalogs and handbooks that gave him information about student life in an American college. He spent close to three hours in the library before he returned to Umuahia.

Three months following his application, Jamike received an admission letter along with the Eligibility Form I-20 that would enable him obtain a student visa to the United States. Also in the package was approval for his application for tuition remission scholarship. He planned a trip to the United States embassy in Lagos, Nigeria's capital city, for the following week.

About five o'clock on a Sunday evening, he set out for Lagos. The headmaster and Jamike rode two miles on a bicycle to the major road to catch the night bus. The headmaster judged that since Jamike had no where to pass the night in Lagos, his best bet would be to take a night bus so that he would arrive early the following morning. After conducting his business at the embassy, he would catch another late bus to return home, arriving back the next morning.

Jamike arrived in Lagos in time enough to be at the embassy at ten o'clock that morning. What Jamike saw in Lagos was nowhere near what he saw in Enugu. Right from about five miles to Lagos the landscape began to change. The pace of activities quickened. He saw more people, more cars on many lanes, slum areas, pedestrians boarding public transportation, people spitting verbal abuses on each other as they struggled to board filled buses, different kinds of buildings, and wires crisscrossing poles and buildings. When his taxi stopped in traffic on Cater Bridge, Jamike was mesmerized by the skyscrapers on the horizon and wondered how long it would take someone to get to the top floors. He feared that all those cars on the long bridge would cause it to collapse into the river. Meanwhile, hawkers on the bridge pressured passengers with aggressive sales tactics. Jamike wondered if there were no markets where these individuals could display their goods.

Once he was inside the embassy compound, Jamike

joined a long line of visa seekers, some of whom had arrived there an hour or more earlier. Jamike saw a couple of people with sad faces as he approached the big iron gate. One of them was cursing the embassy official that refused him a visa. A young lady whose husband was a student in the United States was crying in a corner. On enquiry, Jamike learned that she was refused a visa, though she claimed that her husband had sent all the necessary documents. His heart sank. He took a number from an official and sat down to wait for his turn. Jamike entered the office of the consul in trepidation. He collected quickly from the floor the two documents that fell from his nervous hands. The man who motioned him to sit down had a stoic expression on his face. He summoned enough courage to present his papers. Fear did not allow him to observe anything in the consul's office, but he prayed for God's help.

The consul took a quick glance at the first document.

"Jamike Nnorom is your name?"

"Yes, sir." He turned the page over.

"Do you know anyone in the United States?" Jamike decided to answer in the affirmative.

"I know one Mr. Paul Laski, a member of the American Peace Corps who taught in a school in my village."

He turned the pages forward and backward as if searching for any document from Mr. Laski. Jamike wished he did not say he knew anyone in the U.S. Looking straight into his face, the consul asked,

"What are you going to study in the U.S.?"

"Philosophy and Political Science."

"How many years will your studies last?"

"Four years, sir." As the consul very carefully examined each of the applicant's documents, Jamike's heart raced. When the white man gave a nod as he turned the papers Jamike didn't know whether it was a positive sign or that he saw something suspicious. His heart beat faster. The consul pulled out his desk drawer and brought out a stamp. Taking care to center the stamp on the passport page, he imprinted a student's visa for "Duration of Stay" on Jamike's new Nigerian passport. The consul congratulated him, shook his sweating hand, and wished him well in his studies in the United States. Jamike was surprised at the man's kind disposition.

Jamike missed a step as he hurried out of the room. He rushed to the gateman to pick up his traveling bag. On his mind was to hurry out of the compound before the consul would find there was something wrong with his documents or that he made a mistake. A waiting taxi took him back to the motor park. It was four o'clock in the afternoon. He ate some bread with Fanta orange drink and spent time wandering in the vicinity of the motor park since his bus would not leave until nighttime.

Six

Jamike was twenty-seven years of age when he left for America. Villagers gathered in the compound on the morning of his departure. There was movement of people here and there. Some huddled to talk. It was not difficult for an outsider to perceive that something important was going on. Passersby stood around the entrance to the compound trying to find out what happened. People moved about, some with their hands clasped and others with gloomy faces. Uridiya wept with both joy and sadness as she embraced her only child, now a man.

Jamike was ruggedly built with broad shoulders. He was a charming young man with a broad face and a full crop of dense hair that reminded older villagers of Nnorom, his late father. Since his childhood, Jamike often heard people say that he was every inch like his late father. The only resemblance to his mother was his large eyes. Jamike's body exuded strength. As he grew older, especially in his late teens, his height and perceived strength enabled him to ward off people who might have had any intentions of doing harm to his mother.

With tears in her eyes, hands trembling, Uridiya knelt down, clutching her son's legs in her hands. Looking up at him, she raised her two open palms to his face, and said:

"Jamike, look into my heart and into my soul. Remember your mother. My life is in your hands now. Do not do anything that will cause my death if I hear it. I want to stay alive and live long enough to hold your child, my grandchild, on my lap. Remember the headmaster who helped you. Know that without him you would not have been able to complete elementary school. If you forget everyone else, do not forget him and his family. He saved us many times. I know you will not forget anybody who took me for a human being. Almighty, the creator of heaven and earth, will guide and protect you."

Tears welled in Jamike's eyes. Relatives and passers-by that witnessed this spectacle were moved beyond words. When they learned that he was going to be away for many years, the emotions were mixed. The first son of the village to study overseas was leaving for America. It was a thing of joy, yet some looked sad, as if they wished he would stay in the village with them. As a teacher his presence in the village was a thing of pride and conferred some status on them. Some of the old kinsfolk were downcast because they probably thought they might not see him again. He felt the same way, too, as he embraced old kinsmen and women—some of whom walked with canes.

Many relatives followed him to walk the two-mile distance to the tarred road junction where he boarded transport. Uridiya would have preferred not to see him board the bus. The trip to Onitsha from Aludo took nearly three hours. At Onitsha he boarded a bus that made the Lagos journey in ten hours. A contact the headmaster had made with an old schoolmate bore fruit. Mr. Kamalu was at the motor park and had waited nearly two hours before Jamike's bus arrived. It was his second time at the motor park that Friday. The description Jamike had of Mr. Kamalu made it easy to recognize him. It was almost eleven o'clock at night when they got to Kamalu's home in Apapa. It was the next day that Jamike met his host's family.

Mr. Kamalu arranged for the taxi driver who took Jamike to Lagos International Airport, where they arrived at six o'clock in the evening. The driver was a neighbor, and Mr. Kamalu gave him strict instructions not to stop anywhere but the airport. Once he came out of the taxi Jamike was harassed by porters who wanted to carry his small suitcase through the throng of passengers, panhandlers, pickpockets, and thugs to join the check-in line. He held on tight to his suitcase as he entered the terminal building. Jamike was overwhelmed by the huge airport terminal, the large number of people, the hustle and bustle, restaurants, stalls filled with crafts and assorted goods travelers might need, shoe shiners, male nail manicurists seeking business, money changers, and, perhaps, money-doublers too—all manner of people.

At exactly eight o'clock, check-in began. Once he was checked in, Jamike went through customs and immigration and proceeded to the waiting area. He did not talk to anyone, because he did not know anyone. He was still apprehensive about whether or not his suitcase that was taken from him at the check-in counter would be in America when he got there. He consoled himself because other passengers gave their luggage to the check-in clerk. Boarding began at ten o'clock, and it was past midnight when the aircraft's turbo engines began to rave as it readied to move. Many thoughts ran through Jamike's mind as he sat quietly in his economy-class seat.

"So this is it. I am leaving home," he mused. "Leaving with no idea of when I will be back. I wish it was not midnight so I can see the bushes and trees on the horizon." What he saw instead were dazzling, colored lights on the runway and the blinking lights on the wings of the airplane. Jamike Nnorom was not sure whether this was a dream or reality. He believed that God has a plan for everyone and it is etched on the palms of each person's hands. His people call it "akalaka" and believe that a person's fortunes and tribulations are in accordance with the meaning of the configuration of the lines on his or her palm.

Pan American Airways Flight 114 to New York moved slowly in a slight drizzle on the silent, undulating runway, sometimes almost slowing to a halt. It took one turn, and then another before it finally came to a squeaking halt. The runway it faced was studded with blue light bulbs and looked so straight and tapering it seemed it ended in infinity. The aircraft heaved, raved, and roared to a deafening sound as it sped away at breakneck speed, shattering the silent night. Jamike made the sign of the cross, covered his face with his palms and prayed as he always did whenever he set out on a journey. The plane lifted itself up and was airborne. Already he was overwhelmed by the size of the supersonic jet and the hundreds of passengers on board and wondered how it would keep itself in the air for the number of hours he was told it took to be in America.

Jamike Nnorom, the son of Uridiya, a widow, who struggled hard to survive with her child, despite the rancor of devilish relatives, was on his way on a journey that would change him forever. He was in an airplane that no one in his entire village had seen before. Jamike remembered that as children they would rush out of the compound to strain their eyes looking up in the high sky if they heard the rumble of a nearly invisible airplane. The only thing they would see was a tiny object thousands of feet in the clouds. At these times the youngsters and some old women prayed the pilot for some generosity. Some would say, "Aeroplane kindly drop a bag of money to me." And others said, "Aeroplane kindly drop a bag of money to us."

Jamike, who had an aisle seat, wished he sat near the window so he could lean against it and sleep, but he did not know he had to request it at the check-in counter. The passenger occupying the window seat was an elderly woman who, he later found out from her escort, was visiting America for medical treatment. Her face appeared painful. Her jaw was out of symmetry, perhaps, due to a recent stroke. She appeared anxious and nervous. Jamike took a quick look at the woman and greeted her, but he might as well have been speaking to a wall. He came to the realization that when people are in pain or preoccupied with life's uncertainties, response to a stranger's greeting would not be of priority.

It was not long before a man came and spoke to the woman in a language not understood by Jamike, apparently to find out if she was comfortable. The man introduced himself as the woman's escort. He covered her with a blanket up to her neck and appealed to Jamike to assist the woman who he said was going to receive medical treatment in America. He tried to engage in a conversation with Jamike, but his thoughts were on what he was experiencing and on the village he'd just left. He was not prepared for that conversation. The first time in an aircraft, going to an unknown land, Jamike's mind was occupied with his own private fears. He was thinking about what he would do if this aircraft fell into the water, because he learned that they would be crossing the Atlantic Ocean. He thought about what he feared to think about, whether or not he would see his mother again. To Jamike, engaging the man in conversation rather than being concerned with his inner thoughts would amount to chasing a mouse that ran out of a burning house instead of focusing on putting out the fire, as his people would say.

Once he was fairly comfortable, or rather had adjusted to the discomfort of his narrow economy seat, Jamike kicked off his shoes and stretched his legs under the seat in front of him. Now and then he would try to sleep, but whenever there was a noticeable turbulence of the aircraft, he would open his eyes to check on the reaction of other passengers. Since the pilot informed them that the flight to New York was across the Atlantic Ocean, Jamike had focused some thought on that. He did not know how to swim. What would happen if the plane fell into the ocean? If any such thing happened, he thought, that would be the end of him, and as an only son their household and lineage would permanently come to an end after his mother passed away.

Jamike's other thoughts were of the village and the people he had known, and the village square that was the center of his childhood and adolescent life. When would he be able to see all that again? What would his mother be feeling that night and in the days to come? She must have been lost in thought of him. But Jamike was glad the headmaster would check on her the following morning. What of the old village church where he sometimes taught catechisms to small children? What of Oriaku, the old blacksmith, for whom he used to fire the mud furnace when he was a youngster? Again, he thought about his inability to swim as they were crossing the Atlantic; he remembered that knowing how to swim might not be helpful to even the best of swimmers, because they would not know where to swim to in the vastness of an ocean with no horizon in sight. These and other thoughts interfered with his attempt to sleep. He kept awake and reminisced.

As he relaxed, Jamike reminisced about the farewell party that the villagers gave him in the church hall. The remarks made by the elders contained a litany of what Jamike should do and should not do when he gets to America. As the elders spoke, Jamike's mother lapsed deep in thought, both palms holding her chin, a favorite position when in thought, her facial expression wavering between sadness and joy.

Ikonne, an elder, who spoke at the reception, told Jamike never to forget his origin, village, or his country. There were many good things, they heard, that were sweet in America. He should not allow himself to be deceived by such things. A second elder told Jamike that they had heard that American women were very beautiful, their skin so shiny it reflected the image of the beholder. "So are our own women, too, if you look carefully and closely," he told him. "Remember, if you say your mother's soup is not good enough, people will believe you and help you spread the word." He continued:

"Do not go there to marry a foreign woman. I say to you, look around this hall. Apart from the young ladies here who are related to you, there is no type of woman you will not find among them and in all Aludo. Big ones are here, so are small ones. Tall women are here, so are short ones. There is no shape you will not find. As you see them here, so will you find them in all the villages from which we marry. Just point to the one, and we will marry her for you before you come back. Or if you want, we can send her over there. You know, if you marry a wife from there your mother will die of heartache before you bring her home. American people have a language we cannot speak or understand. If you marry one of them, you have to bring Uridiya to America to learn the language too." There was plenty of laughter.

As these remarks were being made, Uridiya murmured a few sentences to the effect that if her son would want to cause her death, he could go ahead and marry a foreign woman. One of the oldest men in the village stood up to speak. The hall was now rowdy but he was not going to allow that to deter him. He kept standing with his walking stick in hand, waiting for the noise to die down. That did not happen until the headmaster stood up and clapped his hands many times to get their attention.

Raising his wine cup made from a cow's horn, the old man invoked the spirits of the ancestors in a libation. He implored the spirits to share in the food and drink. He committed Jamike to their hands, asking them to protect and guide him as he set forth on a journey that was just a dream to the villagers. Since this had not happened to them before, it might be for the good of the village. To everyone's surprise the old man added, "Everybody has given you all kinds of advice. I am sure your ears are full by now. They have all told you not to marry an American woman. But I tell you the opposite. If they are human beings like us here, nothing stops you from marrying one of them if the two of you agree. If we cannot hear what your wife says, maybe she will teach us."

He joked that by the time Jamike would return to his fatherland, he too could be talking like American people, and they all might need an interpreter to understand him He turned to Jamike's mother and told her,

"If your son comes back with an American woman and you do not know what to do with your daughter-in-law, you can send her over to me. My wife has been long dead as everyone in this village knows," he said, "I think an American woman could prolong my life, and those waiting for my death would have to wait longer or even die before me." Continuing, he added,

"There are many things a white woman can help me to do. She can stoke the fire so I can keep warm at night. I can teach her how to rub my aching back. I don't have to speak her language to do that. She too can teach me the rascality men and women engage in these days. I am not too old to learn that. I know some of you are expecting my funeral, but I tell you, I am not dying yet, not if you give me a woman from the white man's land to take care of me." He sat down and the hall broke loose with mirth!

Jamike was about to respond to the advice given to him, when the traditional head of the town arrived. He greeted all the people in the traditional way with his wide leather fan adorned with peacock feathers. Once he sat down and was recognized, Chief Ekele made his remarks.

"I greet all who came to this happy occasion. We are glad that Jamike has passed all the examinations required to go overseas to study. Your son, Jamike, has done what no one expected. We thank him and advise him that the road that has been opened for him should not be closed. He should not close it for others as some people would do, but instead he should keep it open. America is not for one person, and we will like for others to go there too. As our custom goes, the Chief's council will meet to set a date to prohibit everyone from harvesting their palm trees. This prohibition will last for eight weeks." He continued,

"After this period, the village will harvest them communally, and money realized from the sale we will send the sum of one hundred pounds sterling to Jamike." Then he asked them, "Is this our custom or not?" The villagers answered that it was their custom. He continued, "I believe we have done this for one or two of our sons studying in our country. We now have to pray for good harvest. Anyway, I know that those making it possible for Jamike to go to America will see that he completes his education. Going to America is not a play matter for a mother and her child, as we say. Carry on and enjoy the merriment, as I have to leave because I came out in the middle of a meeting to be here. You know that the absence of the Chief from this type of occasion would be misunderstood."

Chief Ekele left the hall without eating or drinking. When Jamike began to speak he thanked the chief who had already left, for his presence and kind words. He said that he has heard all their advice and remarked that he would only pray to God to hear their prayers for him. He told them he would not forget where he came from and he would not eat up everything presented to him in America. He would surely save and bring back some to them, as only a sensible child would do. Whatever achievement he would make in America would not be for him but for them.

Then he added that as the elders said, "When a child picks a snail in the bush, it belongs to the child, but when he gets home, the snail belongs to the village. Marrying or not marrying an American or foreign wife is not the reason I am going to America. I recognize that my primary mission is to receive an education, and that is what I am going to face when I get there."

Recollections of his send-off party in the church hall that Sunday afternoon came back to Jamike vividly as he sat in the plane. He thought of his mother and prayed that God would keep her until he returned. Jamike looked at his watch, a gift from Mr. Ahamba and his wife, Asamuka. The headmaster was around to comfort and encourage Uridiya the morning after Jamike left for a place she referred to as "white man's land," where Uridiya already said neither her hand nor her voice could reach any longer. To the villagers, anywhere overseas was regarded as white man's land.

Distance meant nothing to Uridiya. If America were nearer, maybe her voice would reach there. When Jamike was a youngster she would call him at the top of her voice if he went to a faraway bush to cut firewood, or even to the stream deep in the valley to fetch water, and failed to return when she expected him. Uridiya would walk up and down along the village dirt road and narrow paths, stretching her voice to call Jamike while passersby would wonder if she was sane. In those instances, she would tell them, "I am calling my only seed from God, and I am not calling him with your voice. You have to bear with me; you know the elders said that if a blind person fails to pick the *Udala* that he felt with his foot, how could he be sure he would stumble on another."

Seven

Jamike woke suddenly from a bizarre dream that gave him a slight headache. It was three o'clock in the morning, and New York was seven hours away. He rubbed his eyes and took a look at his watch. If he were at home, he thought, he would have slept for six hours or more. He knew villagers were accustomed to going to bed early. There wasn't much to do after supper. On a moonless night there would be utter darkness and dead silence. Occasionally the silence was disturbed by the periodic cry of a night owl or the echo of the sound of mournful music coming from a faraway village, indicating the beginning of the ritual mourning of the death of an elder of the clan.

Jamike's thoughts of the village wandered farther. He remembered how a villager once disturbed the peace of the night in search of a goat that broke loose and did not come in for the night. The old man hit his gong hard repeatedly—kom, kom, kom, kom—telling the story of the missing domestic animal along the village road to the entire neighborhood. Jamike recollected him saying, "I am searching for a black goat. Has anyone seen a black he-goat? He left my compound this evening. The goat has a white mark on the right hind leg. I know he is in this neighborhood. If you are keeping him, set him free. Be informed that the goat in question is a sacrifice to the god of thunder. If he is not released, whoever keeps him will suffer the vengeance that the god will visit on their family." The old man would move about a hundred feet at a time, hit his gong once more, and repeat the same message.

People who had been awakened by the persistent sound of the gong would chuckle in their squeaky bamboo beds and wonder how anyone could be so foolish to think they would succeed in seeing a black goat in the dark. Whoever thought so would go against the wisdom of the elders who advised that "one should start to look for a missing black goat when it is still daylight."

Jamike drifted back to sleep, and it seemed that he soon got into deep slumber, because he began to snore. When he woke again it was because the woman in the window seat needed to go to the bathroom, and he had to get up for her. Her escort was standing in the aisle. While she was gone for what seemed like a long time Jamike dozed off. When she returned, her escort tapped Jamike, who stood for her to get to her seat. Jamike went back to sleep, this time for a long period, only to be awakened by the stewardess who distributed United States immigration and customs forms. Soon the captain announced that they were beginning their approach to New York.

Shortly after, through the aircraft window, Jamike beheld the dazzling Manhattan skyline. It was six o'clock in the morning. Lights high and low, multicolored, brilliant in their clusters in varying geometric patterns shone everywhere. Jamike could feel that the aircraft was beginning to lose height, descending lower and lower to land at Kennedy International Airport in New York. This couldn't be true, he thought, because this whole American episode had seemed to him like one big dream that could dissolve any time. Suddenly his head became heavy, as if it was going to burst. The pressure in his ears became painful with a roaring sound. He shook his head sideways a couple of times to get relief but none came. He endured the discomfiture until he stepped into the immigration hall, when his ear canals opened with a rush of air and he heard meaningful sound. He shook his head one more time to ensure he was okay.

Pan American Airways Flight 114 had a smooth landing

at Kennedy International Airport. While passengers were in the aisle waiting to disembark, Jamike was still seated. Now and then he would bend down in a way that seemed as if he was either picking up or searching for something. He was attempting unsuccessfully to get his swollen feet back into his shoes. Shortly after the aircraft was airborne in Lagos, he had removed his shoes, which were a little tight on him because he had bought them only a few days earlier and had not broken them in. After over ten hours of sitting in one place, he could not put the shoes back on.

To quickly join the queue that had progressed toward the exit door, Jamike forced his feet into the shoes and squashed the back of each shoe thus turning it into an improvised slip-on.

The awkwardness of the shoes caused him to shuffle along the aisle. After a few steps, the shoes would slip off slightly, and he would stop to push his feet into them. Coming all the way from seat number 32B where he was, with a stop-and-go movement, a couple of flight attendants and the cockpit crew waited patiently for their last passenger. Once at the door, the crewmembers bid him good-bye almost simultaneously.

By the time he joined the queue at the immigration line, Jamike was at the tail end of one of many lines for non-immigrant aliens. But because there were over twelve immigration officials in attendance, the lines moved quickly. He walked along carefully, and no one noticed he had any difficulty with his shoes. The official beckoned on him.

The immigration officer took a look at Jamike's passport, gave a quick glance at his face, and in a mechanical fashion leafed through a hefty reference book, in search of what Jamike did not know. That done, he opened the sealed envelope Jamike had received from the United States Embassy in Lagos. In this envelope was the very important Form I-20, which stated his eligibility for admission to college and gave other pertinent information supplied by the college to show that he could enter the United States as a student. The officer examined this document with cynical interest and said to him, "You are going to Regius State College?"

"Yes, sir," replied Jamike with some apprehension. The official asked the question as if he knew where the college was. He quickly stamped his papers, including his passport, with the speed and dexterity of a postal clerk. Handing them over to him, he wished Jamike well. "Good Luck," he said, as he motioned the next passenger to approach his desk.

After he collected his luggage, a customs official directed Jamike to an inspector who rummaged through his suitcase, which contained few belongings, and allowed him to go. As he approached the huge exit door and before he could reach to push it open, it swung open automatically. As he walked out, he looked back at the heavy iron door that he did not have to push open and saw that it had closed itself rapidly. No question about it, he was in America, the home of wonders, he thought. He remembered the itinerant magicians that came to perform for students when he was in the primary school. He again recalled their chant:

Come and see America wonder
Come and see America wonder
Come and see America wonder

It was after he came through immigration that Jamike was truly in America. He beheld a spectacle that would forever remain indelible in his memory. There were so many people moving in every direction. They were coming and going, some were embracing and kissing, some huddled around their loved ones just arrived, some hustled, trying to sell some items to anyone who gave them attention. There were those pushing carts loaded high with suitcases to the taxi stand. Jamike wondered what those with these huge suitcases could be bringing to America, where it was said one could get everything in the world. So overtaken by the vastness of all he saw, he almost forgot he had to find his way to the Allegheny terminal in order to catch his flight to Franklintown, Pennsylvania, where Mr. Laski would pick him up. Franklintown was an hour's drive from Regius.

It was eight o'clock in the morning. The next Allegheny flight to Franklintown was not until 4:00 P.M. Jamike had time to wander around and feast his eyes on curiosities. With his suitcase in hand, he stood and watched every moving or stationary object around him. He saw a limousine outside and couldn't believe a car could be that long. He wondered how the car would turn corners. He moved closer to peep into it, but instead saw his own reflection. The windows on the passenger sides were tinted dark, and he wondered why anyone inside a car would like to stay in darkness while moving on the road during the day.

Jamike came back into the terminal building and sat and looked with amazement at everything. A man, who had been looking at him from a distance for a while, approached and called his name in a loud voice, "Jamike! What are you doing in America?" Jamike, recognizing him instantly, jumped from his seat and equally shouted, "Nnamdi, what are you doing here? Were you on the plane?" They embraced, shook hands, and looked at each other as if to learn how well they looked in the years since they had parted ways. They were students together at Teacher Training College.

"Please sit down," Jamike said to his friend, pointing at the seat next to him. "You couldn't have been on the same flight with me or I would have seen you in Lagos."

"No, I was not on the flight. I live here in New York."

"When did you come to this country?"

"I came right after the civil war. I worked for Biafra Relief Services in Gabon during the war and came to the United States after the war ended."

"That's wonderful. Do you live far from the airport?"

"Not too far. I live in Queens." "So why are you here? Are you on a business trip?"

"I came to attend Regius College in Pennsylvania."

As they talked, Nnamdi kept looking in many directions.

"Are you looking for someone?" Jamike asked him.

"Yes, I am here to meet a cousin who was supposed to be on the same flight with you."

Nnamdi abruptly excused himself and headed toward the customs exit doors as a large number of people streamed out. His expected passenger was not among them. Each time the huge customs doors swung open, he moved closer to see if his cousin was in the group of passengers coming out. He asked those whom he could identify as Nigerians by their speech or attire, if there were any more persons still left behind in customs from the Nigerian flight. At one point the number of passengers exiting came to a trickle.

Eight

While Nnamdi looked for his cousin, Jamike internalized everything he saw around him at the airport. There were people of different nationalities, speaking different languages. Many times he would shake his head as if to confirm to himself that he was really in a foreign land. He overheard some black people speaking English with a different accent and tone. He stared at them occasionally, wondering if these were the American Negroes he heard about in Nigeria. He did not see any difference between them and the people back home. In fact, Jamike thought that each one looked familiar.

However, in the course of his stay in America, Jamike came to realize that there was a great deal of difference between the experiences of the black people he saw in America and those back in his home in Africa. He would find out that the experience of racism, oppression, and discrimination against black people in America would color their perspectives on life and society in general. It was in Regius that the clothing store merchant insulted Jamike the week he arrived by telling him that he was not like the other black students who make away with his merchandise. Jamike had gone to buy some clothing, when the merchant who had been watching his movements suspiciously approached.

"May I help you find something, sir? Are you looking for anything in particular?"

"I want to get some clothes for the season."

"Oh, where are you from? You have a beautiful accent."

"I am from Nigeria."

"Boy, you have traveled a long way from home. Isn't that country somewhere in Africa?"

"Yes, it is West Africa."

He was showing Jamike the various items of clothing that would interest him, when suddenly he said in low tone.

"Your accent shows you are not from here. You know, those black kids from Pittsburgh, we watch them closely when they come into the store because once they leave, our goods disappear. You are not like them. You are all right." Jamike was shocked to hear his comment but went about making his selection while he thought over the remark that took him unawares. After he paid for his merchandise, Jamike said to the store man:

"I am new to the college, but I think what you said is not good."

"That's your opinion. Have a good day." He began chatting with other customers.

Through this and other encounters, Jamike realized that he would need to identify with the black students in Regius, whether or not his experience was similar to theirs. As long as he shared the same skin color with them, his nationality would not matter; instead, race would matter because he was black. He would become as much a target of racism and discrimination, as the clothing store merchant had shown. By telling him that he was better than American blacks, Jamike felt that the clothing merchant and other racists would try to put a wedge between blacks from the continent and those born in America. He concluded that by using the tactic of divide and conquer, blacks from Africa were encouraged to remove themselves from the group they belonged to. This first encounter with racism would sensitize Jamike to always be on his guard whenever he came in contact with people who had similar stereotypes of black people. Jamike would find out more.

As Nnamdi looked for his cousin, another passenger was looking inside the same building for him. He was a businessman who was on the flight from Nigeria. He had a letter for Nnamdi, which informed him that his cousin could not travel because the date on an important document he had had expired. He was disappointed after he read the letter. He then rejoined Jamike.

"Man, what did you say brought you to this land?"

"The man I saw you talking to was on the plane with me because I saw him in Lagos. Does he know anything about your cousin?"

"He had a letter for me. The American Embassy did not give my cousin a visa. And do you know what? It is because his Form I-20 was overdue for just one day. Can you believe it?"

"I can believe it! I was warned that embassy officials would not bend the rules about school deadlines. The deadline for reporting to school should be in one of the letters the school sent him. I am sure he saw the date. That is a pity."

"Do you think one day is enough to deny him a visa?"

"I don't know, but I heard embassy staff is serious about adhering to stated dates. I was warned about it. You should know better than I, because you live here and know the system. It seems that Americans rigidly stick to rules in official matters." Jamike kept his eyes with interest on a woman obviously agitated as she made a phone call and talked loudly in a foreign language.

"You talk as if you are one of the embassy officials."

"No, Nnamdi, I speak as a teacher who knows what rules and regulations are. Rules should be followed once they are made, or there would be no need for them to be made. Suppose he was allowed to travel with expired documents and upon his arrival in New York the immigration officials refuse him entry and send him back on the same plane. I hear they can do so. That would not only be a big waste of money but also would cause embarrassment and shame at home. Most people would misunderstand it; they would think he had committed a crime already to be sent back home. You know how some people think."

As the friends talked, three uniformed New York police officers including a female officer, appeared and moved briskly among people in the terminal, looking around, apparently in search of an offender. Jamike stood up to watch them. Nnamdi's eyes followed them. The officers entered a room and shortly after came out with two men whom they led away in handcuffs.

"You are right Jamike," Nnamdi said, continuing the conversation. "To be sent back would be the worst situation and would definitely cause embarrassment." They stood watching the police until the apprehended men were put in police cars outside and driven away.

"Did you say you are here to go to school?"

"I will be attending Regius State College, in Pennsylvania."

"Oh, Regius State College. I know where it is, in Pennsylvania. I know a co-worker who went to college there. It is a good school."

"You call it college but it is a university. You know when Nigerians at home hear one is in a college in America, they wonder how you can enter college again after you have completed college at home. They expect you to enter a university, a post-secondary institution."

"A college here is a post-secondary institution. The high school here is what we call college or secondary school back home."

"I heard that some time in the past, Nigerians who received their education in Britain did not think much of American degrees. I don't know if it is because they were awarded by colleges. Some people, it was said, returned to Nigeria with American degrees and had difficulty finding work. It seems their degrees were not regarded as equivalent to similar British degrees."

"That is pure ignorance on the part of the people who have this mindset. It is what is called a colonial mentality, our belief in those days that anything or any system that came from the British, our colonial masters, is the best. You see, some people like to see that notion perpetuated. Anyone who wants to know about American colleges and the quality of the degrees they award can find that out at the United States Information Service offices in Nigeria.

Let's talk about something else. What is your plan from here on?" They sat down.

"I will travel to Franklintown, Pennsylvania, at four o'clock this afternoon. A good friend of mine, Mr. Laski, a white man, will be waiting to pick me up. He said I should call him collect from the airport so he can come for me. I don't know what a collect call is or how to make it. I am sure you know what it is and you can help me."

"Calling collect is easy. I can show you that. When you call collect, the person you are calling will pay for the call. But you may need a quarter to initiate the call."

"What is a quarter? He said he would pay the cost of the call."

"That is true but you still need a quarter, a coin you will use to call him collect."

"Where will I get it? Who will give it to me? The money I have is in traveler's checks."

"Don't worry about that Jamike; you are not leaving for Pennsylvania right this minute." Nnamdi tapped Jamike on the shoulder. "What time is your connecting flight?"

"My flight is at four o'clock, but I plan to walk around in the airport until that time. There is so much to see here."

Nnamdi thought about asking Jamike to spend the weekend with him before leaving for Pennsylvania. He wanted to catch up on the years they had not seen each other since they were both students at the Teacher Training College. Besides, he had planned a small reception for his cousin and invited a few friends to the house that evening. Jamike might as well be his guest of honor, Nnamdi thought.

"Jamike, do you have to be in Regius today?"

"Do you want me to be late like your cousin? Why?"

"Do you know the exact date when the college will open for fall?"

"I know I still have two weeks. I wanted to come early to participate in the foreign students' orientation." Jamike opened his suitcase and brought out an envelope containing some documents from the college.

They looked at the college academic calendar and confirmed that school would actually start in three weeks.

"You are okay. You have time to spend with your host family in Regius before school starts."

"Now, if I have to spend any day with you, it is important that I inform my host in Pennsylvania. I will like us to do so from the airport. He is waiting for me, and if my plans change he ought to know. He might have made some preparations for my coming. It is only fair that he knows."

Jamike was thinking that he wouldn't want to displease his friend immediately on arrival, and moreover, if anything happened to him in New York he would be blamed for stopping short of his destination to be with a friend he had not seen in years. Jamike was concerned and it showed on his face.

"Can we call him when we get to the house?"

"Nnamdi, I think I owe it to him to know right away."

"That's fine, but calling him from the pay phone here will be expensive." Jamike reached for the inside pocket of his jacket and brought out an envelope that contained his passport, airline ticket, and traveler's checks. He handed a traveler's check to Nnamdi.

"Here, you can change this to get the money for the call." Nnamdi shook his head.

"Oh, no, this shouldn't cost you anything." Nnamdi brought out his wallet and pulled a Visa credit card.

"We are in good shape. We can call your friend from here. I have a credit card I can use. Jamike didn't know what a credit card was but his interest lay in the call and not how it was made. Nnamdi took Jamike to a pay phone and placed a call to Paul Laski in Regius, Pennsylvania. Nnamdi introduced himself and asked Laski to take a call from a friend who had just arrived from Nigeria. Jamike smiled broadly and in a loud voice said,

"Mr. Laski, this is Jamike Nnorom."

"Jamike?" he asked excitedly.

"Yes, Jamike."

"Good heavens! I am so glad to hear from you. Where are you?" Laski thought his friend was calling from Franklintown as arranged.

"I am at the New York airport."

"Oh, you are not in Franklintown. Did you just arrive?"

"No, we arrived early this morning."

"Do you know how to get to the Allegheny terminal? Your best bet would be to take a taxi." Nnamdi was next to Jamike, listening and wishing he could talk to Laski and tell him up front what he wanted to do. He put his hands in his pant's pocket and paced the floor.

"I want to tell you that I have a slight change in my plans. I met a friend I knew in Nigeria at the airport. He would like me to spend the weekend with him before coming to Regius. I would like to do that, if you don't mind."

"That's fine with me. How did you meet this friend?"

"He came to the airport to welcome a cousin who was supposed to be on the same flight with me. His relative did not make the trip. It was such a coincidence. He invited me to be his guest for the weekend. When I looked at some college documents with me, I found out I have three weeks before I can enroll in school. On the basis of that I accepted his invitation."

"I am glad you met someone you knew back home. That's wonderful. Remember, you need to be in Regius for the foreign students' orientation that starts in a week's time. It is required. Also, I would like to spend some days with you, too, before you start your studies or move to the dormitory."

"That is all right. I will be here for the weekend only and come there on Monday."

"That's good. I will be waiting. Call me from the airport on Monday when you arrive in Franklintown." Laski was pleased that Jamike was in the United States. His efforts for him had borne fruit. He telephoned a friend to inform him that his Nigerian friend had arrived in the country. Jamike handed the telephone to Nnamdi to put back in its cradle.

"I knew your friend wouldn't have any problem with your staying the weekend in New York. He will like you to have a good time. Americans love a good time."

"Am I here for a good time?"

"That's okay, just relax."

"I am happy I informed him of the situation. I can now stay with you in a happy mood and don't have to worry that he did not know."

"It is good that you talked with him." Nnamdi took Jamike's lightweight suitcase, and they walked to the parking lot.

Nine

As Nnamdi put on his seat belt, he asked Jamike to do the same. He showed him how to do it and helped him with it. Jamike moved his body sideways in the belt. It felt restraining.

"You don't think this will tie me to the seat?"

"It doesn't tie you. It secures you to the seat so that you do not hit your chest on the steering wheel or your head on the windscreen, if not fall through it in an accident." Nnamdi moved the car.

"I think this belt would restrain me from jumping out fast if there was fire or even an accident."

"I don't know about fire, but in an accident you have a chance of being saved if you have your seat belt on. It has been proved." Jamike showed shocking surprise as they drove through a wooded area of the highway.

"I thought there were no trees or bushes in America."

"Who told you that?"

"From what one hears or reads about America back home it is hard to imagine there are bushes here." Nnamdi laughed.

"It is a misconception. People have a fantasy idea that everywhere in America is paved with concrete. I don't know what they think will be here in place of trees and bushes or the type of buildings they imagine. But America is a place where you can experience nature too like any other place in the world. There are bushes and wooded areas, even forests like in Africa."

Two motorcyclists, one on the tail of the other, rode

past their car with very high speed and deafening noise. Jamike thought the two men were heading for a crash. They passed many other cars and disappeared out of sight.

"You can't imagine the risks people take with their lives. These are the people who need belts to tie them to the motorcycle. According to what you said, in an accident they would be blown to pieces."

"Sometimes they have serious accidents, and some can be fatal. But you can see they have helmets to protect the head, which is most vulnerable in a crash." They came to a stop sign.

"Now I know there are bushes here like we have back home. People in their imagination think that America is a land with every good thing in life. They even think there is money everywhere to pick."

"Well, you know how many dollars you have gathered since you arrived."

Jamike kept quiet for some period of time, but in those moments when he was silent, his eyes roved from one side to the other, observing and internalizing what he saw.

As they drove through some parts of Queens, the neighborhood began to change. Jamike began to see many black people. Some of the houses seemed to be in a state of neglect. He noticed that this part of town was different from the areas they came through as they drove from the airport. Jamike noticed signs of poverty and squalor as he looked at buildings that were not maintained. A number of black people stood in front of these buildings in little groups and talked. Two children pursued another around the corner of the building. One or two people looked familiar to him, a situation Jamike would encounter time and again; some black people he would encounter looking like people he knew back in his home.

Nnamdi turned three regular locks and a chain lock to open his apartment door.

"Do you need all these three locks and a chain for your door, Nnamdi? I understand people carry guns in America; if someone with a gun was after you, and you needed all this time to open a door, I don't think you would have a chance."

"That may be true, but if you don't have these locks you may also not have a chance with anyone who would want to break into your house. You can easily be harmed if it is that simple to gain entry into your apartment." Nnamdi's beige painted apartment had two bedrooms. The living room was considerably spacious and furnished to good taste. The sofas were black leather, the carpet was semi-dense maroon red, and the glass coffee table and side tables matched. Three paintings with an African motif hung on the walls, while figurines of different kinds adorned the top of a five-foot bookcase.

Nnamdi asked Jamike to feel comfortable as he took the visitor's coat and necktie to hang in the closet.

"What would you like to drink?"

"Whatever you have. I can drink water." Nnamdi got out assorted drinks from the refrigerator. After he did that he placed two pots on the stove; one was water and the other was soup. In no time the scent of okra soup with stockfish and chicken, which he made the previous day, permeated the air in the apartment. One could almost fill his stomach with the aroma alone. Jamike looked around the room, touching and feeling some objects. He moved nearer a wall to take a closer look at some family pictures. Meanwhile Nnamdi was moving in and out of the kitchen, getting food ready.

In a short while, a big mound of fufu made from flour and two bowls of soup were on the table. Steam rose from the hot fufu and okra soup and dissipated in the air. Jamike's mouth watered; he was surprised to see his native food prepared in America.

"Where did you get okra from?"

"Okra is in America. You can buy it in any supermarket. Americans eat okra but they prepare it differently. Many other special food items can be found in Spanish or Caribbean stores. Some people from South America eat some of the things that we eat back home."

"That is good to know", Jamike said. "It means that I will find the type of food I am used to."

"America has food in abundance. But you will get used to American food after a while, and you will even love some of it." Jamike loosened the belt of his pants.

"Who cooked this good food?" Jamike squeezed and rolled into a round form a good-sized piece of fufu. He dipped it in the meat-rich slippery okra soup and swallowed. The zest with which he ate showed he liked the food and was happy. He cleaned the little sweat on his forehead and nose with the back of his palm. When he saw Nnamdi pick up a napkin, Jamike reached for one also to wipe his mouth.

"I ask you again, who cooked this food, Nnamdi?"

"It is my cooking. I learned it from my mother."

"If you cook this well, you may not bother about marrying," Jamike teased him.

"Is that why people marry?"

"No, I don't mean that to be the only reason, but a wife needs to know how to cook. People in the village would ask what type of wife she is who couldn't cook."

"Oh, Jamike, is that the reason your father married your mother, to cook for him?"

"You should know better than that. The main reason is to bear children. Then, of course, she needs to know how to cook so her husband and children may eat." Nnamdi went into the kitchen and came out with more fufu and soup.

"Well, you are now in America. By the time you spend a year or so here, you will know that it is not the children or the cooking that are the only reasons for marrying. There are couples who choose to be childless in America. And there are couples who eat already prepared meals in restaurants most of the time. These are choices people make, and they have reasons why they do so. People marry because they love each other and want to be together and share their lives. Of course, they will have children if they so choose. I know people back in the villages have your ideas about marriage and the role of the woman in it and in society in general. You will change many of these ideas, I can assure you." Jamike went into the kitchen to wash his hands.

"I hear that people change when they come to America. Will you change what has existed since the days of our forefathers? If a wife does not produce children for the man, then that particular household and lineage is closed forever. If she does not cook for the family, I wonder who would. Is it the man?"

"Of course, her husband can do the cooking."

"Her husband? You are out of your mind, Nnamdi," exclaimed Jamike.

"Come on, this is 1970s. Times have changed. Yes, her husband will help her with cooking."

Jamike was a typical village man. His life experience, despite his teacher training education, was rooted in the custom and practices of his people and his views were strongly held.

"This is a change and new knowledge to me. This means I have a lot to learn."

"Let's not worry about this, Jamike. I know you are traditional, coming from a part of the world where men feel superior to women, dominate and suppress them. You will change these views, and you will someday help the woman in your life to cook. It is only a matter of time."

The food was delicious, and both had their fill. Jamike thanked his host for making him feel like he was still back home.

Ten

Nnamdi and Jamike talked a lot, reminiscing about school days. Nnamdi was excited about news from home and about a few people they knew. Nnamdi had not been back to Nigeria since he came to America immediately after the civil war, though he had been in touch through letters. He inquired about classmates and other people they knew while in Teacher Training College. As they talked, Jamike's tiredness showed in his eyes, so Nnamdi advised him to sleep for a while before the friends he had invited would begin to arrive.

When Jamike woke up after a couple of hours, Nnamdi's friend, Brenda Lewis, was in the house. She was a beautiful and slender black American woman in her early thirties. She wore glasses and had on a black cotton turtleneck with long sleeves and beige slacks. The sheen on her Afro hairdo glowed under the bright living room light. Nnamdi was anxious to introduce Jamike and Brenda; however, she was on the phone. While she talked on the telephone, she waved what Nnamdi thought was a nonchalant "hi" to his guest and continued talking and laughing. After she hung up the phone, Brenda enthusiastically embraced Jamike. They were talking while still standing when Nnamdi came out of the bathroom. "You were on the phone for a long time, Brenda," Nnamdi said.

"I was talking to Rita, she's got some problem."

"You and Rita are friends again? I have always felt she was irresponsible."

"I think it is rude to call my friend irresponsible. I don't call any of your friends irresponsible. You don't have to tell me who to talk to or how long I should be on the telephone with them. I don't appreciate you disrespecting me before your guest. I do whatever I want to do."

Jamike looked at Brenda with surprise as she talked to his host. Her tone was not cordial for a moment, he thought. Nnamdi made no reply but rather went ahead to introduce them.

Brenda was excited as she continued talking with Jamike. They sat down to drink some beer and orange juice. Brenda put some rum in her orange juice.

"Tell me, Jamike, what do you look forward to most in America?" Brenda pronounced his name in a funny way. Nnamdi corrected her, and she pronounced it better.

"What I look forward to most is my studies. But from what I have seen between the airport and now, I think I have a lot to learn about America and the people."

"You should come back to New York for Thanksgiving. Do you celebrate it in your country?"

"What is it, and how do they celebrate it?" Brenda explained it to Jamike. He thought he had an idea.

"We have something similar to it," Nnamdi interjected as he continued to set edibles out on the dining table.

"From your description, it is very much like our new yam festival which we celebrate yearly when we thank the gods for good harvest." Jamike said. Nnamdi agreed, still busy moving between the kitchen and the dining table.

After a while, three more guests arrived. Nnamdi explained to them that his cousin did not make the trip and why.

"But I met a dear old friend from Nigeria," he continued, pointing at Jamike. "He is on his way to Pennsylvania. Please meet Jamike. Feel at home and ask him questions about Nigeria. Food will soon be ready."

Coming out of the kitchen one more time, Nnamdi urged his guests to start eating. He put a Nigerian "high life" music album on the turntable and it played in a low tone while they ate and conversed.

Jamike felt he was still back home because of the company, conversation and food. He wished his stay in America would continue in this fashion. Some of the introductions prompted Brenda to ask Jamike for some explanation.

"You call Nnamdi your relative. Are you really related?"

"We are from the same tribe; he is, therefore, my brother."

"I know that you are from the same tribe, but Nnamdi has introduced so many relatives, brothers, and sisters to me. Are you really related?"

"Well, our tribe is united by language, custom, and tradition, and whenever a member of the group meets another outside our homeland or in a foreign land, there is a bond and a sense of brotherhood," a guest explained.

"Don't get me wrong. We in America, especially among blacks, refer to each other as brother or sister. But I think it is a totally different concept. It is a solidarity thing. Americans don't consider themselves as relatives unless they are actually related. I guess this might explain why there is more sense of cultural cohesion among you." As the conversation went on, more guests arrived, made themselves comfortable, and joined in the food and discussion.

Some couples danced to the music, while others indulged in pleasant conversation. Jamike was fascinated by the ease with which Brenda spoke English and her intonation. He showed Brenda some "high life" music steps and danced with her. As they danced, his mind kept going back to the response she gave Nnamdi when he chided her for being on the telephone rather than be introduced to him. A lot of their conversation centered on life in general in Nigeria, with Jamike answering their questions. Everyone had a good time.

All the guests left around midnight. They thanked Nnamdi for his generous hospitality and wished Jamike a safe trip to Pennsylvania and academic success in his studies. Nnamdi walked Brenda to her car. He kissed her goodbye and requested her to call when she got home. Instead of taking the elevator, Nnamdi ran up the stairway to his third floor apartment; it was his way of exercising. When he got to the apartment, he saw Jamike dancing to the music by himself.

As they tidied up the room, Jamike said to Nnamdi,

"I enjoyed your friends. Some were really funny. Do you get together like this often?"

"Oh no, just once in a while. But more often during the summer."

"I hope to be able to return to New York and enjoy your company again. You know, Nnamdi, I like your friend, Brenda; she is very extroverted and funny too. However, I was surprised by the way she responded to you before you introduced me."

"Don't mind Brenda, she is sometimes silly."

"She rebuked you, saying you don't have to tell her what to do."

"That is the way she is. She means no harm."

"Do you plan to marry her?"

"I am thinking about it, but we are not engaged yet. We have discussed marriage. I know what you may be thinking about. That has nothing to do with what she said to me earlier. American women feel free to say whatever they want to say. Usually if I think she is being unreasonable or rude, I simply ignore her."

"She seems a very nice person, but her disposition is too brash for me, and I can see that she may not listen to you or obey you as a wife. I may be wrong, however."

"Women are assertive and independent today. I don't want her to obey me, Jamike; I am not God. I think you still have old-fashioned village ideas about men and women, Jamike. Sooner or later, you will change some of those ideas, especially about women."

"Oh, you don't want her to obey you. You want her to be headstrong. Well, if that is what you want, that will be what you get," Jamike said, going into the bathroom.

"I think it is time to go to bed," Nnamdi told Jamike.

"I am not sleepy. It is morning in Nigeria at this time. Let's talk more on this issue. It is interesting."

"No, I have to go to bed. You are suffering from jet lag. But I tell you, you have a lot to learn and quickly too, or these old-fashioned ideas you have will get you into trouble with Americans. Remember when you are in Rome you do as the Romans."

"What is jet lag?"

"It is what happens to you when your body system is disorganized because of the difference in time between Nigeria and America. For the first few days your body will believe it is in Nigeria, so you tend to sleep when we are awake and be awake when we are going to bed. But after a while your system will adjust to the time here"

"That is what is happening to me then. I don't feel sleepy at all. What do you mean I have a lot to learn?"

"It is with regard to our discussion. Women here are different from those at home in many ways, as you will discover. They are educated and liberated and assert their rights. They are also independent and some are self-sufficient. You must keep this in mind as you live in this country."

"Nnamdi, you talk like you do not know where you came from and you seem to have forgotten our tradition. Remember, the elders say that a runner cannot out-run his buttocks or a dog its tail. In the same way, you cannot run away from our customs and beliefs, or easily tear yourself from your roots. You cannot pay all that money to marry a wife only for her to disobey you. It costs a lot of money to marry a wife."

"See what you are saying. Did you say 'pay all that money'? It does not cost the man anything to marry a wife here. I mean there is no bride price to be paid. I could not afford it if I were to marry a woman in the village now."

"How do you do that here in America? Take a man's daughter away as a wife and pay nothing. Are you serious?"

"What are you paying for, a commodity or what? I won't pay money for a wife I want to marry."

From their discussions Jamike was convinced that Nnamdi had adopted American views and ways because he seemed to see traditional African values in a different light.

"In fact, in this country, not only does the bridegroom does not pay a bride price, his parents-in-law pay for the wedding." Jamike was in a state of disbelief.

"No, you can't be serious. You mean the father of the bride, after giving his daughter away to the man, then turns around and pays for the wedding? He might as well buy them a bed and mattress too. What else could he want from his in-laws?"

"That is just the way it is here."

"Well, that may be the case here, but nobody could make me pay for my daughter's wedding. If a man cannot afford to marry, he shouldn't even try. To marry a wife is a costly affair and, maybe, the prohibitive cost makes the man take it seriously and value his wife and the marriage. Remember what the village lunatic said about marriage?"

"What did he say, Jamike? Are you now going to lie on the poor lunatic?"

"Why would I lie on one who occasionally says wise things without knowing it? The lunatic said that what is scarce in the world is money and not wives to marry."

"He told you that? Jamike, you are really a village man, and I feel sorry for you, because you are in for some cultural shock in America."

"I know I am from the village and have village ideas. It may be acceptable for women to talk to you anyhow, but it is not so where you and I come from, and you know it. But—"

"Jamike, you are what is called a male chauvinist, but the good thing is that I know you will change this narrow-mindedness sooner than later. You will realize that women have feelings and need to be treated with respect also; they think and have their own opinions and need to express these too. This is the 1970s; women today can do most things men do. And no one needs to keep others down or impose themselves."

"Don't get me wrong. Women are treated well and held in high esteem back home. The African woman is our pride, and she is accorded great dignity. She is the queen of the household and a priceless jewel."

"You don't think the price paid for a wife will make her husband treat her as an expendable commodity, and in fact, she may have no say, in the relationship and—" Nnamdi did not finish his statement before Jamike cut in.

"It is the other way round. The bride price, as I said before, will make the husband value his wife. What I want to stress is that I will not give my daughter away in marriage without a bride price. How much is this bride price after all, compared to the cost of raising a daughter and giving her education? The bride price is only a token, if you want to say that."

"So what the husband pays for is the cost of raising his wife and putting her through school?"

"No husband can afford to pay for all that, and that is why it is a token."

The telephone rang. Nnamdi picked it up. It was Brenda calling to inform him that she got home safely. He thanked her for coming to meet Jamike, and after a few words of affection, said goodnight. She extended her greetings to Jamike before hanging up.

Eleven

By Sunday morning when he woke up, it dawned on Jamike that he was no longer in his home country, though he dreamed he was in his village during the night. Sometimes he would feel a kind of chill go down his spine when he thought about the fact that he had really left Nigeria and particularly that he was no longer in Aludo, the village he loved and where he had spent all his life. It was hard for him to imagine that a village boy, who grew up in poverty, raised by a widow, was actually in America! He was aware that his life would not be the same after this experience.

Each time he reflected, Jamike could easily recount some things that happened while he was a boy, things that brought unpleasant memories to mind. For example, he recalled the time in primary school when Uridiya needed to borrow some money to complete his school fees. A kinsman who traded on provisions and was well off by village standards refused to help her. His reason was so ridiculous that the young boy could not erase it from his mind. This kinsman told Uridiya to find the money somewhere else, because anyone who educates a poor boy other than his parents would be creating a future enemy, because protégés soon turn to adversaries. The incident was so devastating that he still remembered it.

After breakfast, Jamike asked Nnamdi if they could attend church service anywhere in the neighborhood.

"You must be joking. My job does not allow me time for that. I work Sundays most times. You will find that quite a few people here don't have time to go to church on Sundays."

"Well, if your employers are Christians, they should know that Sunday is a holy day that forbids work."

"Jamike, let's not get into that. You will find out all these things yourself. Sometimes people have two or three jobs, some of which they go to on Sundays and don't have time to go to church and worship. Besides, there are many denominations here. Not everyone worships on Sundays."

"Nnamdi, I think everyone should have time to worship God. I don't claim to know the purpose of creation, but I believe the Creator ought to be worshipped by all."

"Jamike, it is rough here. It is not that they do not want to attend church service. People work nearly round the clock in order to pay bills for rent, food, medical expenses, school fees and a host of other things. I am not saying that these things should substitute for worship. All I am trying to explain is that there are many reasons why many people do not go to church as often as they should. It is different back home where Sundays are free. You know that people can also worship God in the privacy of their homes."

"But the white man who wants you to work on Sunday brought Christianity to Africa. It seems the missionaries tell us one thing and do another thing in their country. In Nigeria, they tell us it is a sin to work on Sundays. Here, work on Sundays is acceptable."

"Jamike, you know well what the old folks say back home, that the geese of every nation crow differently. This is applicable to things here."

"You are right on the mark with that proverb. The geese in America crow differently indeed. That is an excellent saying. I have always been fascinated by proverbs and the condensed message and meaning in them. One can find the entire belief system of a people in their proverbs. To understand a people's philosophy, one should pay attention to their proverbs."

"I like proverbs too, but I wish I knew more of them. They enable speech to flow, and if used properly, one can be spared an hour or more of speech-making. With them, you can cover things you would find otherwise difficult to say in normal speech. My father once said that when a matter had been discussed, decided, and closed with a proverb, the uninitiated would want to know the date for the next meeting."

"I guess he will hold the meeting all by himself." They burst out laughing.

"Back to our discussion, the truth of the matter is that the missionaries who came to Nigeria seem to possess double standards; they do not practice what they preach," Jamike said.

That Sunday evening, Nnamdi took Jamike out to a really nice restaurant. Hardly had they sat down when the waitress asked what they would drink. Jamike wondered if the waitress already knew they were coming and, therefore, was waiting for their arrival. After they placed their order, the waitress returned promptly with drinks. They toasted to health, happiness, and prosperity. By the time Jamike finished his second beer, he needed to go to the bathroom urgently. Nnamdi told him to ask the bartender to show him where to go. Jamike got up and tightened his loose belt. He had a habit of loosening his belt a notch or two before he took food or drink.

Jamike walked up to the bar. "Excuse me, sir," he said to the bartender, "where is your lavatory?"

"Beg your pardon?" the bartender replied. There was anxiety in Jamike's voice. "I want to use the lavatory!" The man was having difficulty both with Jamike's accent as well as the meaning of the word he used. "I want to urinate," Jamike said to him, this time with a sense of urgency.

"You want to what?" the bartender asked in a louder than conversational tone. Jamike clutched his crotch as if to entreat his bladder to hold on for a while. Nnamdi noticed he was still standing there and sensed some problem. He approached the counter and asked for the restroom where he and Jamike went.

When they returned to their seats, Jamike wanted to

know from Nnamdi why the bartender could not understand him.

"What did you tell him you wanted?"

"I asked him to show me the lavatory."

"I believe that was the problem. I don't think he understood that. He would have understood you if you said you wanted to use the restroom"

"What is a restroom?"

"In this country, the lavatory is generally called the restroom. Then there is the men's room for men and the ladies' room for women. You will hear these names often or see them written in public places."

"I am surprised to know this. You would think a restroom would be a room where people go in to rest."

"That's true too. I remember Rest Houses in some major cities in Nigeria. They were built by the British during the colonial time and served as restaurants and lodging accommodations," Nnamdi said.

"I didn't even know this. I had not been to any major city in Nigeria until I was at the United States Information Services in Enugu. Your parents lived in Enugu, so you were used to big cities. The next time I was in a city was when I went to the American Embassy in Lagos for my visa. Is the word 'restroom' in the English dictionary? Nobody would think it means what you say it means."

"I am sure it is in the dictionary. There are some differences in the names that refer to the same thing or object in America and in Britain. Differences are also seen in the spelling and pronunciation of some words we learned from the British."

"That is quite interesting. Do you have some examples?"

"Take for instance, cars are sometimes called automobiles in America; the lift that takes one up a tall building is called an elevator, and so on. In spelling, a word like 'honour' is spelled h-o-n-o-r and 'colour' is spelled c-o-l-o-r."

Jamike scratched his head and thought for a while

"If you think about it, to spell 'honour' and 'colour' the

way you say Americans spell them makes sense. The letter U does not seem to fit in the spelling of either word. You know, I had difficulty understanding the bartender. His accent was different."

"You will come against this time and again until you get used to it."

"Do both the whites and American Negroes speak the same way?"

"They speak differently. Another thing, black people in this country are no longer called American Negroes. They are called black Americans. Negro is the name that the white people gave them during slavery, and it is not a complimentary term. Do you know that the bartender you spoke to is a black American? He is not a white man, even though he looks like one by his complexion."

"Do you mean that man is a black man?" Jamike pointed in the direction of the bar.

"Yes, he is, and there are many of them like that. In fact, some of Brenda's relatives on her mother's side are very light in complexion."

"Are you serious? Is this another American wonder: white is black, and maybe black will be white?" Jamike asked.

"Yes, I am serious. Some of them are very light in complexion but they are blacks. What you have to do in order to understand Americans, both white and black, is to train your ears and pay attention to what they say and how they say it. It will be difficult at first, but you will eventually understand everyone."

"Do you think I will ever understand everybody well?"

"Yes, you will. Every foreigner that came here went through that difficulty. But remember that many Americans will have even more difficulty understanding what you say. In time, it will be easier for you to understand them than it will be for them to understand you. You must also be prepared to spell your name out for them in many instances. Don't feel insulted or even irritated by this. It is the only way to avoid mistaking you for someone else. As for your accent, it won't go away. You just have to improve your speech communication skills. You have to speak slowly, clearly, and distinctly when interacting with Americans," Nnamdi advised his friend.

"You know, I can certainly see how being misunderstood can be frustrating. Spelling your name all the time or constantly repeating it is not fun."

"You are right. But you are not alone. People from other parts of the world, for instance—South America, Vietnam, Arab countries, other African countries and non-English-speaking parts of Europe who come here— have the same problem with the language. After a while, however, they won't even think about it. Give it time. After one or two semesters at the college, you will be fine," Nnamdi said.

"Semester? What is that? I read it in the Regius College handbook but decided to leave it alone until I get to the school."

"Oh, it is something like a term. The university school year is arranged by semesters. Two semesters make one academic year. You can call it two terms, if you will. Your academic advisor will explain all this to you."

"I think I understand it now."

Jamike learned a lot from Nnamdi about living in America. It was close to midnight when they left the restaurant to return to Queens. He woke up late in the morning, but he had time enough for a shower. He ate and had conversation with Nnamdi before setting out for the airport. They called Laski in Regius to inform him that Jamike would arrive at the Franklintown airport by two o'clock in the afternoon. It was past noon when Nnamdi and Jamike got to the Allegheny Airline terminal for the flight to Franklintown, Pennsylvania. After check-in, Nnamdi waited to see Jamike go through security to board the aircraft before leaving.

Twelve

The small Allegheny commuter plane seemed worn out from years of use on the Franklintown-New York route. The seats were cramped, and the single aisle was so narrow that one of two persons moving in opposite directions had to step completely out of the way for the other to pass through. When the aircraft door was pulled down, it turned into a staircase. Jamike already knew that the journey to Franklintown would last close to an hour, because his friend Laski had told him so. Silently he wondered if the aircraft would make the journey, judging from how it vibrated and shook on the runway, but the small plane took off smoothly into the enveloping clouds.

Once the aircraft was airborne and steadied itself, Jamike closed his eyes and dozed off. It wasn't quite ten minutes when the hostess tapped him to ask if he wanted peanuts and a soft drink. Jamike declined the offer and closed his eyes again; nothing but sleep mattered to him at that point. He woke when the captain announced their approach and descent into Franklintown Airport and requested all passengers to return to their seats, place them in an upright position, and fasten their seat belts. Flight attendants were advised to take their seats.

As Jamike approached the baggage claim area, he recognized Paul Laski despite the fact that he had gained weight; part of his hair had grayed, and his moustache had grown bushier. Taking quick steps, they embraced each other and held each other's hand momentarily, both beaming with smiles.

They watched the luggage roll out on the conveyor belt, and it took no time before Jamike's suitcase was out. Laski was happy to see him, and both commented on how well the other looked. Once the suitcase was retrieved, they left the airport and were soon on their way to Regius.

"How was the flight?"

"Good. The plane shook a lot in the air but we are here"

"Yes, it is a small commuter plane and you experience turbulence a great deal in it. Otherwise, everything is okay? And you enjoyed your stay with your friend in the Big Apple?"

"What is big apple?

"Oh, that is what New York is called. It is a nickname, if you understand what I mean. So, how is the principal, Father Murrow? Quite a man."

"You know, he left the country to return to Ireland after the civil war. He never came back."

"I guessed as much. Even when I was teaching at the school, I thought he was tired after all the energy he put into building the school and running the parish as well."

"Even if he wanted, he could not have returned to Nigeria. The Federal Government ordered all Irish priests—in fact, all foreign Catholic priests who worked in Biafra during the war—to leave Nigeria because in their opinion their help for suffering Biafran people amounted to support for their war effort and, therefore, helped prolong the war."

"That does not make sense. Anyway, somehow I miss the fun of the village. Do they still have the annual festival and bring out those masquerades that scare women and children? It is funny that women are not allowed to see them."

"Yes, those masquerades are imbued with magical powers that frighten the opposite sex. That is why they are not allowed to see them. Otherwise everything is still the same, nothing has changed. It still rains continuously during the rainy season, and the scorching heat of the sun still causes oil-bean pods to explode on the trees during the dry season."

"That's funny. What of my friend, the carver? He sold many carvings to me at a cheap price."

"Oh, the old man died. His son took over, and he is even more creative than his father. This is what the villagers say."

As the yellow Volkswagen station wagon made its way along the narrow two-lane country road, winding through the farmlands of western Pennsylvania, Jamike admired the countryside.

"This part reminds me somehow of parts of Nigeria. The scenery is in direct contrast to what I saw in New York, where there are many tall buildings."

It was early September, and the leaves were beginning to change colors, thus giving the countryside a beautiful, picturesque landscape of golden hues. As he looked on both sides of the road, Jamike remarked,

"These are beautiful colors on these trees. Are they always this colorful?"

"No, they are this way only at this time of the year. We are now in the fall season. The leaves will fall off later, and winter will set in, bringing snow with it." Jamike did not understand the meaning of fall or winter but did not ask.

Laski's townhouse was within a comfortable walking distance from the campus of Regius College. It was a medium-sized, two-bedroom house that was tastefully decorated. On two sides of the living room walls hung paintings, some carvings, and different bronze heads of the Oba of Benin, plus some etchings with an African motif. Laski's basement looked like a little shrine of a native medicine man or a fortuneteller's divination room. Among the objects were traditional musical instruments, more carvings, gongs, harps, banjos, and talking drums of various sizes and shapes. There were also various types of figurines, all of which Laski collected while in Nigeria and shipped before he left the country.

Jamike moved around the living room, appreciating the paintings on the wall. Laski was happy to see Jamike.

He took his suitcase from him and took him upstairs to show him his bedroom. He would stay here until school resumed, or for as long as he wished to stay. He showed him the bathroom, the closet, a reading desk and the light switches. Laski asked Jamike to relax, make himself comfortable, and feel at home.

The meal was rice and chicken. Laski thought that would be a good meal to start with. He also prepared some salad to go with it. There was beer and soft drinks. Jamike ate all the rice and chicken that was on his plate and thought the food was good. He did not care much for the raw vegetables before him in a bowl, because he was not used to them.

Laski informed Jamike about his plans for the evening.

"I have invited the few African students on campus to come over to meet you."

"Really? That is nice. I will like to know them."

"Often if I had a visitor from Africa, I would ask one or two to be present. It helps the conversation. And if he is a new student, then I ask fellow African students to meet him. So that's what we will do tonight."

The two friends stayed in the living room for a long while, after which Laski told Jamike he felt a little tired and would like to have a nap before his visitors arrived. Jamike thought that was a good idea, because he too needed to rest for a while and, of course, unpack his suitcase. They both went upstairs. Jamike locked the bedroom door and changed into a native wrapper cloth and lay down to nap.

Thirteen

There were four African students who came to visit. One of them, Emeka, was from Jamike's Igbo tribe. Another, Okpolo, was also from Nigeria, and there were two students from Ghana, Kofi and Kwame. They were all glad to welcome an addition to their group. Apart from a few words of greetings in Igbo language that Jamike and Emeka exchanged after they were introduced, the language of their conversation was English. Cookies and soft drinks were served.

Laski asked Okpolo to tell Jamike about the college and what to expect.

"The community is a small one. People here know practically everyone. The school is their pride, and they are involved with its activities. Apart from the black students on campus, only a handful of black families live on the outskirts of Regius and are hardly seen around, because there are not places they can be gainfully employed," said Okpolo.

"The college is small too, and the professors know the students well," Emeka joined. Jamike watched each person as he spoke.

"The college has a little over five thousand students," Laski said

"One thing you will find perhaps frustrating is that you may not be able at this stage to understand your teachers or fellow students easily when they speak with you. You may have to ask them to repeat, and I am sure they will constantly have you do the same," Okpolo continued.

"Should I try to speak like them?"

"Oh, no, once you begin to feel comfortable with the American accent, things will become easier for you both in class and in the community. Are you going to live in the dormitory like us?" Emeka asked. Laski was listening as the students spoke to Jamike and nodded in agreement with what they were telling him. "I don't think he plans to do that," he said.

"You will be better off if you can afford off-campus housing, because the food in the dorm is horrible," Emeka told him.

"I don't think I want to live in the dormitory. I will like to cook my own food and eat whatever I like," Jamike said.

Okpolo told Jamike about Regius International Association.

"We have an organization called Regius International Association. It is open to all foreign students. Members meet regularly to discuss common problems and foster unity. Their members help with orientation of new international students. They also help new members with registration for classes. You will need some help on the day registration begins in two weeks."

"We all belong to Regius International Association. You should join too," Kwame told Jamike.

"I will like to join the association, because from what you said about it I will benefit from it."

"Are you pre-registered? It is the only way that matters will be easy for you on registration day."

"No, he is not pre-registered," Laski said. "He will go through the registration process." Registration for classes is usually an ordeal in the college auditorium. Students and faculty alike swarm the place where all processes are conducted. Telephone wires crisscrossed the floor in different directions, hooking departmental stations in the auditorium to the deans' offices. Hundreds of pieces of paper are littered. It looks chaotic but you will be just fine. You will get some help," Kofi told him.

The evening in Laski's house was spent sharing and enjoying each other's stories and experiences. It was a most informative evening for Jamike, because he learned so much about the students, the college, and the community. Laski and Jamike spent Sunday mostly at home. In the evening they went to a movie.

On the day of registration, Jamike got the needed help. Kofi and Kwame, two of the friends he met at Laski's house, were there to take him through the process. He got all but one course, Introduction to Social Problems. The dean's office was called, but the secretary said the course was full for all sessions. Jamike had fifteen credits already that included courses in philosophy and history. He still wanted the additional course whose title interested him. He was advised to attend the class for the first two or three days nonetheless, in case someone needed to drop it.

Shortly after classes started, Jamike began to look for an apartment of his own. He decided it would be best to move away from Laski's house, because he was afraid that the longer they stayed together, perhaps there would come a time when one could be in the other person's way. Jamike did not want anything to jeopardize their relationship. Laski tried to persuade him to stay longer, or even live in his house while he attended college if he chose to do so, but he graciously declined. Jamike wanted to be able to eat whatever he liked, the quantity he desired, and to eat whenever it suited him.

In truth, while he lived with Laski, Jamike supplemented some of his meals with bread and margarine that he kept inside his suitcase. The loaf was in his suitcase away from his host's eyes. After some meals and upon retiring to his room, he helped himself to bread and milk or a soft drink. Jamike missed his heavy meals of fufu and soup. One time at the supermarket, Jamike offered to pay for groceries, but Laski declined. Some days, before a meal was prepared, Jamike would tell Laski he did not feel hungry. He felt that purposely skipping meals occasionally would save his host some food. He did not want to appear like a parasite to his friend. The few times he acted this way, he was already full with bread and soft drink.

Laski was concerned about the types of food he ate. He was more interested in eating a balanced diet, more quality than quantity. Vegetables formed a substantial part of his meals. However, when it came to food, Jamike liked quantity more; for him, a bulging stomach signified fullness and satisfaction.

The thought of moving into his own abode was exciting to Jamike, who did not want to wear out his welcome. He knew it was advisable for a guest to take leave of his host while both were still friends and on good terms. He did not lose sight of a saying among his people, that if an honored guest overstayed his welcome he might soon be asked to hold the baby while his hosts took care of other things. It was a situation he did not want to be in.

Jamike found a privately owned off-campus building, the Jefferson Apartments, located on Main Street. Its grounds were contiguous with the campus, and that made going to classes easy.

It was on a Saturday, late in the fall, that Jamike moved into his furnished one-room apartment. Laski used his station wagon to help him move. Apart from some new shoes, clothing, and books he bought since he arrived, his property consisted mainly of what was in the suitcase he brought with him from Nigeria, now including two loaves of bread and a can of margarine. Laski gave him utensils, cutlery, some bed sheets, and two pillows. The apartment was already furnished with a couch, two chairs, and a dining table; a bed, a dresser, and a mirror. Jamike was really thrilled and thought the one-room apartment was what he needed. His concern then was if he would be able to get his native food in Regius. The time required for moving was the twenty minutes or less it took to drive from Laski's house to Jefferson Apartments. After Jamike put his belongings in place, he and Laski spent some time chatting before his host left, wishing him well and promising to come by some other day and take him out to dinner.

Fourteen

A short while after moving into the apartment, Jamike went to visit his fellow Africans in their dormitory and informed them about his new home. When they came to see him the following Saturday, Jamike was getting ready to go to the stores. They drove to nearby Riverside Supermarket and bought ingredients to prepare okra soup for a housewarming meal. Everyone participated in the cooking. Emeka chopped the okra, while Kofi sliced the vegetable. When the soup was done Okpolo prepared the fufu. They talked while they cooked and ate, telling interesting stories about their experiences. After they ate, they all stayed to talk some more. Jamike showed much interest in their stories, laughing and asking questions.

"There are quite a number of black American students on campus. How do you relate to them?" he asked.

"I nod my head when I see them. There is a black student in one of my classes, but he leaves the room quickly after class. I have not spoken to him but we do acknowledge each other."

"Most of them are unfriendly," said Okpolo. "You will find this out yourself. They always stay together wherever they are and hardly approach you—whether it is at lunchtime, after class, or anywhere on campus. My feeling is that they do not like Africans."

"When I first arrived on campus, I would take a detour while walking to the library or going to classes, just to avoid them. At times they looked at me in a strange manner, and I would not approach them because I could be rejected," Kwame said.

"But, Okpolo, their staying together or bonding on campus does not mean they do not like other people. I have been here for sometime, and to be among only a hundred or less black students in a school that has close to five thousand white students can be overwhelming," Emeka said.

"As for them sticking together," he continued, "it is important for their own survival. Some of the white students do not care about them because of racism. And moreover, I hear that the few black students here are mostly from Pittsburgh and, perhaps, they knew one another from attending the same schools."

"Even so," Kwame said, "that is no reason for not speaking to someone. It is the white students that will stop you on campus and want to know where you come from and show interest. Some white female students would even admire African outfits and compliment you."

All the while Jamike was listening and tidying up, but he had something to say though he was new on campus. He said:

"If it is true as you said, that most white students do not care about the black students, it then makes sense if the black students stay in the group in which they are comfortable to socialize with each other. As it is said back home, if everyone abandons you, you should not abandon yourself. So no one should blame them. This is what I would say about that."

Kofi challenged Jamike to try to be friendly and he would see for himself what he was talking about, because he was sure Jamike would be disappointed. The evening they spent together was very helpful to Jamike who had been at the college less than three months. Each of the students had attended the school for more than a year.

"I think we will be heading back to the dormitory," Emeka said. "Can we do this again? It is so much fun. I have enjoyed it. Feels like we are back home, eating our native food and saying whatever we like."

"You are welcome here anytime. This is our home. Even if I am not here, I will give the key to any of you if I know you will be coming over," Jamike said.

"Okay, why don't we decide to come over every Saturday unless most of us can't make it? So let's agree on how much we will contribute for food and drinks whenever we come together," Emeka said.

"We are five. I think ten dollars each will do for our get-togethers. That comes to fifty dollars for buying the food and drinks. We will all participate in the cooking as we did today. Anyone who can't help in the cooking can do something else, like setting the table and washing plates," said Kofi. They all laughed.

"If I get the money earlier, I can buy the ingredients on Friday evening," Jamike said.

"No, we don't want anyone to buy it for us. We will all go to Riverside Supermarket together and buy it. That is part of being together for the day," Emeka said.

The five Africans had found a home away from home. Although they came from different ethnic groups and countries, a special brotherhood had developed among them.

Jamike spent four eventful years getting his degree in philosophy at the college. He was well known on campus by students, faculty, and administrators. His maturity was evident as he interacted with the faculty and staff of the college. He received several dinner invitations to their homes and enjoyed the families he visited. The second time Professor Bundy invited Jamike to his home was to help him do concrete work in his driveway. Jamike appeared that Saturday morning wearing good clean pants. Bundy was in old denim work clothes ready to start work. He was surprised that Jamike wore good pants, because he should know that concrete work got one dirty.

"Are you going to work in these clothes? We are doing concrete work. Your good clothes can be messed up quite easily. Do you want something to put over them?"

"I am okay. I can always have them washed. That is no problem." Bundy went ahead to show him what they would be doing. After he brought out bags of cement, gravel, and sand, they opened and began to mix them. The gray dusty cement was all over Jamike's trousers and shirt. He took off his shirt and had his under shirt. His hair was chalky from the cement dust before they poured water to start mixing with gravel and sand.

"I told you that dirt would be all over your good clothes. I know we both will look terrible at the end of the day."

"That's okay."

"Have you done this type of work before?" Bundy asked.

"No, but I can do it. There is nothing to it, mixing and pouring concrete."

At lunchtime Mrs. Bundy fed the workers hamburgers, potato chips, and soft drinks. That gave Jamike energy to continue working till around four thirty in the afternoon when they were done. The work looked professional and the Bundys were very appreciative of Jamike's help. Jamike's undershirt was dirty, and his pants were totally soiled. Mixed cement caked on it in several places. Jamike went to the guest bathroom where he washed his face and hands and dabbed his hair with water to clean off the cement dust for the time being, until he could go home to take a bath later. When Bundy dropped off Jamike at his apartment, he offered him some money for the work he did, but Jamike refused. Jamike did not attempt to wash his undershirt but threw it in the trash and planned to send his pants for laundering.

As Jamike found his way around campus and the town, he made friends and experienced great conviviality with members of the college community. When Jim Donahue and his wife, Natalie, his friends and professors at the college, went on vacation to Britain, Jamike lived in their home and took care of it for two weeks. He felt honored, because he saw it as an unusual trust for a student in Donahue's biology class, someone they did not know for long and who had been a guest at their home only twice. Jamike took care of their home, allowed no intruders, and fed their big dog, Bismark. The Donahues had a small poultry farm in their backyard, and he took care of that too. Jamike enjoyed feeding the chickens. Surprisingly during that period, he and the dog developed a friendship that was not there the two times Jamike had visited the Donahues in the past. Before then, each time he visited, Mrs. Donahue would hold the dog for Jamike to go through to the living room.

Jamike's visits to American families were more social than work. They were always opportunities for his hosts to learn more about Africa, and for him to know what they think about other people. Residents of rural Regius showed interest in foreign students if they encountered them. They were glad the students selected their college as a place to study. People constantly asked Jamike what made him choose remote Regius.

"I chose to come here because I knew someone at the college." The next question was predictable. "You have an accent, where are you from?" Jamike answered that he was from Nigeria. First, they did not know where in Africa the country was located. To them it was "somewhere over" there. They did not know the difference between Nigeria, Liberia, or Algeria. There was an incident when an elderly manager at the Western Auto hardware store asked Jamike where he was from. On learning that he was from Nigeria, his eyes lit up and he got interested.

"I was in your country. Oh, yes, we were stationed in Algeria during the Second World War. Quite a country!"

"So you have been to Africa? That is wonderful. But I think you are mistaking Algeria for Nigeria. I am from Nigeria, on the West Coast of Africa. Algeria is in the north of Africa," Jamike explained to him.

Jamike was baffled by the general ignorance that Americans he encountered showed about geography. He had previously thought that they would know about other countries, but that wasn't the case. He wondered why he studied the geography of the British Isles, Europe, Asia, and North America in secondary school in Nigeria, when people in America seemed to know little or cared nothing about Africa and, perhaps, other continents.

As he took classes and moved around in the community, Jamike realized that Regius was truly a small rural town as he was told, where most of the inhabitants had not left since birth. This was no surprise to Jamike, who did not leave Aludo until he was to go away to college. The center of life and town activities in Regius was on Main Street. It was also on Main Street that the only taxi cab in town was parked. The nearest big city to them was Pittsburgh and going to Pittsburgh was a major event for the town's residents. It was, of course, the place professors frequented for cultural activities aside from what took place on campus.

By spring of the following year, Jamike was settled in his studies. He wrote regularly to his mother; while his mentor, Ahamba, the headmaster, wrote to him occasionally. Ahamba's letters gave encouragement and emotional support that were needed by one in a foreign country. Uridiya was not able to write often to her son, because she depended on someone to write for her. In one of the letters, a fifteen-year-old junior high school student writing for Uridiya expressed to Jamike how depressed his mother would be each time she wrote to him. The letter urged him to assure his mother he was well, so she would worry less about him.

Uridiya's letters usually contained reports about one farm or another, persons mistreating her, and what goat or fowl was missing. She reported on the leaking thatched roof and part of the mud rampart that had fallen on her side of the compound, thus exposing her to thieves. In one letter, she advised Jamike to write to his age-mates, because they were constantly bothering her about various village levies. She complained that one of them had threatened that the next time they came for the levy and Uridiya couldn't come up with the money, they might seize one of their two goats. Maybe, if he writes and tells them he was a student, she said, they would keep record of those levies until he returned.

In the same letter she asked him to be mindful of mosquitoes for fear of getting malaria that he suffered many times in the past. She concluded by giving him the names of extended family members who had inquired about him and sent their greetings. After the letter was finished, Uridiya asked the writer to read it back to her because she said in her mind, "children are too clever nowadays and could write what no one asked them to write."

It was after Easter in his second year that Jamike received a letter that bothered him. He could discern that Uridiya wrote that letter in a state of unhappiness. The traditional head of the village, Chief Ekele, informed her after this long time that the village would not be able to give Jamike the money he was entitled to from his village and which the Chief himself promised him on the day of his send-off. It was the custom in Jamike's village that any student who was admitted to an institution of higher learning, a rare occurrence in those days, would be given a non-refundable one hundred pounds sterling as financial assistance. It was a way for the village to reward and encourage academic achievement.

Before Jamike went to America, this sum of money had been given to two students from the village who were studying in Nigerian universities. One was the son of Chief Ekele himself; the other was the son of the village councilman, Mr. Madu. Both of them were envious that Jamike was studying in the United States whereas their sons were at local universities. It was at their urging that the practice of village financial support was established. Their two sons were enrolled at the University of Ibadan and the University of Nigeria, respectively.

At the time this practice was started the children of the poor or orphans were the farthest away from their minds as possible candidates for higher education. After all, if their parents could ill-afford to pay school fees for primary education, how would they dream to attend secondary school? University education would only be a dreamland for such children.

Jamike was not surprised by the content of this letter, for somehow he had the feeling that the Chief was not happy that he was to go overseas to study. He was late to his send-off, and his comments were not encouraging at all. Jamike was not surprised either at the councilman. He was the trader who several years ago, when Jamike was in elementary school, denied Uridiya financial help when his school fees were overdue. He claimed that anyone other than the parent who educated or trained a poor boy was creating an enemy. Jamike was not sure about any other persons who would want to block this financial assistance but the Chief and the councilman, both of whom he believed had motives.

Jamike promptly wrote two letters, one to his mother and the other to the headmaster, telling them not to bother that the community went back on its promise. He hinted at persons he suspected could block the award and asked that neither his mother nor the headmaster should discuss the matter with anyone anymore. Jamike consoled Uridiya and urged her to regularly visit Dr. Duru at Saint Theresa's mission hospital for medical attention.

Fifteen

Two weeks after Jamike moved into the apartment, Laski came to take him out to dinner. They went to the Tiber restaurant next to the Church of Our Lady of Wisdom, a landmark building on Main Street. The stone masonry church was one hundred and fifty years old and had a bell tower on which stood a massive cross thrust into infinite space. As soon as they sat down the waitress came to take their order, but they were not ready. Jamike had not been to the Tiber restaurant before, though he had seen the building on Main Street. He looked around and remarked on its comfortable atmosphere. Mirrored walls, ceiling to floor drapes, and flowers arranged in oriental vases gave an intimate ambience. The lights on the tables hung down in inverted stained glass bowls from rafters on the ceiling. Portrait paintings adorned plain walls and matched red patterned rugs.

"This is such an elegant place, so different from the Kentucky Fried Chicken across the street."

"Well, this is the type of restaurant where you are supposed to take time and eat in a relaxed atmosphere while you enjoy your food. The one across the street is a fast-food restaurant where you more or less eat on the run. You are not expected to stay there for more than, say, fifteen minutes consuming your food."

Just before Laski and Jamike finished their dinner, the campus ministry chaplain, Reverend Leonard Smith, and his family walked in. They sat at the opposite end of where Jamike and Laski were sitting but faced different directions. Laski and the reverend acknowledged each other. As Jamike and Laski were leaving the restaurant, they walked over to the Smiths' table. Laski introduced Jamike.

"You haven't met Jamike, I am sure. He is our new student from Nigeria." Jane and her children set their eyes on Jamike.

"No, I haven't really. He must be the new student Bob Takea mentioned in the faculty lounge a couple of days ago."

"Jamike, this is Reverend Smith. He is the campus chaplain. I am sure you will be meeting him again."

"How do you do?" Smith stood up and shook hands with Jamike.

"This is my wife, Jane, and my children, Jennifer and Leona." Jane Smith wiped her mouth and hand and shook Jamike's hand.

"Are you in Professor Takea's philosophy class?" Reverend Smith asked.

"Yes, I am."

"He said the new African student makes interesting comments and asked a lot of challenging questions."

"Jamike, your reputation has preceded you." They all laughed.

"Let me get your telephone number. I will contact you." The Reverend searched his pocket for a pen. Jane brought one out of her handbag. "I am involved in a program at a church in town that I think you will be interested in. We are asking for food and monetary donations to send to Africa. I am sure you know about the Sahel and the problems of drought there."

"Yes, I was aware of it a little bit before coming here."

"We are arranging for food and other supplies to be sent to the drought-stricken people of that part of the world. We will talk more about it. I will call you, and maybe we can engage you."

As they drove out of the parking lot and turned right, Jamike requested Laski to stop for a minute. Laski slowed to a stop.

"Any problem?"

"I want to take a look at the church bulletin box." The lighted box was situated off the pavement a few feet away from the church's entrance.

"Do you want to see anything in particular?"

"I want to see what times they have Sunday service. I think I want to attend service here tomorrow." Jamike found out that there was a second service at ten thirty in the morning.

As they drove home Laski asked Jamike how familiar he was with what the reverend alluded to.

"I heard of the climate catastrophe of the Sahel while in Nigeria and saw some of the refugees, but I have read more about it in newspapers and *Time magazine* since I have been here. The last issue of *Time* and, I believe, *Newsweek* too, carried extensive special sections on it. I have their copies; it is such a distressing tragedy that is happening in those countries."

"Where is the exact location of the Sahel? I am ashamed of not keeping up as I used to with much of the happenings in that part of the world."

"The Sahel region is a belt of land below the Sahara desert shared by Mali, Upper Volta, Niger, and Guinea."

"I didn't know all those countries were affected."

"These countries have had little or no rainfall for some years, and the resulting drought has devastated livestock and killed off many people through malnutrition. People there are crossing over to neighboring countries, including Nigeria, in search of food."

"That is a tragedy indeed. It is good that people in the United States are concerned and are sending relief. I am sure you would like to be involved. You like that sort of thing."

"Yes, I will like to be involved."

"That's wonderful." Laski pulled into the apartment parking lot about ten thirty. Jamike came out of the car and thanked him for the dinner.

The following morning Jamike attended Catholic church service at Our Lady of Wisdom. The Jefferson Apartments building was about half a mile from the church. He wore his native attire, a two-piece embroidered outfit that drew attention as he walked down Main Street to the church. By the time he got to the church, the first Mass was over and attendees were on their way out. The parish priest stood at the exit door greeting parishioners and shaking hands.

Those coming out of the church glanced at Jamike, and he too looked at them. Something he observed surprised him and seemed unreal. The women did not cover their hair; rather, they had well-styled and exposed hairdos. It shocked him because in his home town no woman came to church with her hair uncovered, even half way. If any was noticed without wearing a head-tie or hat, the churchwarden or the catechist would immediately walk over with an evil look in his eyes and ask her to leave. Jamike recalled that a professor's wife who once came to worship at the local church and had her head-tie pushed farther back from her temple, exposing her beautiful hairdo halfway, fared no better at the hands of the warden. Jamike wondered why white missionaries forbade women parishioners in his home from leaving their hair uncovered at church services, while in America it was acceptable to do so.

Father Murrow's predecessor, Father O'Toole, told the villagers it was a sign of irreverence to God for women not to cover their heads, just as it was for men not to remove their hats at church service or during prayers. Jamike refrained from making any judgment but planned to know the reason from the parish priest or any other American priest he would come in contact with.

As he sat in the pew, Jamike observed whatever met his eyes. He admired the multi-colored stained glass windows and marble statues of saints and holy people. The medieval-style architecture with its high ceiling, frescoes, and arcs overwhelmed him. He looked at people as far around him as was possible and noticed he was the only black head among the people in the service. He observed the celebrating priest and, of course, followed the order of the service, because it was the same in his village Catholic Church service. Jamike did not set out to make comparisons between the Mass service in his hometown and what he was witnessing, but some differences were very obvious to him

He noticed that when it was time to receive the Holy Communion, the communicant stood in front of a man in suit and took the wafer from him by hand, a fact that troubled him. A man in suit, not a priest, held a chalice from which communicants sipped what Jamike guessed could be the consecrated wine. This was entirely different from the practice Jamike knew. When he walked up to the altar, Jamike knelt before the priest, as he was familiar with in his native country, popped out his tongue, and received Holy Communion. He bypassed the man in suit and walked on back to his seat. With his head lowered, palms clasped together on his chest, he missed his pew. When it occurred to him he had gone too far, Jamike stopped to look for his seat, but the spectacle of hundreds of white people in the church disoriented him. Walking back five rows, a man who sat next to him beckoned.

"Maybe the missionaries know why they wouldn't offer us consecrated wine in the village," Jamike thought. "If they did, they would be spending a good sum of money buying wine for Sunday service. Some communicants would go for seconds, if only to drink the wine the white Irish priests had long denied them from sharing. The hundreds of villagers who received communion every Sunday would think that the more they drank the blood of Christ, which the wine represents, the more cleansing and redemption they would get. Sometimes it took upwards of an hour to give out communion, and this would be an equal amount of time for wine-sipping by each member of the congregation. And if the chalice of wine was handed to each communicant, as Jamike noticed, then there would be need for a good supply of wine.

Father Davis, the Regius parish priest, greeted Jamike at the exit door after service and expressed his pleasure that he came to worship with them. He was glad to see Jamike, because it was the first time in a long while that they had a black person in attendance. He hoped Jamike would come back to worship and, perhaps, register as a parishioner. The Reverend Father also informed him of a special fellowship that was being planned for Catholic college students and encouraged him to come.

Jamike spent some more time in the asphalt parking lot with several church members who struck up conversations with him. Some gave him their telephone numbers for him to get in touch with them. Jamike was glad for the warm reception these local residents showed him. He promised to get to know the people better and, perhaps, get involved in some social activities at the church and in the town.

College life was busy for Jamike, with classes and other student activities. He had much studying to do for his five first semester courses that included English, Philosophy, and Art. For his Introduction to Philosophy class he studied Plato's *Phaedo*, Aristotle's *Nicomachean Ethics*, Lucretius' *The Nature of the Universe,* and parts of Thomas Aquinas' *Summa Theologica*. Professor Takea enjoyed having Jamike in his philosophy class, because he raised and argued issues.

The art class that Jamike enjoyed a great deal was called Varieties of Visual Art. He liked Gauguin, the impressionist painters, Picasso, and both classical and neo-classical architecture. He wrote a paper on the influence of African art on Picasso. Jamike made friends very easily with students and professors alike. He was twenty-seven years of age when he arrived Regius, imbued with a sense of purpose, to get a good education, learn as much as he could, and return to his village with a bachelor's degree and, perhaps, teach in the secondary school. He asked many questions in all his classes, believing in the adage of his people, that an inquisitive traveler who asks questions rarely loses his way on a journey.

His accent and fast manner of speech posed some difficulty for his classmates, but the professors in some instances repeated Jamike's question or comment so other students would follow. However, he was aware of his difficulty in coping with the American accent of both the teachers and students but made extra effort to understand and follow. It was funny to him that while Americans said he spoke fast, he too thought they spoke too fast for him. In time he would overcome this problem.

Jamike realized that he was the one who would have to make more effort at understanding Americans, if he planned to follow in class or interact in a meaningful way with people. Sometimes in private, he would try speaking with an American accent, but he sounded funny to himself. If he were at a younger age, he thought, maybe it would be easy for him to learn to speak that way. He was too old now for that, he felt. As it was said back home, he remarked to himself, no person learns the use of the left hand in old age. However, after the Speech Instructor told him in class that his accent was beautiful and urged him not to lose it, Jamike decided not to attempt to speak like Americans so he could be understood, but instead to try to be slow, distinct, and clear in his speech.

Both in school and outside, Jamike was being slowly exposed to American culture. Individualism and expression of one's opinion, rooted in the freedoms Americans enjoyed fascinated him. Sometimes, though, he felt that respect for the feelings of other persons could be affected adversely in the expression of one's freedom. Because he came from a society where obedience to authority was the norm, it bothered him that there was a tendency among the students to care little for authority. This feeling was validated for him by what happened in his Communications class.

Professor Enwright came into the classroom and after a brief introduction to the topic of the day, asked the students to open a chapter in their textbook. By the time he read through the first page and turned to the next, a student raised his hand. Once he was recognized, the student voiced his opinion without timidity.

"I don't appreciate your reading the textbook to us. We have the book, and we are capable of reading. I paid fees to be taught and not to be read to. We are not children." There was momentary silence in the class as students, all taken aback, looked up to see the teacher's reaction. Jamike was in a state of disbelief as he thought that the student was being rude to the instructor. He wanted to say something to challenge the student, but he held back because none of the American students said anything.

"If you give me a chance to get to the end of the next paragraph, I will explain the material. However, if you feel I should not read anymore, you are free to leave the class." The student collected his books and walked out of the class. The professor forced a smile and in less than two minutes got to the end of the paragraph. Dr. Enwright chatted with some students after class about the student's behavior. Jamike could not stay to talk about the incident, because he had another class down the hall. The next day, however, he went to see Professor Enwright in his office.

"Hello, come in and have a seat." The professor shook Jamike's hand and turned his chair toward his visitor. "How have you been? What can I do for you?"

"Nothing, sir. I think you need an apology for what happened in class yesterday."

"Not at all, Jamike. Certainly not from you."

"I believe the student was rude in the way he addressed you. Some of the students I saw later felt that way too." Dr. Enwright turned his face slightly away from Jamike's face and lit up his tobacco pipe.

"I appreciate your concern. Other students who came to see me have expressed the same concern. However, in this country, students, like other people, have the right to voice their opinion."

"I thought he was rude, anyway. In my country if a student showed rudeness that way, the professor would report him to the dean and he could face suspension."

"You can't do that in this country. Everything he did was within his right. Now, if he disrupted the class, that would be another issue. The educational system in your country seems to have more discipline. I think it has merits. So does the system here that encourages freedom of expression without breaking the law or being disruptive. Like every other thing in life, it has its drawbacks." As they talked, two other students came to the door.

"Okay, sir, I am leaving." Jamike stood up to leave.

"Thanks, Jamike, for stopping by. See you in class tomorrow." You would think Professor Enwright was pronouncing Jamaica.

Sixteen

Several weeks after Jamike was introduced to Reverend Leonard Smith at the Tiber restaurant, he called to invite him to their home. Smith was a man of slender build with a shining and balding head, and he had a slow manner of speech. Dinner was already over in the Smith household, and the Smiths were relaxing in the living room. The reverend was reading while his wife, Jane and the children, Jennifer and Leona were watching television when Jamike arrived. Jane remembered Jamike from the Tiber restaurant.

The Smiths had a three level four-bedroom townhouse on Cypress Street. It was tastefully furnished with blue upholstered chairs and a blue center rug that highlighted the highly shined wooden floor. Books and papers seemed chaotic all over, yet there was order in the living room. There could be no doubt that the room was lived in.

The Smiths welcomed Jamike warmly to their home and offered soft drinks.

"How is school coming?" Jane asked.

"Good."

"It doesn't seem you have a lot of problems like most foreign students."

"I have problems but I am working them out gradually."

"Great! What part of Africa do you come from?"

"Nigeria." Reverend Smith laid the book he was reading on his lap while he listened to the conversation.

"Do you miss home this Christmas time? I bet you do."

"Sure, I do. It is a time of lots of activities in the village. That is when people return to the villages from the cities, and one is able to see relatives and other individuals one hasn't seen in a long time."

"Is Christmas commercialized over there as it is here?" Jennifer sat up and faced Jamike.

"I don't understand what you mean."

"Do people there spend a lot of money buying and buying as they do in America?"

"It is the same thing, those buying spend a lot and those selling make a lot of money too."

"But it must be to a lesser degree," the Reverend commented.

"Do you exchange gifts too, as we do here?" Jane adjusted her skirt and crossed her legs.

"We do too. In the village, Christmas is a time to buy gifts, mainly clothing for women and children. A husband buys for his wife, children, and parents. If he has money he may buy for brothers and sisters."

"How do you celebrate it, though?" The reverend noticed that Jamike's glass was empty and refilled it.

"People go to church on Christmas day. Some people, of course, want to attend church service on that day to show off their new clothes. Children love Christmas because they get new clothes."

"Do you do anything special?"

"After attending church service, people return home to entertain guests. There is usually plenty to eat and drink. Many guests are entertained. Both children and adult masquerades visit various compounds to dance for people's enjoyment, and they are given gifts of money or food. Some people get lots of visitors and that means entertainment."

"Mom, what is a masquerade?" Jane's older daughter wanted to know.

"They are individuals disguised in costumes and wearing masks on their faces, and sometimes they look horrible and scary."

"Do they hurt anybody?"

"No, Jennifer, they are fun, I guess, because they dance and entertain," Jane said.

"That's right, but there are some really devilish masquerades that women and children don't like to see because they are really scary." The reverend and Jane laughed.

"That must be something!" said the reverend. Jane prepared to get up.

"Good seeing you again," she said to Jamike. "Let me leave you and Leonard. I am sure both of you have a lot to talk about regarding Leonard's program. You should come to our church some day and talk about Christmas in your town. People will find it interesting." Jane and the children gathered some papers and books on the floor and went upstairs.

Reverend Smith was an interested listener while his wife and Jamike talked. He went upstairs once during the conversation to get some papers, part of what he wanted to share with Jamike.

"I am sure you are exhausted from talking with Jane. She is interested in different cultures."

"Oh, no, I am okay." The reverend invited Jamike over to the dining table so they would be able to spread out some papers.

"How are you doing, my friend?"

"Doing well, thank you."

"Well, I mentioned to you briefly at the restaurant what the Methodist church down on Wood Street is doing for people of the Sahel. I am involved with them on this project. Maybe you can assist the church in some way in its effort to help those Africans in the Sahel. Are you familiar with the situation? I think I did ask you that question before, didn't I?"

"I did not know much about the situation while I was in Nigeria but I have read more about it since I have been here. Back in the villages you do not get the newspaper often and the transistor radios are only in a few homes. I have sympathy for what is happening in those parts of Africa. Some of the people affected crossed over to Nigeria and other countries as refugees. I am willing to help. What would you like me to do?"

"Good. We are involved in a drive for food, clothing, and money to donate to the people there. We have placed two announcements in the local paper and put flyers in the stores appealing to Regius residents to send whatever contribution they may have to the Methodist Church. So far, we have had a very good response."

"It is wonderful that you are doing this for people in Africa." Jamike was looking at pictures and perusing documents the reverend passed on to him

"The entire world is one big family of God. So what touches humanity in one part of the globe touches humanity in another part too. It is one body."

"That is very considerate. It is one world, if you think about it. My people, the Igbo, put that notion in a proverb which says that when the nose starts crying, the eye will begin to cry too." Reverend Smith laughed.

"That is so true. It is a beautiful proverb. We are planning a fund-raising dinner at the church. I want to know if you would like to speak at the dinner."

"What would you want me to say?"

"Would you tell them about the drought situation and its hardship and appeal to them for donations? That kind of message coming from you will have quite an impact, I believe."

"I will have to read more on that. Nigeria is not directly affected. Do you have any date in mind for the occasion?"

"Not right now, but I will confirm a date and place after I meet with the church council." Jamike and the pastor spent the rest of the evening sharing other thoughts and ideas. They talked about the college, and the pastor wanted to know how Jamike was getting on with school.

The Agape dinner the church planned was announced in the *Regius News* and on the town's radio station. It took place late in the spring. *Regius News* carried Jamike's picture on the morning of the scheduled dinner. As the evening approached Jamike had constant butterflies in his stomach, but he kept promising to do his best and summoned courage. After all, he had read considerably about the situation in magazines.

The dinner at seven o'clock was well attended. Guests brought cans of food and clothing; some donated money. To underscore the need for people to share and show concern for the plight of others, one plate of dinner was served to every two guests. At first, Jamike was surprised as each dinner plate was placed before every second person. He was one of the persons passed over by the waitress. For some inexplicable reason no one began to eat, as there was consternation on the faces of those who had no plate before them. Once the waitresses had finished serving, the pastor told the guests that each plate of dinner was to be shared by two persons in the spirit of giving and sharing. There was applause.

Jamike sat next to a couple who talked endlessly to him. The only time he was able to escape from them was when he was called up to the podium to address the group.

Reverend Smith gave Jamike a good introduction. Jamike's speech lasted about fifteen minutes. He recalled the horrendous suffering of the people who had not seen rainfall in a number of years. On a map of Africa that the reverend provided, Jamike pointed to the location of the countries of the Sahel—Mali, Guinea, Upper Volta, and Niger—that were the worst hit by the drought. He passed around enlarged pictures of emaciated people, especially children, the scorched grassland and the carcasses of cattle that littered the fields. Reverend Smith had made copies of these from *Time* magazine.

"It is a tragedy of immense proportion. Words cannot even begin to express the horror of seeing both the young and old die in those conditions. Lack of protein has made the children develop a disease called kwashiorkor, which is characterized by tiny legs, distended stomach, and a big head. Men and women have eyes sunken into their heads, with necks that look slender and fragile.

"It is a pitiful situation. All of you and your pastors deserve special thanks and praise for what you are doing for people you don't even know. As the pastor told me, it is one family of God, wherever people are on the face of the earth. The way we have been fed tonight shows that there is joy in sharing and the more the merrier. God will reward you for your compassion." Jamike urged them not to relent but to continue to help people in Africa or other parts of the world afflicted with suffering. He finally thanked the group for their generosity, as demonstrated by the heaps of canned food and clothing stacked in one corner of the room. He then took questions from the audience for another ten minutes.

An important question put to Jamike was how donors could be sure that the goods and money donated would get to the suffering people rather than end up in the pockets of corrupt politicians and government officials. Jamike agreed that there was always that possibility of unscrupulous individuals taking advantage of tragedies for personal gain. "The number of people who do this is small and their greed should not be a reason for well-meaning individuals not to be generous in alleviating suffering." In addition to the food and clothing, over a thousand dollars was collected.

The pastor thanked Jamike for what he called a "touching speech," and the people for their generous contributions. After the speech, Jamike conversed and mingled with the guests for a while before he took leave. He had anxiety before the speech, because he worried whether the guests would understand him because of his accent. He prayed over it and tried to counter this concern by speaking slowly. Once he began to speak, though, his butterflies flew away, and he became more confident. As he walked down Wood Street, he tried to assess his speech mentally, based on what he learned in his Speech class.

His professor had told him to slow down when speaking and to be sure to enunciate his words clearly and distinctly. Jamike's problem, though, was the same that most foreign students have. He tended to speak fast and swallow words, thereby losing clarity. Sometimes, however, he became irritated when Americans said that they could not understand what he said. Equally irritating was that practically everyone mispronounced and misspelled both of his names. Even when he spelled his last name, Nnorom, more than once over the telephone, some people still wrote it down incorrectly. He was convinced that they made little or no effort to listen to him.

Seventeen

When Jamike got admission to Regius State College, he also received approval for a tuition remission scholarship from the college for a work-study program that required him to work at the undergraduate library. He worked twenty hours a week at the circulation desk of the Instructional Media Center. At first, combining work with study and assignments for his classes posed a problem for Jamike. But once his work schedule fitted well with his studies, he was able to cope comfortably.

By the beginning of his junior year, the wages he was paid fell short in covering rent, food, books, and incidental expenses. He therefore began to look for an additional job off campus. But the problem he faced was that Regius was a small town, and the only industry where most people in the town worked was the Owens Glass Factory. There were small businesses along Main Street, but most of these were family-owned and run. There was the Riverside Supermarket where Jamike and his friends bought food, half a mile from campus and even less so from Jefferson Apartments. Some Regius College students worked there part-time.

Since Jamike and the other four African students had discovered they could buy food and condiments used to prepare native dishes at Riverside, he stopped there twice or more a week to pick up little things. It was there that he met Bill Sunders, a student in one of his classes. Bill had been working at Riverside as a grocery parker since his freshman year. His work involved bagging groceries and taking them out to the customers' cars. As Bill pushed a cart of groceries out for a customer one evening, Jamike approached him in the parking lot.

"Hello, Bill, I didn't know you work here. I come here often." Jamike was walking beside him.

"Yes, I do. Are you picking up some stuff?"

"Just a few food items, nothing much."

"Good, have fun." Bill rested the front end of the cart on the car bumper and put the grocery bags in the trunk. Jamike followed him as he pushed his cart back to the store.

"Hey, Bill, let me ask you!" Bill drew the cart back and faced Jamike.

"Is it possible to get a part-time job here? Something I can do on weekends or once or twice in the evening during the week?"

"That's cool, I will let you know when they start hiring," Bill said, as he adjusted the loose strings of his white apron and began to move back into the store, stopping by the side of the entrance door.

"I hope you don't mind me asking you this. Do you think they will discriminate against foreigners?"

"I don't think so. If they hire you, you will be the only and perhaps the first black person working here so far. That does not mean that they don't hire blacks. It could mean that none had applied. I have been working here for three years."

"So you think I will have a chance?"

"Sure, the store may actually need some workers now. Two students quit last week. I have got to go." A customer was waiting to have his groceries packed.

"This is good news. I will see you in class tomorrow." Jamike was excited about working at Riverside. It was less than half a mile from his apartment and getting foodstuff would be easy.

Riverside was the only big supermarket in Regius, and that was where most people in the community shopped; they all knew one another, practically. The manager, Mr.

Gambiano, a man in his late sixties liked to offer part-time jobs to college kids, as he called them.

The Friday evening Jamike submitted his application, the assistant manager, Mr. Newton was on duty. His office was a raised cubicle with four steps leading up to it. After Bill Sunders introduced Jamike, Newton took a liking to him instantly. He shook Jamike's hand firmly. He went through the application and, looking up, he asked Bill, "Is he a good guy?"

"He is okay, I guess."

"Good. We had two students leave. We need to replace them."

Bill left Jamike with Mr. Newton and returned to pack groceries for a customer.

"How long have you been at the college?"

"Three years. I come to the store regularly."

"Yeah? I see students come in and out of the store, but I have not paid any particular attention to remember faces."

"So, do you think I will get a job?"

"It is possible. I have to show your application to Mr. Gambiano, the manager. He is the one that will interview you and make a decision. You shouldn't have any problem. Now, Mr. Gambiano was not feeling well yesterday and had to leave. He is not here today. If you want to come see him, please call first to make sure he is here."

"I will do that and keep my fingers crossed."

As Jamike was leaving the store, he watched Bill perform the type of work he might be doing if he were hired. He found the work interesting, observing Bill put food and other items into brown paper bags, taking care to put the eggs and bread last, and then take a bag or two out by hand; -or, if there were many bags, put them in a cart and push the cart to the parking lot for a customer. Jamike liked the work and was confident he could do it.

It was not until Monday that the manager returned to work. Mr. Newton informed him about an African student who submitted a job application.

"Did you interview him? I believe we need two part-time workers." Mr. Newton handed the manager Jamike's application form.

"I talked with him for a while when Bill brought him. He is an intelligent young man, and we need him now that these other two kids have left."

"He knows Bill?"

"They take the same class."

"Go ahead and tell Bill to ask him to submit his class schedule. Let's give him a chance."

Riverside is the town's major supermarket. Everyone shops there and most people who live in Regius meet one another there. Professors at the college and their wives shopped at Riverside and Jamike would meet them and hold conversation as he took out groceries for them.

Since he moved into the apartment, Jamike and his friends cooked and ate together every weekend. His Saturday hours at the store nearly put an end to their get-togethers, because sometimes he worked more hours to make extra money. If he worked on a Saturday, they would then get together on Sunday afternoon to cook, eat, and share their experiences, laughing either at themselves and their mistakes or at any peculiar behavior of Americans with whom they interacted.

Jamike was excited over his job and enjoyed what he did. He was very punctual and liked to keep busy pushing the cart to the parking lot for customer after customer. Customers hearing his accent would, of course, ask where he was from and how he ended up in Regius. He had ready-made answers for these questions. One evening Jamike was taking out groceries for a white woman who had a little boy of about four years with her. Both mother and child watched Jamike with interest as he put their groceries in six brown bags and wheeled the cart happily out of the door to the parking lot. He waited a little bit while the woman holding the little boy by the hand got in front of him.

The customer opened the trunk of the car, and Jamike rested the front end of the cart on the car bumper. The boy watched Jamike's every move as he filled the trunk with their six bags of groceries. Jamike was interested in the little boy who seemingly liked the way he performed his job. A friendly little boy, he must be, Jamike thought. After he shut the trunk, the boy was still watching. Jamike took the child's hand and shook it.

"Good-bye!" he said and turned around his cart. The little boy ran to his mother as she approached the door and pulled her dress. The mother turned. The boy raised his open palm to her as if he had discovered something. She held it instinctively.

"His hand is dirty."

The mother bent down and whispered to the youngster.

"Don't say that. You will get us in trouble."

Jamike heard him.

As Jamike walked away, pushing his empty cart back into the store, he reflected on the little boy's ignorance and concluded that he must have been from a family where race was not discussed or, perhaps, blacks were portrayed negatively.

There were other incidents, but they were funny. Sometimes Jamike would push the cart halfway through the extensive parking lot because an aged customer would have forgotten where the car was parked. Jamike and the customer would then go around the parking lot, filled with cars, from one end to the other, sometimes in circles, before the car would be located. In winter, ice made the ground slippery. Pushing the cart was a little difficult, and Jamike would try to avoid falling and the cart from skidding or turning over. In a couple of instances he was not successful.

Jamike made many friends among the students, both white and black. It was in the spring of his junior year that he invited Melvin Miller, the president of the Black Student Union, to dinner. It was Melvin's last year, and he planned to go into the ministry. He, too, lived off campus. For dinner Jamike prepared rice, plantain and chicken stew.

Melvin had been trying to get Jamike to join the Black Student Union since they met late in Jamike's second year. He attended only one meeting as an observer but he was at most black affairs to which he was invited. In all instances Jamike mingled and chatted with fellow black students and did not get the impression that they disliked Africans. To the contrary, he found the black students to be quite friendly.

"Hey, brother Jamike, how are you doing?" Melvin said as he entered Jamike's apartment.

"Doing well, man, how about you?" They shook hands and embraced.

"Great! I perceived some good food around here. Looks like we are going to have a feast. Hey man, BSU is inviting the Temptations for homecoming. That's wild. You have to be there."

"That is the music group, right?"

"Yeah, man!" Melvin was still standing and admiring the mask carving on the wall.

"I love their music. Didn't they play that tune, 'My Girl'? Their music is great. I will be there for sure. Just let me know the date. Have a seat." He motioned Melvin to the sofa.

Jamike set two bowls of rice on the coffee table.
Melvin ate with gusto.

"Is there any gate fee to the concert?"

"Are you kidding?. Five dollars. It's cheap. You know students don't have money."

"That's right."

"This is good. You are a good cook. I have to invite you over too. I'll probably feed you McDonald's." They laughed. Jamike offered soft drinks and orange juice.

"Are you ready to join BSU now, my man?" He was eating zestfully.

"Still thinking about it. But I have enjoyed interacting with you and others. There are a few misconceptions about American black students that you have cleared for me."

"Like what, brother?"

"You know, not liking Africans or congregating here and there on campus and excluding other students or even African students."

"You know that is not true. American blacks like Africans. They are brothers and sisters, whether from the continent or from here. It is just that our experiences are different. But regardless of that we are brothers and sisters. We originate from the motherland." Melvin found the plantain delicious and ate some more as he responded to his host.

"That is so true, and there is no need to dislike each other."

"As for congregating on campus, white students do so too. But it becomes an issue if black students do so. They do that for social support and survival. Why should anyone criticize them for trying to survive? They don't threaten anyone. You know, brother Jamike, the way black students are regarded on campus is a carry-over from a racist, prejudicial society."

"I have seen groups of students, white and black respectively gathered in between classes to talk. I have always said hello if I recognized someone among them. But I do not know what the reaction would be if I tried to join them."

"You are free to join any group you want to join, brother Jamike. This is a free country." Melvin told him.

"I know, but if I barge in and do not know what they are talking about I will look stupid. I guess that is why I simply say hello, if I want to, and move on."

"This is good food. You are a fantastic cook, man. I have to invite you to taste my cooking."

"I don't want any MacDonald's restaurant, though I love the French fries." They laughed.

"No, brother, I mean real food." Melvin coughed a little from enjoying his meal.

In addition to being the president of the Black Student Union, Melvin was also the leader of the Gospeliers, a black choral group on campus. Periodically, the Gospeliers would sing in black churches in Pittsburgh and in other towns in western Pennsylvania.

"Man, I want to invite you to go with the Gospeliers to a church service in Pittsburgh and to talk to the congregation about the motherland."

"What am I going to tell them?"

"Tell them about Africa. How things are in Africa. Tell them about the hardship and problems in the motherland. There are things we take for granted here that people do not have over there. We eat too much and throw away too much food. We have electricity and water and expect everything to work at the snap of a finger. We just take too much for granted..." The preacher in Melvin was manifested.

"I can do that. I hope they will understand me."

"Oh, they will understand you. I understand you. Other people understand you. Just don't speak to them in your native African language. They will have j-u-s-t a little problem understanding that. Didn't you tell me the name of your language is Ibo or something?"

"You remember the name of my language? That is good. Your pronunciation is not bad, considering."

"Sure, man. I am interested in everything about the motherland. I want to go there sometime in the future."
Jamike accepted Melvin's invitation to go on a trip with the Gospeliers. It would be his first visit to Pittsburgh, a city he had heard so much about.

The trip with the Gospeliers to Pittsburgh, eighty miles from Regius, was made in the fall when the western Pennsylvania countryside was most beautiful. As the bus moved along the winding road that seemed carved out of huge rocks very high on both sides of the roadway, Jamike thought about the spectacle of the rolling hills. The beautiful foliage of brown, orange, purple and yellow was set against a horizon that seemed to blend with the sky. It was a tapestry so picturesque that Jamike marveled at the beauty of creation. He wished the tropical rain forest in his country could sometimes be as beautiful.

Eighteen

The trip to Pittsburgh in the fall was a memorable one. Tree leaves were beginning to turn to shades of brown and yellow. Adam Street Baptist Church, where Jamike was to speak, was in a black neighborhood. A little distance before the church, construction equipment—big beige drainage pipes covering the length of a block or more, concrete slabs, a bulldozer, and some barriers—bespoke construction work going on in the area. Muddy water from an open rusty fire hydrant that possibly burst the previous day was still not dried on the ground. The streets were quiet this Sunday morning, except for a handful of people moving in and out of a breakfast and coffee shop opposite the church. A policeman in a patrol car slowed to take a close look at a disheveled man who staggered along the pavement, and he quickly drove on.

The speech Jamike made at the church once he was called upon to speak, lasted about fifteen minutes and held the attention and interest of the congregation. As he waited to be introduced, he felt touched by the presence of a large number of black people present at the church service, a distinct contrast to the handful of black students at Regius. He felt a particular kinship with the people. As he faced the small congregation with whom he already felt kinship, he held back tears that welled up in his eyes, because he saw in their faces the images of his people back home. He narrated the condition of hardship in countries of the Sahel region of West Africa, including parts of his own country, where rain had not fallen in a couple of years. He explained how the drought had ravished livestock and caused the death of children and old people in particular, two groups that had developed a new disease called kwashiorkor due to malnutrition.

Jamike told them that as he looked at them, he saw the faces of relatives and townspeople he left behind some months ago, and this reassured him that black people are one. He caused laughter when he said that he realized that the only way the American Embassy in Lagos would give this many people visas to come to the United States in so short a time would be if the embassy staff had suddenly lost their minds.

"I know," he told them, "your forebears, who are also mine, came to these shores against their will under unspeakable and insufferable human conditions. This is a fact that should always be remembered. Being conscious of this will enable us to strengthen the ties that bind black people everywhere, and we will become each other's keepers." Jamike urged the congregation to assist their brothers and sisters suffering in Africa because of an act of nature over which they had no control. Jamike was warmly applauded after his speech. The pastor, Thomas Dunbar, thanked him and encouraged parishioners to support the cause. He promised that his congregation would organize food, clothing and money for African brothers and sisters in the Sahel.

Coffee hour was held after service in the basement, and Jamike had a chance to talk to some people individually. The Gospeliers' bus left for Regius late in the afternoon and arrived back about seven o'clock that evening. Jamike returned to his apartment with a feeling of accomplishment. When he lay in bed that night, he thought about his trip, and the emotions he felt about the people he saw made him feel homesick.

Jamike continued to combine work and study as most students did, doing well in both. His dressing had begun to change. He appeared more in western clothes and reserved his traditional clothes for special occasions. He owned two pairs of blue jeans but would not wear faded ones or those torn in the knee that were popular with students at the time. After he bought his first pair of jeans and found out that tennis shoes were more suited for them, he bought a pair. Because of his involvement in activities relating to the Sahel, Jamike's profile appeared in the *Regius Daily News* with his picture in an article captioned, "Nigerian Student on Campus."

It was not long, however, before Jamike faced a challenge on campus. It was in the spring that a white professor of psychology who had been on a year's Fulbright Fellowship to the University of Nairobi in Kenya, East Africa, sent out flyers about a scheduled slide presentation based on his trip.

On the night of the much-publicized presentation, the hall was moderately filled. After an introduction to the continent and its people, Professor Townsend began to share his African experience with students, faculty, and staff. He made remarks on how beautiful Nairobi was during colonial rule and doubted if the Africans who fought the Mau Mau guerrilla war to take over power in Kenya would keep it that way after independence. He saw deterioration in many parts of the city, and the expatriates he talked to were of the opinion that Africans would not be able to maintain the scenic beauty of Nairobi. He said it would be a long time before the Kikuyu and Massai tribesmen would enjoy the fruits of independence, because they were still in the mountains.

The situation in Kenya, he said, was typical of the rest of Africa, where a small group of educated elite was selfishly agitating for independence, or had already got independence, when the masses of their people were still primitive and went on to ruin what was already in place. As he made his remarks, Jamike could tell that the professor was biased and that his slides would most likely be demeaning to Africa and its people.

As he suspected, the slides were made to entertain his audience with a sad stereotypical reinforcement of the Tarzan mentality some Americans have of Africa. For one hour he showed bushes and dusty roads, mud and thatched houses, tribesmen and women, streams and dilapidated village schools. Since Kenya is the home of the African safari, he showed animals in the wild. His pictures also included one of a medicine man and his household with half-clad children, some pot-bellied and bow-legged, and of old men with half-torn shorts or narrow towels worn between their legs and tied at the waist to protect their genitals. There was hardly anything complimentary, except some modern buildings on the campus of the University of Nairobi.

After the presentation, Professor Townsend invited questions and remarks. A professor who also had been to Africa made remarks on the hospitality of the "natives." One student asked to know why the animals were not kept in the zoo. Another wondered about the kind of education school children would get in the ramshackle school buildings he showed in the slides. Most of the questions portrayed stark ignorance. Each question or comment allowed the presenter to elaborate more on what he called a wonderful experience in Africa.

As this went on, Jamike sat there very disgusted and disappointed with what Professor Townsend saw fit to show as his experience. He wanted to say something, but he was very nervous before all those professors and students, especially because what he was going to say would contradict what the professor had said. He was not sure if it was safe to challenge him. Then he remembered the white student in Dr. Enwright's class who openly challenged the teacher for reading the textbook to them. He remembered that when he went to the professor after class, he learned that it was within a student's right to express his or her views, despite what the teacher espoused. The present situation, Jamike thought, was more serious. Jamike decided to raise his hand. He was nervous as he rose to speak but he gained some composure.

"I am from Africa, and I do not believe that what we have seen here is the true picture. We have depictions of naked children with ashen bodies, their genitalia exposed, or unwashed Kikuyu and Massai tribesmen and women with their spears, pierced noses, crude oversized drooping ear ornaments, and fig leaf coverings. This is appalling—"

"No, no, no," the professor interrupted. "Don't get me wrong. I mean no harm. Those are real photographs of real people and real situations, but go on with your comment if you have not finished."

"You say your experience is common all over Africa, but you failed to mention that there are cities like Accra in Ghana; Kampala in Uganda; Lagos, Ibadan and Enugu in Nigeria with modern buildings, homes, and offices, as well as homes with cement blocks and zinc roofs in the villages. This is an unfair and unbalanced presentation. I mean, some of the things you showed exist, but they represent a dying past." Jamike said.

"But he showed the present too," a raised but unacknowledged voice in the audience said in defense of the professor.

"Yes, he showed some aspects, but he neglected to show how things are changing in the Africa of the seventies. If he wanted to show the past to the extent that he did, then he should have contrasted it to the present, thereby providing this audience with a balanced view of the continent. This whole thing is distorted," Jamike concluded.

When Jamike finished his comments, he was sweating and his heart was pounding but he was happy he was able to voice his opinion. He could not bear listening to Professor Townsend continue to make derogatory comments or show anything demeaning to Africa any longer. To his surprise, the professor thanked him for his comments.

"I thank the gentleman from Africa. What country are you from?"

"I am from Nigeria," Jamike said amid several voices that said "Nigeria."

"I am sorry if you feel disturbed by this presentation. I agree all Africa is not like this, and I did not mean to imply that. South Africa or Rhodesia would be entirely different. All I did was to try to show the audience differences between the African and American societies," he defended. But his excuse was not sincere or acceptable to Jamike. A woman rose to speak.

"I think the young man is right to correct whatever impression he believes did not properly represent his homeland. Every society goes through the kind of transition Africa is going through, and it will be nice to show that things are changing for the better. I believe this is his concern." After a few more comments the professor thanked the audience.

"I would like to thank all of you for coming. I hope you got something out of my travel in Africa. By the way, I need to see the student from Nigeria. You should stop by my office in Ballinger Hall sometime, so we can talk more about the good people of Africa."

The audience rose and Professor Townsend packed up his apparatus.

Kwame and Okpolo, two of Jamike's friends from Africa, who were also in the audience, followed Jamike as he left to go to his apartment. They chided him for challenging Professor Townsend.

"We are aware that the professor made some offensive remarks about Africa but I do not think it was wise to challenge him as you did," Okpolo told Jamike.

"Tell me how I would have done it?"

"As we sat there, we both agreed to talk to him on the matter later on," Kwame said.

"You are only a sophomore. Professor Townsend is a powerful man on this campus and is chairman of the Psychology Department. We have had no problems so far in this school. The remarks you made can hurt you later and may jeopardize your education," Okpolo said.

"I don't care if I am suspended or even expelled from this college because of this incident. This nonsense has to stop, this foolishness of portraying Africa as primitive," he told them.

"But you do not know how much that can hurt all of us. They like us here. Your approach is wrong and is bound to create friction," Okpolo said.

Jamike thought his friends were timid and that Okpolo was inclined to be negative sometimes. He remembered that Okpolo was the one who said black students did not like Africans and challenged Jamike when he was new on campus to find out for himself. Jamike found out later that Okpolo had taken a couple of psychology courses from Professor Townsend and had been a guest at his home at Thanksgiving. It was believed that Professor Townsend liked the African students more than he liked black students. Jamike turned to his two friends.

"I am surprised at the things you say. I am not afraid of Professor Townsend. It is all right if he likes you, but that does not warrant his saying those unfounded things about Africa. As for his liking us more than American blacks—that is pure rubbish, and you must be out of your minds. What do you say to someone who likes you but does not like your brother or sister? It is not in the African spirit to ally with an outsider against your brother or sister. To do so is to be against yourself. And let me tell you—" He was interrupted.

"Jamike, do not deceive yourself. Do the black students here whom you defend accept you as a brother or sister? They hardly talk to us on campus. They always stay to themselves. Their female students feel they are too good to talk to us, and you call them brothers and sisters?" Okpolo responded.

"Well, maybe those same female students are shy and that may explain why they do not say anything to you," Jamike said. "Have you said anything to them? Listen to me. You sound narrow-minded, and you have fallen into the trap of divide and rule. Anybody who tells you he loves Africans but dislikes American blacks, who are also Africans in origin, is fooling you. Do you really believe that? You will learn in the end that he is just using you and that what he dislikes is the color black which is his object of prejudice and hate, regardless of which part of the world you come from. I think Professor Townsend has a very distorted picture of Africa. Have you not watched Mr. Laski's slide presentation on Africa? Was it not a balanced picture? Did anyone complain?" He continued:

"After all, Mr. Laski stayed in Africa more years than Dr. Townsend's one year and knows how Africa is. It is true that some American blacks do not care about Africa, nor even want to be associated with the continent; however, the same thing is true of some Africans, unfortunately. If a black person denies his African origin, the question then is where did he or she originate? Whether a black man or woman believes it or not, Africa is his or her ancestral home. Of course, they may not be born in Africa, but they represent a reincarnation of Africa in America and in any other parts of the world where people of African descent may be found.

Black people may be separated by geography, national boundaries, customs and language, but they remain the same in many respects, although some may not agree with this sentiment. From what I have learned so far, I think our destinies are bound. There is no reason to separate us from American blacks. It is through us that they will further learn about their identity and roots."

The conversation continued until they came to a road junction. Kwame and Okpolo proceeded in the direction of the dormitory, while Jamike went across the tennis courts toward the hilly slope that led to his off-campus apartment.

That night, Jamike reasoned that being a powerful professor on campus gave Dr. Townsend no liberty to distort the image of Africa. He saw no reason to apologize to him in the morning, but rather he would call his friend, Laski, who was at the presentation also and heard Jamike's remarks. It struck Jamike, though, that Laski did not make any comments. If Laski was of the same opinion why did he not say so? Maybe Laski could tell his colleague that Jamike did not mean to be rude as such but was merely trying to express his concern, as any patriotic person would do.

Jamike said that Dr. Townsend had no business going to Africa to re-discover it. It was funny and ironic, Jamike further reflected that Europe claimed to have discovered

Africa, a continent that was in existence before the dawn of history and had great empires and civilizations. Africa boasted of great institutions, great cultures, learning, and nobility when the ancestors of the discoverer were barbaric. Africa, while now modern, still retained vestiges of the high culture that made it great—certainly it was not to be viewed as primitive.

Nineteen

Jamike was a superior student even as he combined studies, work, and social activities. He took his studies much more seriously than his much younger classmates in their late teens or earlier twenties, and this showed in his scholastic performance. His professors were impressed with his challenging questions and useful comments in class. He read wide, whatever books interested him in history, psychology, sociology, or philosophy. Each time he went into Carlson Library, he would go straight to the shelves where new books were displayed to browse. Once he discovered *Time, Newsweek, Ebony* and similar magazines, he read them voraciously, and this gave him a wide breadth of general knowledge. He read a little fiction, but it was mainly historical fiction that interested him.

It was obvious that Jamike read more than just his class texts, and this became evident time and again in his various classes. Once in a political science class, on the very first day and in general discussion, the professor posed a question to the students as to whether the statement, "We hold these truths to be self-evident" was from the United States Constitution or the Declaration of Independence. There was silence for a time among the students when Jamike raised his hand. Though he knew the answer, he first hesitated, wishing that someone else would answer the question. He did not want to appear to be the smart one, particularly because he was the only black student in that session of the class, and it was the first day of class.

The teacher, perhaps purposely, ignored Jamike's raised hand. He was looking at other faces with some expectation before he finally recognized Jamike. He then answered that the statement came from the Declaration of Independence. Upon hearing his accent, the professor inquired about his nationality. After he learned that Jamike was a foreigner, the instructor could not mask his disappointment that he was the only one able to give an answer to the question.

In the fall of Jamike's junior year, he was recognized at the annual honors award banquet for magna cum laude and summa cum laude students in the college. That October evening in Churchill Auditorium would remain indelible in his mind. A letter signed by the president of the college was sent to Jamike one month earlier informing him that he would be among the honorees at the banquet to recognize scholastic excellence among the school's five thousand students. It was a letter he would cherish forever, though the importance of it did not dawn on him when he first read it.

Before he left to go to the banquet that evening, Jamike read the letter again and almost memorized the first paragraph, in which the college president praised the academic excellence of students invited to be honored. He was elated. He folded it and put it in the front pocket of his native attire and went off to the venue of the ceremony. It was a grand affair that faculty, students, and staff attended. Jamike was one of eleven black students, in a college of a little over a hundred black students, so honored. Each student was called up and presented with a certificate for academic excellence. It was a proud day for Jamike.

One of the professors at the banquet was Professor Townsend. During the reception that followed, he congratulated Jamike but made no mention of their encounter during his presentation a year earlier. He told Jamike he should be proud of himself and said he would soon be inviting him to a reception he and his wife were planning for their son. As professor Townsend took Jamike's telephone number, the issue of his slide presentation came to mind, but he refrained from raising it. A number of Jamike's teachers were present at the ceremony, and they all came up to congratulate him. Jamike and the other ten black American students who received honors that evening took a group picture.

A black female faculty member who was thrilled to see those eleven black students so honored was Mary Anderson, the black students' counselor for retention, a petite and lively brown-skinned lady who had a broad inviting smile. She had a vivacious manner and wore a big Afro hairdo. She took special interest in Jamike, because he was a foreign student who did well academically. Each honoree had a cumulative grade point average of 3.5 or better.

Mary, who was also a part-time doctoral student at Bethlehem University, a two hours' drive from Regius, admired Jamike's native attire. She wanted to know if a woman could use the same fabric. She told Jamike that she would like to have an outfit made of the same material. In the course of their conversation, she invited Jamike to stop by her office in Tilden Hall some time during the following week.

Jamike visited Mary the following Wednesday. It was during her office hours and she was counseling a student. Jamike appeared at the open door.

"Give me just five minutes. I won't be long," Mary said to Jamike.

"That's fine," Jamike responded. He waited, and in the mean time read materials posted on the bulletin board in the hallway.

As she came to the door, Mary introduced Jamike to the student leaving her office, informing him that Jamike was one of the black students honored last Sunday.

"Come on in. Sit down," she said. "What do you think about last Sunday's banquet? I thought it was a great affair."

"I think so too. I enjoyed it," Jamike said.

"Did you know any of the other black students before

then?"

"No, I did not but we became friends after that. I have talked to three of them already," Jamike said.

"I hope you all will maintain your very good grades till you graduate. You are a summa cum laude student, right? What is your grade point average?"

"I have a 3.9 grade point."

"That is very impressive, Jamike. You have done very well," she told Jamike softly and with a smile. "You keep it up."

"I will try. Thanks for your words of encouragement."

"It was pleasing to see black students right there on the stage honored along fellow white students." Jamike felt good.

"Did you say you would like some African fabrics?" Jamike asked, making good eye contact with a smile.

"Sure, I would like one like you had on Sunday. That was gorgeous."

"I can arrange to get it for you. If I don't get this particular fabric, I will get one similar to it," Jamike said.

"Thanks. Now, let's see..." Mary tapped a pen on a piece of paper on her table, thinking momentarily.

"Have you been outside Regius since you arrived here?"

"I have been to Pittsburgh with the Gospeliers."

"You did! That's wonderful. They sing very well, don't they?"

"Yes, they do."

"Looks like you do get around, don't you? Have you been to Bethlehem?" she asked with a smile. Jamike had his eyes on family pictures arranged on a bookshelf behind Mary's oak desk. He looked at Mary with surprise at the question.

"Bethlehem? No, I have not. That would be a historic place to see. Wouldn't that be a trip by plane?"

"Oh, no." Mary almost choked with laughter. "I don't mean that Bethlehem, if that is what you are thinking. I mean Bethlehem here in western Pennsylvania."

"Do you have a place called Bethlehem in America? I was thinking of the Bethlehem of the Bible, and I wondered why you would ask if I had been there."

Mary hit her hand on the table and laughed uproariously. "No, we have a Bethlehem here too. American cities and towns bear names from the Bible and from Europe. You will hear of places like Damascus, Jericho, Athens, or Rome. There are places with names like Oxford, Birmingham, Cambridge, London, or Dublin. I am sure you have heard names of places like these in other parts of the world."

"Some of the names you have just mentioned I know are in Britain."

"I figured you would be familiar with those. Anyway, I attend classes two evenings a week at Bethlehem University here in western Pennsylvania. Would you like to take a ride with me one evening next week? It's less than two hours from here. I think you will enjoy the trip."

When Mary and Jamike arrived in Bethlehem a week later, they went straight to the university library, where Mary asked him to wait while she attended class. Jamike used the one and a half hours of class to browse and read magazines. By the time Mary came out of class, both were hungry. They decided to pick up dinner at a nearby fast food restaurant. The cashier rang up the bill and told Jamike the amount. While he was getting out his wallet, Mary stepped forward and handed the money to the cashier. Jamike protested, but Mary told him not to worry about it.

As they ate in the car, Jamike told Mary that he was embarrassed when she did not allow him to pay for their meal.

"Jamike, I said not to worry about it. It is okay." Mary was reassuring.

"No, Mary. It made me uneasy, standing there while you paid for both of us." He looked at her and shook his head.

"How do you see that? Is it that a woman shouldn't pay for your meal or what? Tell me."

"I think when a man and a woman go out to eat, it is the man's duty to pay."

"I don't think it is a matter of duty. Either of them can pay for both of them. Sometime they can go Dutch."

"What is the meaning of Dutch?"

"Oh, it means each person pays for his or her meal, but don't worry about this."

"Well, I just want to say your action made me uncomfortable."

"I am sorry if you felt so," she said. "And besides," she turned to him with a smile, "you will find that women in America are independent and can take care of themselves in some of these matters without expecting the man to pay all the time. Sometimes you don't want to feel obligated and besides, you are my guest."

"Really! Is that the way it is here? It is different where I come from. It is expected of the man to take care of the bill and he would feel insulted if it were otherwise."

"Oh, no, don't get me wrong, Jamike." she tapped him on the lap, holding the steering wheel momentarily with her left hand. "Women love it when men take care of them. I guess that's the way it should be. You are right."

"That is what I am saying," Jamike said as a trailer truck overtook them and Mary's Chevrolet Pinto car swayed in the wind.

Twenty

After that trip, Jamike went to visit Mary whenever she invited him. He gave her a carving of the bust of an African woman in ebony wood. She kept their relationship strictly platonic; however, Jamike wanted it to be different. Mary was intuitively aware of his interest and planned to tell him, as soon as she had the opportunity to do so without hurting his ego, that she only wanted to be friends. She believed that Jamike had to be tutored in the difference between friendship and love— a difference—that he, apparently, could not differentiate. She was going to be patient with him because things were, perhaps, done differently in his culture.

One day after they had been to a movie, Mary invited Jamike home for snacks and a drink. At the time they came into the apartment, her favorite television program, "*The Jefferson's*," a black comedy, was already on. As they munched on crackers and peanuts, Mary spread a comforter on the floor rug to lie down on and watch the television that was set on a low stand. She was lying on her stomach, supporting her torso with both elbows, while her hands on a pillow supported her chin. She told Jamike he was welcome to come down on the floor or stay on the chair if he so desired. The comedy was hilarious and they both enjoyed it. Jamike attempted to put his leg across Mary at a point lower from her buttocks. She gently removed it, said nothing, but thought this might be the time to put the African straight. Jamike tried to press his body against hers. Again, she moved slightly. After a while he tried to put his leg across hers once more and touched her gently. She moved both hand and leg with a firm push, as if to tell him to be quiet.

"You don't like me to touch or hold you?" he asked her.

"Why should you touch or hold me?"

"Because I like to."

"Well, Jamike, I do not like for you to do that."

"Why?"

"Because I think you are getting fresh."

"What does that mean?"

"It means you are trying to get romantic. You should keep your hand and leg to yourself."

"No, when I place my hand on your body, I believe I am saying I like you."

"Thanks for thinking that way, but I still would rather have you behave. As a matter of fact, I am curious to know what you think about black American women. Your behavior seems to suggest that you don't care about them."

"What do you mean?"

"I mean, do you think they are loose?"

"Not at all."

"I want to understand, do you see them as sex objects?"

"Why do you feel so?"

Mary sat up and crossed her legs Indian-style and momentarily looked away from the television. She faced Jamike now sitting on a chair and said,

"I feel that way because of your behavior. A girlfriend of mine told me that African men would want to be intimate with a woman the first time they go out with her. That doesn't make sense, and I get that same impression from you. No respectable black woman is going to go for that foolishness. And the person doesn't even know you?"

Mary tucked in her legs farther as she looked at Jamike

"You have formed a wrong opinion. Are you saying you don't know me? I don't understand." Jamike seemed to show surprise. Mary reached for the volume knob and turned down the RCA television.

"That's exactly what I am saying; I don't know you," she said to Jamike, her hands folded. "Do you think I know you well enough to have an intimate relationship with you? Well, I don't know you, and I do not want our friendship to take that shape now or in the future. I am sorry. I like you as a friend, but I am certainly not going to allow you to put your hand and leg all over me," Mary said with firmness. She must be a determined woman, Jamike thought.

"I am sorry. Where I come from we touch people, and you probably misunderstood it," Jamike said as he sat on a chair.

"So you are a touching person, and you touch with your hand and leg on their buttocks? Come off it. You've got to be careful, Jamike. You could get into trouble." Mary got up and sat next to Jamike on the sofa, with ample space between them.

"I like you, Mary. Don't make me feel bad for touching you. You are making me feel awful right now," Jamike said in a subdued tone.

"I like you too, but don't think it will go beyond that, okay?" Mary moved her body slightly to the left to tap Jamike on the shoulder. She could sense that he did not expect to hear what he heard.

"I want your friendship," Mary continued, "but I want you to understand that it does not mean sex. So get that off your mind, if you had it in your head." Jamike was embarrassed to hear her mention the word sex.

"I do not mean it the way you say it, Mary. Maybe you misunderstand me. Next time, I won't touch you. But are we still friends?"

"Sure. I value your friendship. I told you that already. You are welcome to remain my friend if our relationship will be platonic. However, if you want a romantic relationship, you may have to find someone else." Jamike swallowed an inaudible sigh.

"That's fine," Jamike said.

The ten o'clock news came on. After the news, they chatted and laughed in a friendly manner. Jamike told

Mary it was time for him to leave. He helped Mary fold the comforter that was still on the floor. As she drove him back to his apartment, she educated him on the difference between platonic and romantic relationships. It dawned on Jamike that people from different countries think differently on matters of male-female relationships. He would be careful now.

Jamike continued his part-time job at the grocery store. His friend Bill Saunders still worked at the store, though he would be graduating soon. He was a grocery stocker now, and his work consisted of unloading a forty-foot truck full of groceries nightly with other stockers and putting them on the shelves for the next day's business. Jamike too, had been promoted to stocker, a promotion that gave him a slight increase in his hourly wage. He now earned two dollars and fifty cents an hour. The assistant manager praised his hard work as a grocery packer and recommended his promotion. The manager had no hesitation in approving the recommendation. Jamike now started work at six o'clock in the evening and got off at midnight. It took that long to unload a truck and get the contents placed on the shelves. Jamike would now come to work at the same time as Bill on the days when they both worked the same shift.

Two weeks into his job as a stocker, Jamike added to his American experience. There was no truck to unload this particular night. Jamike and Bill had been stocking the shelves for a little over two hours. They were tired and needed to rest, so they decided to go into the staff lounge to take a break. They took off their aprons as they moved down the aisle toward the lounge. Without thinking about it, Jamike took Bill's right hand as they went along the aisle. Before a couple of steps could be taken, Bill forcibly removed his hand from Jamike's grip, saying, "Do not hold me in that manner. Are you all right?" he asked. He looked at Jamike with surprise.

"Yes, I am all right. What is the matter?"

"You don't do that in America."

"Do what?"

They were at the door of the lounge when Bill swung it open and sat down. As Jamike sat next to Bill, he moved slightly away saying, "This guy, Jamike, is crazy."

There were a handful of other workers in the room, men and women smoking cigarettes or drinking coffee.

"What did Jamike do now, Bill?" Sheri asked.

"I am glad you asked him, because he thinks I am crazy, and I know I am not," Jamike told Sheri.

"Come on, man. I don't know what they do in your country, but you don't do that in America."

"Do what?" Jamike asked again.

"I hope you know where you are."

"I know I am in America and in Pennsylvania."

"Go on, Bill, tell us what he did," said Robert.

"We were coming down the aisle to the lounge, and, you know, in full view of customers he actually held my hand and wouldn't let go until I took my hand out of his hold." He then looked toward Jamike and said, "You can't do that in America; only gays do it here. I am sure you are not one." Everyone laughed.

"Did you hold his hand?" Sheri asked Jamike. Sheri was a cashier who took interest in Jamike from the first day he arrived at the store. She and her husband, Mark, had even invited him over to their house for dinner.

"What is wrong with holding his hand? Don't you hold hands here?" asked Jamike.

"Not exactly." Sheri laughed and shook her head.

"Sheri, please explain it to him. Maybe he does not know or people in Africa do not have that kind of problem. Go ahead and tell him," Bill said.

"Okay, do you know the people we call gays?"

"Yes, people are gay when they are jolly, merry, and happy on occasions."

"Are you sure this guy is all right?" asked Bill, laughing.

"No, Jamike, we are not talking about the same thing. Do you know what 'homosexuality' means? You know, men who like men and prefer them to women."

"I know the meaning of 'homosexuality,' but I have not seen any homosexuals before. I have not seen any man where I come from who would prefer men to women. That would be an unusual situation in my tribe and, in fact, considered an abomination. There would be no name in my language to call such a person. Why would a man prefer men? What is he going to do with a man? You talk as if you have that kind of people in this country."

"Well, Jamike, those are the people we call gays. That is another name for them. You either call them homosexuals or gays. Some women are the same way. They are called lesbians; they desire other women. Do you not have these in Africa?"

"Look, this idea is unknown in my society. Our mindset would not harbor that kind of thought. We would be at a loss as to what name to give this practice. I have not heard of any or seen one before. First of all, the English dictionary definition of the word 'gay' does not say it means what you are telling me. In any case, why would a man desire another man in Africa, when there are women to go around and he can take as many wives as he wants? Or why would a woman desire another woman, for that matter, when the reason to marry is to bear children?"

"Well, Jamike," said Sheri, "it is not a matter of marrying so many wives or having children. I know a man can take any number of wives where you come from, but taking a wife or wives has nothing to do with this. What we are talking about here is a lifestyle that is dear to a human being. Though some people have said that it is a behavior that is chosen, others maintain that it comes naturally. Either way, it is someone's lifestyle."

"Well, I am sorry," Jamike said. "I have not seen a homosexual or lesbian before. I do not understand these concepts. Maybe I will if I stay in America long enough." As Jamike talked, the people in the lounge started going back to work. Bill, Sheri, and Jamike were the last to leave. Sheri kept laughing, saying that Jamike had a lot to learn. The two hours before closing time passed quickly as Jamike and Bill kept stocking the shelves with merchandise. They talked no more about the incident.

As he walked home that night, Jamike thought about

the episode. He could not comprehend what a man would be looking for in another man's body. If only he could tell his villagers about this situation. They would not believe it. Then he thought more about it and concluded that the situation could well exist but not in the open.

When he got home, Jamike ate a meal of fufu and okra soup. He thought about his conversation with his friends at the store and noted he must be more careful how he touched people. Jamike felt it was sad that a man couldn't hold the hand of another man or a woman hold another woman's hand because an otherwise sign of friendship could be misinterpreted.

Twenty-One

It had been a bad winter in western Pennsylvania. It snowed nearly every day, and Jamike hated both the snow and the cold weather. This Monday morning in February, Jamike was trying to avoid the snow that was coming down heavily. He cut through Ballinger Hall to get to the Pierce Science Building for a lecture but ran into Professor Townsend in the hallway. Jamike indicated that he did not have time to sit and talk because he was going to class. The professor held him long enough to get his address because he wished to invite Jamike to a reception he was having in the spring for his son, Michael, a social anthropologist who had just returned from a two-year field trip in Africa. "Some faculty members and foreign students will be there," he told Jamike who accepted his invitation and hurried off to class. When he emerged from Ballinger Hall, he held a newspaper over his head to keep off snow flurries.

The reception at the Townsends' started about six o'clock that Sunday evening. Before he left, Jamike debated whether or not to eat. He had been to a number of functions where only light refreshments were served, and it made him hungrier. But he hoped that because this was a celebration, there might be real food. He weighed this in his mind, because he had cooked a delicious meal of jollof rice and beans with beef and cow feet and was tempted to have some. But if he did, then possibly there would be no space for whatever food the Townsend's might serve. In the end, he decided not to eat.

When he arrived at the Townsends' home, there were only a handful of neighbors and the parish priest. The professor's son and his wife, Rosemary, were already talking with some guests about Africa. Jamike told himself he was not going to listen to any stories, in case they said something untrue and he would be tempted to challenge it. Jamike's friend, Mr. Laski, arrived shortly afterward. Jamike wore an embroidered black brocade kaftan, which received many compliments. In time, more people arrived. The guests of honor mingled with the invitees, chatting and cracking jokes.

A buffet of hors d' oeuvres was served in a congenial atmosphere. Rosemary and Jamike talked for a short while before she moved over to talk with other guests. Toward the end of the function, Professor Townsend announced that his son and daughter-in-law would be leaving for the University of Wisconsin, in Madison, where Michael had been offered a faculty position, and Rosemary would be working as a librarian. He thanked everyone for coming.

Among the people present at the party was a beautiful young black lady, Linda Johnson. She and Jamike were among the few black invitees and certainly the only students. Linda was in Dr. Townsend's social anthropology class and had been invited to their home once before. She was slim, about five feet nine inches tall and wore a blue polka dot dress that had white dots. She had a light chocolate complexion and wore a moderate Afro haircut. Her necklace was simple with a silver pendant. She and Jamike at a point looked at each other simultaneously as she chatted with one of her professors. They nodded to acknowledge each other and Jamike wished he would have a chance to talk to her at some point in the course of the evening. Even as Jamike mingled with people, he could not take his eyes away from her. He desperately wanted to move over to her side of the room, but each time he tried to make the move, someone would start talking to him. Linda admired Jamike's outfit and hoped that she would be able to talk with him. She figured he was from Africa.

It was not until she left the people she was conversing

with and approached the table to get some more food that Jamike was able to get to her.

"Hello. My name is Jamike. I am a student at the college."

"Where are you from?"

"I am from Nigeria."

"I like your accent."

"You do? Thanks."

"I am Linda Johnson. I am from here; actually, I am from Pittsburgh," she said in a light mood. She gave him a broad smile when Jamike offered a handshake. It was warm and gentle.

"I think I have seen you around on campus. I am pretty sure about that. Are you enjoying the party?"

"Yes, I am. I have met so many people here. I see you talk to nearly everyone. Do you know all of them?"

"Not really, just having conversation. Three professors here have actually had me in class."

"What are you studying?" Jamike asked.

"I am an anthropology major. Right now I am taking Dr. Townsend's social anthropology class."

Jamike found her interesting and easy to talk to. He would like to keep in touch. As she turned to move back to her seat, he wanted to know if Linda lived in the dormitory.

"No, I share a room with a girlfriend off campus."

"Maybe before we leave I will get your telephone number to call you sometime. Do you mind?"

"Not at all," she said and moved to her seat with a plate in hand.

On his way home, Jamike decided to pay a brief visit to his friend Laski, who did not live far from the Townsends. Laski had left the party earlier, and Jamike figured that he would be home by the time he got to his house. As he went on his way he thought about Linda. He would surely like to meet her again.

Laski answered the knock on his door quite promptly, as if he had been expecting someone. He was still wearing the same clothes he had on at the party. He opened the door to let Jamike in. Shutting the door, Laski turned and embraced Jamike in his usual way and motioned him to sit on the sectional sofa. He offered some drinks, and Jamike indicated he would like a beer. Laski did not go back to his recliner seat, but instead took his drink and sat next to Jamike.

It was approaching ten o'clock at night as they talked about the party, school events, and campus life, when suddenly Laski changed the topic.

"What are you doing for relaxation after studies? I am thinking about weekends," Laski asked Jamike.

"Well, a student has no relaxation," he said with a smile. "Sometimes I go to social events in Churchill Auditorium, and at other times to Newman Center to socialize."

"That is good," Laski said. "it is important that people relax. You cannot study all the time." He continued to sip his bourbon.

"From my experience in Africa, I know people in the villages have a more relaxed life than those in the city. The atmosphere is calm and less stressful. They gather in village squares to sit and chat after they return from the farms. Even at night, especially on moonlit nights, adults gather to share stories, while young boys and girls play games. Sometimes I can visualize bare-bodied young men in shorts, wrestling each other on the sandy square while adults watch. Oh, I think Africans have the most beautiful bodies."

"Do you mean Africans as a whole, or their women?" Jamike asked.

"No, no, I do not mean any women. I mean the men. I have seen them when they bathe in open streams. Their ebony bodies shine like silk. They are simply beautiful and gorgeous."

"If you describe the men in those terms, how would you describe the women, whom I think are most beautiful? They are the ones who are beautiful. I don't suppose men are usually described as beautiful. Don't get me wrong, I do not mean that they are ugly but I would not describe them as gorgeous."

"Why not?"

"An old woman in my village used to say that no man is ugly as long as he is prosperous and able to give a wife the necessary security every woman needs for herself and children."

"She actually said that?"

"I remember one time a younger woman challenged her on that theory, and the old lady pointed at a man in their village who some said they would not take food from his hand because he was considered ugly, but he had a beautiful wife."

"I describe the men that way, because that is the way I saw them. Look at you; see how shiny you look in the face and hands. You are ebony black. One can only imagine how the rest of your body would be," Laski said. The statement surprised Jamike, because he never heard Laski say something like that before. He put down his glass.

"Is that supposed to be a compliment, or what? Among the Igbo people it is an insult to tell a man he is like a woman. It means he is weak, fragile and needs to be protected, as a woman ought to be. A woman's body is smooth and shiny, and it is supposed to be, not a man's."

"Women, I don't care much about them." Laski shook his left leg as he stroked his salt and pepper beard.

"What do you mean by making such statements? Why would you not care about women? Your mother is a woman; do you not care about her? Do you not have women friends? I am shocked to hear you say this."

"The reason is that I can do whatever a woman can do," he said as he tapped Jamike on the lap.

"Ooh, how can you say that?" Jamike snapped at him as he faced Laski.

At this point, Jamike was a little worried over how the conversation was going as he remembered what his friend had told him about homosexuals in America. That some of them play the role of men and others the role of women. No, Mr. Laski can't be serious when he said he could do anything a woman can do, he thought.

"No, no, Laski. Are you saying you are a woman now,

or what? I want to understand this," Jamike asked, his facial expression indicating seriousness.

"I am saying that I can do whatever a woman can do, and this is why I find African men fascinating," Laski said as he moved nearer to Jamike and reached to place his hand on his knee. Jamike moved away from him a little, but he was totally surprised by what Laski was saying and could not understand it. He immediately recalled the episode at the grocery store when he attempted to hold Bill's hand, and the discussion they had about homosexuals. Could Laski be one of them, Jamike wondered.

Jamike stood up and looked at Laski straight in the face.

"I am most surprised that you say all this," Jamike said.

"Why would you be surprised? I am the same person. I am a homosexual and prefer men to women. That is the way I am," Laski said.

"It is not my place to approve or condemn, but I have a question. Is this a lifestyle you choose, or is it part of your nature?"

"People might say it is what I have chosen but it is not so. It is natural with me. I have always been so inclined."

"When did you begin to notice this inclination?"

"I cannot place a date on it. I grew up feeling that way, and that is the only form of intimacy I know. I wish people would understand that and see homosexuality in a different and compassionate light."

"It is certainly different, but I am sure it makes you happy. Would the hugs and embraces you gave me that I took for signs of friendship be an expression of your homosexuality?"

"No, no, Jamike. I like you as a person and am fond of you too. Hugging and embracing you are signs of our friendship as you rightly thought."

"You know I would not have understood it differently. I was new to the country and had no ideas about these matters, having not been exposed to them."

Jamike expressed a desire to leave.

"I think I have to leave now," he told Laski.

"Do you really have to?"

"Yes, I must go now. It is late." As he said that, Jamike got up and headed toward the door. Laski took a few short steps to come to the door to bid him good bye. He stretched out his right hand to shake Jamike but instead of shaking it fully as before, Jamike tapped Laski's hand gently and stepped outside. When he tried to touch Jamike, he warded of his hand. In the past Jamike welcomed such touches as a sign of friendship, as obtains in his African culture. Now that he was under the suspicion that Laski could have an ulterior motive behind his touches, he was not going to allow them anymore.

Jamike made a left turn as he walked down College Avenue and another left into Main Street heading toward Jefferson Apartments. He was occupied with thoughts of the conversation he had with his friend and mentor, the man who made it possible for him to come to America.

As he thought about it on his way home, Jamike again remembered the itinerant magician who had a long scarf tied around his neck and visited his primary school when he was a boy to entertain the children with magic. The magician bamboozled the children by first pulling rabbits from his hat. Then he would follow that with other astonishing magical acts as he yelled his trademark song and hyped the crowd to clap and chant in unison with him:

Come and see America wonder
Come and see America wonder
Come and see America wonder

America is truly a place of wonder, Jamike thought.

Twenty-Two

As Jamike walked home he took a few minutes to appreciate the bright moon that lit up rural Regius. Since his arrival, he had always felt nostalgic on moonlit nights. Whenever it was a full moon, he remembered the sandy squares in the village where young boys and girls would come out to play after supper. They called each other out by whistling their names hard and loud or by cupping the palm to serve as flute to invite each other out. They would come out to play hide and seek at the edge of surrounding farms and sometimes the girls practiced new dance routines or played games on the shiny moonlit sand.

Mothers, whose children were too young to engage in moonlight games, could be seen walking with alacrity to the square to scold and drag back to bed the ones who had sneaked out. Toward midnight they all would troop to the stream to fetch water, meeting other youngsters from other kindred at the road junction. They would chant songs as they went along the dirt road and descended the erosion-laden steep hill that led to the valley where the stream ran. They could fetch water from the running stream, or they could fetch it running with measured flow through embedded heavy rocks that lean toward the stream below and rise up the hill.

These rocks have been there from the beginning of time and spring water made by nature cascaded from them like an unstoppable fall. A hole was chiseled into the rock, and a long cylindrical wooden trough was driven into it to direct water into earthenware pots, gourds, and calabashes of different shapes and sizes. On the ground the falling water formed an almost crystal clear shallow pool from which people drew water for bathing, washing clothes, fermenting cassava, or mixing mud for house building. When Jamike was a child, he and other children would hold their nostrils tightly closed and immerse themselves in the pool for some seconds in a child's effort to find out how suffocating swimming would be. They were usually chased away by adults who reprimanded them for stirring the settled pool.

There were many things that brought memories of his hometown to Jamike but the moon always made him feel nostalgic the most. The only time he left his village was when he went to Teacher Training College. As he walked home and appreciated the moon, he realized it could be enjoyed in other ways, but car headlights and streetlights took away from the effects of moonlight in the city.

Jamike got into bed around twelve midnight. He picked up an old copy of *Life* magazine he bought at a yard sale to read. After a few minutes, he put the page he was reading face down on his chest. Thoughts of Linda came to his mind. He wished he could see her. He felt he had known her for a long time. He remembered how polite and well mannered she was when they chatted at the party. Part of him wanted to call her, but he had reservations about becoming involved with a black American, a foreigner and it was too late to call her. All the advice he was given at his send-off regarding the avoidance of foreign women came back to him. Yet, he still hoped he would run into her on campus.

The only time in the past that Jamike remembered he developed deep feeling for a female was when he met Adaku. She was an elementary school teacher at Annunciation School in a neighboring village. Adaku was a plump and average lady, with a gait so deliberate that the two sides of her buttocks shook alternately as she walked. Some village women said she walked that way purposely to attract the attention of the opposite sex; others said it was pride. Her skin was brown and most often she wore a braided hairdo with different styles. Sometimes the shiny braids were delicately tied and moved to the right side of her head with a woven crop of braids descending over her right brow as if it were a hood. Other times the braids were moved up off her face and tied at the apex, and it looked like a beautiful inverted cone.

It was toward the end of Jamike's third year at the Teacher Training College that he and Adaku met at a women's basketball tournament at the Annunciation Girls' Primary School, where she taught third grade. At the time Jamike met her, she had been an elementary school teacher for five years, but it was Adaku's first year at her present school.

At that basketball tournament between Ave Maria and Annunciation primary schools, Adaku and her friends stood a few feet away from the goal post of the home team. Jamike was there too. As the game progressed and the Annunciation school team fumbled a few times, a conversation ensued between Jamike, Adaku, and her colleagues. After Jamike and Adaku introduced themselves, they held conversation for the remainder of the game. They both said they found each other interesting.

When Adaku first noticed Jamike, she suspected that he could either be a new teacher or, perhaps, a student. She was further impressed when she learned that in another year he would finish from Teachers' Training College. Jamike took an immediate liking to her and wished he could know more about her. She struck him as being a mature, levelheaded woman and he felt he would like to spend some time with her.

After the basketball game, Annunciation teachers and pupils were overjoyed because they won. Adaku and her colleagues were excited to the point that they asked Jamike to come over to the teachers' quarters for a celebration. The female teachers' house was about a hundred yards or so from the basketball field. Soon they were in the large parlor of the big house, which had six bedrooms. It was teachers' quarters built with mud in the 1950s, and after some years it was plastered with a thin layer of cement. In some places on the outside walls large visible cracks showed, exposing the original red mud walls. In the center of the parlor was a long rectangular table with reading chairs, and on either side were three bedrooms. All the teachers shared the common parlor, although most of the time they stayed in their rooms and used the table when they prepared students' lessons or graded their assignments. Their visitors were generally entertained in the parlor, unless they were close friends, in which case they would be taken into their private rooms.

Apart from conversation on the just-concluded tournament, Jamike and Adaku talked about how she ended up coming to that school, how long she had been in the area, where she originally came from, and how she liked the village. Adaku quizzed Jamike on his school and told him how very much she would like the opportunity to further her education. She attended a two-year teacher's college, took a job, and had been teaching ever since. She offered Jamike Mirinda soft drinks and biscuits.

When Jamike left that evening, he promised to return to visit her and did so twice before he went back to school. During his final year at the college, Jamike and Adaku exchanged some more visits. He invited her to his compound whenever he came home on holidays, but when Uridiya was not home. On one ceremonial market day when she was Jamike's guest, the villagers wondered who she was. They knew she was not from their village, because no one seemed to be able to say whose daughter she was. Some people commented that she was beautiful. Uridiya saw Adaku with her son, but she did not think much of it.

She knew Jamike had better sense than going far with Adaku because in the tribe anyone who made a girl pregnant would automatically marry her. Once the parents of the young lady found out they would immediately take her to the home of the young man she named as responsible for putting her in the family way, whether he was ready for marriage or not. But if Jamike longed for a wife, Uridiya thought, all he needed to do was to inform his mother, who would then search and fetch a good wife for him. Many times in the past, Uridiya had taken up the issue of providing Jamike a wife, particularly because he was an only son, but he had always said he was not ready.

The times Jamike visited Adaku, he stayed in the parlor where he was often entertained. As time went on, Adaku began to have more than a platonic interest in Jamike. On one occasion, when Adaku invited Jamike, she prepared a sumptuous dinner for him. Rather than serve him in the parlor that she shared with the other teachers, Adaku set the dinner in her bedroom and invited Jamike to eat. The room was sparsely furnished. In it were a single-spring twin Vono bed, a chair and a writing desk, a wall clothes hanger, a food cupboard, a clay pot of water, and some enamel pots and plates and cutlery stacked on newspaper on the floor in one corner of the room. The only window in the room held a view of a cassava farm the school owned.

Jamike had a physical desire for Adaku but was too tongue-tied to say anything. Adaku was more mature, and she had expected Jamike to say something to her over these several months they had known each other, but he was not forward, being inexperienced. They joked and played card games many times when they were together, and he sometimes diffidently held her and embraced her. Adaku also felt a desire for Jamike many times in the past but did not verbalize such intentions. Jamike got comfortable in the room and wished that he would not have to return to the parlor after the meal. Adaku was not planning on sending him back there, either on that visit or on other visits in the future.

The meal was delicious. When Adaku came back from the kitchen after she washed the dishes, she noticed that Jamike had left the chair and now sat on the bed, leaning on his elbow on a pillow. She sat on the chair.

"Well, I see you moved from the chair," she said.

"Why are you now sitting on the chair? I thought you were sitting on the bed while we ate."

"Because you are now sitting on the bed. You took my

place."

"So, we can't sit together on the bed?" Jamike asked, his heart pounding.

"I thought maybe you preferred sitting there."

"That's true, I prefer to sit on the bed, but with you."

Jamike left the bed and sat on the chair with Adaku. She moved over to the bed. He moved there. She moved back to the chair. The next time she moved to the bed, Jamike rushed and held her there, both of them falling on the bed and laughing. Feelings of intimacy overcame Jamike from holding Adaku close and at times tight, trying to prevent her from going back to the chair. She was enjoying it, and she began to sense the manhood in Jamike. All these months she had at certain times felt frustrated that Jamike was not coming forth. She was sure he liked her as much as she liked him. She desired him, and now Jamike, who was twenty-four years old, wished he would have his first intimate experience with the opposite sex.

They rolled and played on the bed. Then suddenly Jamike stopped and went back to sit on the chair to Adaku's surprise. The thought of going beyond the play to intimacy struck him as not right because of a possible consequence he would not want at that time in his life. He had resisted his mother's constant entreaties to take a wife and raise a family. He would not do that now, because it could ruin his future. Adaku, in her surprise, could not make out what was on Jamike's mind.

It was past nine o'clock at night when Jamike left the teachers' quarters to go home. Darkness had descended on the village, and the sounds that were heard in that stillness were those of crickets and the lone voice of a nocturnal bird. Adaku gave Jamike a flashlight, and he walked straight into the night.

Twenty-Three

Jamike had a combined major in philosophy and political science. He read Aristotle, Plato, Aquinas, Hobbes, Lucretius and Sartre. Sartre's philosophy of existentialism fascinated him. Jamike agreed with the French philosopher that man's existential problem is the dilemma of choice among alternatives, not knowing which is the best. Jamike believed that ultimately each person, in the privacy of his or her conscience, must of necessity make choices, the outcome of which the individual does not know, and that is the existential dilemma.

A week following Professor Townsend's party, Jamike went to the library to check out some books after his morning class. Because he had some time before his next class, he decided to enjoy the sunshine that spring day. He walked to the large square between the college president's mansion and the library. It was usually a meeting or stopping ground for students as they criss-crossed between classes and the library. They would sit on low concrete benches or stand around in small groups to chat and catch up on events, particularly after a weekend or holiday. Once in a while, a student rushing to class along the paved pathway would recognize someone in a particular group and, if he did not intend to stop, would simply shout their name, and maybe, say something smart. He or she would then head either toward the huge library entrance or the double glass doors that led to the bookstore and classrooms and disappear into one of the hallways.

Jamike came to the square and stood momentarily to

see if he recognized anyone in the little groups that had gathered. A handful of black students as well as white students were milling around. Jamike went into the lobby of the library to pick up a free copy of *Regius News*. When he came back out, he stood a couple of feet away from the entrance of the library, just looking around.

As he held up a newspaper to read, a female student on her way to class noticed him and came toward where he was standing.

"H-e-l-l-o!" she said to Jamike. "Do you recognize me?"

"My God, I would recognize you any time," Jamike said. "You are Linda. I could not miss you in a crowd at all. I often thought about calling you. How are you?" Jamike asked.

"Why do you say you couldn't miss me in a crowd? You saw me only once."

"That is true," Jamike said, "but you stand out in any crowd."

"Oh yeah! Tell me about it fast because I am on my way to class," she said with a smile.

Students were crossing pathways, lawns and pavements to classrooms. Some were in a hurry, while others walked leisurely.

"Because you are tall, pretty, and you have a beautiful complexion," Jamike said.

"Oh, thank you. You know how to flatter, don't you?" Linda said.

Jamike learned that Linda was at the library most evenings studying on the second floor. He told her he might be back on campus that same evening and would look for her. Linda told him she would surely be there. She needed that discipline to do her work, because between her refrigerator, her roommate and the telephone she could not do much study in her apartment. Linda looked at her watch.

"I must leave now; I have two minutes to be in Professor Hill's European History class. He is teaching the French Revolution, and I love it." Jamike folded the Regius News and tucked it inside his book bag as they walked off in different directions.

When he returned to the library that evening, Jamike went straight to the second floor. He searched the floor looking for Linda. Twice he passed the carrel where she was studying, and he was about to leave when she stood up to stretch a little bit. She had been studying for some hours. Jamike gave her a friendly pat on the shoulder.

"Hi, have you been studying long?" Jamike asked her.

"Kind of. I am already getting tired. I am supposed to wait for my roommate and another student who are studying on the third floor. We had planned to take our break together. If you want to wait, I'll run up and see if they are ready."

While Linda went up to the third floor, Jamike flipped through her textbook in social anthropology. It did not take any time before Linda returned with two black female students. One was short and looked athletic and had an unusual hairstyle. The other was of average height, with a rather high-pitched voice.

"Meet Kathy Boardman, my roommate, and Lisa Stone." Linda said to Jamike. "We are all from Pittsburgh. I have known Kathy since high school. I met Lisa here at Regius."

"Hello, my name is Jamike Nnorom. I am from Nigeria. Nice to meet you both," Jamike said.

"I am sorry I did not mention your name when I introduced them."

"That's okay," Jamike said. "I thought you did not want to mispronounce my last name. Once you say it a few times, though, it becomes easy."

"Well, where shall we go?" Linda asked the girls.

"Let's go down to the lobby and we can decide as we do that."

They took the elevator down and walked through the lobby where there were already some students standing and talking.

It was already eight o'clock, past the time Linda and her friends had planned to take a break. They decided not to leave the building, but instead they sat in a corner of the lobby. Their conversation was spirited. Kathy said she was always pleased to meet Africans, for she liked their accents. Her family always spoke of Africa as the place they all came from originally. Her parents called Africa "the motherland" and hoped to visit there when they retired and had leisure time. Kathy wanted to know what part of the continent Jamike was from.

"Do you come from a tribe? I learned that there are many tribes in Africa."

"I am from the Igbo tribe, in the southeastern part of the country."

"I hope I will be able to go there someday. It must be an interesting place to visit. I would love to see elephants and other animals," Lisa said

"I think you would want to meet the people first before you see the animals. You will see elephants and other animals in the zoo if you want to. They don't live with the people or just run around. I am surprised that the first thing to come to your mind when you think about Africa would be wildlife."

"I don't think she means it in that sense," said Linda. "Of course, there are people there and she would like to meet and interact with them too. I guess she wants to go to Africa as a tourist and I suppose that is why she talked about seeing animals."

"That's okay," Jamike said. "The people and their culture are an attraction too. Our way of life is different from yours, and that is something you will like to experience as a visitor from another country. You will see manifestations of the people's creativity in art. You will see traditional dwellings as well as modern; all these are, perhaps, more interesting than wildlife."

"In fact, when it comes to wildlife," Jamike continued, "you will probably see the same animals at the Pittsburgh Zoo as you see in Africa. The only difference is that in some parts of Africa they are in their natural habitat."

"All right, Jamike," said Linda, "don't be defensive. I don't think any offense is meant. We just want to have an idea of what to expect if we went to Africa as tourists." As the conversation went on, Linda looked at her watch and told the group that it was time to get back to study. They studied for another hour before finally leaving.

As he lay in bed that night, Jamike found himself thinking of Linda. His first impression about her was confirmed. He found her good-natured and courteous. She was very friendly and laughed easily. She seemed intelligent and studious. Above all, she had a shapely, curvaceous body to which Jamike was attracted. He would like to know her more. Sleep did not come quickly to Jamike as he thought about Linda. He hoped these thoughts were passing thoughts and that his feelings would not persist. The admonitions from his people back home interfered with his thoughts. Anyway, he would have to give her a call and maybe meet her one day during the week. Maybe he would ask her out to dinner or, better still, cook for her.

While he lived with Laski, Jamike got used to going to the movies. Laski loved the movies, and he took Jamike a couple of times to the Rex Theater on Main Street. Sometimes, Jamike went by himself. The big screen was novel to him and contrasted with the short documentaries he saw in Teachers College or the government-sponsored films he watched in the village. Once in a long while, the mobile film unit of the Government Ministry of Information and Culture came to select village schools or squares to show films to the people. These were shown on a mobile screen in an open soccer field. Because of the wide publicity given to such film shows in schools, churches, and markets, the field was usually packed full with villagers, some of whom walked miles on bare feet to get a glimpse of the silver screen that they called "celema."

The short documentary films villagers watched once in a long while dealt with educational and agricultural issues. The sound system was very poor and was made worse by the pounding sound of the portable electric generator that supplied electrical power, which ran the projector. Ordinary villagers, though, were not interested in what was being said by the characters in a language they could not understand; they were more interested in seeing people in action on the screen. However, from their reactions, their laughter and comments in the vernacular they seemed to have followed the story line and were able to make intelligent guesses and associations. This was Jamike's only exposure to the silver screen before he arrived in Regius.

In the days and weeks following their meeting at the library, Jamike and Linda talked a lot on the phone. He was able to join her and her friends a few times again at the library. Sometimes she would drop him off at the Jefferson Apartments when the library closed at night, but she declined to come into the building because it was often late. From their conversations, they both discovered that they had a common interest in academics and the movies. Some weekends Jamike would ask Linda to look at the movie directory in the daily paper and pick a movie they could watch together. One of the movies they saw at the time was *One Flew Over the Cuckoo's Nest*, a box-office hit that starred Jack Nicholson.

It was on a Friday afternoon that Linda met Jamike's African friends for the first time. As Jamike approached the entrance to the library after his last afternoon class he ran into Okpolo, Emeka and Kwame. They were taking a course together and were at the library photocopying materials for a class assignment. Jamike turned back and followed them as they left the building, and they all stood in front of the library. They made arrangements about their weekend cooking at Jamike's apartment and carried on conversations about different matters. They were not there quite twenty minutes when Linda appeared from the direction of the bookstore. She stopped where Jamike and his friends were and, moving close to him, gave Jamike a friendly smile. Jamike introduced his friends to her. They were surprised at the way Jamike took Linda's hand and how she came so very close to his body. After she exchanged greetings with them, Linda turned to Jamike.

"I have to run. I am behind schedule," she said and kissed his cheek with a smack. The others looked puzzled.

"Well, friend, tell us all about this. Are you hiding something from us?" Okpolo asked Jamike.

He told them how he met Linda at the home of Professor Townsend and how they had become friends since their meeting. He also told them that they had been dating.

"Do you mean this has been going on and you have not told us?" Emeka asked.

"Must I tell you everything I do? Linda is a good friend and that's all. Actually, I planned to tell you about her when you come to the apartment on Sunday."

"How can we come to you when she might be there?" Kwame snickered.

"Why not? There is nothing going on. We will prepare fufu this weekend. Do you know if she likes it?"

"She may like it, or like something other than fufu," Kwame snidely said.

"Have you thought about taking her to Nigeria?" Emeka asked Jamike. Jamike was quick to respond.

"Why do you ask that? Who is talking about taking someone back to Nigeria? Linda is a long way from that experience, my good friends. You don't think the villagers would pull me by the ear and probably chase both of us into the bush?" Jamike quipped.

"You are right about that, Jamike," Kwame said.

"Now, I have to go. I have an appointment to see Laski. I will see you all on Sunday," Jamike said.

"Jamike, do not leave yet. You have not finished telling us about Linda. Remember that if you are hiding something from us, we will find it out later on," Okpolo said.

"The girl is my friend. That is all. You can think whatever else you may want to think."

Okpolo, who was from Benin City, told them that even if Jamike took her back to Nigeria he would be joining others who had done so.

"We better leave Jamike and his lady alone. At least, she is pretty. Some of us overseas would marry ugly foreign women to take back home. I have seen some of them in Benin City, and they looked wretched. I sometimes wondered where they found these wives," Okpolo said.

"You know, sometimes I think that, maybe, these women were married in return for the financial help they were able to give to their Nigerian husbands when they were students, in which case physical characteristics did not matter, but I may be wrong too," Emeka said.

"I know you are wrong in that suggestion. However, if I like Linda enough to want to marry her, it will not be for that reason at all," Jamike said. "But do not jump to conclusions. I have not told you I am planning to marry her. She is intelligent, educated, good-natured and all that. In any case, when I am ready to pick a wife, I will pick one from my home village. Good day, fellows," Jamike said and walked away.

Twenty-Four

Jamike and Linda continued to exchange visits, and the relationship developed more as they spent time together. They studied together at the library. At the football match between Regius and Cheney State College, three black students made snide comments as Jamike and Linda left the Regius stadium.

"Looks that this brother from Africa is serious with Linda," said Kenneth, who knew Linda. "Maybe she thinks we are not good enough for her to cross over to the continent."

"That's his lady. I sometimes see them together at the library," said Terrence, as they made their way through the crowd.

"Man, she has gone international," Kenneth said.

"I don't care for that guy. He looks stuck up, man. You know how these African dudes are. They think they are better than other folks," Kevin said. Linda overheard them and gave a smile.

"They aren't better than nobody. I think we just believe that," Terrence said, as he adjusted his Regius cap, face backwards. When the police at the road junction motioned to the large pedestrian crowd to cross, Kenneth, Terrence, and Kevin followed and headed to campus.

The matter of students from Africa thinking they were better than black American students was an interesting point Jamike and Linda had discussed. Linda told him that some black students held that opinion of Africans at the college. He told her it was a misconception. "What happens," Jamike told her, "is that because the black American students stay among themselves, the average African student would avoid them, not wanting to interfere, fearing he could be rejected. But anyone who was gregarious and friendly would very quickly be accepted."

"After all," Jamike continued, "the oppressors of blacks, or those who discriminate against them do not know nor do they care to know which blacks came from Africa or Haiti or Jamaica. As far as the oppressors are concerned, blacks are blacks, and they do not have the time to separate them by nationality."

Early in their relationship, Jamike promised Linda he would treat her to a Nigerian dish. On this Saturday evening he made good on his promise. He cancelled the usual weekend cooking at his apartment to entertain Linda. Linda called to say she was on her way after six o'clock in the evening. As she drove down Woodlawn Street to Jefferson Apartments, she imagined the type of food Jamike would treat her to and told herself she would eat whatever he cooked. She imagined what things Jamike would have in his apartment. Jamike looked out of his window a few times in anxious expectation as he got the food and plates ready. A man expecting a lady friend has his eyes always on the lookout. He saw Linda's car pull up and unlocked the door. How Jamike heard the imperceptible knock at the door remained a mystery. He opened the door and embraced his guest.

In his one room apartment was a folding couch that doubled as a bed at night. There was a reading desk and a chair and books littered the desk, which also served as a dining table. The room was decorated with two African masks and carvings of an elephant, a giraffe and lions. There was a framed piece of tie-dyed decorative cloth above his reading desk. Linda sat on the couch, and Jamike gave her a photo album, and while she sipped a soft drink and ate peanuts, he explained the photographs. While she went through the photographs, Jamike began to get food ready. He moved between the kitchen, the small dining table and the couch several times.

"What are you doing?" Linda asked, looking up from the picture album on her lap.

"Getting some food ready for us."

"I told you I would not stay long. There are things I need to get ready for Monday's class."

"Have a little patience. I will be done in a minute." he assured her. In a short time Jamike presented a small portion of jollof rice with meat and chicken.

"What is this called?" Linda was inquisitive.

"It is called jollof rice."

"And what is it made of?"

"It is made with rice, beef, and chicken, with tomatoes, onions, vegetable oil and some seasonings. It's really delicious. Next time, I will make fufu for you"

"This smells good. What did you just call it?"

"Jollof rice. It is a popular way of preparing rice in my country."

"Do you prepare rice in other ways?" Linda asked.

"Yes, you can prepare plain white rice and then make stew to go with it."

"Oh, I guess I will find that out later," she said.

"Definitely. I hope you will like Nigerian food. I don't eat hot pepper; do you? You will find that what I prepare has little or no hot pepper at all. I had a bad experience with regard to pepper as a boy growing up in the village. I was scared the day my uncle beat his wife because she put too much pepper in his meal."

"That's cruel. Why would he do a thing like that for pepper? He could simply not eat the food."

"He was very angry, because he said he had warned her on different occasions before that incident."

"Still, that is no reason to beat her. There is, in fact, no reason to beat anybody. It doesn't even make sense. There is something called talking, right? Do you eat a lot of spicy food?"

"No, I don't."

"But I thought Africans liked a lot of pepper in their food."

"No, I don't eat it. Some people do. More than enough

pepper gives me hiccups."

"What? Hiccups? That's funny."

As they talked, Jamike was dishing out more food. At first Linda tasted a little. It was good and she ate more. There was still quite a lot on the plate.

"I am sorry. I can't eat all this. Would you take some back?" she asked.

"That's all right, I can finish whatever you leave on the plate," Jamike said.

"You don't want to do that!" Linda protested.

"It's okay. Just go ahead and eat," Jamike said.

Linda began to eat the rice with zeal. Then she turned to Jamike and said, "This is very tasty, and it doesn't have much pepper. It looks like I am going to finish it."

"You know, it is not funny that I don't eat hot pepper. It runs in the family. I learned that my father did not eat pepper, and so my mother was mindful of that in our food. She always added more pepper to her food. She liked pepper." Linda stopped eating and was looking at Jamike while he talked.

"Go on and eat, don't mind me. I hope you will like the fufu dish when I treat you to it. It is our staple food." Linda looked at her wristwatch.

"What is the fufu dish made of?"

"Actually, a fufu dish is a two-part dish. Fufu is made of dough, which you roll into small balls and then dip each ball in soup and swallow. The soup is made of chicken or beef, or even both, vegetable, onions, crayfish, salt and pepper and seasoning condiments."

Linda stayed longer than she had intended. It was now close to eleven o'clock at night. Jamike rode back with her to the apartment she shared with Kathy Boardman. He planned to see her to the entrance and walk the mile or so back. However, Linda wanted him to come up the steps with her, in case there was an intruder. Her roommate was away for an athletic tournament at another university. They climbed the steps up to the second floor, into what looked like an attic apartment. It was an ample space for two students, however.

"Well, this is where I live. We like it because it is cheap and it serves our basic needs; besides, the low rent allows me to save money to augment what my parents give me. The lady who owns the building is nice but picky. When we first moved in, she told us she did not want parties or loud noise and there hasn't been any."

"Who would want to have a party in a room with a low ceiling? Anyone close to six feet in height like me cannot stand up straight in this room, let alone dance," Jamike said.

"Come on, Jamike, that is an exaggeration. You can stand straight in some areas."

Linda opened a small portable refrigerator and brought out a bottle of orange juice. She poured a glass for herself. Jamike looked at his watch, and it was already past midnight. He moved his chair back a little bit and turned to Linda.

"I think I should be leaving."

"Why do you have to leave so soon? I was going to show you some pictures of my own family. We are not a large family. It is me and my sister, Cynthia, and my parents. I have a couple of relatives."

"I thought you might want to sleep. Isn't it late for you," Jamike asked.

"No, no, Jamike, I am actually a night person. Sometimes I stay up until two or even later in the morning studying or watching late movies." She brought out a big photo album plus a fat envelope of loose pictures. "Would you like to see my album?" she asked.

"Sure," Jamike said. "I would like to see the pictures of my relatives?" Jamike kidded.

As she pointed out her parents, Bill and Wanda Johnson, and her younger sister, Cynthia, Linda leaned on Jamike. Mr. Johnson was a supervisor at the U.S. Steel Corporation in Pittsburgh, and her mother was an elementary school teacher. They lived in a middle-class neighborhood in suburban Pittsburgh. She showed him pictures of family vacations in Mexico, in the Bahamas, and in Florida, Hawaii, and California. Jamike was impressed by her travels. She talked with interest and had humorous stories to tell about the places where the family vacationed.

"These are wonderful pictures, Linda. You should visit Africa too. You would love it," Jamike said.

Jamike had an urge to kiss her, but he held back. He felt as if he was being pulled back and forth. After all, she was a foreigner, someone he knew he could not be involved with. Jamike felt that getting involved with Linda would trouble him because of the admonitions he was given when he was leaving his country. He wondered if his people would understand should he get seriously involved with Linda, a foreigner, who was black like him. These were the thoughts going on in his mind as he sat there with her. Would he get involved as his heart desired and dictated and then betray the expectations of his people back home, or would he stifle the emotion he was feeling for a beautiful black woman whose ancestry went back to the land of his birth?

As he flipped through the pages of the photo album his mind reflected on this matter. Jamike also thought about his African friends at the college too. When they first met Linda on campus, they read unwarranted meaning into their friendship. Would it embarrass him if they saw him in a changed relationship with Linda? They already had something against American black students. If they knew he was romantically involved with her, they would think he had made positive statements about American blacks only because he was already dating one of them and hiding it. Jamike dismissed this thought about his African friends, because he was not accountable to them. It was for them to resolve in their own minds their feelings about black Americans. He had chosen to identify with them and that was that. His concern now was how to handle Linda should his acquaintance with her develop further.

It was now well past one o'clock, and they were still looking at photographs. The pictures were numerous, with Linda running a commentary on some of them, especially those of her and her family. Jamike would look at his watch, and each time he suggested he might be leaving,

Linda would say she was not feeling sleepy yet and requested him to stay a little longer. As they looked on, Jamike turned to her and said,

"You are so beautiful in these pictures."

"Do you think so, or do you flatter me?"

"I am serious. You are very photogenic, looking good in every picture. No, I have no need to flatter you, and I would not say what I did not believe in."

After a lot of hesitation, and with a fast heartbeat, Jamike turned toward Linda and put his arm around her. He tried to kiss her, but she pulled away. Rather, she looked at him straight in the eyes and talked to him.

"Do you think you like me, Jamike?" she asked him with a smile.

"I think I do but, again, I am not sure about what I am doing. I have not felt this close in my heart with anyone since I came to this country. I mean, I have not felt what I am feeling now. I had a platonic friendship with a female a year ago, and that's it," he said.

"Exactly what way do you feel? Can you explain it?" she asked him.

"It is a little bit hard to say. I know I like you, but I have certain inhibitions I do not plan to discuss at this time. Perhaps at a later date you will learn about them," Jamike told her.

"Well, I will wait and hopefully I will learn about them."

"I don't think you understand what I am referring to," he told her.

"Are you worried that you are sometimes seen around with me?" Linda asked Jamike pointedly.

"Oh, no, it is not even that. Why should I be worried? I am not accountable to anyone here, nor do I have to explain my actions. Why would I worry about anyone seeing me with you? It is more complicated than that. But I will tell you about it later on, I promise you."

"O-k-a-y."

Jamike was still holding Linda as they looked at more photographs. It was close to two o'clock when Jamike stood up and stretched. Linda was still not feeling sleepy.

He pulled her up and hugged her. He told her he had to leave.

"You can stay longer if you like," Linda told him. "After all, tomorrow is Sunday; no, excuse me." She looked at her watch. "It is Sunday already, and we can even watch a late movie on television." The movie they watched had already begun. As they watched, Linda allowed Jamike to hug and kiss her on the cheek. Before the movie ended, she changed into a nightgown, ready for bed. It was well past three o'clock in the morning. Jamike who slept on the couch, did not get back to his apartment that night.

In the morning Linda offered to drive Jamike home, but he told her to sleep more since they went to bed very late. Jamike came down the staircase, shut the door behind him, and stepped into the street. He walked down Woodlawn Drive and in a little while crossed over to Main Street. He thought about his visit to Linda. He enjoyed Linda's company. They had good conversations in which she proved intelligent and positive. She had a good family. What was he going to do now? Was he getting involved beyond his better judgment, or what? There was no doubt in his mind that he liked Linda. The only doubt he had was whether or not he would be able to handle the situation now developing, and not allow it to get out of hand.

Jamike and Linda attended a Nigerian wedding ceremony in the spring. It was held at Our Lady of Sorrows Catholic Church, in Orient, Pennsylvania. Jamike noticed that Linda was excited about his asking her to come along. According to the invitation card and program, it would be a mixture of both western and traditional African wedding styles. The service would be the usual Catholic wedding nuptials but the reception would have traditional elements. The traditional part of the ceremony would be the breaking of kola nut and the pouring of libation with the invocation of Igbo ancestral spirits, which an elder person in attendance would perform.

Orient was only two hours from Regius. They drove up Saturday morning and made good time. The church was not difficult to find once they were in the city. As they walked up the steps, Linda told Jamike that they should sit as close as possible to the altar, so she could observe what differences there were from weddings she had attended. To her surprise there were none. It was the same Catholic nuptial ritual. Both the bride and the bridegroom were Igbo like Jamike.

Linda found the reception at the Ambassador Regency Hotel very enjoyable. She had never seen any wedding reception that grand and in fact began to wish to have a similar wedding. It would be wonderful, she thought, to have such a wedding with Jamike. A lot of things fascinated Linda, like the colorful outfits of some of the women, and their head-wraps. Orient had a sizeable number of Africans, and it seemed they were all at the wedding. Some men were in suits, while others wore traditional clothes of different colors with caps that either matched or showed contrast. All danced with their partners to Nigerian highlife music. Some American tunes were also played; in fact, the couple entered the reception hall marching to a western love ballad.

Dancers wiggled and gyrated. Jamike did a couple of highlife dances with Linda, teaching her the steps and the graceful side-ways movement of the body as they danced. She picked up a few steps pretty fast and enjoyed herself. She did not particularly care for the speeches or the litany of advice given by friends of both the bride and the bridegroom. Once she got into the dancing mood, she wanted it to be dance all the way. Jamike told her that the speeches were necessary to advise the couple about the joys and trials of married life. The meal served was rice, chicken and vegetables. Cake, ice cream, and hot tea and coffee were available for dessert.

After the church service, and also at the reception, Jamike and Linda greeted the bride and bridegroom and chatted with them. When Jamike introduced Linda to Nnenna, the bride, she thanked them both for coming and teased a little bit.

"I hope we will be coming to your own wedding sometime soon?" Nnenna asked Linda.

"We will see about that," Jamike answered.
Nnenna then said something in the Igbo language to Jamike.

"Are you going to marry her, or are you playing and wasting someone's time?"

"My sister, I don't know which I am doing, to tell the truth," Jamike replied in their native language.

"You are asking him this right here?" Obi asked his new wife.

"Do I have to convene a meeting to ask a question?"

Linda held on to Jamike's right arm as the conversation went on. After Nnenna spoke to Jamike in Igbo, Linda was curious.

"It is nothing much. I will tell you later," Jamike told Linda.

As they walked to their seats Jamike reflected momentarily on the advantages of marrying someone who spoke the same language, someone he could share cultural jokes with. He thought about how this would constitute a handicap if he loved Linda enough to marry her.

They left Orient by nine o'clock that night, going back to Regius. Conversation centered on the ceremony they witnessed. Linda was glad and appreciative that Jamike took her to the wedding. She probed Jamike, wanting to know if taking her to the wedding meant anything special to him. He told her he thought she would enjoy it, and he also wanted her company on the trip. She asked many other questions. Jamike told her that the kola nut was important in an Igbo household. It was used to welcome guests to the home. It signified unity and bonding and it was believed that partaking of it would bring life, health, strength, longevity, and many other things asked for as one prayed, holding the kola nut in hand.

Linda said she wouldn't mind going to other ceremonies like the one they went to. In her mind she said that, perhaps, one of those would be hers. Linda told Jamike she would like him to meet her parents.

"The next time I go home for the weekend, I would like you to come with me. I told my family about you, and they would like to meet you," Linda said. Jamike turned toward Linda and said he would be delighted to meet them.

It was past ten o'clock when they got back to Regius. Neither Jamike nor Linda was tired when they came back to Jefferson Apartments. They watched some television together before Linda, noticing that Jamike felt sleepy, decided to leave. He needed the sleep because he planned to attend church service early the following morning.

Twenty-Five

It was a bright holiday weekend, the Friday afternoon that Jamike and Linda set out for Pittsburgh, a distance of over a hundred miles from Regius. The breeze was gentle on this spring day. The trees already flushed with leaves, swayed as if in a slow dance. The scenic beauty of western Pennsylvania against a backdrop of undulating mountain range, with acres and acres of farmlands and crops, kept Jamike's eyes on the landscape.

"This is a beautiful countryside, Linda," Jamike said, putting his hand across the driver's headrest.

"Just wait until we get off the I-80 Interstate, and you will see how wonderful this part of Pennsylvania is. I love spring. It is cool and nice at this time of the year."

Linda likes to speed. Jamike cautioned her to slow down. But she had a reason for driving fast. She wanted to get to their home before her parents would arrive from work. In that way, Linda felt, Jamike would already feel comfortable and maybe engage in a conversation with her sister, Cynthia. Linda knew that her mother, Wanda, was usually the first to arrive from work. She therefore wanted Jamike to meet her mother first. Linda had already told her about her African friend and on that day her mother concluded their conversation by advising caution. Wanda told her daughter, "Be careful, we will see you any day you and the young man from Africa get here."

Jamike and Linda laughed and amused each other as they conversed and drove through rural Pennsylvania heading for Pittsburgh. Jamike's eyes roved right, left and ahead as they talked. He was enjoying the picturesque scenes on both sides of the road and in front of him in the distant horizon. He was doing some thinking too as he was internalizing nature's beauty. He became a little worried about the visit to Linda's home. What was the importance of this visit? Did it mean any commitment on his part? Was he going too far in the relationship? He was not sure of the implications for Linda. As they entered suburban Pittsburgh, Linda turned to him and said,

"We are getting close, in less than fifteen minutes we will be at my parents' house."

Jamike turned to Linda and asked, "Are you sure this visit is okay?"

"What do you mean, Jamike?"

"Are you sure it will not create any problems?"

"I am positive. I told you I have already told my mother about you and how I feel. Even my sister, Cynthia, knows about you too."

"What of your father? Is he aware that I am visiting and spending a night? Does he know how you feel about me, as you put it, whatever that means?"

"Dad will like you. My sister was really excited when I told her that I would be coming with you. When I mentioned to Dad that I would be bringing down an African friend, he did not object. He simply said, 'okay.' They are always supportive of me, especially when I do the right thing, and, of course, they disapprove of what they consider wrong. I do not think this is anything wrong, do you? I am not going to hide you. I know what you are thinking about. Ignorant and narrow-minded persons may have problems with Africans, but my family will treat you like family," Linda said.

Cynthia, who came to the door when they arrived, saw their car as it took the turn into the driveway. She quickly opened the door, and there was Linda with a friend in simple African attire. Since she already knew Jamike was coming with her it was no longer a surprise that he was with Linda.

"Hello," Jamike greeted Cynthia.

"Hi," she responded.

"Jamike, here is my sister, Cynthia," Linda said as she faced both of them.

"This is Jamike, Cynthia. He is from Nigeria, from the Igbo tribe. Did I pronounce it right?" she asked Jamike.

"You get better each time, Linda," Jamike said nodding.

"Hi," Cynthia said to him again. "Did you have a good trip?"

"The scenery was marvelous as we drove through the countryside. I enjoyed it," Jamike said.

"It is usually nice at this time of the year in this part of the country." The Johnsons lived in a two-level, five-bedroom house in the suburbs. It was a good section of the city. Almost all the houses here were painted white, off-white, or light blue. The lawns were so meticulously mowed that, from a distance a visitor would think a large artificial grass roll covered and extended from each frontage of homes in the neighborhood. Linda took Jamike's garment bag into the guestroom on the ground floor, and took her small suitcase to her own room before joining Jamike and Cynthia in the living room.

"I know you have many questions. He knows a lot about Africa," Linda said to her sister.
Cynthia looked at Jamike and said,

"Good, tell me everything you know about Africa then."

"How can he tell you all he knows about Africa? That will take weeks or months. After all, he has lived there all his life," Linda quickly cut in.

"Well, let him start somewhere," Cynthia said.

"You are the one that told her I know a lot about Africa," Jamike said to Linda. "Why are you surprised at her asking me to tell her everything I know?" They all burst out laughing.

"I know I am going to be telling my life story over and over again this weekend. Maybe we should wait until your parents come back because I know they too will have similar questions about Africa and about me. In that way I save myself the trouble of repetition," Jamike said with amusement. Actually Jamike was beginning to resent the questioning wherever he went, but he had not made that known to anyone, not even to Linda.

"Okay, don't tell all; just a little bit. I know Mom will have many questions for you too." Cynthia was very excited as she talked with Jamike.

Jamike talked about himself and how he came to America. Sometimes he wished he had written it down or taped it, so that if any person asked him about himself and Africa he would hand them a little pamphlet to read or a magnetic tape to play on their own time.

"Well," he said, my name is Jamike. I came to Regius to go to college. Why Regius? Because a friend there made it possible for me to come. I am studying philosophy and political science."

"Philosophy, that's neat," Cynthia cut in. "My English teacher used to talk about philosophy. He said philosophers do a lot of thinking about the world. Do you?" she asked.

"I am not a philosopher. I am just studying it as a subject."

The conversation came to an abrupt end when Cynthia announced that their parents were turning into the driveway. Linda looked out and turned to her sister to ask what happened to their father's car, because they drove in their mother's car. The car pulled into the concrete driveway. The engine fell silent. Mr. Johnson and his wife, Wanda, came out. They came into the living room. He was dressed in a gray business suit, a white shirt, and a matching striped necktie. He stood a little less than six feet tall, with salt-and-pepper hair that gave him a distinguished look. Wanda, who was an attractive woman of forty, wore a purple short-sleeved dress. This particular evening, Linda noticed her mother looked rather tired from teaching and controlling elementary school children all day long, but that tiredness disappeared after she met Jamike and engaged in conversation with him.

"Hi, guys," Mr. Johnson said, animated as he came in the door with his wife. Linda smiled at her Dad and said,

"Mom and Dad, meet Jamike. Jamike is from Nigeria."

"Hello, how are you?" Wanda said.

Mr. Johnson moved closer to Jamike, shook his hand warmly, and said,

"Linda told us you might be here this weekend. Welcome to our home. I hope you had a good trip." Jamike made good eye contact with Mr. Johnson.

"Yes, we did."

"Was Linda driving fast as usual?"

"I don't want to talk about that. She made me afraid, that is all I can say."

"Make yourself comfortable. I will be down in a moment." Mr. Johnson excused himself to go upstairs. Wanda went into the kitchen and had a drink of water.

"We are pleased to have you in our home. I am glad you had a nice trip."

"It was very nice. I got a chance to enjoy the scenery of the countryside. It is almost like some parts of my country, with farms, trees, and forests. The mountainous background makes the scenery absolutely aesthetic."

"I think it is, you are right. What are you taking in college?" Wanda asked, looking at him with admiration.

"I am taking philosophy and political science," Jamike answered.

"That's good and what do you plan on doing?"

"I will probably work for government or go into politics."

"Here or in your country?"

"I don't know yet."

Mr. Johnson came down from upstairs, having changed into more comfortable clothes. After he joined them, he went into the kitchen and came out with drinks for all.

The subject of conversation was, of course, Jamike. They asked him how he liked Regius, how he liked American weather and other recurring questions.

"Do you plan to go back to your country after your education, or will you stay here?" Mr. Johnson wanted to know.

These were all familiar questions to Jamike. He answered that he did not know yet if he would go back to his country after his education. At this time, Linda interjected,

"Dad, he is thinking about staying here after he graduates."

"That would be wonderful too. I guess there are more opportunities in this country than in your country. What country in Africa are you from?" he asked.

"Nigeria," Linda answered.

"People from all over the world come here. They enrich this country in many ways, and it doesn't matter if their culture, language, or dress is different. Whether you decide to stay in this country or go back, you just do what is right for you."

Their conversation was interrupted when the nightly news came on television. Jamike was relieved from having to talk and answer questions. Following the news there was a dinner of rice, steak, vegetables, and bread rolls. The conversation was general and relaxed.

Twenty-Six

The next day, Saturday, Linda and Jamike went shopping and sightseeing in downtown Pittsburgh. Linda, a native Pittsburgher, gave Jamike a quick tour of a few places of interest in Pittsburgh, a city of rivers, bridges, and historic architecture. She first took him to her father's place of work, the sixty-four-story U.S. Steel Towers, one of the tallest buildings in the United States, located in the golden triangle. They then went to the campus of the University of Pittsburgh where Jamike was awe-struck by the famous Cathedral of Learning, standing forty-stories tall.

Later they went to the Three Rivers Stadium, home of the Pittsburgh Pirates and the Pittsburgh Steelers, and then they did some shopping. In the evening they explored the Brentwood neighborhood, where the Johnsons' house was set on an elevation along Addison Road. Behind it was a backyard lawn that went down a slight slope with shady trees. The temperature, above seventy degrees, was unseasonably high for April. Jamike and Linda planned to enjoy the weather. It was early evening when they went down the slope. They sat down under a shady umbrella-like tree on a comforter Linda brought with her.

They talked about the setting sun, golden on the horizon and about the beautiful neighborhood with lawns mowed so perfectly it looked like rolled-out green carpet. Since they first met, Jamike and Linda had often talked about the subjects they took, how they enjoyed their classes, and also about the idiosyncrasies of their professors. As they sat and talked Jamike remarked that the serenity of their backyard, coupled with the setting sun on the horizon, was so perfect it could spur the creativity of a poet, a painter, or a philosopher.

"Is that right?"

"Yes, because poetry, painting, or philosophic speculation call for reflection in a serene setting. I had a class called Varieties of Visual Art and enjoyed it thoroughly." Maybe I should take a class in philosophy. I need some electives. Can you recommend a course?"

"It depends on what you want out of the course. Philosophy deals with the meaning of life. It asks questions and addresses such concepts as beauty, freedom, justice, truth, and the like. It can deal with anything, because there is a philosophy of everything. You should start with a basic introductory course. It will expose you to issues or problems of philosophy."

"I think I will like it. I like to think about things. When the schedule of classes comes out for the fall semester we will look at it together so I can pick two electives from philosophy, but I don't want to start with the problems of philosophy. That will be hard," Linda said.

"No, no, a course in the problems of philosophy will address the kinds of issues philosophy deals with. That is a good starting point and I think you will be alright." School and what happened on campus were always of interest to Linda and Jamike. Linda's friends referred to her as a bookworm. While they talked, Linda slapped her ankle twice.

"What is it?" Jamike asked.

"It must be some bug or something. We have to leave here now. It is getting a little cool, anyway. I hate bugs. When they bite me, they leave bumps on my skin. Let's go." Jamike was the first to get up. He took Linda's hands and pulled her up.

Jamike picked up the comforter and shook it twice in the air to get rid of dry grass on it.

As they came up the slope, Jamike felt a sinking feeling in his stomach as he thought about where he was. He wondered about who would locate him if he got into something like an accident or if he was harmed in any other way on the trip. No one in Regius knew he was coming to Pittsburgh; none of his Nigerian friends knew his whereabouts. He shook his head, and for a split second questioned himself. From the kindness accorded him, he believed the Johnsons were good people. However, at the subconscious level, he was not sure he was doing the right thing by coming home with Linda. He worried that he was getting too deeply involved in their relationship. He worried it might be difficult to end it if there should be need to do so.

After they returned to the house, they decided to go get some ice cream. Cynthia went with them to the Dairy Queen. Jamike loved vanilla ice cream. Going inside the store, Linda held Jamike's hand till they sat to eat ice cream. Linda asked Cynthia if her parents had said anything yet about Jamike.

"They haven't said anything in particular, but I think Mom likes him," Cynthia said.

"What of Dad?" Linda asked.

"I will say he likes Jamike too because they had an engaging conversation. If he didn't like him, he would not have shown the kind of interest he has shown in him." Jamike kept on eating his vanilla ice cream and not paying particular attention to what the two sisters were talking about. But he heard them. By the time they came back from the Dairy Queen, supper was ready. It was after the ten o'clock news that the family retired for the night.

Linda did not go to bed immediately. She always said she was a night person. She tidied her room and put together clothes that she had laundered and wished they did not have to return to Regius the next day.

Around eleven o'clock, Linda went to the guest room to talk to Jamike, as she did not feel sleepy yet. She sat on the bed and told him how much she would miss him if he ever went back to Nigeria. Jamike told her that it could be possible to take her to Nigeria at some point in the future. The thought was exciting to Linda, because such a trip would give her a sense of connection to Africa.

Jamike gave Linda a kiss on the cheek and held her close. She was very responsive. Jamike then determined to hold himself. He suddenly let go his hands and sat straight.

"What is it?" Linda asked as she looked at him. "Is anything wrong?"

"I am just thinking about us."

"What about us?"

"Oh, so many things, but never mind." Linda tried to lean her head on his chest while they sat on the bed.

"O-k-a-y," she said, sitting back in an upright position. After a while she said, "I think I better go get things ready for our trip back." She kissed Jamike good night and shut the door behind her.

Jamike was not one to waste much time in falling asleep. Though he would fall asleep easily, any little movement would wake him up. He slept lightly. His mother used to tell him that he slept with one eye open like a dog that wakes with any slight movement. This habit of sleep was a useful endowment in the village, because thieves could come at night. But on this particular night when he lay down, sleep did not come quickly. The unfamiliar surroundings might have been responsible for this. He turned toward the wall and lay on his right side with his right hand under his head on the pillow, as if the pillow were too low to rest his head. He lay there, thinking about Linda and where he was. When he met Linda at the home of Professor Townsend, little did he know that it would lead to his coming to Pittsburgh and spending a whole weekend at the home of her parents.

Jamike mused that human beings sometimes never know where the road they travel might lead them. Though rational, humans are sometimes swept up by events beyond their control and, like in a tide, they flow until they reach their ultimate destination. He pulled the sheet up to his neck and thought about home.

This time of the year, April, was the rainy season in his village. He remembered the melodic clatter of the rain on thatched roofs that sang in his ears, putting him to sleep. But if awake, he would hear the unrelenting beating of the raindrops on broad leaves of farm crops in surrounding farmlands outside — and the frightening lightning that preceded many a thunderstorm, which made villagers fearful. This was the time when a mother would get up in the middle of the night to check up on the children sleeping on mats on a clay floor or on creaking bamboo beds, to make sure they were all right. The children were deep in sleep, oblivious to the rain, lightening and thunder that bothered the adults. Sometimes, an older child had pushed a younger sibling away from the mat onto the dry dusty floor or simply had his heavier leg on him. A mother noticing this would gently carry the child back onto the mat or with extra care move the heavier leg away. Such thoughts occupied Jamike as he finally drifted into sleep.

The morning was cool and pleasant. The family had breakfast together. Jamike was getting more accustomed to his hosts and feeling more at ease and at home with them. But it was now time to start heading back to Regius.

"Oh, Linda, you know I almost forgot to invite your parents to the International Day gala." Jamike turned to Mr. Johnson. "Mr. Johnson, foreign students are having their International Day in two weeks, and I am inviting you and your family."

"Dad, it is usually a nice affair, and Jamike and his Nigerian friends will be making some presentation."

"That sounds interesting," said Wanda. "Maybe we can come to that."

"Hopefully, I can come too," Cynthia said.

"I know you will probably come to the International Day gala. But, Cynthia, I would want you to later on enroll at Regius as a student," Jamike said.

"I am beginning to think about it. I had Pennsylvania State University in mind. But you all want to make me change my mind. Not yet, though," Cynthia replied.

Linda and Jamike left for Regius after lunch. They talked a lot as they drove back, remembering some things that happened on the trip.

At one point Jamike kept an unusual silence, lost in thought.

"What is the matter?" Linda asked with concern on her face.

"I am okay," Jamike told her in a calm voice. He was reflecting on the trip and was still worried that he might be going too far too soon with Linda. The admonition not to marry a foreign woman was ever present on his mind. As far as villagers were concerned, it didn't matter that Linda was black or any other color for that matter, but as long as she was from the white man's country, by their terminology, they regarded her as not only foreign but called her a white person. This was based on their conception that people who lived overseas were white. They could not see how black people could inhabit "white man's land." Jamike took a philosophic view of his dilemma, hoping an outcome he could deal with would present itself.

The thought came to Jamike about the possibility of this relationship progressing to the point where he would ask Linda to marry him. He shuddered. No, he could not do that, or his people would never forgive him for what they would consider a betrayal. They had advised him not to marry a foreigner. Linda may not have cared about the nationality of the person she would marry, but it was of great concern to Jamike.

Before Linda dropped Jamike off at the apartment, they stopped to get some ice cream. Jamike had developed a taste for ice cream. He told Linda he enjoyed the trip and was glad to meet her family. They were very friendly and anxious to know about other cultures and people. He recalled Mr. Johnson's comment that the differences in human beings enriched the world. He said no person should feel awkward or embarrassed because they spoke differently, dressed differently, ate something different, or had different customs. If anything, these attributes should make the individual unique and special. Linda was glad Jamike enjoyed his visit to their home.

When they got to the apartment parking lot, Jamike asked if she would like to come in for a few minutes, but she needed to go home and unwind. She drove off with a screech of the tires as she turned onto Main Street and disappeared from sight in her burgundy Oldsmobile Cutlass Supreme. The car was a high-school graduation present from her parents.

Apartment 201 was stuffy from three days of absence. Jamike opened the windows to let in fresh air.

Twenty-Seven

The Saturday that Jamike and Linda were in Pittsburgh was the day he and his African friends would have cooked dinner together. He informed them he was going out of town but did not tell them where. They arranged to meet the following day, Sunday. It was an important meeting because they needed to start discussing preparations for Regius International Day, which was coming up later that spring. They would make a special presentation at the event, and they needed to know what it would be and the responsibilities of each person. International Day was usually a day of festivities when different national groups at the college presented aspects of their culture in food, music, dance, and artifacts. It was a day that was given much publicity on campus and in the town, and attendance was usually considerable. The college president, Dr. Albert Gilchrist, was usually in attendance and would make brief remarks about the importance of cultural diversity on campus and how each international student enriched the school.

When Jamike's friends came on Sunday, they prepared delicious okra soup and fufu for their lunch. Okpolo and Kwame prepared jollof rice with coconut juice, which gave it a good aroma and a good taste. Emeka did not arrive in time to help in the preparation, but he came later with a case of beer. As he entered the room, he told them,

"Listen, people, it is easy to know the apartment where an African lives, because you can smell the soup as soon as you enter the hallway. A visitor who was looking for the apartment number would be led directly to the door by the smell of the soup." They all burst out laughing.

Jamike thought of inviting Linda to join them, but he feared she might feel out of place among his African friends. She would not understand Pidgin English, which they spoke when they got together; the topic of their conversation, which would invariably center on their country and tribes, might not interest her. Jamike thought Linda would easily be bored if he invited her.

While they ate, the phone rang, and it was Linda. Jamike beamed with a broad smile as he answered. She wanted to come over for a while, but he told her he had company and he would call her as soon as they left. She figured they were his Nigerian friends. She knew they came over on weekends to cook their Nigerian food. As he continued to talk and smile, his friends teased him, because they too suspected it was Linda.

"That must be your girlfriend who makes you smile so. Is she coming over?" Emeka asked.

"Emeka, not while you are here. You might make her uneasy."

Kwame, who was usually not talkative, asked Jamike what he planned to do with his American girlfriend after college.

"Before we know it," he said, "you will tell us you are getting married to her and taking her to Nigeria to join those other foreign wives your compatriots brought home from overseas. Maybe you were not advised against marrying a foreign woman. My kinsfolk gave me plenty of advice on that."

"What did they tell you? I know the advice they gave me."

"You know there is no end to what they will say to anyone going to study in a foreign land. I don't think anyone listened to more advice than I did. It was a litany of admonitions, and my ears almost fell off." They laughed.

"Let's hear what they told you." Emeka said.

"Well, it goes like this: Be sure to face your studies. Do not marry a foreigner. You are not going there to indulge in excessive drinking or womanizing. If you need a wife, send us a message, and we will select a suitable one for you, one that will be obedient and give you peace. Do not think you can find a good wife by yourself. No matter how educated you get, we are the ones to select a wife for you. Return home as soon as you get your education, and remember you are an investment — not only to your parents but to the whole village.

Then they threw in a proverb. Remember what our people say: namely, that if a child finds a snail in the bush, it belongs to the child, but when he or she brings it home, it belongs to the community."

"I think you have covered it all," Jamike interrupted.

"No, he has not covered it," Emeka said. "I had more advice than he had, but it is hard to remember it all except when an allusion comes up that jogs my memory."

Everyone laughed as Emeka went through the list of advice given to him. They shook their heads. Jamike acknowledged he was given all that advice too, and that the old man who poured libation gave him a special blessing that was poetic coupled with the advice. Said he:

"My son, may you not meet bad luck.

May you not stumble on the road you take!

May danger always be behind you and not in front of you!

May your head be filled with knowledge!

May the evil ones, man or spirit, not come your way!

We pray for your life.

Whenever you are ready to take a wife, may it be someone we will hear what she says. Let her be from our tribe.

Those of us you leave behind, may we not be in want of what to eat, and as you eat there, do remember us.

When you come back, may you find us as you left us, in health and strength."

The old man seemed to have gotten carried away, because these invocations kept pouring out of his mouth in a cadence. After each statement of supplication the crowd roared "A-m-e-oo..." for "Amen."

"They told you not to bring home a foreign wife too?" Kwame asked.

"Yes, they did," Jamike admitted. "But they failed to realize that in choosing a wife, each woman should be judged individually. It is wrong to generalize about women or any group, race, or nation."

"Jamike, you may be falling in love with an American woman, if you say so," Okpolo said. "But seriously speaking," he continued, "I think their primary concern is that a foreign woman would not speak the same language as they, and even more importantly, the villagers believe that this person will not understand their culture. They also believe that foreign women do not make obedient wives, and that they want to be equal to the man. There is also a litany of other things they are accused of."

"It is possible some of these things are true, but a lot of what they say about foreign women are assumptions and suppositions; in fact, hearsay," Jamike said. Kofi, the student from Ghana then said.

"Well, I believe the knowledge of what they say comes from what they have heard about people married to foreigners. You know how news about such matters travels across villages. It may have been one person who, perhaps, heard the story on a visit to a city or a distant village and came home to tell the story of what he heard and it spread from there. And by the way, I know someone from my town who studied overseas and returned with a foreign wife."

"Can you tell us what the people have against a foreign wife?" asked Jamike.

"For one thing," Kofi began, "they say foreigners do not allow their husband's relatives to come close to him anymore. She dominates him and dictates what happens in the home. His parents cannot come to visit and stay as long as they choose. If his parents should visit, they have to give them some months' notice. The moment the parents step foot through the door, they are asked how long they will be staying. They think this is unheard of; a man's parents should stay as long as they want in their son's house."

"Wait, wait, some of our women married to Nigerians do exactly that, so what is the difference?" Jamike interrupted.

"It is said a foreign wife would not allow the husband to extend help to brothers and sisters, and discussion about financial help to relatives causes disagreement all the time. When they return to the man's country, it is believed that after some time she would take the man's children and return to her country, and that the man may not see his offspring again. In addition, she never fully considers herself as part of the husband's extended family. If there were a problem, and relatives came in to settle it, she would consider it an interference. They do not realize that where we come from, one man does not marry a wife, the whole village marries her. They are not embarrassed to sue for divorce, and, if the couple lives in the wife's country, she is awarded the house and custody of the children while the man is left with nothing. This is what the villagers heard. I tell you, our people have a lot against marriage to foreign women."

"But you see," Jamike said, as he dropped his spoon, "I don't know where they get all this. These people are ignorant and have generalized from the behavior of one or two foreign wives they have heard about, and then they ascribe that behavior to a group. That, you know, is stereotyping, and it is wrong. This is exactly what black people complain white people do to them. How can we do it to ourselves? These villagers could even be imagining these things. A woman from anywhere in the world can have these attributes. Just as there are good and bad foreign wives, so are there good and bad African wives. In fact, those African wives who come overseas and learn these practices our people are against, are worse in their application. Some of the things they say may be true, but it is not a behavior pattern limited to women who do not come from Africa."

"You know," Emeka said, as he swallowed a piece of rounded fufu, "one old man in my village, a stark illiterate, suggested that the foreign wives we bring back may be the ones no one was willing to marry in their own country. He said that if it were up to him, his advice would be that we should go ahead and marry them, but let them be so beautiful as to stir the groin of any man. He even put it as the Igbo might say in a proverb: if anyone wants to eat a toad he should be sure it is a juicy toad so that if he is called a toad-eater, he will assume the name with pride. He advised that anyone who wants to marry a woman from the white man's land should wash his eyes squeaky-clean and get a woman that is fatty and juicy."

"Well," Jamike said, "Linda is beautiful and bright. She is intelligent. And by fatty, I think our people mean that she should look well fed. So, if I should be called a toad-eater, I will proudly answer to the name."

"Jamike, you are not the one to tell us that your lady has all the qualities you claim. Allow us to tell you that," Kwame said, laughing.

"How are you supposed to know if she has all the qualities I said she has, unless I tell you so?" Jamike said, with food in his mouth.

"Do you not remember the adage of our people, that a ripe corn is known by just one look? That is why you should leave that to us," Emeka interjected. "Anyway, now that you tell us she is beautiful, intelligent, fatty, and juicy, are you going to marry her?" he asked.

"Let's leave that topic alone. As our people say, it is the person who is under a palm tree who can tell if the nuts are ripe. We will cross that river when we get to it. Let's continue to eat and enjoy the evening," Jamike told his friends.

Jamike's friends did not leave until ten o'clock at night. Their discussion ranged from their experiences in America to issues of concern in their respective countries. In the meantime, one half a case of beer had been consumed. They reached agreement on what to prepare for the International Day event. As was their practice, they would contribute money to buy the food items and other ingredients. While they shared duties, they lamented the fact that there were no female students among them to give the dish a female touch.

As they were leaving, Emeka noticed a yellow post office slip held on the refrigerator door with a magnet. He commented that he was familiar with those yellow slips from home, and that they always contained heavy stuff and more advice than anyone would care to pay attention to.

The yellow slip was for a letter from Jamike's mother. She had not written often. Jamike understood that finding someone to write letters was sometimes difficult for Uridiya. So whether or not she replied to his letters, Jamike wrote once a month to inquire about his mother.

Twenty-Eight

The heat had cooled off on this Orie market day, and the sun, now a red bowl, was setting on the horizon. Uridiya Nnorom, returning from the market, met the woman appearing in her dream who would become her future daughter-in-law. Along the road she was walking were dust-covered cassava leaves that looked pale from the heat that scorched them earlier. Hordes of black birds coasted in the sky above Uridiya, heading to a destination only they knew. Fowls that went into farms and bushes in the morning in search of food were tiredly making their way back to family chicken coops.

Two months earlier, Uridiya had suffered a severe attack of jaundice from which many believed she would not recover. She had relatives scared, and some even suggested that the priest be called to administer the last sacrament. Two native doctors worked very hard to restore her to health. Ritual sacrifice was made to propitiate the god that was responsible for her illness. Uridiya stayed away from the daily market and from her farms for two weeks. That illness gave her grave concern because she worried that she might die without carrying Jamike's child on her lap. But she became well again and began to go to the market to sell small amounts of crops harvested from her farms.

Chioma Adibe was returning from a visit to her aunt who was living in Aludo. Uridiya saw a beautiful, copper-complexioned young lady. The twenty-two-year-old was plump and full of life. Her plaited hair was tied in the front. She wore a simple floral dress and was riding her bicycle on a sandy strip of the road. When pedaling became difficult on the sandy road, she dismounted and pushed her bicycle along. Uridiya, who was returning from Orie market, went passed her. After passing each other, Uridiya turned to look at her. Suddenly Uridiya stopped and brought down the basket of fruits and vegetables she could not sell, and she looked back in the direction the girl was going and called her.

"Daughter, daughter, look this way," she called. There was no answer.

"Daughter, daughter with a bicycle. It is you I am calling." Uridiya's tone was louder. She got no answer. Then she raised her voice a little higher. "Young lady pushing the bicycle, you behave as if you haven't heard me. Is it not you I am calling and nearly losing my voice?"

Chioma turned in her direction. "Mama, are you calling me? Is everything okay?"

"Everything is okay, my daughter. I want to ask you a question."

Chioma used her right foot to push down the bicycle stand. Uridiya walked back to meet her.

"Mama, did you say you have a question for me?" Chioma asked as she approached Uridiya.

"Yes, my daughter, who are your parents in Aludo."

"I am not from Aludo. I am from Ndioma."

"Who are your parents in Ndioma?"

"I am the daughter of Adibe."

"Which Adibe? I hope it is not the church warden."

"That's my father."

"Oh, my God. I knew he would have a beautiful child like you." She came closer and embraced her. Chioma did not respond to the embrace but was rather embarrassed.

"Everyone knows your father and mother. So, they have a daughter like you. Tell me child, what do you do?"

"It is not long since I left the P.T.C. I am teaching now."

"My daughter, explain what 'tee-tee-tee' means. I did

not go to school."

"I completed elementary school and went to Teachers College for one year. It is called Preliminary Teachers College or P.T.C."

"I don't know which is which. Where are you teaching now?"

"I teach kindergarten at the local government school in Ndioma."

"Kindagadi, which one do you call 'kindagadi,' my child? Chioma laughed.

"It is the very little kids."

"That seems right for you, child. Someone like you will be perfect for the young ones. You will be good for my own young ones too. Beautiful child," she held her hand. "Is anyone marrying you now?" Uridiya continued. "I am looking for a wife for my son."

"No, Ma, I am not married. It is not long since I completed school. Marriage is not what I am thinking about now."

"My son I am talking about is in America. You don't know him. He left for America four years ago."

"Your son is in America?" Chioma asked.

"Yes. He asked us to look for a wife for him. Will you agree for him to marry you?" Uridiya asked.

Chioma blushed and looked down.

"Give me an answer. I am getting him a wife today or tomorrow. I am serious and in a hurry too about this."

Chioma looked up.

"Do you want me to give you an answer on the road? This moment? I have to see the person." She was unconcerned.

"How will you see him? I said he is in America. Any wife we marry for him will be sent to him. If you want to see him, I will bring you his picture. He is a strong young man. He wants a young girl like you who is strong too. Marriage will fit both of you."

"Mama, I have to go now, it is getting late."

"Did you say you are Adibe's daughter?" Uridiya asked.

"I will not lie to you; there is no reason to."

"What did you come to our village to do?"

"My aunt is married here."

"Who is she? In whose household is she married?"

"Her name is Agnes. She is married to Mr. Luke Onyewu."

"My God, are you related to Onyewu's wife? This whole matter is over then. I am going to see her. If I don't see her this night, I will see her in the morning. We belong to the same women's meeting. Listen to me, beautiful. You will be my daughter-in-law. God brought you out today so I can meet you. My son, Jamike, has a wife today."

"Have I agreed?" Chioma asked Uridiya.

"My daughter, it is not you who will agree. I will see your parents. It is they who will agree."

"Let me go then, until you see them. I hope you will marry them too," Chioma said sarcastically.

"You can go, my child. I have seen what I have been looking for. You will see me soon with someone familiar to your parents before the next Nkwo market day."

Chioma picked up her bicycle and pushed it some more distance down the road. Once she passed the sandy area, she rode again. Uridiya fixed her eyes on Chioma until she disappeared from sight. Since Chioma was a little child, everyone said she was beautiful. Men and women who saw her said they would marry her for their son. When Chioma became a teenager she would be stopped on her way to the stream to fetch water, to the market, or to school, by old men and women who wanted to know her. They would ask whose daughter she was and said they would see her parents. Those who actually approached Adibe or his wife were informed that Chioma had not reached the age of marriage and was still in school.

As Chioma rode home this evening, she thought about her conversation with Uridiya and chuckled. "These old women will not fail to stop me as I go about my business. If I had not excused myself from this woman she could have delayed me, telling me what I cannot make out, something I have no interest in. I wonder how many husbands I am going to have."

Uridiya carried her basket up, balanced it on her head and walked away, filled with thoughts of Chioma Adibe. She began to see Chioma in her dreams as Jamike's wife, her daughter-in-law. When she visited the headmaster a few days later to inform him about her new find, he told her he knew the church warden and that Adibe's daughter would be a right choice for Jamike because she has been given a good upbringing. Jamike, he said, would need a girl from a good home. He did not remember the young lady very well, but if Adibe was her father, that would be the only recommendation they needed. He promised he would go with her to approach Adibe on the matter. The headmaster told her to be sure to ask Akudike, Jamike's uncle, to come with them to represent his father, because that was the custom.

A week later, Uridiya, Akudike, and the headmaster visited Adibe and his wife, Ihuoma, to inform them that they were interested in having their daughter's hand in marriage for Uridiya's son who was studying in America. Okeke Adibe was a religious man, and his baptismal name was Julius. He and his wife, Ihuoma, were well known in the church as they involved themselves in various religious activities for men and women. Ihuoma was the leader of the Christian mothers who swept the floor of the church every Saturday, donated eggs, pots of water, firewood, fruits and vegetables and other things to support the parish priest. Adibe joined the men to cut bushes around the priest's house and maintain the lawn. It was common knowledge in all the villages in Aludo that Adibe and his wife gave their children good upbringing. There was no doubt that the daughter, Chioma, received excellent home training, as evidenced by the exemplary good manners of the Adibe children.

On this visit, Akudike took a calabash of palm wine. Adibe was pleased to see the headmaster. After they were presented kola nut and palm wine, the visitors said what their mission was.

"Adibe, thank you very much for the kola," the headmaster started. "Akudike and Uridiya asked that I accompany them on this trip. Because it is about something good, something I support, I could not say no." He turned to Akudike. "Now, Akudike, you are the leader on this trip, tell Adibe what brought us to this household."

"I accept to be the leader as you said, but Uridiya and her son brought us here. We are here in your household, Adibe, because my late brother's wife, Uridiya, is in search of a wife for her son. She saw a young lady who appealed to her, whom she would like to live in her household." All eyes were on Akudike. "This young woman told her that she is your daughter. Uridiya says it is she or no one else as wife for her son. That's why we are here." There was a momentary silence. Adibe and his wife looked at each other.

"You say the young woman is from Adibe's household?" Adibe asked, after he breathed out.

"Yes, that is what we say," Uridiya responded. Adibe asked his wife to send for his brother, Duru, to be a witness to what he and his wife were hearing. After Duru was briefed, he asked.

"Where is the young man in question? The one you are talking about? Did he send you here while he stayed home? Is he the one marrying, or you three?"

"The person we are representing is studying in America," the headmaster said.

"We have his picture here," Akudike said.

"Let us see the picture of this individual," Adibe, his wife, and Duru almost said at the same time.

After Uridiya showed them Jamike's picture, the two brothers, facing each other, looked at each other but said nothing. They talked with their eyes as villagers often did in such matters.

Ihuoma, Adibe's wife, looked over the picture of Jamike thoroughly. She gave Uridiya a smile and looked at her husband.

"This is your son?" she asked Uridiya. From her body language, she seemed to have approved the visit. She stepped outside to ask Duru's wife to join them. Adibe talked about his daughter.

"Many suitors have pestered me and my wife over Chioma since she was a little girl. But we have not asked any of them to proceed beyond mere inquiry."

"Will that be our fate?" Uridiya asked. Everyone in the room said something.

"I welcome you all. We have listened carefully to the purpose of your visit. We will not answer yes or no to your request until we have had a chance to talk to our daughter.

"How long will this take? I want a wife for my son, like today or tomorrow." Uridiya said.

"We will be able to give you an answer, one way or the other, in two weeks."

Adibe told his visitors that Chioma finished elementary school and attended one year of a teaching training course in a Preliminary Teachers College. The headmaster commented that that was a significant educational achievement for a village girl at the time, because it qualified the holder to become an elementary school teacher and was preparation for further training in the teaching profession.

Although Adibe did not show any signs of his pleasure when Uridiya came to ask for his daughter's hand in marriage, he did not have second thoughts about its potential. He and his wife already looked into the future and saw the possibility that their daughter and Jamike would someday be in a position to help them educate and train their other children. They might even make it possible for their son, Mbakwe, to join them in America.

When Adibe and his wife talked to their daughter, it was to inform her of their consent to the present suitor and to make her aware of the benefits such a marriage would bring to their household. Chioma replied that if it suited them, it would suit her. She added that they were her parents and she would not contradict whatever they said. Adibe said to her, "By your statement you prove you are my daughter. If you had any reservation I would have wondered whether or not I am your father."

Twenty-Nine

The yellow post office slip for a registered mail that Jamike received on a Saturday afternoon came from home in Nigeria. It was too late for him to collect it that same day. He was always anxious to read letters from home. Not that the contents of the letters were usually urgent or even important, but because they carried ordinary village news that connected him to his people.

Registered mail was supposed to be important, but the villagers would register any letter going overseas, whether its contents were important or not. They registered them to ensure they were delivered. Villagers were afraid that non-registered letters might get lost in transit, and they were often lost. Sometimes in his anxiety, Jamike would open and read a letter from his village right there at the post office. He was anxious to know the condition of things and to learn about his mother. If the letter came from one of his age-mates, it would definitely have humor. They liked to tease him and he enjoyed that.

One time, a bosom friend and age-mate said in his letter that no matter how much knowledge he acquired in America, he would still be able to wrestle Jamike to the ground, just as he used to do at the market square when they were adolescents. He told Jamike not to think that his book knowledge would make him any stronger than before. Jamike liked these teases from his friends who might envy his education, but would be quick to tell him that regardless of all his knowledge, he would still be one of them and engage in native customs and rituals. When Jamike was attending Teacher Training College, his age-mates, though proud that one of their own was receiving higher education, were quick to inform him that his education would not place him above them as long as he was a member of their age group. They would remind Jamike that no member of the age grade rises above the other, or that no finger is too big for the nostril.

Though he was now far away from them in a land they could only imagine, one age-mate teased Jamike that regardless of how many years he stayed overseas, his age group would still claim him when he returned. It was Oriaku, another age-mate, who reminded Jamike of the story of the beautifully colored rodent that sped across the dirt road into the bush as a lunatic walked up and down the same road. The lunatic clenched his index finger between his teeth and cursed the creature that fled from him. However, he secured a low stool and positioned himself in ambush at the point where the rodent entered the bush. He shook his head and pointed his finger in the direction the rodent went. "A traveler must come back someday," he reminded the animal that eluded him. Despite their teases Jamike's age-mates were proud of him and awaited his return to rejoin them.

The package Jamike received on Monday afternoon came from the village headmaster, Ahamba. His name was conspicuous on the envelope as the sender. It was a thick overseas airmail envelope with short blue and red stripes around the edges. The cursive script handwriting on the envelope was meticulously done as only an old headmaster would do. The fat envelope had more than one letter. One was from the headmaster and the bigger one from Jamike's mother. Looking at his watch, Jamike judged that he could only read one of the letters before going to class. He decided to read his mother's letter right away. After he read it, he wished he had saved it for later, because the content was not the kind to read while standing or walking to class.

He recognized the handwriting. The person who wrote

the letter for his mother was his distant cousin, Onyema, who was in junior secondary school. Uridiya always said she liked the manner in which the young man wrote letters for her. After each paragraph, he would repeat faithfully in the vernacular what Uridiya asked him to write, as she was in the habit of asking him to repeat each sentence to make sure he wrote down exactly what she said. Onyema always omitted unkind statements or whatever might upset Jamike but memorized them so that when asked to read them back he would give back the message exactly as she had said it. It was because Uridiya believed that Onyema wrote down every word she intended for Jamike that she preferred him to compose her letters. The letter Jamike opened was a bombshell.

Uridiya sent greetings and asked about Jamike's health and studies. She told him she was in good health again, following an attack of jaundice. She was still experiencing some aches and pains for which the native medicine man was giving her some herbs. She said that the man had a gifted hand in medicine, because of all the treatments that the native doctors gave her, only Nwogu's herbs had worked. Then she told him how she thought about him constantly and prayed to God to keep her alive until he returned. She continued:

"I have been thinking much of you since the headmaster informed me that you are nearing the end of your studies.

Please read all the books you can, so that when you return you will have no need to go back there for any other thing you forgot to read. You know about the gigantic Iroko tree, which is so huge that no one since the beginning of time has been able to climb it twice. Remember what the Igbo say, that if anyone is strong enough to reach the top of the Iroko, he should procure all the firewood he can lay his hands on, because no one is able to climb the Iroko tree twice in a lifetime.

"I have been telling you since you became a man that you ought to marry. Time waits for no one. All your agemates in the village have married. I cannot wait any longer. Each time I see your mates with their families, I regret ever agreeing for you to go away to learn more. I saw with my eyes all the books you read while in school. The knowledge you had before going to America was enough. Anyone who doubts it can come and count the books in this house. I do not know what else you are going to add to it."

"My happiness will not lie in how many more books you read to have more education. My happiness, Jamike, will be for me to carry my grandchild on my lap. I want to be able to do this as soon as possible, because I do not know when my god will send for me. You know that nothing is guaranteed in life, and I am sure you read about that in your books too. You should not wait to obtain all knowledge before marrying. If anything should happen to you right now, you would have nobody to succeed you, and our lineage would end. The headmaster told me about something you educated people do with women that is called engagement. I hope you have not done that with any woman. Anyway, I know you would not do that in a land where the only person you know is the white man that took you there."

Uridiya asked Jamike if he remembered Okeke Julius Adibe, the church warden. "Well, his daughter who was a young girl while you were at home has grown into a beautiful woman. She is so beautiful that if beauty were to be eaten, no one will waste any time in eating her. She is like a creature from the sea, a mermaid," the letter continued.

"We are looking at her as the woman who you will live with, and she will bring you happiness. What you want in your life is happiness. As you know, her father is a very truthful man. We heard that the young lady is hot in her brains. She is always first in her class. She is very polite and respectful and greets everyone she meets, whether it is in the morning, afternoon, or night. She is very obedient to her parents and definitely will be obedient and submissive to the man whom she takes as her husband.

Everyone in her village likes her, and they think she will make a very good wife. We have asked her to take a picture which I will send to you." Continuing, she informed Jamike that she and some relatives have already carried wine, as required by custom, to the girl's parents to inquire about her and seek her hand in marriage for him.

"I need a quick reply from you, for nothing will make me happier than a good daughter-in-law who will look after me very well as I am getting old now. Since I have no daughter of my own, your wife will become one for me. I have heard that you will finish your education at the onset of the rainy season, which will be the fourth month of the year here. I am pleased to hear this. My eyes are on the lookout for your reply. It is my prayer that I will be alive when you return, so I can see you with my two eyes."

Jamike shook his head in disbelief after reading the letter. He folded it and placed it back into the envelope. Usually attentive in class, Jamike must have reread the letter three times during the fifty minutes of class period. After class was over, he stayed back to read the headmaster's letter. Mr. Ahamba sent greetings and inquired about Jamike's upcoming graduation. He asked about his plans for the future. Was he going to return immediately or work for some time to save some money before coming back? Was he planning on more studies? Whatever he planned to do, he should arrange to return to see his mother. But the sooner he came back home for good, the better, as nowhere can be better than one's home. Another man's country would always be another man's country, he told him. The headmaster informed Jamike of his mother's desire to have him take a wife as soon as possible. He did not see anything wrong with this wish, because Jamike was at that point where he should be thinking seriously about marriage.

The headmaster told Jamike that he knew the family of the young lady that his mother was courting for him. "She is the daughter of a man of God who has raised his children in the fear of the Lord. The girl is brilliant, down-to-earth, and good-natured. I believe she will make a good wife, unless the devil steps in. Her family has welcomed the move by accepting the first round of wine carried on her behalf without hesitation. As soon as we hear from you, we will go to the next stage in fulfilling marriage customs. In fact, it is possible to complete all necessary customary requirements in time before you return, or, if you cannot come home anytime soon, your wife would be sent to you. Then you and your wife can spend a year together before returning to the country."

As Jamike folded the letter, he held his forehead, took a deep breath, and then let it out. He slowly shook his head sideways. He knew it would come to this someday. His mother was definitely going to start something like this. But Jamike hardly thought she could begin any such process while he was still overseas. Again, he took a deep breath and exhaled. He wasn't going to think about this now, he told himself; he would deal with it later.

Thirty

International Day was held on a sunny and beautiful Saturday with the temperature above seventy degrees. Flowers of delightful colors bloomed around Randolph Hall. Evening activities for the day started at five o'clock in the neo-classical turn-of–the-century marble building with huge white columns. Linda's parents and sister arrived earlier in the day. Members of the organizing committee of the Regius International Association, including Jamike, made sure that food and drinks, art exhibits and costumes were in place and dancers in readiness. The president of the association, Mr. Wong, moved around in the hall directing and putting finishing touches to all they planned to do that evening. Randolph Hall was decorated on the outside with colorful balloons, buntings, and flags of the different countries represented at Regius.

Wanda and Cynthia sat a few rows away from the platform, where they had a good view of the speakers. As the organizers got ready, the event got started. The association president greeted the audience and welcomed them to the college. He thanked the college administration for giving international students the opportunity to share aspects of their various cultures with the college and the Regius community. He thanked those parents and friends who came to share with them, especially from out of town, and hoped they would enjoy the rich diversity that foreign students brought to Regius and the college. He then introduced the Dean of International Students, Dr. Hammond Abrams, who welcomed visitors to the college and wished them a happy evening on campus.

The president of the college, Dr. Albert Gilchrist noted how the presence of international students changed the complexion of the college and how the various cultures enhanced the vitality of the college community. He shared some of his experiences when he spent a year in France as a Fulbright scholar and talked about how that one year enriched him. He commended members of the Regius International Association for what he knew would be a wonderful event and hoped everyone would enjoy the evening.

There was a polka dance by six students, followed by a Japanese dance and an Irish jig. There was a colorful array of assorted food from every continent. Jamike and his Nigerian friends had their usual jollof rice and chicken. The president and members of the faculty mingled, moved from one table to the other, sampling different types of cuisine. Mr. Johnson, Wanda, and Cynthia moved around with Jamike. They told him how much they were enjoying the occasion and complimented him and the other students on having everything run so smoothly. Jamike told the Johnsons that he would visit with them at the hotel before they left the next morning. Both Professor Townsend and Laski, Jamike's friends, were there too. Jamike walked over to Laski with Mr. Johnson and Wanda and introduced them.

"Jamike has told us so much about you. How nice of you to make it possible for this young man to come to the United States," Wanda told him.

"He is a good fellow. When I met him in Africa, I knew he would benefit from an American education. I am glad he is here and likes it. I hope his people will benefit from his education and exposure in this country when he returns home."

"Our daughter, Linda thinks so much of him," said Wanda.

"He is a nice gentleman, without a doubt," said Mr. Johnson.

"Are you enjoying the evening?" Laski asked them.

"It has been very pleasant. It is wonderful of the students to put this together," Mr. Johnson said.

"Yes, it is. I hope you continue to enjoy it. Jamike, go on and show them around. Nice to meet all of you," Laski said. Jamike and the Johnsons moved on to mingle in the crowd.

Both Laski and Townsend were supporters of the Regius International Association, and at every annual festival they had given the students carvings, musical instruments, and any other materials they thought would be of attraction to their guests. The masks that were exhibited came from Laski.

The sun that appeared on Sunday morning was gentle. Its delicate rays were soothing and were an invitation to bask a little in its cozy warmth. Linda and Cynthia picked up Jamike and took him to their parents' hotel for breakfast. Linda dressed in a crisp navy blue dress with a broad white collar and cuffs. Cynthia had on a flowered and elegantly fitted dress. Jamike wore a pair of gray trousers, a blue shirt, and a plaid jacket. Mr. Johnson and Wanda were ready when Linda knocked at the hotel door. They ate brunch at the nearby Howard Johnson restaurant.

"I think it was nice that Jamike introduced the person who made it possible for him to come to this country," Wanda said, turning to her husband.

"He has a good heart, obviously. I don't believe many people would do that. One has to be of selfless character to think of bringing another from a foreign country to obtain an education so he can return and apply his knowledge to solving the problems in his own country."

"Dad, I know you would do that if you had the opportunity, wouldn't you?" Cynthia said to her father.

"I believe I could do that, if the opportunity presented itself," Mr. Johnson replied.

Jamike told them that when he first met Laski and he talked of the possibility of bringing him to America, he did not believe it. It was too much for him to imagine. It would only be a miracle, he thought. But the miracle did happen, for he found himself in America. He was thankful to this man and to God who made it all possible. He told them that when he first came to the country, the end of four years of college seemed so far away. He wondered how he would make it; but here he was already in his junior year.

"You will be graduating next academic year. Have you thought of what you plan to do? Will you be returning home, or what?" Wanda asked.

"He is going to stay right here in America, Mom," Linda said smiling, not letting her mother finish the last sentence, even before Jamike could answer.

"I have applied to some graduate schools and, in fact, both the University of Chicago and the University of Maryland have given me admission."

"What do you mean he is staying here in America?" Cynthia asked her sister.

Mr. Johnson looked on as the conversation was going on between his family and Jamike.

"I have not made any decision on what I will do after graduation. I have a number of options. First and foremost, I will like to return to Nigeria after my studies. If I stay longer after my graduation, it will be to work and gain some experience. This will be after graduate school, though; but before all that I would want to visit home to see my mother after I complete my degree."

"You will have been away for four years from your home and your mother by the time you graduate. I bet you get homesick sometimes. I would." As Wanda was finishing her statement, Linda interjected.

"Mom, what would you say if I moved to live in Africa?"

"In Africa?"

"You have to tell us why you want to move to Africa. We will probably support it if you have a good reason," Mr. Johnson said.

Linda looked at Jamike, then at her mother and back to Jamike, as if there was a conspiracy between the three.

As a mother, what was going on with Linda did not come as a surprise to Wanda. Linda's admiration of foreign lands and people began very early in life. She had always been fascinated by the exotic, always interested in people, and liked to read the *National Geographic* magazine. Each time Linda and Cynthia traveled with their parents on vacation to Latin America or the Caribbean, the Johnson children had always treasured the experience, shared it with classmates, and talked about it with each other and with their parents. It would be no surprise to Wanda if Linda would think about marrying a foreigner. The family had once played host to a foreign student who was on an exchange program through an organization to which Wanda belonged. However, Jamike was the first student from the African continent whom they knew this closely.

Wanda believed that her daughter was in love with Jamike. Linda somehow gave her that impression when they were visiting in Pittsburgh. Mr. Johnson and his wife had always supported their daughter in the choices she had made. When Linda decided to major in anthropology instead of law, which was their preference, they did not try to change her mind but instead supported her. When she changed her mind to attend Regius State College rather than Pennsylvania State University or Wanda's alma mater, Spellman College, in Atlanta, her parents had no problem with her decision. The possibility of marrying a foreigner is one idea that had crossed their minds. They knew, however, that Linda would be able to adjust and live in any country that interested her, just as she would live in the United States.

As they ate brunch that Sunday morning, Wanda and her husband in their conversation implied that their daughter could live wherever she wanted after graduation as long as it was her choice and she was safe. Linda was quick to remind them that Africa or even Europe may seem far, away but anyone living there could visit or call often. Jamike sat through all this conversation full of smiles and feeling a little embarrassed at what was going on between Linda and her family. After brunch, they went back to their hotel room and the Johnsons prepared to leave for Pittsburgh.

Jamike helped to bring down their luggage and had it loaded into the trunk of their car. They departed at about two o'clock in the afternoon. As the Johnsons drove home, they discussed the very clear possibility that their daughter could marry Jamike. While it was not particularly troubling to them, they were still puzzled that Linda would be in that frame of mind at this time. However, they were of the opinion that Jamike was a very respectful and levelheaded young man, whom they felt would make a good son-in-law, if it came to that. Wanda even said that if they got married it would give her an opportunity to visit Africa. She remembered that a colleague at school had once mentioned that she and her husband were planning to go on a trip to Africa to visit their daughter who was married to an African. Wanda now intended to seek this colleague out and have a conversation with her about her daughter's experiences.

Thirty-One

Wanda wanted to know more about Jamike and Africans after she and her husband returned to Pittsburgh from the International Day program. The following day in school, she had a conversation with a colleague, Walleta Brown. Walleta's daughter, Sharon, was married to an African, an architect from Ghana. She and her husband with their two children had lived in Brooklyn, New York, before they moved back to Kumasi in Ghana.

While Wanda and Walleta had lunch together, Wanda told her about Jamike, an African from Nigeria, with whom her daughter was having a serious relationship. She told her how nice she and her husband felt he was. Since Walleta's daughter was married to an African, Wanda wanted to know how her daughter's marriage was working out, because she did not want Linda to make any mistakes. Of course, she wanted her to be happy in marriage.

"I don't think it is a matter of making mistakes. It is a matter of whether or not she will be able to make the necessary adjustments if she is married to a foreigner, whether an African or not. You know, cultures are different, and people see certain things from the perspective of their culture. That makes a big difference," said Walleta.

"You have to educate me from your daughter's experience, so I can tell my daughter, Linda, things to look out for," Wanda said.

"Actually, it is better for your daughter to experience it herself, because people's experiences and the way they react to them differ. Sharon loves her husband very much, but foreigners have been conditioned from their culture, and it is so hard for them to change, even in a country like America where they receive their education," Walleta said.

"What are some of the problems?"

"It is a matter of adjusting to their ways. Sharon told me Africans find it hard to adapt to American ways in the manner they treat their wives. She had complained about some things when they lived in Brooklyn, but we encouraged her to give the marriage a chance. I was divorced from her father, and I did not want the same thing to happen to Sharon. It was so painful. But when he formed a habit of beating her, I said no, that's taking it too far. It is time for a divorce, and I couldn't care less."

"He lays his hands on her? That is certainly unacceptable. In what other areas did they actually have problems?"

"Sharon told me and her step-father, Andy, that she had concerns about many things. In fact, Andy first suggested that she had no business being in such an unhappy relationship. He wanted her out and fast too, but I had a different view on the matter. Leaving the marriage would be running away from problems that they should work together to resolve. I thought I probably was hasty with my own divorce. But I was wrong."

"I wish Linda could talk to her. In what country in Africa do they live?

"They live in Kumasi, Ghana."

"Oh, but that is not Nigeria?" Wanda asked.

"True, it is not. But Africans, Sharon found out, treat their wives, and women in general, in similar ways. When they lived in Brooklyn, we used to visit them and she told us that whenever the African wives came together the complaints were the same, whether their husbands came from Ghana, Kenya, Nigeria, or other African countries."

"Well, Linda has to be aware of these problems," Wanda said.

"It makes me sad," Walleta said, "because they expect their American wives to accept things women would definitely not accept in the United States. She told me that at one time her husband's brother, who had lost his wife, came with their baby to live with them in their apartment and had no plans to leave. He did not work but stayed home all day. He invited his friends, and they did nothing but drink beer and talk in a language she could not understand. Besides, some of them physically abuse their wives and children. It has to do first with the problem in the relationship between the man and his wife, then his parents and a whole lot of relatives and friends and, of course, money and who should decide how to raise the children. It's an entirely different culture."

"What did Sharon tell you about living in Africa?" Wanda asked with concern.

"The most basic thing is that you have to adjust to lack of regular electricity and water. I believe that would be a shock to any American woman. It is not even the lack of these amenities that is the issue. It is this matter of beating her that drives me crazy. Sharon said it happens whenever she talks back to her husband or challenges him. The last time it occurred had to do with the kids. He felt Sharon was too liberal with them. For anything they do wrong, as any kids their age would do, he flogs them. When Sharon raised concerns about that manner of punishing children, he told her he was not going to allow her to raise his kids in what he called her crazy American ways. They got into an argument, and before you knew it, Sharon's face was swollen from a slap in her face. He does not want her to challenge him in any way. She must agree to whatever he says, which is the law."

"She did not call the police?"

"In Brooklyn, before they went back to his country, the police came a few times, but she did not press charges. You know how that goes. You call the police, he is arrested, and you go to get him out. You make love and make up. Sharon said that the police in Kumasi wouldn't do anything, because she understood that all men, including the police, beat their wives as they please. I guess that is one sure way they know to get their wives to do their will. Sharon said Kojo told her she was neither an obedient wife nor a good mother. You know, he actually makes all the decisions himself and does not believe she should contribute any ideas. Their first battle was about money. He wanted a joint account, so he could send all her money to his family just as he did even before they got married, when he constantly borrowed money from her and never paid it back. His family made tremendous financial demands on him. He sent most of his earnings home."

"Did he marry her for money then?" Wanda asked.

"Some of them marry for the money, but I don't think it is the case here. He didn't even marry her to obtain the Green Card. They were in love."

"Did you say Green Card? What is that?"

"It is a card that the U.S. Immigration department gives to foreigners to allow them to stay in the United States permanently. Some foreigners marry American citizens for the convenience of getting the Green Card, so they can remain here."

"They do? That is very interesting. So your daughter's husband did not marry her for this card?"

"Oh, no. Part of the problem is just that he wants to dominate her in every way. His relatives and friends would drop by anytime without notice, and he would start to entertain them right away, and they stayed as long as they wished. Even if it were their last money, he would entertain them with it to impress. They would speak in his indigenous language without caring whether or not she understood what they said. That, I think, was most discourteous; simply disrespectful. When they lived in this country, he used to help her with the children and with some domestic chores. Sharon said she hardly sees him these days in Kumasi. In fact, she thinks he is keeping a woman somewhere in the city. She is not sure about this. You know, some of them marry two wives and keep them in different homes. Sharon said that while they lived in the U.S., a couple of Kojo's friends had American wives and wives back home too."

"What nonsense is that? Isn't that bigamy?"

"Not if nobody knows and they don't live together in

America. Women accept polygamy in their culture."

"Can the women there marry two husbands also? No American woman would accept that."

"Sharon has stories to tell about this marriage, I can tell you that."

"Her life sounds terrible, so why does she still stay with him?"

"I know. That's why Sharon is getting a divorce. She plans to return to the States with their children."

"She should, for sure. Nobody will treat my child in that manner, no way," Wanda emphasized.

"You know, one time he wanted to bring his mother to the United States. Sharon told him they were not financially able to do so. He did it anyway, and that put them in a financial bind. When Sharon refused to give him money, they had a fight."

"His mother stayed one year, and she didn't speak English. Sharon never understood a word of whatever he and his mother said. She said she thought they were always saying things against her, but Kojo said it was not true. This was stressful to her. Whatever she did, according to Sharon, his mother always gave her an evil eye as if she had stolen her son from her. She would take the grandchildren and try to speak to them in her native language, but the children would be staring at her and soon began to cry. Still, Kojo would force them to go to her."

"The children need to go to her. She is their grandmother. The fact that she did not understand what they said did not mean they were necessarily speaking against her," Wanda said.

"That might be true too. Right now, Sharon says that she has joined a support group of American wives who meet regularly to share their experiences. You can believe their stories are the same."

"This marriage seemed doomed from the beginning," said Wanda. "They have been married five years. Sharon loved Kojo, and she was optimistic they could eventually work things out when he realized his mistakes. But you know it is said, the leopard never changes his spots. It is hopeless."

"My daughter loves her African boyfriend very much, and I doubt very much that she will believe these things. You know how love blinds us women. However, I will still mention them to her so she will watch out for signs."

The school bell rang to signal the end of the lunch period. Walleta and Wanda left the lounge and went into different classrooms. Wanda thought she would like to talk to her daughter in person about the issues she discussed with her colleague. She knew it did not look possible because Linda was having her final examinations, but she hoped Linda would call.

Linda called on Friday night at approximately nine o'clock to find out what time her parents planned to arrive in Regius the morning of Jamike's graduation. Wanda was getting ready for bed, expecting her husband back from a board meeting, when the phone rang. She informed Linda that they would be getting into Regius in time to get good seats before the ceremonies would begin at eight o'clock in the morning. Before Linda hung up, Wanda asked if she had a couple of minutes more. She wanted to talk to her.

"I am glad you called, Linda. I had wanted to call you and share a couple of things. Not that it will change anything, but just for your information," she said.

"What is it, Mom?"

"I have a colleague at school whose daughter is married to an African. I talked to her to find out a little more about Africans, now that you and Jamike have committed to each other."

"What did she say, Mom? I am curious."

"She said a whole lot, but I think I am most concerned about a few things."

"First of all, do you think Jamike wants to use you to get what is called a Green Card?"

"I don't know what that is, but I do not think so, as he has not mentioned it. I don't think he even knows what that is."

"I understand that it is a card that the U.S. government gives to qualified immigrants to allow them to have permanent residence in this country. She also said that some African husbands beat their wives, that they are dominating, and that whatever they say is the law in the home. She said also that their relatives are a big problem. She said other disturbing things, for instance that they could be married in their country and still marry Americans only to get the Green Card."

"Mom, I have heard some of these things from conversations with friends who know I have a relationship with an African, and I have discussed a couple of these same issues with Jamike. I have not heard about this Green Card stuff. All I know is that there are a lot of misrepresentations, and I would like to discover their culture myself. He is not a violent person, Mom, and he would not hit me. From our conversations, I understand that the most important person in his life is his mother. She is a widow who has been mistreated by relatives. I don't think he has relatives who would bother him. He doesn't speak well of them, anyway, and may not allow them to our home."

"Did he ever mention to you that men might marry more than one wife in his culture?" Wanda wanted to know.

"He said it is practiced in their culture, but he does not agree or condone it. He doesn't plan to do so. I think I will be happy with him."

"If that is the way you feel, I hope it works out for you," Wanda said. "As your mother I am naturally concerned about your happiness."

"Mom, I understand, and I thank you. I will be on the lookout for any signs of the things you mentioned. You can be sure I will."

"Yes, Linda, it is important that you do."

"Okay, Mom, I thank you for telling me what your colleague shared with you. I am going to meet some friends. I have to go." Wanda heard a turning of the door lock. When Mr. Johnson entered the bedroom, he gave his wife a kiss. It was close to ten thirty. After he changed into his pyjamas, Johnson held conversation with his wife for a while before he tidied some papers and laid down.

Thirty-Two

Langley Forest was an hour's drive from Regius. Set in the idyllic woods of western Pennsylvania, it was a deer hunting ground in the winter and a tourist delight in the summer. Regius residents as well as students took day-trips to enjoy walks in the forest during the summer. Its winding and rustling stream meandered between rocks, with white pebbles that lay shining crystal clear in its wooded path. Visitors liked to sit on protruding huge boulders to watch and enjoy nature.

Jamike and Linda had been planning to take a day's trip to Langley Forest for some time. He had postponed it because he wanted to first complete his upcoming examinations. Jamike knew that his last two courses in sociology of organizations and philosophy of the human person required a lot of reading, and he was not the kind of person who placed pleasure before business. At the same time, he was preparing for the Graduate Record Examination in philosophy and sending out applications for graduate school admission. Linda shared with Jamike the view that their relationship should not interfere with their studies. Jamike was studying even harder this last semester to maintain his summa cum laude grade status. He did not want to become complacent because of the outstanding grades he already had. But having now completed his exams, Jamike wanted to enjoy some relaxation with Linda. The timing was right for the visit to Langley Forest, because Linda had a break in between summer school sessions.

The weather was rather auspicious the pleasant Saturday morning in July when they made the trip to Langley Forest. The sun rose bright and early. It emerged from the distant horizon and burst like sunflower, with rays slashing through trees, casting early shadows and spreading delicate light on the quiet neighborhood. Jamike was excited about their trip and so was Linda. He agreed with Linda's suggestion that they should leave around eight o'clock in the morning. Since they would spend just the day and return to Regius, not much was needed in terms of preparation. But they had sandwiches and soft drinks.

They drove through winding roads dotted with beautiful bungalows spread on ample acres of rural land. Though the sun now shone with a glare in the morning, its effect was gentle along the wooded road to the forest, where they were already among the early morning visitors. They parked the car and started strolling. Linda and Jamike followed a beaten pathway that had witnessed millions of footprints on its pebble-strewn ground. They walked and picked up pebbles that they threw at tree trunks and on the boulders.

Linda ran a few yards ahead and threw pebbles to Jamike to catch. He would throw them farther behind her, and she would run to pick them up. They threw pebbles back and forth until they came to a huge fallen tree trunk. Its smooth shiny surface showed that it had been sat on by many a tourist over a long period of time. They decided to sit down. Linda was panting from running back and forth, trying to pick up pebbles Jamike purposely threw beyond her.

After they settled down on the tree trunk, Linda commented on how exciting and wonderful it was to be there. It was a trip she always desired to make.

"Jamike, you know, this place will look gorgeous in the fall with leaves of different shades of color on these trees."

"It is equally beautiful in the summer as you can see."

"That's true," she said, adjusting and moving closer to Jamike. "Oh, you know, my parents invited us back to Pittsburgh. I suspect Dad might invite some of our neighbors over."

"What makes you think so?"

"He did that when we had an exchange student in our

house. He wanted our neighbors to meet her too."

"I don't mind returning to Pittsburgh because I enjoyed our last visit. I felt welcome. It took me time to relax, but I did so finally."

"I did not realize you did not feel relaxed at some point."

"That's okay, it doesn't matter now."

It was in the midst of this discussion that Linda reminded Jamike of the question he had asked her the previous day.

"Oh, you wanted to know if I would like to live in Africa. Why did you ask that?"

"It was just a question I threw out, to see how you would feel about living outside your own country. I didn't think you still remembered it. I guess I should have known that women never forget anything, unless they choose to," Jamike replied.

"Yes, women don't. You have a reason for asking the question, and I think I would like to know that reason."

"So would you like to live in Africa?"

"Jamike, remember, living in Africa is different from visiting it."

"I know that."

"Well then, I would not mind living in another country, but I would like to know why I should live outside America. Would I be going there by myself or with some other person?"

Linda focused intently on Jamike's face. Two long-tailed birds flew over their heads, one with a shrill sound that suggested that it was in flight from a chase by the other. It might have been mating season. Their eyes followed the birds until they disappeared from their sight in the woods, dodging and ducking tree trunks and branches along their wooded path.

"Well, I will like to take you to Africa, and I do not suppose you would live there by yourself," Jamike replied.

The thought came to Linda that Jamike might be proposing to her, and the woods of Langley Forest would be an idyllic and memorable place for that to happen. Jamike continued to measure his words and statements, pausing from time to time. He believed that Linda would make a good mate. In the three years they had been dating he found her bright, intelligent, caring and understanding. They both had interest in learning and also enjoyed the theater.

Jamike knew that taking a wife would please his mother because she always looked forward to a daughter-in-law and grandchildren. Uridiya had said in the past that she would reserve some choice palm trees and a farmland to pass on to her daughter-in-law, in the hope that she would live in the village to farm. She also hoped and often said that when the time came for Jamike to take a wife, she would wash her eyes very clean and select a good and worthy wife for her only child.

Jamike turned to Linda. He held her close as they sat on a weatherworn tree trunk. Looking into her eyes he said to her, "Linda, I want you to be my wife. Will you marry me? I will take you to Africa." Linda's eyes were misty with tears. He held steady so they wouldn't fall backward from where they sat.

"Oh, Jamike, do you mean this? I will marry you. That will make me happy, very happy. I can't wait to tell my mother."

Jamike kept a steady look at her.

"There will be obstacles along the way. There may be difficulties, but let's not focus on that now. I will fight for us."

"I know what you mean," Linda replied. "If we love each other we will be able to overcome whatever obstacles there may be. A marriage like ours does not occur ordinarily, but it is no one's business. The important thing is that we love each other, don't you agree? We will create the type of world we want for ourselves and enjoy it. We want no interference from anyone. Oh, Jamike we will be good for each other and so happy together," Linda stated and then embraced him.

Jamike sat there listening to Linda, feeling and thinking that the kind of talk coming from her was the very fear of his people. It was why they warned him against marrying a foreign woman. This idea that whatever is done in the marriage is nobody's business, and the belief that marriage is just the man, his wife, and their children, if any, in their own world. He knew the extended family rather than the nuclear family was what his people believed in. Jamike would put Linda straight about her ideas if she plans on becoming an African's wife.

"You know, Linda, marriage practice is different in my tribe. Marriage is the business of the families of the bride and bridegroom in the way my people see it. Even relatives, who accompanied the bridegroom and were witnesses when the father-in-law handed his daughter over, would feel an obligation to see the marriage succeed and thrive. No one would give his or her daughter's hand in marriage if the groom presented himself alone. His closest relatives and members of his family must be present. His future in-laws would like to know that the suitor was not an only tree that never makes a forest, and that he has a family. When finally the husband brings home his wife, she is regarded as married to every member of the family. It is common to hear the husband's age-mates and older male relatives address her as 'my wife.' "

"How will your family and relatives feel about me?"

"I know my mother would be shocked and ready to disown me for wanting to marry a foreigner, but she is my mother. I will get someone to prepare her mind for the news."

Linda Johnson was overjoyed by Jamike's proposal. She jumped down from where they were sitting and pulled Jamike. They kissed and continued to wander and explore the forest, talking to students they recognized from the college. The rest of the time they spent in Langley Forest, Linda clutched Jamike's hand and would not let go. Her face glowed with a special charm and vibrancy.

The journey back to Regius was made as the radiant sun was receding into the horizon. The evening was cool and calm. She suggested they announce their engagement during his graduation party at the end of the semester.

Linda's parents would be at the party and they would give them their blessing. The idea of announcing their engagement at the party was not unwelcome to Jamike. Linda dropped Jamike off at Jefferson Apartments. When she got home, she telephoned her family in Pittsburgh to break her good news to them. Cynthia picked up the phone when it rang. Both of her parents were in. Linda was almost hysterical when she requested Cynthia to get her mother on the phone. Wanda, never in a hurry, took her time to get to the phone, and an excited voice rang out from the other side.

"Hi, Mom, I got good news for you all!" she said in a somewhat choked voice.

"What is the news, Linda? You and Jamike are getting married?"

"Yes, Mom, Jamike said he would marry me. I am so nervous and excited. You guessed right, Mom. How did you know that?"

"I am your mother."

"That's all?"

"That is enough, don't you think so?"

"Oh, Mom!" Linda said ecstatically.

"We kind of thought you two were heading in that direction. Even Cynthia said so after we came back from your International Day program."

Linda wanted to know what she meant by "we" when she said they had thought about it. She hoped that "we" included her father, whose facial expression never betrayed his inner thoughts. Wanda told her daughter that she and her father as well as Cynthia noticed that she and Jamike were very much in love and made a handsome couple. They knew that marriage was a distinct possibility. She asked Linda if she would like to speak to her Dad. Wanda handed the phone to her husband.

"Hi, Linda," he said. "You seem to be happy. What is the news? Anything I need to know?"

"You heard it already, Dad."

"Well, I want to hear it from you, honey. Go on and tell me. Cynthia is beside me here bubbling with, would I say, enthusiasm and smiles."

"Dad, Jamike and I will be getting married sometime in the future, maybe in a year's time. When we went sight-seeing at Langley Forest, he proposed to me. Oh, he is so wonderful, Dad!"

"I am happy for you, and you have my blessing. It certainly calls for some celebration, doesn't it?"

"Thanks, Dad," she said.

"Are you both still coming to Pittsburgh sometime?"

"We will, but it won't be for a while."

Mr. Johnson told his daughter that they would look forward to seeing them soon. He handed the phone back to Cynthia, who continued the conversation with her sister. Cynthia was happy for Linda and asked if she would be going to Africa to live after they were married. Linda had no answer for her younger sister. They kidded for a while before hanging up.

Thirty-Three

Jamike, who wrote his mother often, did not reply to Uridiya's letter about Chioma for over a month. He was disgusted with the letter but could no longer put off a reply to it. He knew the delay would not solve the predicament he was in but instead cause him more anguish. He made the tone of his letter fitting for a mother concerned about his welfare and future. He gave her the usual greetings and inquired about her health and other family matters. He told his mother about his upcoming graduation and how happy he was that his studies were coming to an end. He urged her to continue to pray so that they would reunite before long. He spoke of how homesick he had been feeling of late and how much he missed her, his relatives and friends alike. He wrote:

"I know it is time for me to take a wife, and I appreciate your worry about it. Maybe it is even overdue as you say. I know someone has to succeed me in the family and carry on our name and lineage as you always told me. Mama, it is not my plan at this time to take a wife. I know getting married now would make you very happy, and I want to make you happy and proud of me. I promise that you will carry your grandchild on your lap one day as you have always wished. But I would like to do so when I am ready."

"I have heard what you said about Chioma, who you say is the daughter of the church warden. I would like to see her when I return, but in the meantime I want you to hold on from further customary marriage rites on her.

Mother, you do not know, but there are some young ladies here who will make good wives like Chioma. I know how much you have sacrificed for me all my life.

"I really would like to pay for all traditional rites and ceremonies on behalf of the woman I will marry. I will like to pay the bride price for my wife by myself. What I would like you to do for me is to pray for me as I always pray for you. When I write you next, I will discuss an important matter with you. Regarding Aunt Ebere, I will meet her when I come back. The relationship with her that you tried to explain to me seems complicated, but give my regards to her, anyway."

Jamike was aware, and this had been so ever since he was growing up, that his mother vowed to do for him what his father, Nnorom, would have done if he had lived; that is, send him to school and give him a wife when he came of age. Uridiya would do this even if it meant selling all her farm lands and fruit trees. After she saw Chioma and liked her, she vowed the young lady would be her daughter-in-law.

While she waited for her son's letter, Uridiya proceeded with fulfilling the customary requirements of marriage in their part of Igboland. She first sought for a kinsman of the Adibes who would act as middleman between the two families. She was introduced to Chibuzo, a loquacious man given to argumentation, a gift that suited him well in his new role. His first assignment, usually, was to ensure that the suitor was made aware of the requirements that must be fulfilled according to custom. He would make sure that no unusual demands were made on Uridiya's family by the Adibes, and also that Uridiya would fulfill the necessary requirements. Uridiya sold two pieces of land and pawned another, promising the local trader that Jamike would redeem the land on his return.

After Chibuzo informed Adibe of Uridiya's intention to undertake the first official ceremony of taking wine to her in-laws, a suitable market day was appointed. Uridiya and Akudike summoned their Umunna, as custom required, to inform them that they would need to accompany Uridiya to

Adibe's home for the betrothal of Chioma to her son.

On arrival at Adibe's house, they were welcomed and presented with the traditional kola nut and alligator pepper to go with it. It was handed over to the oldest man among the Ndioma villagers present. The old man prayed with the kola nut and poured libation with palm wine to seek the protection and guidance of ancestral spirits in their deliberations.

Akudike opened the discussion. He introduced himself, Uridiya, the headmaster, and other relatives present. He told them that there was some "young thing" Uridiya discovered and had her eyes on in Adibe's household and would like to take to reside in her household. When he was interrupted and pressed to give the name of this "young thing," Akudike told them he was talking about a beautiful young female who lived in that compound. He traced Uridiya's encounter with Chioma and how she made inquires and discovered that she belonged to this reputable compound. Akudike cleared his throat and asked if there was anyone by the name of Chioma in Adibe's household. A couple of voices in the room answered in the affirmative. He was interrupted a few times, but he put his point across.

"We have been to this compound before and made initial contact. We liked what we saw." He was referring to the first visit in which the headmaster accompanied him and Uridiya to seek out Chioma's family and indicate their interest. He continued, "Uridiya would like to marry the lady called Chioma for her son who is in the white man's land, getting education."

To confirm what he just said, Akudike turned to his relatives and asked, "Umunna, isn't it why we came?" They all answered in one voice: "It is so." There was momentary silence as Uridiya brought out Jamike's picture. It was different from the one Adibe and his wife saw on their first visit. She handed it to Akudike, who gave it to Adibe and his wife. They studied it for a minute before passing it around. From comments like, "He looks well-fed," "He looks strong and healthy, "He is full of life," all agreed that

Jamike was a strong young man who looked well and would make a good son-in-law.

A member of Jamike's family told the group that it was important for them to see Chioma, so they would know that they were talking about a human being and not a spirit. They wanted to find out from her if she welcomed their proposal. Someone objected, saying it was too early to bring her out for such questioning. An elder pointed out that although it may be true that Uridiya had seen Chioma, they should not forget that their forefathers said in a proverb that an ordinary snake seen by one person is usually described as a python. They too would like to see the person who was the reason for their visit.

After this statement, Adibe and his wife, Ihuoma, left the room for a few minutes. When they returned, Chioma walked shyly behind them and took a seat beside her mother. Once seated, her father addressed her:

"Chioma, my daughter, these people from Aludo are here because of you. The reason they came is not new to you, though it has not been made public till this time. They say they want to marry you and now inform me that they have a question for you. From my understanding, it is only you who can answer the question they have, not me or your mother."

Chioma would shyly lower her head and raise it again to look at her father as he spoke. One of Jamike's relatives spoke.

"My daughter, your name Chioma is a beautiful one. You have heard your father. I cannot add to it except to say that you know why we are here and to ask you: do you welcome our proposal?" Chioma did not answer the question but rather looked at her mother. She was shy. Some relatives answered in the affirmative on her behalf. But that wasn't enough, because the family of her suitor would want to hear the answer from her voice. In a rather low tone, and not looking at any person in particular, she answered, "I welcome your proposal." Someone began to clap and there was applause.

After that, Adibe asked his daughter to go back to her

room while the adults continued with the ceremony. Uridiya and her people were pleased that Chioma gave her consent as she did when Uridiya first visited with Akudike and the headmaster. A change of mind now would have been a betrayal of her parents.

As already said, Uridiya sold two pieces of farmland and pawned another to be able to cope with the cost of the items that would be needed to fulfill the requirements for what she had embarked upon. Once every two weeks for the next month and half, Uridiya and Jamike's Umunna would visit the Adibe family, carrying palm wine, yams, bags of rice, heads of leaf tobacco, bar soaps, fabrics, stockfish, and little sums of money in keeping with custom. It would be after the ceremony on their fourth visit that custom required Chioma to go to the home of her future husband and spend four days. Following this would be the last visit of Uridiya and her Umunna, after which ceremony Chioma would go home finally with them as Jamike's wife.

This four-day visit would be a time for Jamike's family to get to know her closely and even test her. She would demonstrate her ability in domestic work, required of a wife, showing also how economical and resourceful and amiable she was. For instance, she would be expected to wake up early in the morning to sweep the entire compound, even up to the road leading into a neighbor's yard, to show her broad-mindedness. They would watch to see if she was flexible enough in the waist to bend low to sweep thoroughly. That ability she would need as a wife, to bend down to cook, to do farm work, to do native dances and things of that nature. During these four days, they would find out if she was a pleasant person, if she respected elders, if she was friendly with members of Jamike's family, if she was a woman who greeted neighbors, and above all, if she was caring toward her future mother-in-law.

On the fourth visit, when it was time for Jamike's Umunna to depart, Ihuoma brought her daughter, Chioma, to the parlor carrying her small suitcase so her father would hand her over to Jamike's uncle and mother to commence the four-day visit in their household. While they were still in the room, Ihuoma noticed her daughter tried to push back the tears that welled in her eyes.

"What is this foolishness?" she asked in a low chastising voice. "No one is going to harm you there. It is only a visit and for four days. It is our custom."

"I know, mother. But the next time they come wouldn't it be the final"

"Wouldn't it be what?" Ihuoma cut in, taking a step toward the door ahead of her daughter. "Come on, they are waiting for you."

Adibe handed over his daughter to Jamike's uncle, Akudike, saying, "I leave my daughter in your hands. Go well and may you meet only good luck and no bad luck on the way."

It was a little before midnight when they set off on their journey back to Jamike's village. The night was dark, made even darker by thick forests on both sides of the road. Apart from their chatter about the events of the day, the only other sounds in the silence of the dark night were of crickets and occasionally of owls and other nocturnal birds. No one from Jamike's family had remembered to bring flashlights or lanterns. Ihuoma provided a lantern while Chioma came along with hers. Men with bicycles did not ride but pushed them along with faint flickering headlights. The rest of the group walked behind them and those with the lanterns.

On the third day of Chioma's visit with Jamike's mother the mailman brought a letter from America. It had taken nearly a month to arrive. He gave it to Akudike because Uridiya and Chioma had gone to the market. When Akudike handed the letter to Uridiya when they returned in the evening, she smiled with pleasure on learning that it was from Jamike. Over the years, she had come to recognize a letter from America on sight if it was an aerogram, but this letter came in an envelope. She hoped Jamike would be glad to hear that a wife was being selected for him.

"Come, my sweetheart," she said to Chioma. "It is a letter from your betrothed. Read it for me, daughter."

Uridiya sat on a long narrow bamboo bed while Chioma sat on a wooden stool.

Chioma read through the letter once before translating it to Uridiya. She could not conceal her surprise when she read the contents. Uridiya noticed her facial expression and felt she must have read something unpleasant. She told her to read it carefully, because she did not think that the young man, Onyema, Chijioke's son, who used to read, write, and translate for her, did a very good job.

"I want to hear every word in that letter. Onyema used to read things that were not in Jamike's letters. From the replies I got from Jamike, I think that he would write what came to his mind and not what I told him to write to my son." Chioma began to read the letter.

Uridiya listened carefully to the contents of the letter. The part where Jamike said there are women in America who would make good wives made her burst out laughing. "Oh," she said, "Jamike has not yet outgrown his childishness. Who told him that there are good women to marry in his America? How will they know our customs? Jamike is like a baby who starts bathing his body from the belly." Chioma pretended as if she did not pay attention to what Uridiya was saying and continued to read the letter. She folded it back in the envelope and handed it to her.

"No, he will not marry over there. If he does, I will commit suicide, and it will be on his head. I know he hasn't done it, and he will not attempt it. Tomorrow, I will write to him. I will let him know that no other person than his wife is writing my reply. If he hears that I have finished the customary rites about you, he will come home and take you, or we will send you to him over there. But I know he will come home."

"Mama, you know that there is no place in the world where there are no women to marry. What he said is true. After all, the men over there do not come here to marry. They marry the women who live over there. Maybe he found someone else."

"I know, my child that there are women everywhere. But remember what the elders say, that the firewood that exists in a particular land is what the people there use in cooking. You may not understand this proverb. What I mean is that the women there may be suited for the people over there, but they are not suited for my son. He is not from there; he belongs here. He said he would have good news for me soon. What good news would he have for me? I am the one with news for him. I have got him a wife. That is good news. Unless he would tell me he had finished his studies and is ready to come home to take you. That would even be better news."

Chioma was taken aback by what Uridiya was saying.

"Mama," she said, "he does not know what you are planning or doing for him here. He may even not like me when he sees me. Did you send that picture I gave you?"

"My daughter, you will break my heart if you say he may not like you. My child has no idea who will make a good wife and who won't. I am his mother, and I am the one to tell him. Yes, I sent your picture. It is a beautiful picture, and that is what you are, beautiful. It is in his hands right now. I know the good news he will have for me. The headmaster told me Jamike would finish his education soon. That is good news. The only news that is better than that is you. Oh, I wish his father, Nnorom, were alive today to see the good things happening in his family. His only child is in America, and a good wife has been selected for him."

Chioma handed back the letter to Uridiya and got up from the low kitchen stool and asked what they would eat for dinner. It was time to start cooking dinner.

"Sit down, my love. Cook whatever you like, my beloved daughter. As long as you eat, I am satisfied. Since you have been here, I can assure you I no longer feel hungry. Joy and gladness have filled my heart, and I have put some flesh on my body," Uridiya told her daughter-in-law. Chioma laughed with a blush. Then she said inaudibly, "I have become food that fills the stomach. This is wonderful!" Uridiya sensed Chioma said something. She got up and got closer to put her hand across the young woman's shoulder

"Were you saying something, good daughter?" she asked

"No, Mama, I was talking to myself."

"I just wondered if you wanted to say something to me."

"No, Mama." Chioma got up and went into the kitchen. Uridiya heard her blowing the fire, and the smoke that emerged was followed by flame. The clay pot was set to cook with its contents of yam, palm oil, crayfish, and plenty of vegetables for yam porridge.

On the fourth day of her stay, Chioma's uncle, Nwaobasi, came on his bicycle to take her home. When Chioma was ready to leave, the women and children in the compound came out to bid her farewell. They were pleased with her humility, pleasantness, and overall fine disposition. Once her suitcase was tied to the bicycle carriage, Chioma sat precariously on the frame. Nwaobasi rode off on the narrow and earth-crusted bush road.

Thirty-Four

A couple of weeks before graduation in May, Jamike informed Linda that he would not be able to spend an entire weekend at their home in Pittsburgh. He needed to be in Regius to take care of a few personal matters if he hoped to visit Nigeria after graduation. He told her that a day's visit would be all it would take to personally present her parents with the invitation to his graduation ceremony. Linda's parents, however, wanted them to come for a weekend and had hoped to invite some of their neighbors over to introduce Jamike. After they discussed it, Linda agreed that it would be better to go on a Saturday and return the same day. By doing so they would not totally disappoint the Johnsons, who had already included them in their plans. Linda was to let her parents know of their decision.

Jamike actually was uncomfortable about another trip to Pittsburgh due to a disquieting dream he had. In that dream he saw a jubilant crowd chanting songs, waving palm fronds, and dancing along the road that leads from the market square to his home in the village. Uridiya, Chioma, and Jamike's close relatives were in front of the crowd. They were bringing Chioma home in music and celebration. When Jamike saw them, he quickly moved to bring his mother aside from the crowd to talk to her. As he proceeded toward his mother, he woke up and realized that it was a dream. This dream bothered him. Judging from the contents of his mother's letter, she could bring Chioma home any time soon. That was what Jamike feared most, and that was what his dream was about. Though he was able to brush it aside saying that it was only a dream, it stayed in Jamike's subconscious and weighed heavily on his mind as they prepared to make this second visit to Linda's parents.

It was on a Saturday in April that Jamike and Linda drove up to Pittsburgh. He wanted to obtain graduation invitation cards from the student affairs office before making the trip. Wanda and her husband had just finished a late breakfast that morning when Linda's car pulled into the gray concrete driveway. Mr. Johnson answered the door, and Linda walked in with Jamike.

"Hi, Mom. Hi, Dad." She gave each a kiss. "Where is Cynthia? Is she still sleeping?"

"Hello, Jamike." Mr. Johnson shook Jamike's hands and exchanged pleasantries while Linda and her mother engaged in a conversation.

"Cynthia did not feel too well yesterday. We thought she was coming down with a flu or something," said Mr. Johnson. While Jamike sat down to talk to Wanda and Mr. Johnson, Linda went to Cynthia's room to see her. "What is the matter, girl?" she asked. Cynthia explained she had not been feeling well for a day and thought she might be coming down with the flu. Linda told her she and Jamike came to bring their invitation to the commencement. Linda spent a few minutes with Cynthia. As she left the room, she said, "Take care, Cynthia. Let me get back to the living room and see what Mom and Dad are up to with their favorite son, Jamike."

As she entered the living room, Wanda was talking to Jamike about staying the weekend. Linda immediately interrupted.

"Mom, we are not staying. Jamike has so much to do. But since we promised to visit again before graduation, we wanted to keep our promise and bring the invitation cards to you. You know graduation is in two weeks and so much is going on in the campus."

As they conversed, Jamike handed three invitation cards to Mr. Johnson. He suggested that they arrive in time, in order to get good seats. They could come a day before or drive up to Regius the morning of commencement. He told them there would be a small celebration in his building's party room afterward. Wanda said they would get up early and drive up to Regius the morning of the graduation.

As they ate, conversation centered on what Jamike planned to do after graduation. He informed them he had admission for graduate studies at the University of Chicago and the university of Maryland. But since he had heard terrible things about the severe cold winter and snow in Chicago, he had definitely ruled out Chicago and would accept the admission to Maryland. However, more than anything else, he would like to return to his country to see his mother who was advancing in age and he was worried about her well-being.

"That would be a good idea," Mr. Johnson said with a nod to Jamike. Linda nudged Jamike gently. He guessed what was on her mind but chose to ignore her.

"Tell them what you plan to do at your graduation party," she told Jamike.

"What do you mean what I plan to do? I plan to have a party."

"Okay, Jamike, if you won't tell them, I will."

Since Linda informed her two close friends at the college that Jamike had proposed to her, they would tease him wherever they see him on campus. It embarrassed Jamike. Because he was reluctant to say what Linda wanted him to say to her parents, she told them that they plan to announce their engagement at the party. Jamike put on a smile, adjusted himself on the sofa, and said,

"Don't mind Linda, she likes to make an issue of everything. I told her I would like to announce our engagement during the party, and she wants to make a big deal out of it. It was just a thought."

Afterward, the topic of discussion changed to other general issues. They had an enjoyable visit. Jamike and Linda left for Regius quite late in the afternoon. Jamike planned to stop over at the home of his mentor, Laski, once they were back in town. He now wanted to share things that were happening in his personal life with Laski, and he thought it might be appropriate to take Linda along.

Jamike and Linda got to Laski's house in the evening. Laski met Linda at the International Day program and was introduced to her. He opened the door and shook his guests' hands and tapped Jamike gently on the shoulder. Many times in the past he would embrace Jamike and tap his buttocks. Jamike was prepared to push him away if he attempted that. He did not have to do so, however.

Laski asked what they would drink. Jamike wanted a beer, while Linda asked for a soft drink.

"Where are you all coming from?" He handed her a glass of soft drink.

"We are coming from Pittsburgh. We went to give my parents their invitation cards to Jamike's graduation."

"Are you a senior too?"

"I am, but I will be graduating in December." She took a sip.

"What are you majoring in?"

"Anthropology," she said, looking at Laski as if expecting him to comment on that.

"Very good. That is a good major."

It was at this point that Jamike told Laski that the reason they came to see him was to tell him that he and Linda were engaged to be married.

"Oh, that is so wonderful. She is beautiful."

"Are you still coming to my graduation party?"

"Sure, I will be there." Laski got up and brought some more crackers.

"We should actually be leaving now. We want to catch a movie. I plan to announce our engagement at the party."

"Great." He looked at Linda steadily, sizing her up. "Thanks for bringing Linda over. I am sure your mother will be happy for you."

"I have just written a letter to her. I plan to write the headmaster too. I owe him a letter." Their visit ended after an hour.

As they left, Jamike thought about the way Laski looked at Linda at some point. Could he be thinking of how Linda was going to be able to make the adjustment as an American wife living in Africa? Laski had firsthand experience of Africa, having lived in Nigeria and visited Uganda and Zambia. Was he thinking about several amenities taken for granted in the United States such as electricity, good running water, telephones, good roads, and the like which are hard to come by and in some cases non existent? Maybe he was thinking about his days in the Peace Corps when he did not consider lack of those amenities to be deprivations due to youthful idealism. Jamike thought that Laski might be feeling that Linda was too young to be able to cope.

As they headed for the movies that evening, Linda was silent for a moment. She had not yet talked with Jamike about the conversation her mother had with a colleague at school. She started,

"Jamike, I have been meaning to ask you about some comments I have heard about African men, and to find out if they are true or just hearsay, another Tarzan story. But you have to be honest. Do you promise?" The look on her face was serious.

"Let me hear what it is. I will be honest with you," Jamike promised. He wondered what it could be.

"Remember you told me right after we met and I came to visit you, that your uncle beat his wife? Would you do a thing like that, really?"

"Is that the question? Of course, I would not be that stupid. It does not make sense, for beating solves nothing. If you love someone, why would you lay your hands on him or her? No one has the right to hit someone else." Jamike held Linda affectionately and promised he would never do a thing like that.

Linda quipped, "My parents never laid their hands on me, and nobody is going to do that. They could get hurt."

"By whom?" Jamike asked.

"Definitely by me. If they want to hurt me, I'll hurt them first. I heard that African men dominate and smother their wives. Why is that?" Linda asked.

"Who has been telling you all this stuff?"

"My mother talked to a colleague whose daughter was married to an African."

"Was married? Are they no longer married? Let me get the tickets." He took steps toward the theater ticket window.

"I am not seeing any movie. This is important, and I need answers." She was forceful. He stepped back.

"Linda, I don't care what African men may or may not do. I only care about what I am going to do with you. I have enough education and exposure to know that marriage is a partnership between two people. There is no question of domination. We will plan and work together for our own happiness. I will never hit you." His face showed frustration.

"Listen, I know that if we love each other, there is no reason why we cannot work together. You know people say these things, but each individual is different, as are couples."

"I am glad you understand these important issues," Jamike said. "However, one thing I have to say to you," he continued, "is that I love and live for my mother. She was widowed early in her life when I was only two years old. She has made many sacrifices to see me through. I will want the wife I marry to love her and to do everything possible to make her happy. She has been longing for a daughter-in-law ever since I was a youngster. Were it not for my unwillingness, she would have had me take a wife over fifteen years ago. If you do that for me, I will love you forever. But if you don't, then we will have problems." He was forthright.

"You don't have to worry about that, Jamike. I will love and respect my mother-in-law. I promise you we will get along well. I know she may not understand what I say to her initially, but that will be for a short period. To be sure, love overcomes all barriers," Linda said.

There was silence for a moment. Linda was framing in her mind how diplomatically to pose the next question, when Jamike asked,

"Can I get the tickets now? The film showing now will be over in less than fifteen minutes." Jamike was exasperated.

"What we are discussing is important to me. You will see the movie alone if we don't discuss this fully."

"And why do you think this is the best place for this discussion?" Jamike asked as he tapped his foot.

"I don't know there is any best place for it."

"Go on then." Jamike resigned himself.

"What about this talk of two wives? I understand many Africans have two wives or more, and that even some of those who are married here in America, with all their education, have other wives back in their own country. Is that true, Jamike?"

Jamike scoffed at the question.

"I think we better sit down to talk about this, since seeing a movie may not be possible."

"We still have time." Linda was determined.

"W-e-l-l," he said, as if he was in search of what to say, "It is true that some Africans marry more than one wife. Let me back up. In the old days, it was necessary for wealthy persons, chiefs, and other important men in the community to have many wives, which usually led to the propagation of many children. The wealth of these individuals at the time we are talking about consisted of the population of their household and the expansiveness of their yam barns. Since their wealth was equated to their numerous farm lands, they needed many wives and children to serve as farm hands in order to cultivate their farms."

"In fact, the respect and reputation of those chiefs largely resided in the number of human beings in their households, in addition to the number of domestic animals -sheep, goats and cows that roamed the compound and how extensive the yam barns were. Women cultivated cocoyam, and the wealth of each wife, meaning the wealth of her husband also, was measured by how large her annual cocoyam harvest was. So there were also many practical reasons for having many children at the time. Excluding purely economic reasons, these children also provided protection from challenges by outsiders who would make trouble for the family. Any such challenge would need people to counteract it and thus maintain family honor. It used to be a common saying that there is always all manner of people in a chief's household to meet every kind of challenge."

"So the main purpose of marrying then was to bear children for farm work? That is terrible," Linda said.

"You might say that, but it served its purpose at the time. Remember we are talking about the traditional rural society," Jamike said. "Even now, there are people who still marry more than one wife and believe in the antiquated idea that the main reason for marriage is to have children. Quite frankly, I believed so when I was growing up. I am not ashamed to admit it, because it is part of my culture."

"Let me correct myself here. I believed so until I came to this country and realized through my studies and what obtains here that a woman is an equal partner and a helpmate in marriage. Her duty in the world is not to breed as many children as her husband wants, nor is she a piece of property to be paid for. As partners they together decide how many children they want. So I am saying that having many wives or children in traditional African society was in part economic. Life was simpler then. Now, however, the world has changed and no one can have that many wives or even children without incurring severe social and economic difficulties. Today we send children to school, not only to farms. Women go outside the home to work-not just stay home to have and rear children." Jamike looked at Linda straight in the face. "Do you understand what I am saying to you?"

"You don't have to be ashamed to believe in a practice that is a way of life in your culture. Anyway, you no longer support the idea of more than one wife or many children, do you?" Linda asked.

"No, I don't think more than one wife is a very good

idea. It may have served its purpose at the time, but today it is definitely anachronistic. The same goes for having many children. But you know what? At one time I discussed marriage in Africa with some married American men. When I told them that in my part of Africa a man can marry more than one wife, they showed a lot of interest, and some asked me how much the airfare to Africa was. They said they wouldn't mind moving over there."

"That is funny. What about Africans who are married here, who may have wives back home?"

"I actually don't know of anybody in that situation, neither do I care. I don't know why they would want to have a wife here and a wife there too."

"That would be bigamy."

Linda pressed Jamike further. "You may think I am silly if I ask you this. Do you have a wife in Nigeria like some of your people here?"

"Cut it out, Linda. I don't know who has been feeding you all this. The answer is no. I don't have a wife in Nigeria, and whether I marry here or over there, it will be to just one woman. Don't worry about that. I have learned so many things in this country and it is amazing the way my thoughts on some things have undergone what is quite a metamorphosis. I even accept that couples can opt not to have children at all. That is their prerogative or personal choice. But no matter where we live, I want you to be pleasant to my relatives and friends when we marry. You know—"

Linda cut in. "Like Emeka and the rest of them here? Do I have to? How many relatives and friends do you have?" she asked pointedly. "I have to be pleasant to them, even if they get on my nerves?"

"You need to control your nerves, because you will be seeing many of my relatives after we get married and return to Nigeria."

Linda stood up. "I don't think you want us to see this movie if you are going to talk like that. I am leaving." She picked up her handbag.

"Come back, Linda." Jamike stepped up toward her. She

walked fast to the car, entered, and slammed the door.

"Why, this is not necessary," Jamike said as he entered the car.

"What did I say that made you so angry? Tell me." She took away the hand he placed on her.

"We need to talk about this further." She dropped Jamike at the Jefferson Apartments parking lot and drove off. Jamike was shocked. He was at a loss as to how to interpret what had just transpired. After all, they had gone to visit her parents. Who might have talked to her? Jamike wondered.

Back in Nigeria, Jamike's arranged wife, Chioma, had just returned to her parents' home after the customary four-day visit with her mother-in-law, Uridiya. It soon began to rumor in both Aludo and Ndioma that Jamike would soon return from America to take his wife. It was Chioma's visit that fueled the speculation.

On an evening when the compound was quiet and most people had gone to the local market, Ihuoma Adibe decided to have a talk with her daughter. She asked Chioma to bring a bench seat to the veranda for her. Chioma sat on a low kitchen stool. They faced each other with a little space between them as Ihuoma questioned her about her four-day visit with her future mother-in-law. Chioma said she thought the visit went well and that Uridiya was a fine, kind, and adoring old lady, the type that could easily spoil a daughter-in-law. Ihuoma said to her daughter:

"Well, you know that all but the bride price ceremony have been completed on you. After the bride price is negotiated, settled, and paid, Uridiya's family would like to take you with them even before your husband would come back from America. It is obvious to me that if Jamike comes back, he would like to return to America with you. I don't know how soon this will happen. Since this is so I just want to have a mother-to-daughter talk with you, so I can explain some important matters to you. It is my duty.

"I can tell you this, there is always a special time for

every woman and your own time has arrived. Your father and I have given you the upbringing that is our duty to give you and you will not do anything that will bring us shame when you are in America. Remember, Jamike is now your husband; you must always listen to him and obey him. We do not want to hear of any quarrel."

"Any household he enters is the one you will enter; the one he does not enter, you cannot go into. Avoid this and that friendship. Friends can mislead you by teaching you bad behavior. Do you hear me?"

Chioma did not say a word. Rather, she looked at her mother occasionally but had her eyes fixed on the polished-earth floor as her mother went on and on.

"Of all things I say to you today, the most important is obedience. Cook good food for him, because a man is happy with a wife who feeds him well. Do not lie to your husband. Do not speak harsh words to him. When God blesses you with a child, I will come and take care of you and the baby for a short while, as is our custom. At that time, I will teach you how to take care of a newborn. Remember, Jamike is an only child, and his mother talks about grandchildren all the time, so be ready for a house full of children," she said with a smile. Chioma did not find that statement funny as shown by her body language.

As Ihuoma continued giving advice to her daughter, the repeated sound of a bicycle bell was heard. It was Adibe announcing his arrival at the gate that led into the compound.

"I think that sounds like your father's bicycle bell. We will leave this discussion for now. I will have another occasion to talk with you, especially how you should relate to your mother-in-law. You need to learn a lot about that too. Now, I must go to the door and welcome your father. Please run inside the kitchen and stoke up that fire so we can get his food ready. He must be hungry by now, because he left quite early this morning."

Ihuoma tried to persuade Adibe to put something in his stomach before he left that morning, but he said he had to be at the mission on time. She had told him many times before that it was important to eat something in the morning, no matter how little. She used to say that her parents taught her that the worst thing that could happen was for a person to go to the land of the spirits on an empty stomach. She would admonish her husband that "whatever a person has in the stomach is what goes to the land of the spirits with him or her." But like a typical village man, Adibe did not think a woman's talk amounted to much.

Thirty-Five

Commencement in May was held in Alexandra House, which was also used for basketball games and other tournaments. It was packed full with students, parents, relatives, and friends. In addition to Jamike's other friends, Mr. Johnson, Wanda and Cynthia were there. Jamike's graduation was the proudest moment of his life. By seven o'clock in the morning, he had lined up with other graduating students on the tennis lawn next to the stadium, dressed in his black academic gown, hood on his neck, and cap with tassel on his head, ready to march into Alexandra House. Uridiya's son! Soon he would take his seat with others in the huge basketball arena decorated with flags and buntings, ribbons and balloons.

Then the call came: Jamike Nnorom, Bachelor's degree in Philosophy (Summa cum Laude). The Johnson family all got up in jubilation as his name was called out. Linda's yelling voice could almost be picked out from the cheers and applause that came from the crowd. Jamike stepped on to the stage where he was handed his degree certificate. Camera lights flashed as he shook hands with the president and the dean. Jamike was now a university graduate; a village boy's dream had come true. He has bagged the proverbial Golden Fleece, a degree in philosophy with the highest praise and a certificate in his hand to prove it. His mind raced back to that meeting with Paul Laski in his village. Jamike was filled with self-confidence after his graduation, and he wished his mother or the headmaster were in the audience to witness it all.

Jamike's graduation party was held in the Jefferson Apartments' party room. About twenty or so people were there, including Mr. Laski, Professor Townsend and his wife, Linda and her family, and, of course, his African friends. Linda had been quite busy for the past few days as she helped Jamike with plans for the party. She made the arrangements for the food platters from the supermarket, while her friends helped her to decorate the hall with balloons and congratulatory messages. There was an assortment of food and drinks, something for everyone. Emeka was the master of ceremonies; he and his Nigerian friends prepared a rice dish and bought the drinks.

When called upon to make some remarks, Jamike thanked everyone who was present and the many friends he made in his years at Regius State College. He placed on record his indebtedness to the professors responsible for his education and personal development. He thanked the Black Students Union and the Campus Ministry, all of whom played a role in his life at Regius. He would miss all of them, he said, as he proceeded to the next level of his life in graduate school.

He paused, took a breath, and continued, "Apart from the news of my graduation, there is another good news I would like to share with you." He beckoned to Linda, who approached him with smiles in quick successive steps in high heel shoes. He held her hand and told his guests that they had become engaged to be married. There was applause. Wanda turned to her husband with joy and a smile.

"Isn't that beautiful?" She gave her husband a peck on the lip. "Wonderful." Mr. Johnson held his wife close. They were happy parents.

Jamike pointed to the left side of the apartment hall to recognize Linda's parents and their daughter, Cynthia. There was more applause and the party continued. At about seven o'clock, Linda's parents took leave to begin the trip back to Pittsburgh, leaving Cynthia behind. Mr. Laski and the Townsends left shortly after.

By ten o'clock, some more people left to attend other

graduation parties. Linda and Cynthia stayed back to help Jamike clean up the hall after the party ended. Jamike went to bed completely exhausted. As he lay down, he thought through his whole life in a matter of minutes. He thanked his mother and God for having brought him this far. He also thought of his mentors, the headmaster and Father Murrow. Other teachers who influenced him came to his mind. No one in his village would have believed this could happen to a poor widow's child. The next day, Sunday, Jamike went to Sunday service. When he came back, before some visitors would arrive, he wrote two letters, one each to his mother and the headmaster. The letters would take two weeks to reach their destination.

Back in the village, life moved on, its slow pace unchanging. The mailman, Ojilere, rode his bicycle in mid-afternoon heat to deliver the day's mail. Nearing the market, as he rode on the side of the road, he heard the sound of a vehicle. He looked back and saw a decrepit lorry coming down the road that passed through the middle of Afor market. As it came nearer, Ojilere could read the epigram boldly written on the lorry's discolored, weather-beaten gray wooden board above the windshield: "NO CONDITION IS PERMANENT." He dismounted his bicycle when the lorry came closer. He cleared from the roadway and completely moved outside the tarred road. The lorry lurched to the right as it avoided a big pothole and almost knocked him down.

Ojilere thanked God he was safe but kept watch as he pushed his bicycle along. As the lorry very slowly made its way through the road, market women who displayed their wares practically on the road scampered to move them as the vehicle approached. Both the mailman and market women cursed the driver who put them in a state of panic. The driver brought his head and bare torso out of the wooden half-door of the driver's compartment of his vehicle, stretched his neck and cursed them back. He spat back and dared them to leave their commodities on the road next time he came passing through. An old man slipped and nearly hurt himself, trying to get away from the lorry. He cursed the driver and in a loud voice wished him an accident before the end of the day. "May you and your lorry burn to ashes," the old man concluded.

The mailman pushed his bicycle through the market crowd. He mounted it again and headed toward Jamike's home carrying letters for villagers. One of those letters was from Jamike.

Uridiya was still getting ready to go to the market when Ojilere dismounted his bicycle at the gate. She was never this late to the market. The mailman rang his bicycle bell twice in quick succession and loudly called out Uridiya's name as he entered the compound through its unlocked gate.

"What man or woman would call me this way? Am I indebted to you?" Uridiya responded in an equally loud voice from her veranda.

"Come out and receive a letter from your son." As she emerged from her house, Ojilere added, "Now, you can see you owe me for delivering this letter. Don't you know I would rather be at the market drinking palm wine like the others, instead of delivering letters?" the mailman said.

"Come, my son, pardon me; you know it was a joke. If I don't owe you who bring me letters, who else would I owe?" Uridiya apologized.

As he was about to leave, she asked the mailman if he could read the letter for her, and he accepted. As soon as she heard that Jamike had finished his studies and graduated she jumped up and shouted joyously in a loud voice. She called out members of the household to hear the message being read to her. She began to sing. Passersby on their way to the market stopped to know the reason for that much joy. The mailman appealed to her to have patience and listen to the rest of the letter.

In the market she was accepting congratulations. The women who knew her would raise their hands and slap Uridiya's open palms above their heads to give high five. They wanted to know when Jamike would come back and she told them soon. "A woman has been married for him," she told them. "He has to come back to take his wife. I don't have the strength to look after that young woman."

"You have married a wife for him?" one of the women asked, surprised that she could afford the expense.

"Oh, yes, what I want now is for Jamike to come home to find out what a lucky man he is. Chioma is as tender as the embryo of an egg. She is ripe. If he crosses his leg on that child, I can assure you I will have twins on my lap. Anyone who takes a look at that child's hips can tell she is fertile. It may not stop at twins. I have heard some women have four at a time. God, I say, look at my heart and soul and give me that kind of blessing. I want a house full of children. I cannot wait to see the day, because I am ready. It is in your hands, God, not in Uridiya's. We are but poor and humble creatures and are incapable of doing anything without you. The power is yours."

A few of Jamike's relatives who heard the news in the market and saw Uridiya accepting congratulations were inwardly jealous of Jamike's achievement. When Uridiya returned from the market that night, she went over to Jamike's uncle with the news, but his grandson had already given him the information. A handful of kinsmen came over to Akudike's house that night to find out more about the news circulating in the market. After Uridiya gave them the message, they thanked God and heaped praise on their able son for making them proud. Akudike presented them with kola nuts and some leftover palm wine. Ajaegbu, the oldest man among them, poured libation and evoked the blessing of their ancestors.

He said, "Spirit of our forefathers share this drink with us." He poured a little on the earth floor. "God the father, you are the beginning and the end. There is nothing we can do unless you approve of it. You have seen it fit that this honor reaches our kindred through Jamike, the son you gave us. We thank you and thank him who has made it possible for us to have this joy. You have made it possible for a widow to see better days. You have blessed her by sending the angels that took her son overseas, and now you have enabled him to realize his quest in a foreign land."

"Forefathers! We know you are all there interceding for us; see to it that only good luck comes to this village. May this luck that has reached the household of Nnorom come to us one by one. And we say as our forefathers said, that the hawk will perch and the eagle will perch, both on the same branch. Whichever does not want the other to perch, may that one lose a wing. Jamike, you have brought us joy and made us proud, may you be blessed." The rest of the people said, "Amen."

"The power and strength are yours, Lord," he continued. "May the spirit of Nnorom, and all our forefathers, partake of this drink." The libator stepped up and poured more wine out of the door. As he did that, a younger man in the room challenged Ajaegbu.

"I hope you will not give all this little wine to our ancestors, while we who are alive do without."

"Are you envious of our ancestors for partaking of our drink? Our reason for joy has never happened in this village before, so let our ancestors drink to their hearts content if they so choose."

"Well, let them have the calabash too." There was laughter.

"If you want our ancestors' wine, you may need to join them to get it and not be here with us." It was not much wine, but everyone had a little bit.

In the days following his graduation, Jamike felt increasingly homesick. He had been feeling this way since the beginning of his last year in college. Later, he would say it felt like hunger, but a different kind of hunger, the longing to go back to one's homeland. It was a pull he never felt before. His mind was now set on home. In his relaxed moments, he could visualize himself in his hometown and among his people. Sometimes when he would be with Linda, he would seem preoccupied. When asked what the matter was, Jamike told Linda his distraction was due to exhaustion from studies. Sooner or later she would know the real reason. He loved Linda and did not want it to appear that the only thing on his mind after graduation was going back home. She would not understand the longing for one's homeland after years of absence, he thought.

Linda had looked forward to the time when he would have more free time to spend with her, as he promised he would do after graduation. She gave Jamike a lot of space while he wrote his senior year research paper, and during finals, but now he was almost obsessed with going back home and seeing his mother. He had dreams in which either his mother appeared to him or he was in the village square with his people under a huge shady tree as the adults chewed bitter kola and drank palm wine while they discussed village affairs.

The last dream in which he saw his mother looking very much older than when he left home caused him pain. She spread her hands entreating him to come home before she dies. She told him she had labored so hard for him and hoped he would not want to see her as a corpse. Uridiya informed Jamike of a dream she had in which her ancestors were beckoning her to join them, but she told them she was not going to join them until she saw her son. The dream frightened Jamike and caused him to wake up. He was glad it was only a dream. He rubbed his eyes, went to the bathroom, and came back to bed but could not sleep again. He lay there on his back, looking at the ceiling, and recalled his life. It had been four years since he'd seen her; he must go home to see her. His mind was made up. As for the matter of Chioma, he was not going to worry about it.

Jamike and Linda discussed his dream when she came to visit.

"You know, Linda, I am very concerned about the kinds of dreams I am having these days." There was a worried look on his face.

"What are they like?"

"One dream frightened me. In it my mother appeared very old and entreated me to come home before she would die," he said in a subdued voice.

"I am worried too."

"She then informed me in the dream that her long

dead ancestors were beckoning her to join them in a dream she had."

"Please don't say that. It is frightening." She shook her head, horrified.

"I will feel guilty for the rest of my life should anything happen to her before I can be with her."

"What are you going to do now, Jamike?"

"The problem is that I came to the United States on a student's visa and I am required to depart the country at the end of my studies."

"Isn't that in theory, though? I know that there are Africans and other foreigners who finish their studies from the University of Pittsburgh and stay in the city to work."

"Maybe they changed their visa status. The only way I can continue to stay in America would be if I go on to graduate school. But I want to first go home to see my mother for a while and then come back for graduate school. If I leave without changing my visa status, I will not be able to return to the country." He tapped a pen on the coffee table.

"There must be a way out of this so you can go home on a visit. I don't have any knowledge in these matters. Maybe you have to make inquires. I think you need to," Linda advised.

"You know what? I have an idea. I have a friend in New York. I will call him." Jamike brightened up.

"Who is that?" Linda's somber mood changed as she saw Jamike's countenance lighten up.

"He is a friend. I don't know if I mentioned to you at some point that I met a friend in New York when I first arrived in the country four years ago. That was before I came to Regius. In fact, I spent a few days with him before I came to stay with Laski. Nnamdi would know about these things. He has lived in this country for a long time."

"Call him then, if he is still in New York. He may be helpful."

"I will do that. I don't believe he has left New York," Jamike said as he got up and moved toward the kitchen. After Linda left that evening, Jamike searched and found

Nnamdi's telephone number. That night he placed a call to New York and spoke to Nnamdi. They discussed his situation at length.

The next morning Jamike called to inform Linda that he spoke to Nnamdi.

"What did he say? Does he have any good ideas?" She was curious.

"I would say yes, but it needs your participation."

"I would do anything. What is it?" she asked anxiously.

"It's what we need to sit down and talk about. I can come over this evening."

"No, no. I will be right there."

Linda knocked and turned the knob. The door was unlocked. Oftentimes Jamike would leave the door unlocked anytime he knew Linda was on her way.

"So what did your friend say? I am anxious. Is there anything I can do to help?" She sat down, trying to get her breath. He bent and gave her a kiss. He sat next to her.

"Well, this can be done in one of two ways..."

"Did he say which one is easier? The one that will get you home and back? It is important that you go and come back. You know you can't leave me here too long." He smiled and held her.

"I can wait until I enroll at the University of Maryland and then get a Form I-20 to travel in the summer of next year. That is one way."

"What is Form I-20?"

"It is an immigration form that enables a foreign student to come into the U.S. to go to school. Each time he wants to visit home, a new one is issued."

"You can't get it from Regius now?"

"No, I am no longer in school."

"Oh, dear! And nothing can be done about it?"

"Nothing. The other way to go, Nnamdi says, is to marry an American citizen. That will solve my problem instantly, because the marriage will make it possible for me to get what he called a Green Card. The Green Card will make me a permanent resident in America, and I will be able to travel in and out of the country anytime."

"This card is green?"

"I know nothing about it, and I have not seen one before. I would think it is green to call it a green card."

"Did you tell him about us? And what did he say?"

"I told him about you, and he suggested we have a court marriage and see a lawyer immediately to begin processing the immigration papers. He said a Green Card should be ready in six weeks, and I could go home and be back in time for graduate school."

"We can have a court wedding. It should be no problem." Linda said it in a voice that gave relief to both her and Jamike.

"This will be pushing things faster than we may want, you know."

"What is the difference? We will need to do it sometime, anyway. So it doesn't really matter."

"What will your parents say to this now?" Jamike asked with hands folded across his chest.

"We will let them know. It is real, just that we did not plan for this to happen now. But we have a problem we need to solve." She was convinced. They decided to have the court wedding as soon as possible. It was agreed Jamike should brief Emeka, the only Nigerian student from his Igbo tribe, while Linda would inform her roommate, Kathy.

The two witnesses, Emeka and Kathy, were at the courthouse the Wednesday morning the wedding took place. The following day, the couple went to see an immigration lawyer.

Once the process of changing Jamike's immigration status was in progress at the law offices of "Rosenberg & McLean" in Regius, preparations for his trip began in earnest. Jamike and Linda informed her parents that Jamike would be visiting his country. Linda also told them that Jamike would like to spend the night before his travel date in their home so it would be easy to get to Pittsburgh International Airport in the morning, rather than bear the stress of driving up from Regius. That was fine, Mr. Johnson assured his daughter.

Thirty-Six

It was at the first crow of the cock in the morning that Uridiya set out for the home of Okeke Adibe to give her in-laws the happy news that Chioma's husband had completed his education and was ready to come home to take his wife. Her persistent knock at the wooden gate of the compound woke Adibe from sleep. He came out with a bush lantern, a machete in hand, to let her into the compound and then into the parlor.

"What would bring you here when it is not yet day-break?" Adibe asked her.

"It is almost daybreak; the palm of the hand is already visible. I saw some women already on their way to faraway markets"

"You have to be careful at night when you have no lantern," Adibe advised. "You could step on a snake or even be attacked by evil spirits."

"The snake I may worry about. As for evil spirits, are we not all spirits?"

Uridiya's high-pitched voice brought Ihuoma to the parlor.

"I hope all is well, Uridiya? What matter would bring you here so early in the morning?" Ihuoma asked.

"Nothing bad has happened; I have brought good news, instead. Your son-in-law has finished his education." She brought out the letter she received from her son and all were filled with joy. As they conversed, day began to break outside, and the sleeping village woke to a new day; one could hear cocks crowing from chicken coops in every household. Two relatives came promptly to hear the good news. Adibe blessed and invoked ancestral spirits with a half-dried kola nut. Uridiya informed them that it would not be long before Jamike would return from overseas. She gave them notice that within two weeks, she was coming with her kinsmen and women to complete final marriage rites. When Chioma joined them, an old relative in the room suggested that she should write to congratulate her husband.

"I don't know what to write. Who will I say I am?" Chioma asked.

"Tell him you are his wife. He will be happy to hear that," Uridiya said to her daughter-in-law.

"He does not know me and has not seen me before."

"Well, if you do not know what to tell your husband in a letter, what will you tell him when you see him?" the same old relative asked.

"You want me to tell you right here what I will tell that man when I see him?" she asked, somehow irritated.

"Are you calling your husband 'that man' or are you referring to someone else?" asked another relative.

Before Chioma excused herself, Uridiya requested her to come over in two days time to write a reply to Jamike.

Writing a letter for Uridiya was not an easy task. At intervals she would ask Chioma to read it back to her in the vernacular to make sure what she said was written down. The letter began:

"I thank God for the joyful message you sent. Since your letter arrived we all have been dancing. Your chi is awake and you should thank him. Thank also the man who took you there and showed you the way. Pray to God to keep me alive until you return. No one thought you and I would survive, because some of your relatives chased us in every way to put our heads in the ground." She paused for a few seconds to put a pinch of snuff in each nose. She inhaled deeply, exhaled and continued.

"The person whose good handwriting you read is Chioma, the lady I have selected to be your wife. I know God will bless you two with abundant children. Now, listen to me, in two weeks all the marriage rites will be completed, and she will become the wife of Jamike Nnoromele. Nnoromele is your father's full name; it means, 'I will live long to see what life will bring.'" She continued:

"Now, we have lived to see this happen. Praise to the Creator! You now have to come home to take your wife. I will like to see my grandchildren soon. You are an only son; you should have a house full of children." Chioma did not write this last statement. "When you see the wife I have selected for you, you will know that I went all the way to the source of the stream to fetch this beautiful crystal clear water." Uridiya continued, "she is a ripe corn that is recognizable by just one look. I dream of you everyday and wonder if I would still be alive until you return. I put it in the hands of the creator." Chioma wrote nothing about a ripe corn.

Then she continued: "The headmaster said Chioma could stay with his wife for training, to learn how to take care of a husband and other duties of a wife until you return. Many husbands send their wives to Ahamba's wife for training. When these young wives complete their training, they are ready to bring joy and happiness to their husbands and families. I want the same joy for you. The reply I expect from you is the date you will set foot in this village." She then informed Jamike of Aunt Ebere who is the great grand daughter of his grand-father, who paid her a visit and brought two big yams. "She is someone you need to thank when you come back. Her heart is full of kindness," she told her son.

The letter went on about her condition in the village and about those who were still mistreating her and forgetting she has a son like Jamike. All this, she said, would end soon, and that gave her hope.

"Those who mistreat me will soon be on the run. Chioma is waiting for you. She is a ripe pear ready for sucking, and you should come to pluck it, my son. God be with you. I am your mother, Uridiya." Chioma did not write anything about the ripe pear. She understood the meaning of the metaphor and felt flattered. But she chuckled and remarked to herself: "Old women think they can say whatever comes to their mind. How can she describe a person as a pear to be sucked?" Chioma read the entire letter back to Uridiya, and was clever to remember the sentences she did not write. Uridiya was satisfied with what her daughter-in-law read back to her.

Two weeks after Uridiya took the news of Jamike's graduation to her in-laws, she was ready to return to them to complete the final marriage rites. She gave official notice of her intention through the middleman, Chibuzo.

The sun was still hidden in the heavens, but its gleams of gold shone dull with gentle rays on the waking village the morning Uridiya visited her in-laws. It was a typical morning in the village, about seven o'clock. There was a burst of activity already, as some women and older children swept the compounds while other women already carried baskets on their heads, on the way to distant farms or simply to throw away trash in nearby bushes and farms. Cocks and hens took measured steps as they emerged from their quarters, excreting carelessly along their path as they did not have to clean up after themselves. They left the compound and headed for surrounding farms to scratch the earth for food.

It was a common spectacle this early morning to see big red-combed cocks give quick pursuit to lowly hens, both stumbling now and then. Once caught, the hen succumbed, and the cock would press down his victim and climb on top in a matter of seconds, holding the fluffy neck of the hen strongly with his beak and mating. Dogs moved in a group, settling at a road junction, the male dogs circling the female ones to mate. Sometimes cyclists riding through would disperse them, but the dogs would quickly come together again. Those already mating and knotted in opposite directions would pull each other sluggishly out of the cyclist's way.

It was time to get ready for the day. Anyone who looked into a compound could see the man of the house sharpening his machete before he would head in one direction or the other to work on the farm. Some village men and bare-bodied young adults, with their machetes, would enter nearby bushes to cut some fresh palm fronds, green twigs and small tree branches to bring home to the goat shed for goats to feed on. Others would be seen taking the sheep out to the bushes where they were tethered to graze for the day. Still others would be seen climbing palm trees to tap wine for the day's market.

School children would soon be on their way to the mud-walled village primary school in their uniforms of khaki shorts and white shirts, some of which had nearly turned brown. Some would be seen carrying palm fronds from which they would make brooms during class handiwork sessions. Others carried pots of water for the teacher or sticks for fence construction. The village in the morning bustled with activities.

It was later, well before noon, on this typical morning in the village, that a good number of the village men and women went with Uridiya, as was the custom, to visit her in-laws and complete the last marriage rite. They took with them commodities that were required as written down in the village register of marriage customs. In addition, the men contributed palm wine while the women prepared edibles. By mid-day the sun had become harsh, and all of a sudden the clouds darkened and rain threatened. There was a rumble in the sky. Some people said they felt rain drops.

Villagers saw the slight drizzle that preceded the beginning of the ceremony as a shower of blessing. It did not last long, and once it cleared the sun came out again. As the ceremony commenced, the men and women met separately. The items—yams, soft drinks, clothing and head wraps, heads of leaf tobacco, bags of salt, bags of rice—were inspected to make sure they were of acceptable standard. There was haggling and argument on the adequacy of some of the items. Sometimes it seemed that a fight would break out as voices were raised, but it was all in good spirit to ensure that everything was done right and each party got their due.

The highlight of the ceremony was when the bride price was negotiated and agreed upon. Villagers set the bride price according to the level of education and training of the bride-to-be. Girls who were uneducated fetched a smaller bride price. Even at this, parents would hike the bride price of their daughter regardless of what she was worth to see if they could get away with it. Chioma's relatives set her bride price very high, at five hundred pounds sterling. They claimed that she was worth that much because she finished primary school and completed one year of Teacher Training College. The negotiation took a lot of time and sometimes got into angry argument. However, after much bargaining, the sum of three hundred pounds sterling was agreed upon by the negotiators as a fitting sum of money for Chioma's bride price.

There was agreement among the negotiators that this money should be given to Adibe and his son in the privacy of their room. They feared that thieves might pay them a visit before dawn if it was given in public, a worse prospect than needy relatives who would come to borrow money from them the next day. Relatives wishing to borrow money from the Adibes would conveniently forget that this money would be needed to pay for a wife for Mbakwe, Adibe's son, or to start a trade for him or even pay for the rest of his education. Worse still, it is a truth well known in the village that the cheerfulness with which such money is borrowed usually turns sour when it is time to pay back.

Adibe sent for a wide enamel tray. Jamike's uncle turned a worn-out raffia bag upside down to empty currency notes that filled the tray. When it was counted, it was a little over three hundred pounds sterling. Akudike put the surplus back in his bag.

When the money was given to Adibe, he asked that it be handed over to his oldest son, Mbakwe, who disappeared into their inner room with the tray as soon as it was in his hands.

The merriment went past midnight. Everyone agreed that a lady with a good upbringing had been selected for Jamike. Adibe's second daughter, Nneoma, was even being eyed by some of the men as a possible bride for their sons. When it was time to leave, Chioma and her parents conferred for a long time in the bedroom. Chioma's mother and sister helped pack her belongings. When she came out her sister was carrying her suitcase. Chioma's eyes welled with tears.

"What is this stupid girl crying about?" Her father scolded her for being childish. Her mother cut in.

"She is still a child and does not know much about these matters." Even Chioma's sister, Nneoma, held back tears. Adibe asked her daughter to kneel before him. She did, and he placed his right arm on her head and prayed for abundant blessings to be bestowed on her and her husband. He put grains of sand in her open palms, signifying both longevity and prolific fertility, and prayed.

Adibe noticed Eze and Ibe, his young relatives, suddenly get up from their seats and rushed to hold on to Chioma's suitcase. They said Chioma was not leaving until their demand was met. Two other men from Jamike's family challenged them and tried to repossess Chioma's suitcase. All four people had their hands on the suitcase. Chioma stood there at a loss as to what the matter was. Adibe sensed what was going on and calmed everyone in the commotion that ensued. He took possession of his daughter's suitcase.

"Wait, everyone! I say, wait. Everything has gone so well so far. What is the matter? Our in-laws should leave in peace with your sister." He appealed in a calm voice to his young relatives.

"Aludo people want to take our sister away without giving us the six packets of cigarettes due to us. That is not acceptable. If we don't get what is due to us, our sister is not going anywhere." Eze stated emphatically.

"Oh, is that the matter? That is a simple one." Adibe smiled. "My in-laws, you should know that custom requires that you give these young men the six packets of cigarettes due to them, or you give them the money for it."

"How is it that we have just paid you three hundred pounds sterling here and now, and you hold us back for a mere six packets of cigarettes? You can take back your sister and give us back the bride price. We are leaving," a contentious relative of Jamike said in a vexatious tone as he moved toward the door and motioned other family members to come along. A few relatives rose and made moves as if they would go along with this man's exhortation. That wasn't going to be. They were not going to leave without their prized bride, for whom they have sweated, some said, and spent all day, far into the next morning

"Wait! Wait a minute, my in-laws. I ask everyone to step on the brakes. This is not a difficult matter to resolve." Adibe appealed again to all. "Young men," he addressed his relatives. "One of you should come to me tomorrow morning for your six packets of cigarettes. Our in-laws have had a long day and have quite a distance to travel home so late in the night." There was peace.

Adibe stepped to the center of the obi where the people were and put the suitcase down. He took his daughter by the hand while Ihuoma sat and watched. She had one hand across her chest, held under her armpit while the other hand supported her chin.

Ihuoma whispered to a woman next to her that she could recall the day Adibe came to take her from her own parents very many years ago, and that she knew what her daughter was going through. Adibe handed Chioma to Akudike, Jamike's uncle. The suitcase was by Chioma's side. Adibe said:

"Look at me. I am giving my daughter to you today because you have fulfilled all the requirements of marriage according to our custom. She is now your wife. I hope we all will remain good in-laws, the type that would continue to exchange visits, being good to one another, and caring about one another's welfare. I wouldn't want you to be the kind of in-laws that would turn their backs on the parents of the bride once they take their wife away. There are quite a few like that. We want peace and harmony."

He turned to Uridiya and said, "Look after our daughter who is now your daughter as well. We know our daughter well; she will take good care of you. The relationship between a mother-in-law and daughter-in-law is an important one. Keep her under your wing, and keep her for your son. If for any reason you no longer find her suitable, send her back to us. We will accept and love her. As a matter of fact, some of her earlier suitors do not speak to us anymore. They did not see why we should give Chioma in marriage to you instead of to them. The fact is that they know what they want, and my wife and I know what we want. I have no doubt that Chioma will do well in your family. God bless you all. Go well."

Akudike took Chioma by the hand and thanked his in-laws and promised that all would be well. With those words, Uridiya put her hand across Chioma's shoulders and embraced her beloved. It was well close to two o'clock in the morning when Aludo villagers jubilantly began the journey back, with hurricane lamps and flashlights lighting up the way home. No one rode but pushed his or her bicycle in the darkness of the night while the rest walked. Uridiya got one of the men to tie Chioma's suitcase onto his bicycle's carriage. Some women carried some other of Chioma's belongings. The remaining property with which Chioma would start life would be delivered later on.

Two days after, the headmaster, Mr. Ahamba and his wife, Asamuka, came to Uridiya to take Chioma so she would begin her domestic training.

Thirty-Seven

It was during the sixth week following their visit to the immigration lawyer that Jamike's Green Card arrived in the law offices of Rosenberg and McLean. Jamike chose to use their address for security reasons. It was after he and Linda picked up the Green Card that it became certain that Jamike would visit home. He was full of excitement and expectation. To see his mother again after four years! From then on, Jamike rarely slept well as he dreamed often about his village. He found himself in familiar places back home and met people he knew, friends and family alike. In real life, he imagined how things might have changed since he left.

He remembered the huge Ubeagba tree under which he and other age-mates played when they were kids. He saw the village market in session with women moving in the surging crowd and hawking their wares on their heads, some with wrapper tied just above the breast and exposing the upper part of their chests. Jamike amused himself when he recalled how people in the market quickly made way and yelled to others to do the same for a woman carrying a big uncovered pot of red palm oil. No one wanted red oil spilled on them in case the woman tripped as she made her way briskly through a throng of buyers and sellers.

After he received his Green Card, Jamike and Linda went to Globe Travel Agency to book his flight to Lagos through Pittsburgh International Airport. He sent a telegram informing his mother and the headmaster of the date of his arrival. His plane would arrive at the Enugu airport in the southeastern part of Nigeria. Excitement filled Jamike without bounds now that it was a reality that he would visit his country and reconnect with who and what he left behind these four years in a foreign country.

A week before his departure, however, Jamike received a yellow post office slip for Uridiya's registered letter. Because it was too late in the day to claim the mail, he went to the post office the next day with Linda. As was his habit, he opened the letter in the post office lobby. Some letters from home gave him joy; some depressed him, as was the case with Uridiya's last letter about Chioma. But they never failed to make him anxious, because he worried about his mother.

Jamike learned that Chioma wrote the letter for his mother. She was now with the headmaster's wife for training and was waiting to join him in America. He should plan to come home as soon as possible to collect his wife, the letter said. Jamike could not believe what he was reading, that a wife had been married for him and that she was waiting to return to the United States with him. He read and reread the first page again and his face puffed with anger. He folded it and put it in the book, *Native Son,* by Richard Wright, which he had just started reading and planned to take on his trip.

Linda saw the change in his countenance and asked to know if everything was okay back home.

"Nothing much. Just my mother and her problems," he said.

"Is she okay?" Linda asked.

"Oh, she is all right and expecting me back today," he answered sarcastically.

"That's fine. You are going home, anyway, and you have sent out a telegram to inform them. It has not reached them yet, or she wouldn't write this letter," Linda said.

As Jamike walked down the post office steps, Linda doubled her steps to take his hand. He slowly disengaged her hand as they walked on the sidewalk. He put his hand in his pocket instead and was lost in thought. How dare his mother do this? Did he ask her to choose a wife for him? He was a grown man and knew what was good for him. Did he not ask her to put a hold on that plan until he came back? He was married already, and if Uridiya wanted to live with Chioma, that was her choice, but he was not going to be a part of it. She probably thought he was still the same person who left home four years ago.

Jamike was familiar with the practice of having an only son marry as soon as possible, but he did not think that his mother would be able to do this on her own, given the high expense of marrying a wife in his tribe.

Jamike reread his letter many times. As the day of his trip drew nearer its contents occupied his thoughts. He wished it were a dream. The thought of the situation sometimes dampened his spirits. He would not let Linda know what his mother wrote, as it would confirm her worst fears. He swore he was not going to give his family a chance to present Chioma to him. This was his frame of mind until the day he left Regius to travel to his homeland.

Jamike and Linda arrived at the Johnsons' home in Pittsburgh late on Friday evening. His luggage was put in the guest room. He was still not totally packed. After dinner he and Linda took time to put everything he was taking home in two suitcases. His briefcase would be his hand luggage. It was already eleven o'clock at night, and he needed to get some sleep since the flight was as early as nine o'clock in the morning. Linda kissed him good night and closed the guest room door behind her. Jamike read the letter one more time and put it back inside his book, which he placed under the second pillow and drifted into sleep.

Jamike's dream of his village and its people was interrupted two hours later. Linda walked quietly along the dark hallway toward Jamike's room. The rays from a distant streetlight that pierced through the heavy living room curtains provided the only gleam in the house. She groped her way past Cynthia's room and in that quiet night sauntered toward the guest room where Jamike was asleep and dreaming. She gently turned the doorknob and stepped inside. One could hear a pin drop. She bent over and kissed Jamike's exposed cheek and whispered into his ear. He opened his dreamy eyes and murmured something. Linda tapped her forefinger imperceptibly across his mouth and said,

"It is okay; it's me. We are legally married now." Jamike made way so she could get into the bed. She felt the book under the pillow and leaned over him to drop it on the floor. Jamike looked at the table clock. It was past one o'clock in the morning. He kissed her and drew her close to his body. An hour later she used the bathroom. The stillness of the night was disturbed by the hissing sound of the tap water Linda turned on. As she gathered some bedding and a pillow off the floor, her foot pushed Jamike's book under the bed and out of view. Then she felt her way to the door and disappeared into the dark hallway. Thereafter, utter silence descended on the home of Bill and Wanda Johnson.

As if he was holding on to a fading dream, Jamike struggled to retain the words, "It is okay; it's me. We are married...," which Linda whispered in his ear, but in no time he was deep in sleep again.

In the morning, Linda and her family went to the airport to see Jamike off. After he checked in, he took Linda aside and held her close.

"I will miss you, but I told you I will be gone for only two months."

"You call it only two months? You know what? I wish I were traveling with you."

"Do you mean it? You would really have come with me if I had asked?"

"I would have loved to meet your people."

"You know I don't have money. Who would pay for your ticket?"

"You shouldn't worry about that. My parents would gladly pay for it. Remember that next time."

"I had it in my plan for the next trip I would make, but

I did not think you would be ready so soon. It is wonderful that you feel this connection with my people and my homeland."

"I do, Jamike, I really do. I am family now." Her voice almost choked.

"You know what I am thinking? Now that I have my Green Card, based on what the lawyer said, I could even take off a year to work and make some money before going to graduate school."

"It is a good idea. We can both work and save money toward our wedding and, maybe, have enough to travel to Africa too. But try to come back in good time if you plan to go on to graduate school. You know I need to spend time with you also, unless you would want me to join you there."

"I understand how you feel. My main purpose of traveling home is to see my mother." But he understood what she meant.

Soon the announcement came that the flight to New York was boarding. In New York, Jamike would connect to another flight to Lagos, Nigeria. He shook hands with Mr. Johnson and hugged both Wanda and Cynthia. He gave Linda a tight embrace. He slung his suit-hanger over his shoulder, went past the metal detector entrance, and emerged on the side barred to non-passengers. He turned, waved good-bye, and disappeared into the crowd heading to Gate D 2. In Lagos, he would take a local flight to Enugu.

After the Johnsons came back from the airport, Linda went into her room and closed the door, because she wanted to be alone for a while. She called Kathy Boardman and informed her that Jamike had left to visit his home country. Kathy cheered her up and promised she would visit to spend a few days with her. Later in the afternoon, Linda went into the guestroom to put away a few personal belongings Jamike decided at the last minute to leave behind in order to avoid excess luggage. Before dinner, she went to tidy up the guestroom and gather the sheets for laundry and set the bed back into a sofa. There was an eerie feeling of emptiness to the room when she entered.

As Linda folded the bed, she saw Jamike's book under it. She felt sorry that he had forgotten the book he planned to read on the plane. She would save his book for him. She put the book with some other things that she planned to take to her room and vacuumed the floor. Maybe she would read the book. She was familiar with *Native Son* by Richard Wright from high school. The book could make her feel Jamike's closeness when she was ready for bed.

Linda turned off the ceiling light and turned on the bedside lamp and lay down. She saw Jamike's book on the dresser and decided to browse through it. As she opened it, she saw Uridiya's letter. She knew it was personal, and it would not be right to read it. But she always wanted to know more about Jamike's people and his country and could not resist the urge to read it.

The letter informed Jamike that the person writing for his mother was Chioma, the wife his mother had selected and married for him. Jamike should plan to return quickly and take her back with him. Meanwhile she informed him that Chioma was with the headmaster's wife, undergoing training on how to take care of a husband, children, and mother-in-law. The letter went on and on along that line.

Linda was numbed momentarily. "No, this can't be," she said. She reread the first half of the first page. Then she came to, "Chioma is now waiting for you to come home and bring her to America." Linda's head turned around. She got up and sat on the bed. As she held the letter, chills came over her. Goose pimples covered her body. The letter fell off Linda's sweaty hands and she felt like screaming. Could this be real? She needed to talk to someone but feared talking to any member of her family. The conversation her mother had with a school colleague came to her mind.

Linda lay back in bed and covered her face with both hands. She wondered if Jamike was part of this arrangement. She knew that what was between them was real. She wondered how Jamike would handle this. Could he go against his mother's wishes? Many questions came to her mind. Would Jamike ever write? What would be the content of such a letter? Why did he not tell her? Suppose he did not make contact with her anymore? How would she handle the situation?

Linda got very little sleep that night and the night that followed. She thought of breaking up the marriage and about what her mother told her she had learned of African husbands, and she wondered if she was not making a mistake with Jamike. But she loved and trusted him and would like to hear from him. Maybe he would write.

As passengers waited for the plane to take off, Jamike's thoughts were about Linda. He already began to miss her and thought how it would have been to bring her along. One day in the future that would surely happen, he assured himself.

When the plane steadied at a cruising speed and altitude, and the seat belt sign turned off, Jamike brought out his briefcase from the overhead compartment. He opened it to discover that the book he planned to read was not there. He realized immediately that he had left Uridiya's letter in it. He shook his head and blamed himself for not putting the letter in his coat pocket.

He wondered if Linda had found it, or, worse still, if she would read it. How would he explain the contents of the letter? She would never understand it. If only she knew that he was innocent in this whole plan. He wished the plane could turn back so he could just pick up the book and letter and continue on the journey. He would have to write her as soon as he arrived to reassure her and ask her not to pay any attention to the contents of the letter.

Jamike kept hoping she would not read the letter, though there was nothing he could do about it now. He adjusted the aircraft seat fully backwards and closed his eyes. He knew it was useless to agonize over it but he could not bring his mind to shut it off completely.

He thought about telephoning Linda but knew that would not be so easy, because he would have to travel over a hundred miles from his home to the city of Port Harcourt to use the government external telecommunications line. There he could wait for hours and may or may not be able to get a call through to anywhere overseas, in addition to the frustrations this could cause him, having been used to placing a call through in seconds. He made up his mind to telephone rather than write Linda a letter that could take over two weeks to reach her.

Thirty-Eight

The local flight from Lagos to Enugu took only one hour. Waiting for Jamike at the airport terminal were Uridiya, Chioma, Jamike's Uncle, Akudike in addition to Headmaster Ahamba and his wife, Asamuka. There were also four other relatives. Recognizing Jamike from a distance through a glass wall as passengers filed into the arrival building, Uridiya shouted,
"It is him, it is him, it is my son." She turned and embraced Asamuka, held her tight in excitement, and then let go. There was jubilation as Jamike came into the terminal building. Uridiya rushed up and squeezed her son to her bosom, saying, "Is this really you? How many years have passed? Oh, I have lived to see this day!" Uridiya knelt down on both knees. She beat her open palms on the ground twice and raised them. "Almighty, I thank you." She was oblivious to people around. Women who were there to meet other passengers looked at her in delight and shared the joy she displayed upon seeing her son.

She held him close again, then pushed him a little bit away from herself. "Let me see how tall you have grown! Oh God, it is my son! My God has done everything I wanted Him to do for me." Jamike moved over to the headmaster and held him and his wife in a prolonged embrace. He embraced his uncle and each of the relatives he recognized. As he shook hands and embraced Chioma, Uridiya quickly told him that she was his wife. He suspected she was, but paid her no special attention.

Jamike and his mother sat on the front bench seat of

the covered Peugeot pickup utility vehicle as it pulled away. The rest of the people sat in the back. A glass and wire mesh partition separated them. As Jamike and his mother settled to talk, she said to him,

"I know you got my letter. The young lady you embraced is Chioma, your wife. I already told you who her parents are. I believe she is destined to be your wife because she had many suitors, but she vowed to live in our family."

"Mama, this is not a discussion we should get into now. I am not going back to America tomorrow morning. We will have time to talk about it. Tell me how you have been these four years. I want to hear about the things you wrote in your letters." Uridiya ignored what he said and went on. "The reason I am telling you about Chioma ahead of time is because the headmaster and his wife will present her to you this very night. You will have a wife tonight. Oh, I am so happy. I long for a grandchild to carry on my lap," Uridiya said appealingly.

"Mama, leave that matter alone for now. I have just arrived. You say Chioma is with the headmaster and his wife. Well, let her stay there until we discuss matters relating to her." Jamike placed his hand on his mother's head and tilted it. "I hope there are good doctors here, because I plan for them to give you a thorough medical examination. Before I leave back for America, I will see to it that you are in excellent health. You have to leave the native medicine man for a while."

"That will be wonderful, my son; however, the most important thing you can do for me is to take Chioma, your wife, to America. As to my health, those of us in the village are used to illnesses. We get sick, then we get well; we get sick again and get well. If there is no sickness, the doctors will have nothing to do. To tell the truth it is not the doctor who cures; only God can cure. As to the medicine man, I will say he is the one keeping me alive with the help of my god. Without him, I would not be alive to see you today. When you settle down, we will pay him a visit as I promised him. He is someone you need to know and to thank."

When they came to the village square, Jamike asked

the driver to drop him off so he could walk the two hundred yards between the square and his compound. The journey from the airport had taken a little over two hours. As he left the car, the rest of the passengers came out of the vehicle too. Jamike took his time, looked around, stretched, and inhaled. He immediately observed that the village road, on which he and his age-mates had played on moonlight nights when they were youngsters, seemed narrower and the sides overgrown with bushes. The vegetation was lush and green, and there seemed to be all kinds of trees, including coconut and palm trees everywhere. Everything changed in his eyes; nothing seemed as it was before he left.

When the horn of a motorcar was heard repeatedly, villagers, some awe-stricken, half-clad youngsters, and women carrying infants by their sides, or tied to their backs rushed out to the road to know the business of this motor car in their kindred. When they learned that it was the car that brought Jamike home, they all tried to get a good look at him as Jamike walked up the road and entered their compound. Some of the excited children were very young when he left for America; the little ones who ran to the car were not even born then. One of the women who came to welcome Jamike was Ebere, a primary school headmistress at the Aludo Girls' Primary School, who was related to Uridiya. She was a woman of small stature who appeared talkative. She and Jamike conversed for a while and Jamike, who took instant interest in her, thanked her for her generosity to his mother.

There was a festive atmosphere and merriment. Akudike fired two shots in the air from his locally made gun. That brought in even more people, including passersby who joined in the rejoicing. Kola nuts and garden eggs were available in abundance, and so was palm wine. Village women who came around were jubilant. Uridiya introduced them with joy. As twilight came and people began to disperse Uridiya informed Jamike that a bucket of warm water was ready for him to take a bath in a thatch bathroom in the backyard, adjacent to the pit toilet that was in use when he left the village go to America.

It was night when the headmaster, Ahamba, his wife, Asamuka and Chioma arrived at Jamike's compound, carrying a bush lantern. Uridiya sent for Akudike who presented them kola nut and palm wine. They also ate dried meat with red pepper mixed in palm oil. After a brief discussion, Uridiya sent for her son. Jamike's house, attached to his mother's, was a short distance from the obi where discussion was taking place. Jamike almost tripped in the darkness over a stone on which children cracked palm kernel earlier in the day and left in the way. Everyone agreed he should have asked for a lantern. They joked that his eyes were not like theirs anymore, because he had got used to electric light in America. "We are in darkness here and used to it," one man quipped.

His uncle Akudike spoke first. He greeted and blessed all that were there. He faced Jamike and talked about situations his mother had endured during his absence. He said she was a strong woman who loved her son and always placed his welfare foremost. She had done what only a man with means could do; marry a wife for him in the belief that his father's lineage would continue. He turned toward Chioma and asked Jamike to take a look at the beauty that was his wife. Though he would have preferred not to look, Jamike found himself turning his head in Chioma's direction. Husband's and wife's eyes met momentarily.

Uridiya told her son that his chi was awake because he has been blessed both in America and in his family; he obtained that for which he went to the white man's land, and here at home a wife was waiting for him. What else can a young man ask for?

"The reason we assemble here tonight," Uridiya told her son, "is to hand over your wife to you." As she talked, Jamike held his chin and looked at his mother stoically. Uridiya told Jamike that handing his wife over to him was a moment that she dreamed of for so long. And with regard to Chioma, she has written everything about her in letters to him.

"So, here is your wife. She is all yours," she told him, making a hand gesture toward Chioma. Headmaster Ahamba spoke next, touching on so many things, especially the sacrifices Uridiya made on Jamike's behalf. He urged him to pray for his mother's health and long life, so she could reap the harvest of the seed she planted. The headmaster told Jamike that Chioma had been living with his family, and they found her very caring and would be the envy of any man in search of a wife.

Jamike asked the headmaster to step outside with him for a while. He told Ahamba that he would appreciate it if Chioma were sent out of the room, so that he could respond to what they said and not embarrass her. When he came back into the room, Jamike thanked them for their kind words about his mother.

"You all helped in keeping her alive so that she could see me. I thank you, Mama, for your love. You know, there is nothing in this world I will not do to please you. I thank you for all your concern, especially thinking that I am of the age to marry. I have never lost sight of the fact that I am an only child, and that I have cultural obligations and expectations thrust upon me by that fact. But, Mama, we were not in any agreement that you should look for a wife for me. How can you marry a wife for me, Mama? You do not know if I will like her or not? I don't understand this. You know I will not do anything to break your heart but I believe that I should be allowed to select the woman I will marry because I am the one to live with her. You don't even know if I am already married. With a voice, firm and yet sensitive, he held everybody speechless.

"If you marry an American woman, I will kill myself!" Uridiya cried out.

"I will not let you kill yourself, Mama. I love you."

"Why are you doing this to me, doing this to me?" She hit a clenched fist twice on her chest. "How can you love me and yet break my heart? I will not live to see this," she cried.

"Mama, you want me to get married. Let me tell you this; maybe it will please you. I am now married. It is someone I love. You will love her too, and she will love you," Jamike told his mother. There was silence. It was broken by the persistent bleating of a she-goat that jumped hither and thither in the goat shed avoiding a he-goat that pursued with a menacing cry to mate. Akudike's wife hit a stick a couple of times on the wooden gate of the shed to bring about temporary calm.

The headmaster heaved a sigh. No one was sure if it was for relief or disappointment. He then asked the country of origin of this wife. Jamike told them she was American and black. Uridiya interrupted, "Did you say you are married in the white man's land, Jamike? Is that what is coming out of your mouth? I will not live to see this." Uridiya threw herself on the hard, crusty earth floor, hitting her chest in quick succession with a clenched fist. Asamuka, who sat next to her, reached down immediately and held her. She and the headmaster got her up and sat her down while Asamuka held her.

"Are you all right?" everyone asked her almost simultaneously. She was okay.

"Mama, don't do this to me," Jamike said, looking very distressed. "I thought you were happy I came home to see you."

"My son, if I am not happy to see you, who else on earth would I be happy to see other than your father? But that I know will not happen today or tomorrow." Uridiya calmed herself, looked her son in the eye, and said calmly, "what can an American woman do for me, Jamike? We will not hear what the other says. What does she know about our customs and habits? What am I going to do if you reject Chioma? It will shame me in this village, and all my effort will be in vain. What will this American woman know to do, as she has not been educated in our ways? No, this will not happen, my beloved son. Look into my heart and soul and have mercy on your mother. It is your welfare I am concerned about. I don't have much time on this earth."

There was worry on the faces of Akudike, the headmaster, and his wife.

"It will be all right, Mama. She will learn all the things you expect her to know, if she is taught."

"I don't know how this will be all right, my son. You know that in Igboland if you reject a wife, you will not be refunded even one penny from the bride price or anything at all from all the gifts to her and her family. But if at some point she rejects a man who has put down money toward marrying her, her parents will refund every penny. No, this discussion will not end this night. Asamuka, take Chioma with you. Bring her back tomorrow night about the same time. Before then, I will have a conversation with my son in private." They dispersed. The mood was somber.

When they left the room, Uridiya took Chioma from Akudike's parlor where she was waiting and talked to her. "My daughter, the headmaster and his wife will take you home. They will bring you back tomorrow. Your husband is tired. He needs time to rest and time to hear how I have been living during these years he was in America, when some of these people who pretend to rejoice today mistreated me. I have told you all about these bad people already." Chioma nodded. "Have a good night, my beloved," Uridiya said, rubbing Chioma's shoulder as they stood outside.

Before noon the next day, Jamike sent someone to the girls' primary school to invite Aunt Ebere over for discussion. Despite the fact that many people were coming to see him, Jamike found time to brief his aunt on the marriage situation and what his feelings were on the matter. He offered her Fanta orange drink and biscuits. Jamike cleared his throat and went straight to the heart of the matter.

"I don't know if you heard that my mother selected a wife for me while I was in America?"

"I knew about it, and I gave her praise for it. Your mother is equal to ten men put together, as the adage goes." Ebere was not sure what the concern on Jamike's face was about. She thought he ought to be happy.

"There is a problem. I knew nothing about it."

"You don't? Who gave her the go-ahead?"

"She took it upon herself, and that has created a big problem. She thought she was doing a wonderful thing for her son."

"It is wonderful all right, but I am worried both of you were not in agreement on this. No, she must not treat you like a child."

"I am already married in America, you see." There was a momentary silence.

"To whom? Did we hear about this?"

"To an American woman."

"Are you honestly saying that you looked all around Aludo and the entire tribe and couldn't pick out a wife other than this white woman?" The puzzled look on her face wasn't what Jamike expected.

"She is not a white woman, Aunt Ebere. She is a black woman. And even if she is a white woman, what does it matter?"

"They are all foreigners and are the same to us. I don't know how this is going to be handled. I agree that a wife should not be selected for you unless you so desire. But you have to convince us why you think this woman is better than all the women in Aludo and the neighboring villages." Jamike did not show his irritation.

"The headmaster and his wife are bringing this woman tonight, and they will try to persuade me to take her as my wife. But I can't. If you are not busy, I will like you to be present when she is presented to me. You are educated, and I am sure you may have some advice for my mother and our relatives." The tapping of his foot on the cement floor was audible.

"I have a conference with a parent late in the evening, and I don't know how long that will last."

"Do your best to be present, but if you can't make it I will understand."

"I can't make you a promise, my dear. I will endeavor to be there but if I can't make it, I am hopeful all will go well." A little girl came to the door to inform Jamike that someone was waiting to see him,

"Let's leave it at that and hope you will make it."

Aunt Ebere left. She felt Uridiya was wrong in not consulting her son over the young lady she married for him but at the same time thought Jamike has made a big mistake.

Thirty-Nine

The following night, the headmaster and his wife arrived without Chioma. Two elders were invited as well as Onyeneke, Jamike's best friend. Also present were Akudike and Jamike's aunt, Ebere, whom Jamike had briefed on the situation earlier in the day. After presentation of kola nut and palm wine, Uridiya informed them of the seriousness of the situation and urged them to convince Jamike to marry the woman she had selected for him. The first elder, Uzosike, told Jamike that he had been married for over forty years and knows that what one marries in a woman is character, and character is beauty, and Chioma has character. He said to Jamike,

"Although you might be an educated man, you do not have enough experience to determine which woman would make a good wife. Even if you stayed in the white man's land for a hundred more years, you could not learn it. It is this type of knowledge that sets us in the village apart from those of you who have been to school where you were supposed to learn and know everything in the world but you do not. I encourage you to marry Chioma and to plan on raising a family immediately. That is what we want from you."

The second elder took over. "I want to ask you, Jamike: Is your behavior what you are taught where you came back from? It seems you don't think and behave like your kinsmen anymore. Is it because you have been to the white man's land? Well, if that is the case, the next time any of our sons wants to go there, we would have to take a second look at it and, if necessary, tie a rope around his waist and hold him here so he could learn to be wise." The headmaster chuckled. There was silence. The elders' pleading was to no avail. Jamike emphatically stated that he was married and that there was nothing he could do about it. He continued:

"The wife I married is an American woman, and she is black like you and me. She does not speak our language, but she can learn it. After all, is language not learned? Not one of you spoke Igbo from birth. As for knowing our customs and tradition, she will learn them also. I am asking all of you to accept my wife and break the news to Chioma and her parents as soon as possible, in any way you see fit. I am not marrying two wives."

Jamike's aunt, Ebere, sought permission to speak. She looked Jamike in the face.

"The concerns of your mother and relatives are in order, but I blame this confusion on the lack of agreement between you and your mother before Uridiya started selecting a wife. You have married an American. You should know that our way of life is different from that of American people, because they would not understand the customs and traditions we hold sacred." Aunt Ebere then turned to the headmaster and his wife.

"He has already made up his mind on what he wants to do. I will appeal to all of you to allow Jamike to marry the woman he selected for himself. After all, whether he marries Chioma or the wife he is telling us about, he will be the one to live with her. I hope you will not think that I am having a different view from you because I am a teacher and as such, educated. Far from it, I value the customs and traditions of our people, but we can reach some understanding and accommodation here. I believe I speak your mind on this."

Jamike was calm, his arms folded across his chest, listening to every word that came out of Aunt Ebere's mouth. He looked at his mother and saw her grow pale.

There was pain on his face now; he loved his mother, but he thought he needed to be true to his commitment. Uridiya developed a sudden fever as she sat motionless listening to Ebere. Aunt Ebere turned to Jamike a second time, and in a firm voice, with open the palm of her right hand stretched toward him, she said:

"Now, you see how far we have come, whether your wife is black or white, there can be no compromise on educating her properly on our customs and habits. She must be schooled on the behavior of a good wife and most importantly, how to live happily and peacefully with a husband. I hope you know that what we are doing is trying to save you from anything that will trouble you or make you unhappy in the future. It is important that you invite her immediately to join you so she can start learning our customs and way of life. Do you think she can come?" Before Jamike would make a reply the headmaster signaled to speak.

"What teacher Ebere suggested is what I wanted to say. Everyone here tonight will see that as a way to take care of your mother's concern. Her concern is mainly for your future happiness in marriage, no matter whom you marry. We all want to see your wife and for your wife to see us." Uridiya was now tired. She forced a statement.

"I am agreeable to all you have said. I belong to you and so does my son. It is my desire to see this woman today or tomorrow. I want to talk to her. Let her come and learn our ways. I want to put my only child from God in her hands. Mistreating him will result in my anger." Jamike, who listened intently, spoke.

"I thank you, my people. If what it will take for me to marry the wife I have chosen for myself is to bring her home, I will send for Linda immediately." Jamike's voice was subdued. Aunt Ebere continued,

"There has been so much testimony about Chioma's good character. Nothing is greater than for a young lady to have good name. A good name is superior to wealth. And let me tell you, if it is her destiny, she might still be the future wife of someone who lives in America, and she would still be able to travel to the white man's land someday. Did our people not say that when one door closes, another one opens? It could even be a better one. The night is far spent." Uridiya had her hands still clasped across her stomach, holding her sides tight as if she was shivering.

"I am tired now," she said. "I would like to know the name of this white woman who you say is your wife. I hope she has a name I can pronounce, since as you all know, I did not attend any school. I am what you who went to school call 'illikerate.' " The headmaster, his wife, and Ebere laughed. Jamike forced a smile.

"Mama, she is not a white woman," Jamike said.

"If she is not white, what is she? I thought you went to the white man's land. Are the people there sometimes white and sometimes black? Are you sure you know what you are saying?"

"Mama, I told you already, she is a black woman. There are both white and black people in America. The great-great-grandparents of the black people who live in America today were taken there from our homeland. They were our kit and kin from all over Africa who were sold into slavery."

"Is this a story you are telling me, or what?" Uridiya asked. An old man among them commented that what Jamike said was true.

"Have you been there before?" Uzosike asked him. The old man continued.

"Some of you remember nothing. When we were young, we were told that in those days when people were sold, the white man laid ambush early in the morning to catch villagers going to their farms, and roped them." Then he added, "Sometimes, they would shoot their gun in the air in a crowded market and, in the stampede, they would catch some people to take with them." One would think the old man was teaching a history class.

"To tell you the truth," Jamike continued, "some of our people in those days of slavery were sold by our chiefs. In exchange for human beings they received such silly things as tobacco, gold, mirrors, guns, and cheap trinkets, thereby aiding the white man to take their subjects into slavery, and these were shipped to America and other parts of the world against their will." Uridiya was completely disinterested in the story. Jamike gave the name of his wife as Linda, who he said came from a good black family and looked to Africa as her ancestral home where she would find acceptance." Uridiya took a deep breath and let out.

"Mama, I will send a message to Linda to come and I know she will love you and will be good to you too," Jamike told his mother. "I will do nothing to break your heart. You want me to have a wife so you will see your grandchildren and I can assure you it won't be long before your wish is fulfilled. I promise to repay everything you spent on Chioma." Jamike's tone was emotional, placing his hand on his mother's shoulder.

The headmaster stretched himself and gave his wife a slight nudge to keep her awake. "I think this matter is rested," he told them.

"Our forefathers put it aptly when they said that if you do not find the firewood suitable, you should send it back to the bush from where it was fetched. The firewood we have is good but the person for whom we fetched it wants a different kind. Jamike has made his choice. It is better that he refuses to marry Chioma now, as painful as it is, than to marry her only to send her away for any reason after they might have had children together. You know it is not our custom to do that."

The headmaster told Uridiya and Akudike that Chioma will stay with his family until they meet with Chibuzo, the middleman. They will all put their heads together and hear his advice on the best way to send the message to her family. He knew it would be an embarrassing situation and also difficult. Luckily they would not be asking the Adibe family to refund the bride price or any other expenses, because neither Adibe nor his daughter, Chioma, is the reason why the marriage should not go on.

They left the matter in the headmaster's hands, because as a teacher, they thought, he would know how to put the issue across.

"This thing is about marriage, not death," the old man, Uzosike, said, as he got up with the help of his cane. The headmaster would confer with the middleman who would meet Chioma's father to appoint a date for this sad meeting. Uridiya should visit the Adibe family soon in the company of Akudike, the headmaster, and a few elders seasoned in the use of proverbs to handle such delicate matters."

Early the next morning, before the palm of the hand became visible to the eye, Jamike and Ebere walked over a mile to the nearest road junction. There they caught a taxi to Umuahia, a city fourteen miles away, from where they would take the train to Port Harcourt to telephone Linda in America.

The journey to Umuahia lasted twice the time, because the old beat-up taxi they took was too slow. The taxi dropped Jamike and Ebere off at the railway station.
They boarded a coal-fired locomotive with its string of coaches for the one hundred-mile journey to Port Harcourt. The train was a "local" that made a stop at every station. It made its third stop at Obiala, a minor station located on the outskirts of a village along the bush railway track to Port Harcourt. Hawkers with fruits and other edibles in baskets and enamel trays carried on their heads or shoulders rushed to the windows of the train that pulled in. Passengers stretched down their hands to select what they want through the windows.

Because Jamike was anxious to get to Port Harcourt, he wondered why the train was spending much more time there than it did at the two previous stations. Thirty minutes had gone by. Jamike overheard concerned passengers saying that trains usually waited for only fifteen minutes or even less at that station. Could there be a problem? Jamike wondered.

A man in a brown uniform came into the coach through a door marked "Do Not Enter" and stood right in the middle of the coach. He had a white handkerchief knotted in a scarf-like manner around his neck. He hit a metal hand-held hole-puncher three times in rapid succession on the inside metal roof of the coach. He got attention. He was the ticket master, a short burly man in his late fifties.

"Listen, everyone. There is a problem with the train's engine. A message has been sent to Port Harcourt terminal, our head office. The officials may send another engine, or they may decide to send an engineer to repair the train. You should exercise patience." He moved toward a connecting door marked "Do Not Enter."

"Excuse me, hello, mister!" Jamike wanted to have more information, because the trip was becoming disgusting to him. The ticket master turned with irritation on his face. His piercing eyes met with Jamike's.

"What is it? Is there anything I said that you failed to understand?" Jamike was puzzled by his brusque manner. He almost decided not to say anything, but changed his mind.

"I understood you. But can you give us an idea how much longer we will be here before something is done about the engine." Jamike got a how-dare-you look from him.

"Are you asking me?"

"Yes, I am asking you, because you have just told us the reason why we are stranded here."

"My friend, if you have any questions you can direct them to head office." The "Do Not Enter" door closed swiftly behind him as he quickly crossed over into an adjoining coach.

"I am not your friend," Jamike muttered.

Jamike closed his eyes and resigned himself to the situation. Nearly an hour and a half later, without any announcement, a loud sound was heard as if a heavy object had hit one end of the locomotive. Everyone was startled. The train jerked first backward and then forward with force, leaving passengers wondering what was going on. The engine coupled and pulled off. There was relief. Jamike looked at Aunt Ebere and shook his head. He expected her to say something.

"You know, I was afraid that we might be at this station till nighttime and never get to Port Harcourt today." There was tiredness in her voice.

"Can that happen?"

"It can happen very easily and with no apologies. This is your country."

The coal-fired locomotive whistled and puffed out dark smoke as it sped through the moving greenery of the rain forest, leaving waving hawkers and everything else behind. The journey to Port Harcourt continued.

Forty

Jamike signed in and took a number at the International Telephone section of the Posts and Telegraph Department. It was not quite forty-five minutes when number 14 was called. Jamike wrote Linda's telephone number on a piece of paper and gave it to the attendant. On the first ring, he handed the receiver to Jamike and stepped out of the booth. Jamike shut the door as the telephone continued to ring in the Johnsons' home in Pittsburgh. It was a rather jarring ring, because it rang simultaneously in the kitchen, the den, and the living room. Linda, who had been watching television, picked up the receiver in the living room. Jamike's heart sank into his stomach.

It is hard to say if he would have been happy if no one picked up the phone as he worried over what to expect. Linda was home alone. She has not gone out much since Jamike left for Africa. She had been very worried not knowing what would become of her marriage with him. She had been doing some soul searching, wondering if Jamike would ever call now that he probably knew that she had read his mother's letter and was aware of what she believed was the plan with his mother. Sometimes Linda had wondered if she made a mistake going into this marriage with a foreigner. Whenever this thought came to her, she had convinced herself that she did the right thing because she loved Jamike.

"Hello, this is the Johnsons' residence."

"Hello, who am I speaking with?" Linda had a voice that

was hardly distinguishable from her mother's. She knew whose voice it was on the other end, but she was thinking how best to approach this call. Would she be emotional and show her anger, or just let Jamike talk? She decided not to show anger; perhaps he was not in on this plan with his mother.

"This is Linda; can you wait just one minute?" She was anxious and nervous. Her heart beat fast. Turning off the television, she took the telephone and its twenty-five feet of cord into her room and shut the door. She decided to be firm rather than emotional in what she said to him.

"Hello, Jamike. I thought I would never hear from you again."

"Hello, my dear. How are you doing, and why is that?"

"To be honest with you, I am not doing very well." A bedside lamp illuminated the room. She stood with one hand on the cupboard and the other holding the telephone receiver to her left ear. She would not sit down until she heard what would put her mind at rest. She continued.

"I have been lost in thought since you left. I was afraid you would let me down."

"How in the world would I do that? I know you found and read my mother's letter. But I will explain. I would never betray you because marriage with you means so much to me."

"But you did not tell me you had a wife in Nigeria, and yet had me married to you. You know you cannot have two wives in America, even though that can be done where you come from. It is called bigamy here. When I found that out in the letter, I was furious. Were you playing games with me or what?" Her voice rose above conversational tone. She knew no one else was in the house.

"Linda, Linda, please calm down, you are justifiably upset, but allow me to say something to you," Jamike tried to interrupt. He would keep the conversation at a reasonable tone.

"Let me ask you, Jamike, did you marry me to get a Green Card? My mother told me this is what foreigners do. I hope you did not deceive me into this marriage. Now you have your education, I am sure you have no plans to return to America. If that be the case, I can only wish you good luck" There was momentary silence.

"Linda, can you now hear me out? I know you have read my mother's letter. I know you are upset. I am very sorry. But you need to hear me. I know you are very upset now." Jamike needs now to choose his words. He was afraid to say anything that would further upset her.

"What do you have to say about this grand design of yours and your family?"

"Linda, you accuse me falsely. There is no grand design, and I never married you to obtain a Green Card. Our marriage is genuine, because we love each other."

"That is what I thought, and I have been under that impression from day one."

"Yes, my marriage with you is genuine. First of all, I want you to calm down. You are right to feel betrayed after you read my mother's letter. You are right to feel hurt and disappointed in me. But things did not happen the way you think." His voice was calm. He thought speaking calmly would be a strategy to make Linda bring down her voice that was raised a while ago.

"Tell me how things happened, Jamike. I think I am entitled to an explanation. What is the status of the marriage we entered into? Were you planning to be a bigamist with an American woman? You know that would not happen. I am listening."

"Linda, please calm down. I know how you feel."

"You do not know, and can never know, how or what a woman feels when she thinks she has been betrayed by the one she loves. Go on and talk to me."

"I have not planned to be a bigamist. I did not plan to deceive or betray you. For your information, I have rejected this woman, this arranged wife. It is a long story. I am glad you have calmed down to hear me."

Linda changed the telephone to her left hand, and with the right hand pulled the bedcover back and sat down. She went to the door and listened for any sign or voice of any other person in the house. There was none. She checked the doorknob a second time to ensure it was locked. Jamike continued.

"My family gathered to introduce this woman as my wife the very first night I arrived. I was supposed to accept her and start a family while I was visiting and then return with her to America. My mother was anxious for an only child like me to give her a grandbaby. I fully understand her concern. It is expected in my society that an only male child would marry as soon as he comes of age. It is not uncommon for parents to have a wife married for the only son, as my mother has done, even when this son cannot afford to maintain a wife. But it is the tradition."

"Did I hear you say your mother wants you both to start a family right away, and you kept me in the dark about it? You have betrayed me." She began to cry.

"Jamike, I love you and want to be with you," she said, sobbing.

"Don't do that Linda. I have rejected this lady. I am saying this a second time." Linda cried more, and anyone outside the room could now hear her. She reached for a tissue to dab her tears.

"Linda, please stop crying. My family did all they could to persuade me to take this wife. I told them I am married to you, and I would never have a second wife. They could not believe that I would not want my family to select a good wife for me, as is the tradition. I told them I would have nothing to do with this wife. My mother threatened suicide and become uncontrollable." Suddenly Linda realized that crying would not help the situation and calmed herself. Her tone changed, and she began,

"What are you going to do, Jamike? Are you going to go against your people's tradition because of me? No, you have to take the wife your family has selected for you."

"No, Linda, I will never do that. I am married to you and to no other woman."

"Let me ask you. Is this a legal marriage? If it is legal, then there is problem."

"There is no problem, Linda. What they did is to marry this woman according to native law and custom. It is our traditional way of marriage. It is legal in my society, but I was not part of it, so she cannot be my wife. As far as I am concerned, it is not legal with me. My family can marry her if they choose, but she is not going to live with me. The only legal marriage I know is the one I have with you."

"Jamike, are you telling me you were never a part of this arrangement? I believe there was a process; a marriage does not happen overnight, no matter the society. If you knew your mother was into this marriage, why did you hide it from me?" Linda's voice became softer. She wanted to learn more.

"My mother always wanted me to have a wife while she was alive, so she can carry her grand children on her lap. She never got tired of telling me this, and it has been so since I was in high school. At no time did I pay her any attention. When my mother first hinted at this arranged marriage in a letter, I rejected the idea outright and told her how I felt about it. She explained that as an only child, she was willing to sell her farm lands to marry a wife for me so I could have her grandchildren; particularly, a son who would succeed me according to our tradition in the event of my death, otherwise my family name would be lost forever."

"Well, is what your mother did what tradition required of her? Do you really want to go against that?"

"I understand tradition. I was born and raised in the village. I am a village boy. Tradition did not say that my consent should not be sought and obtained before a marriage process was initiated. I am the one to live with the woman I call wife, not my mother or any of my family members. If tradition says that I need not be consulted over a wife I will live with, then on this issue I will break with tradition. I am not marrying this wife selected for me, and I have told them so, making myself very clear. They heard me." Jamike now thought he was getting somewhere with Linda because the tone of her voice had changed and had become calm.

"Will there be any repercussions on you or on us if you go against this tradition of your people?" Linda now fears for their safety if Jamike goes ahead with their marriage.

"Usually there are repercussions when one goes against the tradition of our people. There may be sanctions by the family or clan, of course. But I believe that in this particular marriage situation that is personal, and in which no one consulted me, I am doing the right thing by marrying the one I truly love and not one selected for me by my beloved mother and my family. This is a woman I do not even know. We are not dealing with a taboo in this case. It is a matter of the heart. I have to go against tradition here."

"So, Jamike, are we still married?"

"The answer is a big yes. First of all, I thank you for calming down. When we began this conversation, I was afraid you would go off the handle on me because of how you felt. I am happy it did not happen."

"I was furious when I read your mother's letter. My problem was how long it would take to hear from you. I could not go on living in a state of uncertainty with the one I care about. I needed to know something fast. I am glad you wasted no time to contact me."

"I know how important it was for you to hear from me. Let me go on with my conversation with my family about you. Family members raised a lot of issues over you and me. I know very well I was advised not to marry a foreigner when I was coming to America. I was reminded of that too. But with my education, experience and exposure, no one is going to choose a wife for me. I choose my own wife.

"Some of the issues though were legitimate I must admit but I was able to argue and make them see things my way and win them over. For instance, the difference in language and culture was an issue. I told them you could learn all that. Then communication with my old mother was an important issue, because at her age she needs a daughter-in-law who she can open her heart to and confide in. I explained you would love her and do for her whatever she wants. Love understands every language. You would understand her."

"How exactly does your mother feel at this time?"

"Linda, first of all, my mother seems to have accepted the inevitable and calmed down. True, what I have done is not what she expected of me. She feels as betrayed by me as you would feel if I accept the arranged wife instead of you. My family feels I have left them in a terrible situation. As to the arranged wife, they will have to find some way to send her back to her parents. I am not going to worry about that. I simply do not want her. Next time, perhaps, when the story is known in all the villages they would be careful over these arranged marriages. They should know that education has broadened people's horizons and exposed them to different cultures and to the modern ways people live and think. Nobody wants anyone else arranging a wife for him anymore than you could arrange a husband for a woman. People want to make their own choices."

"You are very right. Things have changed and will keep changing, the old order giving way to new."

"Linda, there is, however, one point over which my family would not budge."

"Thank you, Jamike, for protecting me. I love you very much. I will love your mother too as well, because she means so much to you. You say there is a point over which they would not budge? What might that be?" She was thinking that, perhaps, his family would not allow him to return to America, having stayed four years away from his clan. They might even require her to join him to settle in Africa. That would certainly be out of the question, she thought, because she was not ready for that now. Jamike continued in a firm voice.

"I am asked to send for you to visit for a while so my family can meet the wife I told them about. My age-mates and older men in my village want to see their wife. Remember I told you not to be embarrassed if members of my age group or older men in my village call you 'my wife' when you meet them. I tried to educate you on this aspect of our culture. You are married to all of them in my village."

"Am I supposed to refer to each of them as husband

too? I am not married to them, I am married to you. I am confused."

"Actually, you are supposed to too, but I know that would be awkward for you. Just be nice to them. Some may even touch or embrace you. When any one of them touches or embraces you, it means that they care about Jamike's wife. Now, do not laugh because my family is serious about this next point. They insist that while visiting you would have to undergo training on how to take good care of a husband, take care of your mother-in-law, and be a good mother and wife."

"Well, that sounds like it would be an interesting experience. Where would this training be and with whom?"

"Usually it would be in the village with an older woman who has been married for, perhaps, thirty or so years. For you, I believe, my family will have to find a mature and educated relative in the city and you would spend a week or two in her home, observing how she generally relates to and takes care of her husband and family."

"And you agreed with them on all this?"

"Linda, this is a compromise I reached with my family in order to appease my mother, so you would be accepted by the whole family."

"Jamike I love you and will forever do. I would do whatever it takes for us to be together. I know I will treat you well as a husband. I already learned that from my mother and father, but I know I will be a good mother and daughter-in-law to your mother too. Jamike, can you explain this training for me?"

"Linda, from my experience, you would live with the woman chosen for this training for about two weeks. You would observe her in her household and learn how to cook basic African dishes. You would learn how an African wife interacts with her husband in their home, how she serves him and the children and how she interacts with her mother-in-law when she visits. You would learn much about our culture and traditional practices in the home. Knowledge of these would make you bond more with me and my family."

"Jamike, my family has always felt kinship with Africa. I will have no problem learning more about her, her culture and tradition."

"Yes, Linda, you can learn all that in general through reading, but we are talking here in relation to life together as husband and wife. My family would like to see you. I promised to bring you to them so we can put this challenge behind us."

"Jamike, you know I love you and would do whatever is right for us. What exactly do you want me to do in the present circumstance?"

"Linda, I want you to prepare to come to Nigeria for a brief visit. I will raise money to send you a ticket. Can you do that for me? I don't know what you would think about it, but I am already going against every advice my family gave me because of you. I am going against tradition because I love you. My mother wants to see my wife, and I promised I would send for you to visit. There have been so many odds and I am going against them. Can you do this for me? Can we set a date?" There was ominous silence momentarily on both ends of the transatlantic telephone line, then Linda began:

"Jamike, I will come to Nigeria to meet your family. I am coming to see my family too. I don't know how this will work out but whatever I learn about your culture and tradition I hope will strengthen our marriage in the future. I would have liked to know if I would live with this trainer or visit her home regularly. I guess that will be worked out when I am there. As for the ticket, I can promise you that Mom and Dad will contribute to it." Jamike muttered "Oh, my God," to himself. He missed a breath. He did not expect the answer he just got.

"Linda, I love you more than ever. You have made me so very proud and shown that you really care about the difficulty I am having with my family over you and want to help me surmount it."

"Jamike, whatever difficulty you have over me is not your difficulty alone but our difficulty. I have to support you in any way I can to work through it. My mom and dad are not here now, but I will inform them of this conversation as best as I can. I don't think they will have a problem with it, and they will believe I would be safe as long as I am coming to visit with you. I may or may not tell them about the training aspect. No, I will, they will find it interesting and may want to know all about it on my return. Can you hold just one moment?"

Linda went to the kitchen and took a calendar from the wall. They agreed on two dates in the summer to be presented to her parents. When Jamike calls again a date would be confirmed. The two exchanged words of endearment. Jamike shut the door of the telephone booth behind him. He was elated.

Auntie Ebere wanted to know what he and his American wife were saying to take all that length of time.

"You know, American women want everything to be explained to them, and they talk a lot too. She asked many questions, so she would not be in the dark about what is going on with my family and me over the wife my mother married. It took time to explain all that and make her understand. I am sorry it took so long. Are we late for the train?

"No, we are okay but we need to hurry up to get a taxi to the station. Is your wife coming or not to begin the training as we all agreed last night?"

"Auntie Ebere, Linda has agreed to visit Nigeria. We have two dates. I will need to return to Port Harcourt to confirm the actual date after she consults with her parents."

"She will come?" asked Ebere who was not particularly hopeful about the visit.

"Yes, she is excited about it."

"Your problems are over, Jamike. Villagers want to see their American wife."

Two weeks later, Jamike left the village a day before Linda's arrival to go to Lagos to wait for her. She would be arriving at the Lagos International Airport the next morning. In the village it was decided that women from the kindred would take a rented bus to go to Enugu local airport to welcome and bring home their newest wife, an addition to their number. The women would be in uniform attire, each wearing a blue wrapper cloth, a white blouse, and a blue headgear to match. Only four men in traditional outfit were to accompany them, as this was seen as a woman's thing. Some women even questioned why any man should come with them. The rest of the men-folk and women were to stay back in the village to prepare for the celebration that would follow on arrival back from the airport.

It was a bright morning when the journey to Enugu Airport was made. The sun burst on the horizon and shed its golden rays on the serene village. Even before the bus arrived village women going on the trip had begun to gather in front of Jamike's compound in readiness for the journey to receive Linda Johnson from Pittsburgh, U.S.A. Village women presented with as many hues of blue and white as were their number. The four men in the group, including Akudike, Jamike's uncle, all sat with the women in the back. Only Uridiya and the driver sat up front with two seats reserved for Jamike and his bride.

The bus arrived Enugu Airport just in time, for within fifteen minutes the announcement was made that Nigerian Airways Flight 628 from Lagos was landing. As passengers alighted from the aircraft, all eyes were in search of Jamike and Linda. Shorter women stood on toes and stretched necks to get a first hand view from a distance, literally climbing on each other.

There was jubilation as Jamike stepped down from the aircraft, with a young woman in a skyline blue business suit by his side. They concluded that the woman by his side, whose hand he held, must be the one, his wife. They were right. Some of the village women wondered why she was not a white woman, because they heard that Jamike had married an American wife. All eyes were on Linda.

Once inside the terminal building, even before formal introduction, Linda was mobbed by the village women, each eager to touch this woman from the white man's land. When Linda was introduced, she greeted and embraced Uridiya as well as every other person in the group.

When she spoke, the women became more mesmerized by one who spoke in an accent that charmed them. There was so much excitement and jubilation. Once her luggage was identified everyone trooped to the waiting bus in the parking lot with Jamike and Linda sandwiched in the middle.

Some women began to sing and made dance moves, a precursor of what awaits Linda in the village where there would be traditional women's dances and a couple of celebratory gunshots in the air. Linda, tall, slim, elegant, and fair complexioned was the love of everyone. Both men and women made comments to one another, saying, "This is it," "She is the real thing," "Jamike got to the head of the stream to fetch this one," and "They look like brother and sister," "She fits him."

Jamike and Linda joined Uridiya and the driver in the front of the bus. Suddenly one woman intoned a familiar song that they sing when a new bride is brought home in the village. Linda Johnson, an American bride, has come home to Africa.

By the time of Linda's arrival, Jamike's arranged wife, Chioma, had been sent back to her parents. It was a difficult assignment that required wisdom, tact and appropriate use of proverbs by the four elders who took Chioma home. Headmaster Ahamba, Jamike's mentor, led the group. The only woman among them was Asamuka, the headmaster's wife. It was the middleman who informed Chioma's parents of the turn of events and arranged the meeting. Though it was an unhappy meeting with an unsavory agenda, Mr. and Mrs. Okeke Adibe received their daughter back with equanimity and love. It was not her fault that she was returned to them. The news circulated in the village but it was talked about in a whisper by shocked villagers. Chioma went back to her teaching job but took a transfer. Two years later, she quietly got married and moved to the United States with her new husband.

N USA
2009
V00002B/82/P